Bloodhunters v3: New Blood

Xine Fury

Bloodhunters Volume 3: New Blood

Contents

Part 1

Part 2

Part 3

Bonus Stories

Part 1

01.00 Introduction

ED.02508.01.15

The robbery had gone off without a hitch, and boy was it the talk of the town. Plenty of people could say they robbed a bank, but how many could claim to have stolen the entire building off its foundation? Tarlos "The Squid" Prozner patted himself on the back for a job well done.

Of course, he couldn't have done it without the boys. His cohorts stood nearby, making small talk while they waited for their buyer to show up. Korbek was the muscle of the group, a gorilla-like Grunthian with natural armored plates growing all over his body. He had four arms, two of which were much larger than the others. He wasn't much of a conversationalist, but Prozner sure felt safer when he was around.

Altoon was a well-armed Vhelran with orange scales. He was Prozner's weapons supplier and demolitions expert. His current outfit held a comical number of weapons, as if he expected a war to break out at any moment. Altoon was quiet, often brooding, and when he did talk, it was usually about conspiracy theories. Prozner wasn't sure he trusted him, but he'd be glad of Altoon's firepower if the cops showed up.

Rounding out the group was Yeela, their tech expert. A human cyborg, she wore cybernetically-enhanced armor and always had at least one drone following her around. The heist wouldn't have been possible without her tech. She had attached antigravity discs to key points around the building, allowing it to float free once Altoon severed the foundation.

Most buildings couldn't have survived such a trip, but this bank had been designed like a giant vault. Prozner chuckled. The very features that made the bank more secure had made it easier to steal. The building now rested in a safe place, buried where no one would think to look for it. They would spend the next couple of months drilling into the multiple vaults, but tonight they were here to sell a single item they'd pilfered from a safety deposit box. A single gem worth more than most people earned in a lifetime.

Prozner felt a little exposed out here on the loading dock. It was dark and foggy, but he couldn't shake the feeling that they were being watched. "Yee, you want to do another perimeter check?"

"You got it, boss," Yeela said, and walked off into the fog.

Prozner took a drag off his vape, nimbly holding it with the tip of a large tentacle. "Time?" he asked.

"Nine oh-two," Altoon answered.

The buyer was officially late. Prozner shook his head. "Five more minutes and we head," he told them. It was going to be a great payout, worth sticking around for. But making the Squid wait? Not smart.

He was about to call it off when he heard a noise nearby. He thought he saw a flash of light from the rooftop of a warehouse. Then his comm unit buzzed. He glanced at the text, then growled. "Up there," he said, pointing toward the rooftop. Prozner and Korbek scaled the side of the building, while Altoon hovered up beside them on Levatech boots.

As Prozner climbed over the side of the roof, he saw that Yeela faced four adversaries. A woman in black, wielding a bow. A punk woman with bright blue hair and two AON daggers. A garishly-dressed young woman with several animal companions. And a guy in a dark blue flightsuit with red armored plating.

Bounty hunters, Prozner thought. And practically teenagers, at that. If the police couldn't bring Prozner in, what made these kids think they had a chance? Prozner stood on four of his tentacles, while the other two drew his sidearms.

The male bounty hunter spoke first. "Tarlos Prozner, you and your team are wanted for the unusually thorough robbery of the Maple First Bank of Gazna City, Galea. Come along peacefully, and none of you will be harmed. Resist and… well, it probably won't be pretty."

"Who even are you people?" Tarlos asked.

"We're the Bloodhunters," the young man said, his voice brimming with pride.

Prozner rolled his eyes and nodded to his henchmen. Korbek roared in fury and charged at the male. Altoon opened fire on the other three, both energy pistols blasting rapidly. But his targets were no longer there. The woman in black somehow vanished into the shadows, and the others ducked behind the stairwell access. Yeela launched a tiny drone from her wrist, and it sped toward the stairwell.

It was four against four, but that didn't mean the sides were even. One side had a vested interest in capturing their target alive, while the others had no such limitation. Altoon held his weapons wide, one aimed at each side of the stairwell, just waiting for a target. Then a glowing white arrow flew out of the darkness, piercing his left hand and making him drop his weapon. With his other hand he fired repeatedly at the arrow's point of origin, wincing in pain.

Korbek chased the male bounty hunter, Parzak, around the roof. The Grunthian was fast for his size, but not very agile. Every once in a while, Parzak would drop to his knees, roll sideways, and try to get a shot off with his stun gun. So far he'd hit his pursuer twice, but the voltage of his weapon was too low to bring down such a hulking monster.

As Parzak neared the far side of the roof, he shouted, "Sekka! Little help?" Then he rolled to the side once again. A flying reptile swooped into view, attacking Korbek's face. The Grunthian swatted at the creature with his lesser arms, still using his greater arms to blindly reach for Parzak. Korbek hit the far edge of the roof and tumbled over the side, still flailing at the winged lizard.

Yeela's drone flew around the stairwell entrance, only to get sliced in half by a glowing blue blade. Vex held out her hand and the AON dagger returned to her grasp. Beside her, Sekka stared into the eyes of one of her pets, mentally giving it an order.

Altoon was tired of waiting for his prey to come out of hiding. He wasn't about to walk around the stairwell enclosure, as he knew his opponents would be waiting for him. Besides, that wasn't how he did things. His pistol couldn't penetrate the steel walls of the stairwell enclosure, but he never left home without at least six ways to blow things up. He reached behind his back and pulled out a small bazooka.

His left hand was too injured to use, and it wasn't easy to handle the bazooka one-handed, but desperate times called for des— *holy harpies what is that?* A boa constrictor, with six eyes and covered in tiny pink feathers, quickly wrapped itself around Altoon's legs. He did not like snakes. Not. At. All. In a panic, he very nearly fired the bazooka at his own feet. He dropped the bazooka and started reaching for something less explosive, but the snake was too fast. In seconds it had wrapped itself around Altoon's entire body, pinning his arms to his sides.

No longer under fire, Vex and Sekka burst from their hiding place. "Give it up, Squid!" Parzak said, approaching from the far end of the roof. Prozner had yet to fire a shot in this battle, expecting his henchmen to do all the work. But now that it was two against four, he reconsidered his reticence. He nodded at Yeela, expecting her to release a burst of deadly drones or something. But Yeela seemed lost in thought.

More of a thinker than a fighter, Yeela had spent the last few seconds analyzing the bounty hunters and calculating the odds of avoiding capture. And now she had reached a conclusion. "You're on your own, boss," she said, and dove off the side of the building. Multiple Levatech emitters in her armor kept her aloft while her jet boots came online.

Outraged, Prozner ignored the bounty hunters and turned his weapons on Yeela. He drained both pistols firing overcharged shots at the back of Yeela's skull, killing her instantly. Her lifeless body floated eerily in mid-air, and would probably continue to do so until her armor's battery ran out.

Prozner turned back to the Bloodhunters. All four of them stood there now, just a few meters away, weapons drawn. Prozner tossed his two empty pistols away, and looked around for an out. The edge of the roof was just behind him, but Altoon's bazooka was also within reach. Fight or flight?

"Oh, no, I liked her…" Sekka said, staring at Yeela's body in the distance.

"Surrender, you big sack of squid," Parzak said.

That settled it for Prozner. They weren't going to take him alive, and he wasn't going to flee from the likes of these whelps. He grabbed the bazooka and aimed it at Parzak. It was close enough range that it would probably kill at least three of them, including Prozner himself, but his pride wouldn't consider any other outcome.

But before he could fire, several thousand jolts of electricity shook his body. He fell over, unconscious and smelling of overcooked seafood. Behind him, a hubcap-sized drone floated in mid-air. Yeela's final defense weapon.

"Man, do we suck at this," Parzak said.

A few hours later, they returned to their ship, the

Bloodwind. Parzak's mentor had given him the ship after she retired from bounty hunting. Glik, the ship's doctor, greeted them on the way in. "How did it go?" Glik asked.

"We caught three of the four alive," Parzak said. "Some injuries, mostly on their side. But we made some mistakes and got lucky at the end."

"You're still learning, Zak," Glik said, compassion in his voice. "Don't be so har… erm… What's that?"

Yeela's drone hovered just over Zak's left shoulder. "It followed me home, can I keep it?" he quipped.

"Okay, but you have to pick up after it," Glik said.

A few hours later, the team sat in the galley, drinking coffee and discussing combat strategy. The galley had changed a bit since the previous owners. The new team had taken out a couple of walls, sacrificing a few storage closets to make the room comfier. It was now both an eating area and a briefing room, with two large couches flanking a rectangular table.

"It's still following you?" Sekka asked. She had changed out of her eyesore of a battle outfit, and now wore pink pajama pants and a white T-shirt with a picture of a cartoon character on it. Her hair was white with pink highlights, and she had white eyes. A pink-furred squirrel slept on her shoulder. Sekka was the youngest member of the group, not counting Wisp.

"Ever since we left Galea," Zak replied. He now wore denim jeans and a dark blue shirt. He ran a hand through his unruly red hair. "I don't know what it wants."

"Let me take it to the lab," Glik offered. "I'll scan it for viruses and such." Glik was tall, about a head taller than the humans. He had bulbous eyes and mottled gray skin with purple splotches. But the most notable attribute of his Bufonid heritage was probably his transparent chest. When he didn't wear a shirt, his organs could be seen through his skin.

"Are we sure it's not dangerous?" Vex asked. She hadn't changed since the fight, but then, she didn't have a specific outfit she wore for bounty hunting. She tended to throw on whatever was comfortable, adding a few accessories if a fight was in the cards. Right now she wore ripped jeans over netted leggings, an off-the-shoulder shirt, and black lipstick.

Vex reached toward the kitchenette area, and an apple flew into her hand. Her neon blue hair flickered when she used her telekinesis. She had specifically picked her hair dye for the way it reacted when exposed to psychic energy. She thought it looked cool. It would probably make her go bald someday, but Vex tended to live for the moment.

"Well, it did save our lives," Zak said, watching Vex take a large bite out of the apple. She held it out to offer Zak a bite, but he shook his head.

"That doesn't mean anything," Glik said. He was the oldest member of the group, again not counting Wisp. He had previously worked as a nurse at a halfway house before it closed down. It was there that he had met Zak and Vex, both runaways, having fled bad situations at home. Even though he was useless in a fight, Glik felt like the group's protector. He had a den mother energy about him that made him feel responsible for the group.

"Yeah, it could be their last revenge on us," Vex added, talking with her mouth full. "Wait until we're all in one spot and then boom!" She sat in a most unladylike manner, legs spread wide, one foot on the arm of the couch. She threw the half-eaten apple into the waste chute, guiding it with her telekinesis. Her abilities were mild – she couldn't lift anything much heavier than an apple – but it had still been enough to break up her family.

"Okay, you're right, you're right," Zak said. "We'll look at it as soon as we're done here. But first... what was all that back there? We almost got killed. If people are going to take us seriously, we're going to have to work on our communication."

"Huh?" Vex said, looking at her nails. Sekka was so preoccupied with petting her squirrel, she hadn't even heard the question. Wisp, who hadn't spoken this entire time, appeared to be lost in thought.

Zak rolled his eyes. "Wisp? You have the most experience, do you have any ideas?"

Wisp sat cross-legged on the couch, staring off into space. She was the youngest-looking person in the room, but her true age was incalculable. She was an artificially-aged clone who had technically only been "born" six years ago, or seventeen depending on how you did the math. But her mind was another story. Originally from the Earth's Middle Ages, she had been reincarnated dozens of times, and had the memories of many lifetimes in her head.

"Wisp?" Zak repeated, and she jumped.

"I apologize," she said, getting to her feet. "But I have to go."

"Go where?" Zak asked.

"It's complicated," Wisp said. "I need to take one of the shuttles. I'll try to be back within a week."

"A week?" Zak repeated incredulously. "But we're just..."

"Look, I'm sorry," Wisp said. "I've been made aware of something, and I have to check it out."

"If it's a bounty you know you have to share it with the group," Vex said.

"It's not," Wisp said. "I just have to... meet an old friend." She started to walk toward the door, then turned around and put her hands on Parzak's shoulders. "Look, Zak. You're doing a great job. Fleeking awesome." Sometimes Wisp's vocabulary jumped around the centuries. "I'll help you when I get back. But this ship still has some extra rooms. It wouldn't hurt to recruit a few more partners. Bring in some extra skills, and you can learn from each other."

Then she turned and left, leaving the others confused.

01.01 *Inauguration Day*

ED.02508.01.20

It was a historic occasion. Janiz Ortina-Z'varan, born on Earth but the daughter of Galean immigrants, was about to be sworn in. She was the first non-human to be elected president of the United States of North America. She was also the first polyamorous lesbian to hold the office, so the day was doubly historic.

On the planet Valos, the Council of Heirs watched the inauguration on a viewscreen. Previous councils would have had no interest in Earth politics, but in recent years Valos had become less reclusive. Two of the current council members had once lived on Earth, and they were eager to witness this piece of history unfold.

The feed from Earth was transmitted through multiple relay stations that used technology similar to warp gates. By the time the feed reached Valos it was about three minutes behind, which wasn't perfect but still a miracle of technology. Venus Vermon, the current head of the council, sat in an ostentatious chair that had been built for someone much more vain.

Six other council members filled out the table. Nazdak Vermon, a man with a head for numbers and the heart of a sheep, sat to Venus's right. Next to him sat Vernach Vermon, an oily-skinned man who constantly munched on snacks, and Karden Vermon, who looked like he'd rather be somewhere else.

To Venus's left sat Lemondrop Vermon, a golden-skinned woman with a sunny disposition. Next to her sat technically-not-a-cyborg Raven Vermon, who tapped her metal fingers on the table in anticipation. Next to Raven sat the newest member of the council, Steve Vermon. Steve and Raven were the two who hailed from Earth, and were the most anxious to see the ceremony. At the far end of the table, there was an empty seat reserved for Sekka Vermon, who had been missing more and more council meetings since becoming a bounty hunter.

Each member of the council had the same father, the late but not-so-great Lord Teykor Vermon, former ruler of Valos. They all had different mothers, hailing from various planets, which accounted for the wide variety of inherited features on display at this table. But there was one feature they all shared – Lord Vermon's white eyes, which often came with mild psychic gifts.

The president was sworn in, and she addressed her citizens. "My fellow North Americans," she began. Raven's comm unit buzzed, flashing "Zeva" in the name field, and "Earth" as the location. Zeva was one of Raven's favorite people, probably her second best friend in the galaxy, but it was still an unwelcome time for a call. Raven sighed and opened the line.

"Zeva, couldn't you wait…"

"Oh my god are you seeing this?" Zeva asked. "This is terri—" then the call cut out. The words NETWORK OVERLOAD flashed on the comm unit's readout.

"What was she…" Raven began. Then, on the viewscreen, they watched history unfold. There was a loud POP sound, and a man in crimson appeared directly behind the newly inaugurated president. He held an AON sword, which glowed a bright red. The blade came down on top of

President Ortina-Z'varan's head, slicing her neatly in half as if she were made of gelatin. Then, with another POP sound, the assassin vanished as quickly as he'd appeared.

No one at the table spoke for several seconds, then everyone started speaking at once. "I think I know who…" Raven started to say, but no one could hear her over their own chatter. Then they heard it again. POP. Everyone became silent, and all heads turned back to the viewscreen. Except this time the sound seemed closer, not from the viewscreen at all.

"Does anyone else smell ozone?" Nazdak asked.

"Where did h-URK!" Venus shouted. A red AON blade now protruded from her chest. Everyone else got to their feet. Behind Venus's throne, a man in red withdrew his blade, then vanished with a loud POP. The room erupted into chaos. Guards were summoned. Everyone shouted. Nazdak hid under his chair.

Amidst all the yelling, Raven gradually realized she could hear maniacal laughter. Everyone lowered their voices, listening for the source. It came from the viewscreen, which now showed a woman's silhouette. "Who needs an army of assassins when you have one who can appear anywhere in the universe?"

Raven knew that voice. She looked over at Lemondrop, who nodded in agreement, her eyes wide with fear.

"Know this, council of traitors," the woman said, in quite possibly the most ridiculously over-the-top voice possible. "Your days are numbered. Your lives are mine. You won't know when, you won't know where. But you. Will. Die." The woman laughed again, and the transmission ended, replaced by the ongoing feed from Earth.

Even if Raven hadn't recognized the voice, the melodramatic flair was unmistakable.

Tena.

01.02   *Unfinished Business*

ED.02508.01.20

As far as the rest of the galaxy knew, Lord Teykor Vermon had died eight years ago. Little did they know that he was incapable of dying. Or he had been. Vermon's and Wisp's origins had been intertwined centuries ago, but only recently had Wisp discovered the secret for ending his life for good. Now that he had been laid to rest – permanently this time – Wisp had an important decision to make.

Have I lived long enough? she wondered. *How does one even answer such a question? What is enough when talking about something like life?* She thought about her past lives. Some were harder to remember than others, but a few really stood out. She'd been a doctor, a police officer, a queen, a space explorer, and a super hero. She'd been a mother seven times, and she'd outlived all of her family lines.

It was fun working with the Bloodhunters, but she worried that she outclassed them. *I've maxed out all my skill trees,* she thought, and laughed. *If I were a video game character, people would call me OP.* Sometimes she felt like the avatar of a deity living among mortals, just trying to fit in because she had no peers of her own. It almost felt like cheating to work with the Bloodhunters.

And this body... it was, without a doubt, the best body

she'd ever been born in. Her Auroran heritage was like winning the genetic lottery. She could absorb light and sound, see in near darkness, and even change her skin color. These natural abilities perfectly complimented the skills she'd developed over her lifetimes. It would be a shame to cut this life short.

She studied the dagger. It was probably the only weapon in the universe that could kill her permanently. This body was as mortal as anyone's, but she'd always wake up about thirteen years later. Her biggest concern was getting separated from the dagger. What if she lived out this life, determined to finish it in the next, only to be reborn on some remote planet without space technology?

She laughed at her own ridiculousness. There were people actually suffering in the universe, and her biggest worry was that she might live too long? *Stop it,* she told herself.

She would live this life and enjoy it to the fullest. She would try to help people when she could. When she got old, she would decide whether to use the dagger. If she died unexpectedly before then, she would hopefully recover the dagger in her next life. Or the next. Until then, she would keep it with her at all times.

She returned to her shuttle, and set a course for the Bloodwind.

Wisp entered the galley and opened her mouth to announce herself, but saw that a meeting was already in progress. Glik stood at the head of the table, briefing Zak, Vex, and a male Galean Wisp didn't recognize. "It was a spree attack," Glik told them. "In the space of an hour, they killed fourteen major political figures on eight different planets."

"What the hell did I miss?" Wisp asked, her eyes wide. She sat down next to Zak.

"And they were all the same assassin?" Zak asked.

"No one's sure," Glik replied. "It was definitely the same body type. Male, humanoid. Red outfit, mask. Same red

AON sword. And the timing tracks. He appeared at one location, killed his target, teleported directly to the next, killed, and so on."

"But no one has the technology to teleport that way," the catlike Galean said. "Sure, we can send ships through warp gates, but teleporting a single person? That far across the galaxy, to such precise locations? Without ripping them apart?"

"It's one of a thousand questions people are asking," Glik said. "Planets across the galaxy are rallying forces. They've also started crowdfunding a reward for the capture of the assassin. Donations are pouring in from nearly every civilized planet. It's the biggest bounty in history. Yes, bigger than Sarr. Whoever catches this guy will be able to buy a planet."

"I wish people would donate some of that money toward helping the families of the victims," Wisp said.

"The families of these victims are already rich," Vex said. "Besides, this guy has to be stopped. Now. Whatever it takes."

"Infinite wealth is a great motivator," Glik said. "But that also means bounty hunters are going to be at each other's throats to catch the assassin first. They will swarm over any lead. If you intend to be a part of this..."

"Like we'd pass this up," Zak interrupted.

"Then you'll have to be creative," Glik said. "Find an angle others wouldn't think of."

"If we do find an angle," Wisp said, "we can't keep it to ourselves. Stopping the murders is more important than any reward. This guy needs to be caught, I don't care by whom."

"Speak for yourself," Vex said. "I could use the money."

"I understand your feelings, Wisp," Glik said. "But if you find a clue, and it becomes general knowledge, hunters and cops alike will trample it to pieces. They'll climb over each other to get there first, and the assassin will get away."

"I promise you, Wisp," Zak added, "If we win, we'll donate a large percentage of the reward to a charity of your choosing."

Wisp didn't like his use of the word "win," as if this was a game. But they were right. It would be safer if they kept any leads to themselves. "So, do we actually have any leads?" she asked.

"Not so far," Glik said. "But we'd better start looking. Not only could there be more murders, but some of the governments involved have started the blame game, and tensions are high. Some planets were already looking for an excuse to start a conflict. The Grunthians in particular are being volatile. If the assassin isn't caught, war is inevitable."

They all nodded, and Glik sat down. The room took on a more casual vibe. Vex and Zak started their own conversation about leads and clues, while Glik introduced Wisp to their newest teammate. "Wisp, Mavu. Mavu, Wisp."

"Call me Midnight," Mavu said, shaking Wisp's hand. He was humanoid, with the facial features of a cat. He had black fur and green eyes.

"Good to meet you," Wisp said. Then, turning to Glik, she asked, "Where's Sekka?"

"With her siblings on Valos," Glik said. "One of the victims was the head of the Council of Heirs."

"Venus?"

Glik nodded. "She'll probably stay at least until they hold the funeral, maybe longer."

While the other four discussed where to start, Wisp became lost in thought. Her mind was a jumble of memories spanning over a thousand years. Sometimes it was difficult to tell if a specific memory was recent or more than a century old. Compounding the problem was the false childhood she'd been given in this lifetime, a decade of memories that had been deliberately fed to her in an attempted brainwashing.

But elements of the assassination did seem familiar. Alterra Sarr, also known as the bounty hunter Whisper, was Wisp's... mother? Twin sister? She was the woman from whom Wisp had been cloned. Wisp had a false memory of Alterra killing her parents, planted as a test to see how difficult it would be to program Alterra's clones. To this day, Wisp felt a twinge of anger when she saw Alterra, even though consciously she knew the feeling was based on an event that never happened.

In any event, it was a complicated relationship. False memories aside, Wisp felt weird around Alterra. This woman was so much like her, but also so different. They looked exactly alike, except Wisp was about ten years younger and had red hair. They had the same voice, but completely different dialects. Hanging around Alterra gave Wisp an uncanny valley feeling, and she believed Alterra felt it too.

But they had spoken some in the past few years, and elements of the assassinations reminded Wisp of some stories Alterra had told her. She took out her comm unit and sent Alterra a quick text. Her reply came back almost immediately.

"CALL ME," it said.

01.03 *Meeting of the Minds*

ED.02508.01.21

"Until we know what to do with this information, it goes no further than us." Raven's voice was cold and stern... pretty much like every other day. But her friends could tell the difference.

They were on Valos, in a secret home owned by Lemondrop. They had scanned for listening devices seven different ways, and hadn't even told the other members of the council about this meeting.

In addition to Raven and Lemondrop, there were ten other people in attendance. Detanna Taush, retired bounty hunter and Zak's mentor. Trenyn, telekinetic cyberneticist and Raven's best friend. Alterra Sarr, who believed she knew the identity of the assassin. Doctor G'Heesh Eshton, a Levatech expert who had a theory on the assassin's mode of travel. And finally the Bloodhunters; Zak, Vex, Wisp, Midnight, Glik, and Sekka.

"Let me get straight to the point," Raven said. "We know who sent the assassin. Tena Vermon is my father's most psychotic offspring. We thought – well, hoped – that she died a few years ago, when we destroyed her gravity cannon. But when the assassinations started yesterday, she couldn't resist the urge to taunt the council. Alterra?"

Alterra stood up. "There are only snippets of the assassin on video, and he's masked, but he sure looks like someone I used to know. Andoro Korr, who sometimes calls himself Crossbones. He's an Auroran like me, which makes him extra dangerous. He has no scruples, and obviously no reservations about killing. Doctor?"

Doctor Eshton stood up next. "Years ago I was in a program involving the implantation of Levatech emitters into IGP officers. The idea was to allow the subject more control over their personal gravity, to aid them in adapting to other planets. The program was a failure. However, one of the test subjects learned how to teleport by warping the space around him. Then he went insane and turned to a life of crime. A few months ago, his body was found. His implants had been removed."

Eshton paused, took a deep breath, and continued. "This assassin's method of teleportation looks and sounds too similar to my test subject's to be a coincidence." Eshton sat down, looking ashamed. He blamed himself for his role in inventing the technology.

"So what we have," Raven concluded, "Is an assassin who can strike anywhere in the galaxy, at any time. And he's taking orders from a madwoman who lives for chaos and is hell-bent on revenge."

"So what do we do?" Zak asked.

Lemondrop took this one. "Until we know more, anyone Tena considers an enemy should go into hiding. This includes the entire Council of Heirs, and the bounty hunters who destroyed her gravity cannon six years ago." There were a few grumbles from around the room. "I'm sorry, but we don't know how Tena's targets are selected, or how accurately Korr can find a target. If you're in public, you're in danger. Also, Doctor Eshton, you'll need to stay hidden. Tena doesn't like loose ends."

Alterra looked glum. When she'd been framed for terrorism eight years earlier, she'd had to hide her identity for more than two years. She didn't relish going into hiding again. But she knew both Tena and Korr considered her an enemy, and she'd be a fool to make a target of herself. All her skills meant nothing against an opponent who could strike so quickly.

"What about us?" Zak asked.

Detanna stood up. "I don't think you're on her radar," she said. "That's why we asked you here. We need some hunters in the field who aren't directly connected to Tena. People we can work through."

We'll be doing our own investigations from a hidden location, Trenyn added, addressing everyone telepathically. *We will feed you any leads we have.*

"Any leads that become public are going to get picked clean by amateurs," Detanna said. "But we have resources the public doesn't have."

"Are you going to share any of your resources with the public?" Glik asked. "We are talking about information that could save lives."

"It depends on the information," Detanna replied. "And whether we believe releasing it will do more harm than good."

"We've already alerted the authorities about Tena and Korr," Lemondrop said. "We know it won't accomplish anything. They're probably in the most secure location in the galaxy. But having a named target might ease the tensions between planets."

Raven turned to Zak. "But while we search for more leads," she said, "I encourage you to keep taking other jobs as well. Follow clues when we find them, make a living in the meantime. If you focus too hard on this one bounty, you might make yourselves another one of Tena's targets."

Would that be so bad? Vex wondered, but didn't say it out loud. She was pretty sure she could handle Andoro in a fight. Across the room, Trenyn turned their head and looked at her strangely.

"Make no mistake," Lemondrop added. "Tena and Korr are top priority. But until we have unique intel, we're just treading ground already trampled by thousands of other bounty hunters and IGP officers. Are there any questions?"

Wisp and Sekka looked at each other, and Sekka raised her hand.

"I know," Lemondrop said. "You two have connections to Tena. And if you want to hide with us, you can. But Sekka, Tena last knew you as a council member, and probably doesn't even know you've been bounty hunting."

"And Wisp," Alterra said. "Tena probably thinks you died when you destroyed the cloning station."

"You both might want to rebrand yourselves," Detanna said. "Come up with different names, always wear masks, and so on. I can help you with that if you like. But I doubt she'll notice either of you out of the thousands of bounty hunters looking for her."

"If there are no more questions," Lemondrop announced, "Then this meeting is adjourned."

01.04   *Blood Drive*

ED.02508.02.11

For the first week, Zak waited by his comm unit. The Bloodhunters took no other jobs, wanting to be ready at a moment's notice. The second week, Zak sent his teammates after unrelated bounties, but he stayed aboard the Bloodwind just in case. By week three, he was over it. There had been no clues and no further killings. Either Tena's stunt had been a one-time thing, or the next stage of her plan required some setup time. Either way, Zak needed some action.

He lay on his bed, tossing his comm unit up in the air and catching it. "I think I have a job for you," said a computer voice. Zak was so startled he dropped the comm unit, which rolled off the bed and clattered onto the floor.

"What have you got, Yeela?" Zak asked, sitting up.

The disc-shaped drone hovered over to him, coming to rest a few centimeters above the bed. A hologram appeared above the drone, showing a 3D representation of the target. "His name is Arnek Nitelocke," Yeela's electronic voice said. "Also known as the Lifedrinker. Wanted dead or alive. He's killed eleven people over the past two years, and now he's hiding out on the planet Montara."

"What's his shtick?" Zak asked.

"Just your run-of-the-mill vampirism," the drone replied. "His species gets high on human blood."

"Lovely," Zak said. "Do they know where he's hiding?"

"He's in a town called Withersun. He's not even being subtle, anyone with half a brain could probably find him in half an hour. So for you, two hours tops."

Zak rolled his eyes. "If he's so brazen, why haven't—"

"Korr. When the assassinations happened three weeks ago, most of the Withersun police force quit to become bounty hunters."

The drone's A.I. was quite extraordinary, but that's because it wasn't A.I. in the strictest sense. Before she'd died, Yeela had backed up her mind into the drone. Her original plan had been to have it transferred into a new body. But for now, she was actually enjoying being a drone. She could fly everywhere, and she never had to eat, scratch an itch, or use the restroom.

"I'll take it," Zak said, reaching for his shirt.

Withersun was about as beautiful as its name would suggest. Located near the planet's southern pole, the town had no full day or night, just a perpetual dusk. The sky was full of dark clouds, but there were two full moons to see by. It was raining when Zak arrived, and according to Yeela, it had been raining for more than a month. Zak walked through the streets with Yeela floating just above his head, acting as an umbrella. It didn't make much of a difference.

The town's buildings were made of stone, with spired roofs and ornate gargoyles. The cobblestone streets curved over hills and under arches, occasionally veering into tunnels that went under houses instead of around them. The town's geometry felt off to Zak somehow. He tried to visualize the road map from above, and he could only picture a tangled ball of yarn.

As if reading his mind, Yeela projected a map of the town into the air above him, with a helpful red dot representing his location. The town's layout still didn't make a whole lot of sense, but at least he could follow it. He hadn't seen a single person since arriving in town, but there were lights on in a few of the windows.

"Where to?" Zak asked, and Yeela put a blue dot on their destination. He followed the blue dot over a few hills, under a couple of buildings, and finally arrived at the constable's office. He knocked on the door and waited. No answer. He tried the knob, but the door was locked. He tried looking in the window, but heavy curtains blocked his view. However, the window was slightly higher than the top of the curtains.

Yeela floated to the top of the window and peeked in, over the curtains. "He's sleeping," she said, and projected a holographic image of the constable's office so that Zak could see. A human male, presumably the constable, slept in an office chair, his mouth wide open. Zak banged on the door loudly and persistently, until the constable finally woke up and let him in.

At first the man was angry at having been disturbed, but he softened when Zak introduced himself as a bounty hunter. "Have a seat! I'm glad you're here, how do you like your tea?" he said, turning on a kettle.

"Thank you, um, however you make it is fine," Zak said. He wasn't a tea drinker, and didn't even know what the options were. But any warm beverage would be welcome right now. "Let me get right down to business. Arnek Nitelocke, also known as the Lifedrinker. My intel tells me that he's in hiding somewhere in this town. I know you're overworked, but do you have any clues as to his location? Anything at all will help, even if it's just a rumor."

"Yes," the constable said, handing Zak a cup of hot water and a teabag. "He lives in that big castle on the North end of town. The one hanging over the lake, with the drawbridge. I believe he sleeps in the East tower. I can call you a cab if you like."

"You already know where he is," Zak said, deadpan.

"Of course," he said.

"I know you're short-staffed, but still…"

The constable sighed. "This isn't my real job," he said. "I'm actually a veterinarian. A few weeks ago, we lost all but one of our lawmen. They went off to grab a piece of that huge bounty, I'm sure you know the one. This left us with a single officer, and he disappeared a week ago when he went to arrest Arnek. I was given this job against my will. I'm not qualified. I've never even fired a gun."

"Have you called anyone from other towns? Or the IGP?"

"Of course," the constable said. "But they have their own staffing shortages. They'll get around to it, I'm sure. But in the meantime, my townsfolk keep disappearing."

Zak nodded. "I'll be back with Arnek," he said.

Twenty minutes later, Zak stood on a stone outcropping, overlooking a chasm. On the other side of the gorge, the stone castle looked ancient and uninviting. Far below, the choppy waters of Lake Miser threatened to engulf anyone who even thought of taking a late night swim. With the drawbridge up, crossing the chasm would be difficult.

"There's no gatehouse, no doorbell, no way to let him know someone's here. How does he get pizza delivered?" Zak wondered. He peered down into the chasm. He supposed he could climb down, swim across, then climb back up the other side. But it would take him all night, and the constant downpour wouldn't make it easy.

"I could look for an open window, and see if there's a drawbridge release on the other side," Yeela suggested.

"That would definitely let him know I'm here," Zak said. "I'm not sure I want to lose the element of surprise just yet."

"Should we go back and get the shuttle?" Yeela asked.

"That would also tip him off, seeing a shuttle flying in," Zak said. Then he had a thought. "Can you hold my weight?"

"I doubt it," the drone replied.

"Let's see," he said. Zak held on to the drone with both hands, and she tried to lift him into the air. She couldn't get him off the ground. Zak let go. "Okay, let's try this, go up a bit more."

Yeela hovered half a meter above Zak's head. He jumped up and grabbed her. She couldn't keep him aloft, but she had just enough power that he fell slowly, like a parachute. Zak rubbed his chin, mentally judging the distance across the moat. "That's a bad idea," Yeela warned.

"Bad ideas make the best stories," Zak said. He held the drone above his head with both hands, took a running start, and jumped. He hit the apex of his jump about a third of the way across the gap, then slowly floated down toward the other side.

He was about two-thirds of the way across when he realized he wasn't going to make it. He was already at chest level with the other side, and still going more downward than forward. He hit the rock wall at the far end of the chasm, releasing the drone so he could get a grip on the rocky outcroppings. He was about two meters below the edge of the landing. As he climbed up, Yeela got below his feet in an attempt to help.

"I did warn you," she admonished.

"I'm here, aren't I?" Zak said, as he pulled himself over the ledge and onto flat ground. He stood up and patted his hands on his thighs. "Now what," he wondered aloud, looking for a way in. He spotted a door right next to the drawbridge, but walking in the front door felt like a bad idea. A rocky outcropping surrounded the castle on all sides, allowing him to walk around the castle in search of other entrances.

There were several to choose from. He picked one on the right side of the castle. It was unlocked and led to the kitchen. Several small pies lay on a marble top island, cooling. Thick red filling bubbled to the top. "I really hope that's cherry," Zak said.

"If it's blood, I'm gonna hurl," Yeela said.

"That would be a neat trick," Zak replied. "Does that really gross you out?"

"I always had a problem with blood," the drone replied. "Of course, I can't get sick now but the psychological hangup is still there."

"Weird," Zak said.

They heard footsteps. Zak hid in the pantry, and Yeela floated up to the ceiling. The kitchen door opened. "I know you're in here. Come out now." The voice was deep and gravelly.

From his hiding place, Zak pulled out his comm unit and sent a quick text to Yeela. A panel on the drone slid aside, and the barrel of a stun gun popped out. Yeela slowly turned in the air, until she had the mansion's owner in her sights. But before she could fire, Arnek jumped up and snatched her out of the sky. He threw the drone across the room, where it banged off the pantry door and slid across the floor.

The pantry door popped open, and Zak waved sheepishly. Then he fired his own stun pistol. Arnek ducked behind the island, narrowly avoiding the stun disk. Zak spotted Yeela and bent down to check on her. Several lights were blinking red, but she appeared to be functional. He would have to worry about the damage later. He stood up. "Arnek, surrender now and GLAFF!" A pie hit him in the face. "Hot hot hot!" He frantically wiped off his face, but before he could open his eyes, he felt a blunt object hit him on the head. "It really is cherrrrrry..." he said as he blacked out.

When Zak came to, he was unarmed and tied to a chair. As his eyes focused, he could see Arnek across the room, sitting in an easy chair, watching television. "How..." he groaned. He had a headache now. "How did you know I was in the pantry?"

Arnek stood up and walked toward Zak. He was tall and gaunt, with pale skin and no hair. His ears came to a point, and he had yellow eyes. He wore black silk pajamas and no shoes. "Nothing happens in this castle without my knowledge," he said ominously.

"Some sort of... vampire sixth sense?" Zak asked.

"No, you idiot. I have security cameras everywhere," Arnek replied. "You have arrived on a very important night. It's the..."

"Some sort of blood ritual?" Zak asked. "I saw there were two full moons, is that when—"

"It's the final episode of my favorite sitcom," Arnek said, gesturing toward the television. "So if you would just shut your yap for half an hour, I'll deal with you then." He turned back toward the chair and sat down.

"Is that Bleepo and Janet?" Zak asked, craning his neck to get a better look at the television. He was a couple of seasons behind, and didn't even know it had been canceled.

"Shhh!" came the reply.

While Arnek was distracted, Zak took stock of his possessions. His most obvious weapons were gone, but he still had a few hidden tricks in his flightsuit. He'd learned from the best, after all. The only problem was that he couldn't reach anything. Each wrist was strapped to the chair by a tight elastic cord. His ankles were similarly bound to the chair legs. He could probably break the chair, but not with Arnek sitting right there. But he couldn't just sit around waiting, either. He didn't know what his captor had planned for him, but it probably involved a lot of bleeding.

SYSTEMS ONLINE

SELF-DIAGNOSTIC INITIATING...

Yeela scanned her environment. She was in a large metal waste receptacle at the bottom of a trash chute. She was covered in discarded napkins, moldy bread, banana peels, and… was that a human arm? Yeela's nonexistent stomach lurched. She tried to hover, but her Levatech emitters were damaged. That was a problem, as it was pretty much her only system of movement.

Or maybe not. She decided to focus on what worked, rather than what didn't. She had a grappling gun hidden behind one panel, and it seemed to work. A small gun barrel whirred into place on her top, and she aimed it around the room. Aiming it straight up, she fired at the top of the trash chute. The magnetic tip flew up the chute, a thin cable trailing behind it. It bounced off the top of the tunnel and fell back into the waste bin. The walls of the chute were stone, not metal.

But wait. The chute was stone, but the door to the chute had been metal. She had scanned the kitchen when they'd first arrived, and she never forgot a detail. She retracted the grappling cord and aimed again. Hmm. She'd need a better angle to hit the door. She fired the grappler at the side of the waste bin, and pulled herself over to the edge. From here, she could just see the door at the top of the trash chute.

She fired again, hitting the door with a clang. Then she pulled herself up the long chute, clattering along the stone walls. It wasn't the most dignified way to travel, but Zak needed her. She reached the top of the chute, and found herself stuck to the back of the door. It was hinged on the bottom, opening outward into the kitchen, and her weight caused it to fall open.

She now lay flat on top of the door, which was open in a horizontal position. She demagnetized the grappling tip and tried her Levatech emitters again. Her left-side emitters were working, but they weren't getting much power. Still, it was something. She used it to rock herself off of the door… and promptly fell back down into the trash chute. *Well, crap,* she thought.

Zak waited for a commercial break to speak again. "So what

are you going to do to me?"

"What do you think?" Arnek replied. "You obviously know who I am and therefore you know what I do. I should probably thank you for saving me a trip into town."

"You're going to use my blood to get high?"

"Is that what they told you?" Arnek replied, giving Zak an incredulous look. "You don't have a clue what's going on. This is going to blow your mind, but... Hold on, the show's back on." Arnek turned back to the TV.

"Oh, come *on*..." Zak started, and Arnek threw a book at him.

Yeela was back in the trash receptacle, positioning herself to fire another grappler up the chute, when she heard moaning. Curious, she fired her grappler at the lip of the bin, then used her one working Levatech emitter to flip herself over the side. She clattered onto the ground and scanned the environment. She was in a garage. Two hovercars sat nearby, one fairly modern, and the other designed to look like an old-timey carriage. There was an open door that led to a hallway.

The door handle was metal, so she used her grappler to pull herself across the room. From her new vantage point, she could see into the hallway, which was lined with four more doors, all with metal handles. One of the doors was open, and it sounded like the moaning came from in there. Using a combination of grappler and Levatech emitter, she finagled herself in that direction.

She made her way into the room. There was a bed with a railing in the center of the room, surrounded by several pieces of medical equipment. Yeela latched onto a metal coat hook and pulled herself up for a better view. A young woman lay in the bed. She was of the same species as Arnek. And she was writhing in pain.

The credits rolled, and Arnek wiped a tear from his eye.

"Can you believe they killed Bleepo's mom?"

"I sure didn't see it coming," Zak said.

Arnek stood up and approached Zak. "I suppose it's time to take you downstairs," he said.

"You were going to tell me the real reason you need blood," Zak said.

Arnek studied Zak. "You're not like the others who came here. They didn't care about why. They just wanted some quick credits. I tried to reason with them, but it was kill or be killed."

"I'm willing to hear what you have to say," Zak said.

"Easy for you to say when you're tied to a chair, trying to prolong your life. But I wonder… would you consider a temporary truce? If I untie you, and show you something downstairs, can I trust you to at least hear me out before you attempt to take me in?"

"Of course," Zak said. "But how do you know you can trust me?"

"I still have your weapons," Arnek said, untying Zak's bonds. "And earlier I took you down with a pie. I like my chances."

"Yeah, please don't tell anyone about the pie thing," Zak said, standing up.

Arnek had Zak walk in front so he could keep an eye on him. "The first seven murders weren't even mine," Arnek explained, as they walked down the stairs. "I needed blood, and there was a serial killer who kept the blood of his victims. I found his lair, but he escaped. So I took the blood he'd stored. And then he managed to pin the murders on me."

"What about the other victims?" Zak asked.

"Those were all people who came after me. I was wanted dead or alive, and I only killed in self-defense. Of course, I still drained their blood. No sense letting that go to waste."

"What do you need the blood for?" Zak asked, as they reached the lower floor. Arnek gestured toward a partially open door, and followed Zak through it. There was a convalescent bed inside, where a young woman moaned in pain. Like her father, she was bald, with pointed ears and pale skin.

"It's for my daughter," Arnek said. Turning to the woman, he said, "I'm so sorry, Lyryssa. Did it wear off already?" Arnek opened up a nearby mini-fridge, and pulled out a vial of blood and a syringe. As he loaded the syringe, he explained to Zak, "She has a condition that keeps her in constant pain. Human blood is a painkiller."

"Aren't there easier ways of getting it?" Zak asked. He spotted Yeela hanging from the coat hook, and pulled her down.

"You'd think," Arnek said. "Insurance doesn't cover it. Sales are restricted on my planet, since it can be used as a narcotic. I tried getting it on other planets, but they think of my people as vampires, which is ridiculous. We don't even eat meat."

"Couldn't you have gone to the police? Surely you have evidence that you're not the killer?" Zak attempted some minor repairs on Yeela as he talked.

"And risk leaving my daughter?" Arnek asked. "I know how I must look to you. No jury is going to believe my testimony."

"So why come here? You weren't exactly difficult to find."

"I ran out of money," Arnek said. "This castle is all I have left. And it's difficult to breach, as you discovered. I know I'm living on borrowed time. Sooner or later the police will come, and I won't be able to stop them. But I don't have a lot of choices. It's hard to be on the run while taking care of someone."

"I understand," Zak said. A thought occurred to him, and he sent a quick text on his comm. A reply came back a few seconds later. After reading the text, Zak said, "I have a proposition for you. I have a friend who may be able to create synthetic blood for your daughter. She'll stay in our care, but you have to surrender to the police. I'll do whatever I can to help you prove your innocence for those first seven murders. The rest, you'll just have to convince the court you had no choice. You'll probably still have to serve some time, but at least your daughter will be taken care of."

"That's risky," Arnek said. "How do I know your synthetic blood will work? How do I know you won't just abandon Lyryssa as soon as I go to jail?"

"The alternative is to stay here until some IGP officer or bounty hunter captures you anyway."

Arnek nodded his head. Then they both turned as they heard a crash from down the hallway.

"The garage…" Arnek began.

"Wait here," Zak said, and poked his head out the door. A man in a silver flightsuit came running down the hallway, his gun drawn. He was at the door before Zak had time to yell a warning. Zak backed into the room as the intruder barged in.

The newcomer was human, with dark hair and a scar on his left cheek. He wore an eye patch over his left eye, and held a Volt-322 energy pistol. Zak recognized the model. It didn't have a stun setting. The man glanced at Zak and dismissed him as unimportant. Then he spotted Arnek and raised his weapon, aiming it at Lyryssa.

"Arnek Nitelocke, you're coming with me," he said. "Come quietly or I'll kill her."

"Vanton Erbek!" Arnek shouted. Turning to Zak, he added, "He's the killer of the other seven."

"Seven that they know of," Vanton said with a grin.

"How did you get across the gorge?" Zak asked.

Vanton pointed to his back, turning slightly so Zak could see his jetpack.

"I've always wanted one of those," Zak said.

"You'd kill yourself within the hour," Yeela replied.

"Shut up, all of you," Vanton said. He licked his lips, the

side of his mouth twitching. He was clearly in a crazed state of mind.

"You won't get away with this," Zak said.

"Won't I?" Vanton said. He looked to his left for a second, as if someone else was speaking to him. "You're right. I won't. Not if I leave witnesses. Arnek is still worth money dead. Kill them all, that's better. Then I get paid for Arnek, and nobody pins anything on me." Vanton raised his pistol at Arnek.

Zak was unarmed, but he still held Yeela. He lifted her toward Vanton, and she fired an energy bolt. This burst of energy activated Vanton's jet pack, launching him into the stone ceiling with a sickening crunch. He was dead before he hit the ground.

"See?" Yeela said. "Jet packs are dangerous. Get yourself some nice hoverskates instead."

Arnek went to prison to await trial. There was more than enough evidence to exonerate him for Vanton's crimes, but the rest of his killings would be trickier to defend. He would probably end up serving time, but the death penalty was off the table.

In the meantime, Lyryssa Nitelocke was put in Glik's care, and given a room on the Bloodwind. Glik was indeed able to synthesize a blood substitute that met her needs. He was even able to isolate the active ingredients and create a more efficient elixir. Eventually he hoped to find the source of her pain and perform an operation, but for now this was an improvement.

When Arnek received word that the treatments were working, he was beyond elated. It didn't matter how long he spent in prison. He wouldn't see his daughter again for a while, but thanks to Zak, he would see her someday. With that to look forward to, his sentence would fly by.

01.05 *Dinner Plans*

ED.02508.02.20

"Thank you for coming, my friends," Lemondrop said. "This meeting of the Council of Heirs will now come to order. First order of business. I want to thank you for trusting in me, by appointing me temporary lead of the Council. But it's time to choose someone to take the spot permanently. Before we vote, does anyone want to be removed from the running?"

"Please remove me," Nazdak said, raising his hand. Right now he was deathly afraid of the assassin, but even in safer times he wouldn't have wanted the job.

"Remove me as well," Raven said. She cared little for politics, and didn't feel she could do the position justice. She was always too busy with her projects in the lab.

"Are you sure?" Lemondrop asked. "Both of you would make excellent leaders." While she addressed both of them, she was clearly being diplomatic. Everyone knew Nazdak couldn't make difficult decisions, including Nazdak. But Raven had proven herself to be impartial without being heartless. She could always be counted on to suggest practical solutions that hadn't occurred to the others. She was creative and fair, and didn't have a greedy bone in her body.

Unlike Vernach, who wanted the position for all the

wrong reasons. Right now he was practically salivating at the prospect of taking over. Lemondrop had no idea what changes he had in mind, but she knew all his ideas would be designed to benefit him personally.

Lemondrop hoped Vernach didn't win, but she also knew what it meant if he didn't. Steve was too new, Karden was more of a fighter than a leader, and Sekka rarely made it to the meetings these days. If Vernach didn't get the vote, and let's face it, he probably wouldn't, the burden would fall to Lemondrop. Which also meant she could be the target of Tena's next attack.

If there was another attack. It had been a month since Inauguration day, and there hadn't been any other attacks. Could it have been a one-time thing? Or was she just waiting for an opportunity? The Council of Heirs had been in hiding ever since the attack, but the rulers of other planets weren't necessarily as careful.

The bottom line was, it was Tena they were dealing with. And she didn't necessarily need a rhyme or reason for her actions. When Tena and Thresh had worked together, they'd managed to build a weapon capable of destroying planets. But Tena without Thresh was something else entirely. Without Thresh to keep her focused, she was a chaotic force made up of random, deadly whims. It was perfectly on-brand for her to kill fourteen world leaders for the fun of it, but it was equally possible that it was the first step in a greater plan.

The council voted. It was unanimous. Most of the council members voted for Lemondrop because she was the best person for the job. Lemondrop voted for herself because she didn't want anyone else to be a target. Even Vernach voted for Lemondrop, having decided that he didn't want to be a target.

"Thank you for your confidence in me," Lemondrop said after the winner was announced. "I promise I will do my best to live up to your expectations. Now that that's out of the way, let's get down to business. I have two pieces of important news, both involving the technology used in the attacks. Doctor Eshton is here to explain. Esh?"

Doctor Eshton had been sitting in a chair off to the side, watching the proceedings. He stood and approached the table. "Thank you, Lemondrop. This first bit of information has not yet been released to the general public, so your discretion will be required. To clarify, your own lives will be in danger if this information is spread." He over-pronounced every word in his stilted accent, as if he was used to being misunderstood.

He studied each of their faces before he continued. "At two of the sites of the attacks, these devices were found." He held up a tiny black cube, no bigger than a microchip. The council members leaned forward, straining their eyes to see it. "We believe it is some sort of transponder. At three of the other sites, they found some black dust that might have been the remains of cubes like this one."

"Did he leave them behind?" Karden asked.

"The cubes were most likely placed there sometime before the attacks. We believe that Korr's teleportation tech focused on them to guide the jumps. This is good news. It means he can't just appear anywhere in the universe at will. He has to plan his attacks ahead of time. Now that I know what we are looking for, I should be able to build a device that scans for them."

"And the dust?" Steve asked.

"My theory is that the cubes are meant to disintegrate after use, so as not to leave behind evidence. But two of them failed to do so."

"We have to keep this a secret," Lemondrop interjected. "We can use this to our advantage. But if Tena finds out we know this, she'll switch methods."

Doctor Eshton continued. "And the other bit of news. I am working on a way to nullify Korr's teleportation ability. I believe I can create a field that prevents his tech from working."

"So you can prevent him from teleporting into a room?" Raven asked.

"No, but I should be able to prevent him from leaving once he arrives."

"What good will that do?" Vernach asked.

"It means we can set a trap," Lemondrop said.

The meeting had been held in Lemondrop's safe house. After it was over, most of the attendees left in unmarked cars to travel to their own safe houses. Vernach, however, had other plans. He was tired of living on homemade food. It had been a month since he'd been to a restaurant. A whole month without a real steak made by a real chef. Slathered in butter, cheese, and bacon. And a side of… hmm… cheese sticks or sarklizard tenders? Oh heck, it had been a month, why not both.

Now that he knew the attacks had to be planned in advance, he was less worried about random assassinations. Vernach confidently pulled up to his favorite restaurant, and was led to his reserved booth. It was his favorite table in the restaurant because it was closest to the kitchen, which meant he got his food a few seconds faster. He gave the server his order, and while he waited, he salivated over the dessert menu.

As he put the dessert menu back in its holder, he knocked it against the napkin dispenser. A tiny black cube rolled out from beneath the dispenser. "What the…" he started to say.

POP. Andoro Korr appeared and grabbed him around the neck. POP.

When the server arrived with Vernach's appetizers, he was nowhere to be found.

"Where is Lemondrop's safe house?" Tena screamed.

"I swear I don't know!" Vernach wailed.

"Liar!" Tena backhanded him across the face, her bony nails tearing a gash in his cheek.

"I have a few techniques that will have him squealing like a pig," Andoro offered.

"Then where's the fun for me?" Tena asked. "But we'll give him a chance to reconsider." She put her hand under Vernach's chin and kissed him. "Think on it, brother. I'll be back in three days." Then she turned to Andoro and ordered, "No food, just water." Tena and Andoro left the cell and locked the door behind them.

"Vernach is missing," Raven reported.

Lemondrop's heart sank. She didn't like the man, but he deserved better than whatever Tena had in store for him. And he knew too much. "We're going to have to change some of our plans," she said. They would need to find a new place to meet, all of them would need new safe houses, and they'd need to go over everything Vernach knew. This was a nightmare.

Vernach sat in his cell, his stomach groaning audibly. It had been three days since he'd been yanked out of his favorite restaurant and into this cell. Three days without any food. The cell had no bed, just a blanket on the floor. There was a toilet in one corner, but other than that the cell was empty, just a concrete floor surrounded by metal bars.

Andoro sat in a comfortable office chair outside of the cell, watching a karate movie on his datapad. Andoro had been in and out the last few days, mostly to bring Vernach water. Vernach had tried reasoning with him, but Andoro seemed to relish in Vernach's discomfort.

Andoro and Vernach both looked up as the outer door opened. It was Tena. She was holding a large paper sack. And she was nude. Andoro stood up and offered her his chair, looking her up and down appreciatively. Tena grabbed the chair while Andoro opened the cell door. She dragged the chair into the cell and sat down. Then she reached into the bag, pulled out a huge bacon double cheeseburger, and took a large bite out of it.

Grease and ketchup dribbled down her chin as she asked, "Have you reconsidered?"

"Please," Vernach said. "Don't do this to me. I can't betray the council." Right now he probably would have betrayed Lemondrop for a raisin, but he wasn't stupid. He knew that he was only useful to them as long as he had information they needed.

"Oh, screw the council," Tena said. "Work with me and you can have anything you want. This…" she held up the burger, "or even this," she gestured to her body.

"You're… my sister," Vernach said.

"Never bothered Thresh," Tena answered.

The thought disgusted Vernach so much that, for once, he lost his appetite. "I wouldn't touch your vile body if you were covered in chocolate," he said.

Tena's mouth popped open, half-chewed food spilling out. She looked shocked, then enraged. She threw the cheeseburger to the ground and leaped for Vernach's throat. In one quick motion, she ripped out a chunk of his trachea and shoved it into his mouth.

"I thought you needed him," Andoro said.

"Whoops," Tena replied, then shrugged. "Oh well." She sniffed her bloody fingers, and a look of pure ecstasy crossed her face. She scanned the room until her eyes fell on Andoro. Her smile made Andoro's stomach lurch. "Want to help me desecrate his corpse?" she asked.

While Andoro thought Tena was perfectly attractive, the setting wasn't exactly a turn-on. But he'd just seen how she handled rejection, and wasn't about to make the same mistake Vernach had. He entered the cell and she started ripping off his clothing. *I hope I survive this,* Andoro thought.

01.06 *Family*

ED.02508.02.28

The statue of Princess Quora was the tallest landmark in Rarity City. The city had been so named due to the abundance of rare gems in its mines, though those mines had dried up years ago. That didn't stop the tourists though, who paid big money for a chance to chip away at the rocks for an hour, hoping to get lucky where so many before them hadn't.

Vex leaned over the railing of the giant left hand, on the narrow concrete path that traveled along the statue's outstretched arms, running from fingertip to fingertip. Noisy tourists brushed past her, some glaring at her for standing still and blocking traffic. Vex didn't care, her mission was more important than their vacation photos. Far below, Vex saw the entrance to the mines, as well as downtown, the outlying suburbs, and all the chintzy attractions that kept visitors from staying within their vacation budget.

She searched the crowd for one being, one needle in this chaotic haystack of pushy vacationers. The target's name was Pythen, and they were a Navoran with light blue skin. Vex looked through her digital monocular, and zoomed in to survey various parts of the city. Wherever she looked, the monocular's software scanned the crowd for Pythen's face.

An aggressive seagull mistook the monocular's strap for food, and tried to grab it as it flew by. Vex was so startled that she dropped the device. Reacting quickly, she reached out and called the monocular back into her hand. She didn't have a huge range on her telekinesis - maybe ten meters at most - but fortunately she caught it before it fell beyond her reach.

She looked around. Had anyone seen her do that? Not that it mattered. Telekinesis was uncommon but it wasn't unheard of. No one was going to burn her as a witch. Her current target even possessed the ability. But she'd grown accustomed to keeping it a secret, and she still felt a flash of shame whenever she used it.

Don't tell your father. The words echoed through her mind. Her mother had said it so many times, it was drilled into her. Five-year-old Vera Xynth never understood why it was so important that her father not find out. She knew it had something to do with the fact that her parents didn't have the power, and that her mother's hairstylist did. But it was years before she put the pieces together. She managed to hide it until she was twelve, when she instinctively used her ability to save her father from a potential injury.

He was not grateful. To be fair, the majority of his anger was directed at Vera's mother. They argued nightly, great shouting matches that kept Vera awake until sunrise. Her parents stayed together, but it would have been healthier for everyone if they hadn't. Her mother started drinking, her father became more and more distant, and Vera felt like everyone blamed her. They stopped praising her for good grades, or punishing her for staying out past curfew. She felt like they no longer considered her their daughter. When she was fourteen, she ran away from home.

Vex no longer felt sad when she remembered her family. She'd found a much truer family with the East Side Daggers, and more recently with the Bloodhunters. She now knew that family wasn't about blood, it was about acceptance.

She put down her monocular and clipped it to her belt. If Python was in Rarity City, they weren't out sightseeing. They had an agenda. Vex would have to think like a criminal to find them. That wouldn't be too hard for her; she'd spent most of her teen years stealing to survive.

Vex followed the walkway back up Princess Quora's arm and into her ear. She took the elevator back down to the street level. The moment Vex stepped out of the elevator, a jumble of images flashed through her brain. This was her other power. It was a mild form of telepathy, but she had no control over it. Her mind subconsciously picked up the surface thoughts from all the people nearby, and predicted the near future based on their short-term decisions. It wasn't exactly precognition, but it was close enough.

Right now it showed her a man playing cards. He was human, but Vex had a feeling he was connected to her quarry. There were at least three casinos nearby. She poked her head into the first one, but it had the wrong decor. The second one looked closer to what she'd seen in her vision, so she went inside and looked around. She knew she wouldn't find Python here. Navorans weren't allowed in most casinos. But maybe this card player would lead her to them.

It didn't take long to find the gambler. He had the highest pile of chips at any of the tables, and he was attracting attention. Not far away, Vex saw a pit boss talking to a floorman, looking in the player's direction. Apparently the player noticed too, because he lost a quarter of his winnings on his next bet. It must have been enough to satisfy the pit boss, because he shrugged and turned his attention elsewhere. But Vex recognized that it had been an intentionally bad bet, to throw off suspicion. The man won the next hand, then announced he was going to quit while he was ahead.

The player stood up and gathered up his chips. Keeping her distance, Vex followed him to the cash-out window. He took his credits and walked out the door. Vex continued to tail him. His next destination was another casino. Vex went in and sat down at a video poker machine, far enough away that she could watch him without arousing suspicion.

It didn't take her long to figure out his angle. Before making any decisions, he always looked lost in thought. Sometimes his lips would move, almost imperceptibly. She'd seen people do that when talking to telepaths. This guy and Python were working together. But where was Python? He couldn't be far, because Navoran telepathy didn't have a very long range. But he couldn't be in the casino. Even standing behind the building would rouse suspicion.

But he could be under it. Vex reached out with her mind, trying to sense if Python was in the utility tunnels below the building. But she sensed nothing, because that wasn't one of her abilities. Still, it had been worth a try. Given the abilities she had now, who knew what else she might be capable of someday.

There was a hallway nearby that led to the restrooms. At the end of the hall, she saw a door marked "Utility Access: Employees Only." There was a keycard reader next to the door. Vex walked around the casino floor, looking for a distracted employee. She spotted a floorman arguing with an older woman about whether the slot machines were rigged. The floorman's keycard dangled from his belt. Vex made sure no one was looking, and held out her hand. The keycard wriggled out of its protective holder and flew into her grasp.

Once again making sure no one was watching, Vex walked down the hallway, swiped the keycard, and slipped into the utility room. It was hot in there, and not well-lit. Steam pipes and fuse boxes lined the walls. She found a floor grate with a ladder leading down into the tunnels below. The grate was locked, but Vex was good with locks.

As quietly as possible, she descended into the tunnel. These passages connected every business on this street. The tunnel stretched as far as she could see in both directions, with many side tunnels branching off the main passageway. Vex knew Python would want to be as close to his partner as possible to keep their mental link. She estimated about where the player had been sitting and searched in that direction. She arrived at a four-way junction, and peeked down the right tunnel.

Bingo. Python sat on a box, staring straight ahead, probably only seeing through their partner's eyes. If Vex was quiet, she might be able to subdue them without much of a struggle.

Vex had only met one Navoran, but Trenyn's powers were considered weak for their species. It was a dangerous prospect, attacking a fully-powered Navoran. They were powerful telepaths, and their telekinesis was unmatched. Vex could throw apples, but Python could probably throw hovercars. But she came prepared. Glik had given her a tranquilizer pistol, but instead of a sedative, the darts were filled with a drug that suppresses telekinesis.

Still crouched at the hallway entrance, Vex took careful aim at Python, and fired. The dart flew straight toward its mark. Then, mere centimeters from its target, the dart stopped in mid-air. Python turned their head and glared at Vex. *Did you really think that would work?* they asked telepathically.

Python stood up. They were about half a meter taller than Vex, had a large head, and yellow eyes. They had two arms but four hands – each arm split into two forearms at the elbow. Their blue skin turned darker, a sign of anger. The dart still hovered near their head.

Vex put on a brave face. "Python, you are wanted for eleven counts of fraud. If you come peacefully… well, it would sure make my job easier."

Python hit her with the telekinetic equivalent of a punch to the face. It didn't hurt much, but it sent her backward with such force that she flew more than ten meters. She might have broken some bones if she hadn't used her own telekinesis to soften the landing. She rolled to her left and got to her feet. Seeing another side tunnel nearby, she sought refuge there.

It was a dead end, but there was a locked metal box fastened to the wall. Vex popped the lock and the box swung open on a hinge, revealing a control panel full of buttons and levers. *There you are,* she heard Pythen think as they reached her passage. She felt a prick in her neck. Pythen had hit her with her own dart.

Desperate, Vex pulled the largest lever, and all the lights went out. It was pitch black in the underground tunnels. Could Navorans see in total darkness? Vex wasn't sure. She pulled out her monocular and switched it to night vision. Pythen certainly looked like they couldn't see her. They appeared to be listening hard for her movement. Vex pulled the dart out of her neck and threw it across the hall. Pythen heard it hit the wall, and turned in that direction.

Vex pulled out her pistol and fired, the dart hitting Pythen in the back. They turned around angrily, throwing another invisible punch in Vex's general direction. She tried to jump to the side, but it still knocked her sideways. Then the drug started to kick in, and Pythen staggered around, disoriented.

The effect was worse for Pythen than it was for Vex. Vex had been taught from an early age to suppress her telekinesis, and even today she treated it like a backup weapon. But Navorans were so incredibly dependent on their powers, losing them was like losing their arms.

The emergency lights flickered on. They could now see each other unaided, but without their mental powers, they were on equal footing. Vex pulled out her AON blades and switched them on. "Last chance," she said.

I'll take it, Pythen answered, their shoulders slumped.

"Oh," Vex said, almost disappointed. She hadn't expected that. She pulled out two pairs of cuffs and slipped them around Pythen's wrists.

Pythen's partner got away, but without a telepathic

sidekick, he was out of business anyway. Python was kept drugged until they could be placed in a special cell that suppressed their abilities. Vex collected her bounty and returned to the Bloodwind.

A few days later she got a message from her mother. At first, she was confused. How did her mother know her address? Then she saw that it had been forwarded from the Bounty Hunter Registry. Pretty much anyone could message any registered hunter that way. Vex's anonymity was still guaranteed unless she replied directly.

"My dearest daughter,

I saw your picture on the news. I'm so proud of you for catching that criminal. I have been following your career. You seem to be doing very well.

I miss you very much, but this is not an invitation to come home. When you left, a weight was lifted from this house. I've stopped drinking, your father and I have reconciled, and we've agreed to put the past behind us. I'm afraid that if you were to come home now, it would upset the apple cart.

But, I would still very much like to see you. Maybe we could meet for lunch sometime, just you and me. Your father doesn't have to know. Just let me know.

I wish you the best of luck in your new career. Be careful and stay safe.

Love you always,

Mom"

Vex did not reply. She already had a family.

01.07 *The Trap*

ED.02508.03.02

"Glorious people of Valos, It has been two months since the series of assassinations that sent us into hiding. In an abundance of caution, we have kept our locations a secret. But I am tired of living in fear. I will be making a public appearance tomorrow on the central stage in Grand Square. I encourage any and all to attend. We will be taking many precautions, and I'm prepared to fight if I have to. So to any would-be assassins – bring it on. I dare you."

Lemondrop finished her speech, and the transmission ended. "Think it'll work?" she asked. She was in yet another safe house, along with Raven and Trenyn. It was sparsely furnished, mostly with card tables and folding chairs.

"She'll suspect we have a plan, but she can't resist a dare," Raven said.

It all depends on what Vernach told her, Trenyn added.

The following day, Lemondrop stepped up to the podium. Six armed guards stood with her on the stage, each in golden armor. A box the size of a moving van sat near the stage, draped in a giant tarp. The large crowd murmured excitedly in anticipation of their leader's speech. Looking absolutely fearless, Lemondrop spoke into the microphone.

"Exalted citizens, thank you for coming. Two months ago, a most terrible tragedy occurred. Not just to Valos, but to eight planets across the galaxy. Fourteen excellent leaders lost their lives in a series of assassinations that forever altered the universe. It may well be the worst terrorist attack in recent memory. Not since the destruction of the IGP space station eight years ago has anyone shown such blatant disregard for sapient life. These terrible crimes were really… terrible."

As she spoke, her eyes kept darting toward the tarp. Earlier that day, they'd found a transponder cube hidden in Lemondrop's podium, and relocated it. If Andoro attempted an assassination today, he'd be teleporting directly into a trap. Raven's voice sounded in her earpiece. "Keep stalling, he hasn't shown up yet."

Lemondrop continued. "It would be a disservice not to honor those who lost their lives. Please indulge me for a moment to honor the victims. The first killed was Janiz Ortina-Z'varan, newly elected President of the United States of North America on Earth. Next was Asahi Suen, Premier of the Associated Asian Nations. Then he killed Mark Koslov, the Prime Minister of the Euro-Russian Union. After that, he teleported to Valos, where he killed our own Venus Vermon, Head of the Council of Heirs. After that, he went to Grunthar, where he killed The Grag Prime Wotharn. He killed two leaders on Galea, first was Jartak Vem-Thee, the Head Chair of…"

"Okay, we've got him," Raven said.

"…and the rest," Lemondrop concluded abruptly. "But now, I am proud to announce that we have caught the assassin!" She gestured toward the box. The tarp was pulled away, revealing a clear chamber. Inside, Andoro Korr slashed at the walls with his AON sword. The chamber was constructed of heat-resistant transparent walls, which were immune to AON weapons. The box was surrounded by an electromagnetic field that prevented him from teleporting away.

When the cheering died down, Lemondrop continued. "He will never harm anyone again. But there's more. Our top scientists have unraveled the secret of his teleportation. We know how to predict his next target. Even if his boss sends another assassin, we'll be ready."

The crowd went wild. Behind Lemondrop, one of the guards removed a glove and lunged forward. Before the other guards even knew what was going on, the rogue guard thrust a clawed hand through Lemondrop's back. Lemondrop looked down with horror as she saw the familiar hand burst through her chest.

Then the guard withdrew her hand and jumped into the crowd. The other guards now had their weapons raised, but they couldn't fire into the crowd. The guard removed her helmet as she ran. Those nearby recognized Tena immediately. As she fled through the crowd, she reached out, slashing at random citizens indiscriminately with her razor-sharp, bony fingernails.

Andoro Korr pounded on the transparent wall of his container, as if to say, "What about me?" But Tena's destination was in the opposite direction. She reached the edge of the crowd and vaulted over a parked hovercar. The hovercar exploded behind her as she continued her getaway. It created a fireball much larger than one would expect from a hovercar, and several nearby citizens were injured.

The guards, the crowds, and even the cameras lost track of Tena after that. Officers swarmed the area looking for her, while medtechs tended to the wounded. Lemondrop was put on a stretcher and loaded into an ambulance. But instead of a hospital, she was taken to a secure location.

"How is she?" Alterra Sarr had just arrived at the safe house. Trenyn was waiting for her. More friends would be arriving throughout the day for an important meeting. The makeshift medbay was separated from the rest of the room by a curtain. Alterra could hear medical equipment beeping from the other side of the curtain.

There's something you should know, Trenyn began, but then the curtain was pulled aside.

"She'll be fine," Lemondrop said, standing by the bed. Another woman entirely lay in the bed, receiving treatment from Raven.

Alterra rushed over to the bed. The injured woman was a good friend of hers, the shapeshifter Dervish. "I knew she would go for the chest," Dervish said weakly. "I made sure she didn't hit anything vital."

"She'll heal quickly," Raven said. "Marae are known for that. Their internal organs are... complicated."

"You were very brave to do that," Alterra said to Dervish.

"I thought about using an android or a hologram," Lemondrop said. "But I didn't think it would fool Tena. Our friend here is an excellent impersonator." Dervish smiled proudly at the compliment.

"Where's Andoro?" Alterra asked.

"He's here," Raven answered. "Why?"

"I want to see him," Alterra said.

"I'm not so sure that's a good idea," Lemondrop said.

"I used to be his fiancée," Alterra said. "I know how to push his buttons. I might be able to get him to divulge something he otherwise wouldn't."

Lemondrop looked skeptical.

"We're from the same planet," Alterra added. "We have the same skills and abilities. I might spot a flaw in your cell design that he could use to escape."

"Fair enough," Lemondrop said. "But not alone. I'll come with you."

"I thought I told you to always wear a mask in my presence," Andoro growled as Alterra sat down.

"And I think *that* was my answer," Alterra replied, pointing at Andoro's eye patch. In addition to the patch, he wore a plain pair of pants and a shirt. Everything he'd brought with him had been confiscated.

"Have you removed his Levatech implants yet?" Alterra asked Lemondrop.

"Doctor Eshton will be here later today to do the procedure," she answered. "Until then, we have those to keep him from escaping." She pointed at several boxes embedded in the walls.

"I've got to hand it to you," Alterra said, addressing Andoro. "You've really ruined your life this time. Right now, fourteen different governments are fighting over your fate. Most want you executed. At least one wants to hire you."

"I'll update my resume," Andoro said.

"I wouldn't bother," Alterra said. "What were you thinking? Tena isn't coming back for you. You know this. She used you, and now you're going to die for her."

"Unless?" Andoro said.

"Right now, several planets are on the brink of war over which one gets the honor of executing you. Their citizens are out for blood. They need a target for their revenge, and you're it. But if you help us catch Tena, she becomes the target. You'll still spend the rest of your life in a box, but at least you'll be alive." Alterra stepped closer to the transparent wall, trying to read Andoro's face.

"Pass," Andoro said.

"But you can…"

"I said pass," Andoro repeated.

It was time to change tactics.

"There's something else," Alterra said with an unsure expression. "I don't know why I'm telling you this… I mean, we're not really telling people yet… but you're almost family, and when am I going to see you again? If you ever make it back to Auroris - which I hope you don't, really, seeing as how you're about to be executed - but if you do, maybe you can relay this news to my mother…"

Andoro groaned. "I'm going to take a nap. Wake me when you get to your point."

"I'm going to have a baby," she said. Lemondrop's eyes widened in surprise, but Andoro seemed unfazed.

"Huh," he said. "I thought your husband had his balls cut off."

Alterra bristled. "Before *she* transitioned, *she* saved some of her semen." Andoro knew how to get under her skin too. But she calmed herself down. It wouldn't do to let Andoro see that he could get to her.

Andoro frowned. "You always told me you didn't want children."

"Well, not with *you*," Alterra said. "Honestly? You're right. I never really pictured me having children. But Detanna's such an amazing person, the universe deserves more people like her."

"You were promised to me," Andoro said.

"You weren't good enough," Alterra replied.

"*I'm* not good enough?" His face was turning red. "Your husband doesn't even know what sex he is!"

"She knows exactly who she is, and she's worth twenty of you," Alterra said. It was time to drive it home. "My family line will produce generations of strong, skilled warriors. Your family line will end the day you are executed. Your own parents will erase the records of your birth. If you are remembered on Auroris at all, it will be as a coward who killed without honor."

Andoro pounded on the wall. "You're wrong, you little—"

"Come on, Lemondrop," Alterra said. "This bug isn't worth our time." Lemondrop stood up, and they started moving toward the exit.

"They will remember me!" Andoro shouted, pounding on the transparent wall. "After the fifteenth, I will never be forgotten again!"

The women froze, their backs still to Andoro.

"And Tena will come for me!" he continued. "She needs

my blood! Without me, she can't..." Andoro trailed off. He realized he'd said too much.

"What do you think?" Lemondrop asked.

"That's the closest we're going to get to a clue," Alterra answered, and they left Andoro to fume in his cell.

"Are you really pregnant?" Lemondrop asked, as they walked down the hallway.

Alterra sighed. "Please don't tell anyone yet. I don't want to jinx it."

Lemondrop wrapped her arms around Alterra and squeezed. "Congratulations!" she said. Lemondrop was known for her sunny disposition, but this was probably the first time she'd genuinely smiled since Inauguration Day.

Alterra smiled meekly. She was less than two months along, having had the procedure just a few days before the assassinations. The galaxy had felt safer then. But now? She wondered if she and Detanna were on Tena's hit list. Most likely yes, given their history. Alterra was no coward, but Tena unnerved her. She couldn't stand the thought of losing Detanna or the child.

She wouldn't get a good night's sleep until Tena was brought to justice.

01.08 *Instincts*

ED.02508.03.10

There was going to be a lot of walking, so she'd had to pack light. For Sekka, that meant no more than six animals. She hiked up the mountain, led by her guide, with various tweets and chitters coming from her huge backpack. The guide's name was Chamlek, and while he was friendly enough, Sekka had developed a rapport with the Kithian red parrot that perched on his shoulder.

Chamlek could only speak Kithian, but his parrot was bilingual. While the bird wasn't sapient, it was still incredibly smart. It knew over three hundred words in both Kithian and English, and could translate simple sentences from one language to the other.

"Kri-Kri," Sekka said to the bird, "How much farther?"

Kri-Kri repeated the question in Kithian, and Chamlek replied. "We walk until sundown," the parrot translated.

"Ugh," Sekka said. It wasn't even noon. Her backpack had been designed by her half-sister Raven. It had a sturdy but lightweight metal frame, which supported two small stacked cages, topped by a horizontal metal perch. It was lighter than it looked, but it was still no picnic to haul for long distances.

Sekka had picked this bounty because it was in such a

remote location. With Tena killing off council members, she didn't want to spend much time in public. But now she felt like it was a little too remote. What if she got separated from her guide? She didn't want to have to call the Bloodwind for help. At least with her abilities, she wouldn't have to worry about the local wildlife.

The target called himself Ursa Major. He'd once been a bear trainer with the circus, until he decided to chuck it all and live in the woods. He still trained bears these days, mostly to raid local campgrounds for supplies. When the park rangers tried to confront Ursa, they got mauled by bears. Once the word got out, the Kithian Park Service found it difficult to hire new rangers. The only choice had been to temporarily close the parks.

Some bounty hunters would have balked at this job. Kithian bears were some of the deadliest beasts in the galaxy. But Sekka wasn't worried. She'd yet to meet an animal she couldn't tame. Sekka had actually bid low for this job, because she didn't want anyone else to take it. Another bounty hunter might have just armed themselves to the teeth with flamethrowers and grenade launchers and such, brute-forcing their way to Ursa with no regard for the lives of the bears. But Sekka hoped to get through this with no lives lost.

The sun was now directly overhead. Every once in a while, a shadow passed by. One of Sekka's pets, a flying lizard she called Lizzy, circled the area looking for threats. Occasionally it would come down and perch on Sekka's backpack, but it only rested a few minutes before taking off again. Lizzy's extra weight didn't usually bother Sekka much, but today she was already tired.

The trail was rocky and hard to navigate, but at least it was a trail. Sekka's feet slipped on loose stones now and then, and she was glad she'd decided to wear boots. Even if they did clash with the rest of her ensemble. The crew had told her to dress less conspicuously, so she was dressed in pink camouflage.

Around two o'clock, they found a makeshift sign. On the flat side of a boulder, someone had written a short message in Kithian. Chamlek read it aloud, and Kri-Kri translated. "GO AWAY."

Instead of going away, they took a break for lunch. They sat down on some large rocks, and Sekka removed her backpack to check on her friends. The top cage held four steelbeak buzzers, which were similar to hummingbirds except more dangerous. The bottom cage held her best friend, a pink squirrel named Nutters. Lizzie landed on a rock nearby as well. Sekka pulled some food out of her side pouch, and fed all of them.

"Any sign of bears yet?" Sekka asked, taking a bite out of a granola bar.

Speaking through Kri-Kri, Chamlek reported that he hadn't seen any. They had passed some bear scat earlier, but it looked several days old.

As if on cue, they heard a roar. Kri-Kri flew away immediately, Chamlek calling after him. Then he turned to Sekka and rattled off a long set of instructions in Kithian. Sekka didn't understand a word of it. She pulled out her comm unit and loaded up the translation app, but it was too late. A huge shape appeared from behind a rocky outcropping, and Chamlek bolted.

Sekka wondered if she should follow him, but she didn't want to leave her animals. "Release the buzzers," Sekka told Nutters, and the squirrel opened the upper cage. The four brightly colored birds flew to Sekka, hovering just over her shoulders. Unfortunately, they sounded like bees, which attracted the bear's attention.

The Kithian bear stood on its hind legs, roaring at Sekka. At its full height, it was a good four meters tall, larger than any bear Sekka had seen on other planets. It had jet-black fur and yellow eyes. Sekka tried talking to it. Her Vermon ancestry gave her the ability to calm and control the minds of animals, making them friendly to her. This bear, however, was either too enraged or too stubborn, and it continued its approach.

Sekka pulled out her sidearm and fired. It was an energy pistol designed to shock humanoids into immediate unconsciousness. But it only made the bear angrier. It dropped back down to all fours and charged. "Get him," she told the buzzers, and they attacked. The four buzzers went for the face, their sharp beaks easily penetrating the bear's skin. The bear swiped at them, but they were much too fast.

"Lead it away from me," Sekka said, and the buzzers complied. The bear continued to swipe at them as they led it down the slope. Sekka ran in the opposite direction, going up the mountain as Chamlek had. The squirrel hopped on her shoulder as she left the backpack behind.

She didn't stop running until she was sure she was in the clear. Out of breath, she sat down in the middle of the trail and pulled the water bottle off of her belt. She took a large swig and then poured some into the cap for Nutters. "I think... we lost him," she said between heavy breaths. A few minutes later, the buzzers caught up to her. Sekka hoped they hadn't hurt the bear too badly.

Sekka continued hiking up the trail, hoping to find Chamlek. And after an hour, she did. Chunks of Chamlek's corpse lay scattered across the trail. Another message was scrawled on a nearby boulder, presumably in Chamlek's blood. Unfortunately, without Chamlek or his parrot, Sekka couldn't read the message. But she was pretty sure it didn't say, "Welcome to my mountain, please enjoy your stay." She continued to follow the trail uphill.

The sun was low in the sky when the end of the trail came into view. On the right, she saw a steep cliff. On the left was a cave. In the middle stood the welcoming committee. Two Kithian bears waited for her, and in the middle stood Ursa Major. He was a big, burly, hairy man with a bushy beard and a wide belly. And he was completely nude. Sekka stared at his face, his beard, the bears, the sky… her eyes wandered anywhere they could to avoid glancing at Ursa Minor. He didn't seem embarrassed, though. He called out to her in Kithian.

"I'm sorry, I don't understand Kithian," she yelled back, still walking towards him.

"I said I don't like visitors," he repeated in English. "Even if they are cute girls."

Sekka shivered at the compliment. This guy looked at least ten years older than her. "Ursa Major, I've come to collect the bounty on your head. Please come without a fight. Pretty please? I don't want your bears to get hurt."

Ursa's booming laughter was so forceful that some of the nearby pebbles shook. "For that laugh, you get to live, little girl. Now turn around and go back to school before you get detention."

Sekka stood her ground and drew her pistol. "You're coming with me one way or another," she said. She really hoped she could take him alive. She had no idea how she was going to move him otherwise.

Now Ursa looked angry. "Get her," he said, and both bears charged. Sekka stared the closest one in the eyes, and suddenly it attacked its partner instead. "I said get *her*, not each other," Ursa shouted in confusion.

Lizzy and the steelbeak buzzers swarmed Ursa. He swatted at them, but they kept drawing blood. Just then Sekka heard a roar. A third bear came running up the trail behind her. Judging by the wounds on its face, it was the same one that had attacked her earlier in the day. "Help!" she shouted, and the buzzers left Ursa to attack the new threat.

With most of the animals fighting each other, Ursa charged at Sekka. Lizzy kept clawing at his back, but he ignored it and kept his head down. Sekka raised her pistol and fired. It hit him square in the chest, and it slowed him down, but he kept coming. Sekka fired again, but missed.

Then he was on top of her, pinning her to the ground. Sekka struggled to breathe under the weight of his body.

Holding her gun arm down with one hand, he started choking her with the other. "Stupid little bi— OWCH!" he screamed. Nutters had bitten him in a particularly tender spot. Ursa rolled over and tried attacking the squirrel, but it easily avoided his grasp. Her hand now free, Sekka fired at Ursa again. This time it knocked him unconscious.

An hour later, Sekka retrieved her backpack. Nutters and the buzzers got back into their cages, and Lizzy perched on top. Then Sekka remounted her bear, which gave her a ride down the mountain. Walking next to her, another bear carried the unconscious form of Ursa Major. Riding down was a lot faster, especially riding bearback, but it was still dark by the time she reached the bottom.

Some officers were already waiting for her to take Ursa into custody and to process her reward. Sekka said a tearful goodbye to the bears and returned to the Bloodwind. She was sorely tempted to keep one of them, but she had the sneaky suspicion the rest of the crew would object. That was fine. She knew where to find the bears if she needed them again.

01.09 Ides

ED.02508.03.14

It was the fourteenth, and they were no closer to deciphering Andoro's outburst. Lemondrop, Raven, Trenyn, Alterra, and Doctor Eshton had lunch together in the Council of Heirs throne room. The council members were no longer in hiding. Now that they could detect the warp transponders, and Andoro's implants had been removed, they no longer felt the need to stay in a safe house.

"To be clear, did he say she would need his blood on the fifteenth, or were those two different things?" Eshton asked.

"He implied something would happen on the fifteenth," Alterra replied. "He also said Tena would rescue him because she needed his blood. I don't know if the two were connected."

And now he won't talk, Trenyn added.

"Have you tried..." Eshton began.

"Yes," Lemondrop answered. "Whatever you're about to say, yes. We tried truth serum, we tried using our freaky Vermon eye powers, we tried making him a deal. At one point we even sent Dervish in disguised as Tena, but he saw right through it."

"We haven't tried torture," Raven said.

Everyone looked at her, mouths open.

"I'm not saying we should," she clarified. "Moral issues aside, it's a notoriously unreliable way to acquire information. I just mean that we can't say we've tried everything. Other planets have been pressuring us to hand him over, planets that would have no qualms about torture. If something catastrophic happens tomorrow, and we haven't tried *everything*, it could look bad for Valos."

"You let me worry about public relations," Lemondrop said.

"Torture wouldn't work on him anyway," Alterra said. "Trust me, I know him."

Could it have been a red herring? Trenyn asked. *Maybe he didn't actually lose his temper. Maybe he saw an opportunity to send us on a wild goose chase.*

"It's possible," Alterra said. "But I don't think so."

"Regardless," Lemondrop said, "they're the only leads we have. Even if he fed us false information as a distraction, we have no other leads he could be distracting us from. We may as well work with what we have."

"What about the blood?" Raven asked. "If she needs Auroran blood, she might go after Alterra as well."

"Ugh, not again," Alterra groaned.

Does Auroran blood have any unusual properties? Trenyn asked.

"Not that I know of," Alterra answered. "Unless she's trying to clone him."

"She wouldn't need a constant supply of blood for that," Raven said. "If Tena planned to clone Andoro, she would have just taken some cells when he first started working for her, and worked with those."

Nithari use human blood as an intoxicant, Trenyn offered. *Maybe Auroran blood has some effect on Tena's mother's species.*

"For that matter," Raven said, "maybe Tena has a Nithari on staff. I wonder what Auroran blood does to them."

"Both Aurorans and Nithari are elusive people," Eshton said. "Very xenophobic. They can't possibly cross paths very often. I don't even know where one could find a Nithari these days."

"I do," Raven said.

"You want me to what?" Glik asked.

Raven's face was displayed on the medbay's viewscreen. "Instead of the synthetic human blood you've been giving her, try some of Wisp's blood," she suggested.

"I won't treat my patient like a guinea pig," Glik said.

"I'm not asking you to," Raven said. "Run whatever tests you need to beforehand. Allergy tests. Toxicity tests. When you're sure it won't hurt her, just give her a little bit at first. At the first sign of any trouble, abort the experiment. But hurry. Whatever Tena has planned, it might happen tomorrow."

"You're asking me to run a month's worth of tests in mere hours," Glik said.

"It's okay," Lyryssa said. Glik jumped at the sound of her voice. He hadn't heard her approach. "I don't mind being a guinea pig if it saves lives."

Glik sighed. "I'll let you know what I find out," he said, and turned off the viewscreen. He pulled out his comm unit and summoned Wisp. She showed up a few minutes later.

"I'm happy to contribute," Wisp said, once she'd been briefed. "I was a Nithari once."

Glik didn't know how to respond to that, and decided to let it go. Once he'd drawn a few vials, he told Lyryssa, "I'm going to take some tissue samples from you now. I'll run a few tests, and see how your cells interact with her blood. If I see nothing dangerous, I'll call you back in a couple of hours and give you a small amount of diluted blood."

"Stop being such a worrywart," Lyryssa said. Before Glik could stop her, she snatched one of the vials, popped off the cap, and poured it down her throat.

"Lyryssa!" Glik shouted.

"Relax," she said. "I'll be... whoa."

"What is it?" Glik said, worried. "Do you feel okay?"

She felt more than okay. For starters, her pain was gone. Human blood muted the pain, but she could always feel hints of it in the background, threatening to return if she missed her next dose. But on Wisp's blood, there wasn't a hint of pain. But that wasn't all. She felt faster. Nithari already had unusually quick reflexes, but now she felt like she could snatch a zapfly out of the air. But there was one more thing. There was a weird tingling in her fingertips, and it was spreading into her hands...

"Oh no, she's disintegrating," Glik said in horror.

Lyryssa held up her hands. Her fingers were gone. For a second she shared Glik's panic, but then she realized she could still feel them. She touched her arm to be sure. The effect continued to travel along her body, and within a few seconds, she was completely invisible. "I'm still here, I swear," she told them. It was odd. Once the effect reached her eyes, she was able to see herself again, though her body had a ghostly, transparent quality.

The others just saw a floating nightgown. "Incredible," Glik said. Occasionally they saw a glint of movement, a minor warping of the air, but nothing they would have noticed if they weren't looking for it.

"I wonder how long it lasts," Wisp said.

"I'd better call Raven back," Glik said.

"So she's planning to use a Nithari to sneak in somewhere," Lemondrop said.

"Or to be her next assassin," Alterra added.

"We should increase the security around Andoro," Raven said. "Make sure any cameras also use infrared scanners and motion detectors. Guards should also wear infrared visors."

"Done and done," Lemondrop said, sending a text to her security team.

"The good news is that as long as we have Andoro, Tena's supply is limited," Raven said. "The bad news is we don't know how many vials she took before we caught him."

Of course, every planet had its own system of keeping time. Some had multiple time zones, while others used a single time zone across the globe. Many countries utilized some variation of Daylight Savings Time to maximize sunlight hours, and some cultures reset their clocks every day at sunrise. Quite often, various cultures on the same planet had different methods of keeping time.

But in situations involving more than one planet, most planets used Earth-UTC to refer to the current time. There were multiple reasons Earth time became the standard, but chief among them was the fact that humans were stubborn. In the long run, it was just easier to get used to Earth Time than it was to convince humans to learn something new.

On the evening of the fourteenth, Earth-UTC time, the citizens of multiple planets held their collective breath as midnight approached. They didn't know what to expect, but they took various precautions. Some people kept their kids home from school. Some avoided malls or other crowded areas. Some people hid in bomb shelters, or retreated to private space stations. Celebrities and politicians went into hiding.

But everyone watched the news, looking for any sign of a terrorist attack. On Earth, there was a minor earthquake in California. It had been predicted weeks in advance, and hardly did any damage, but that didn't stop widespread panic from those who thought it was a bomb. On Kalara, there was a tsunami, with similar results. A mass shooting on Chirminon was first reported to be Tena's armed forces, but was later revealed to be the work of a disgruntled factory worker.

Around noon, a volcano erupted on Vhelra. It was unexpected, as it occurred in an area that hadn't been known for volcanic activity. But it was in a sparsely-populated area, and the citizens were evacuated with little loss of life. It didn't even make intergalactic news at first, as all the news programs were preoccupied with speculation about Tena's plan.

But then, an hour later, another volcano erupted. This one sprang up in the middle of the capital city of Vhelra's largest country. Within fifteen minutes, ten more volcanoes erupted, all in major cities. Within an hour, there were a total of forty eruptions worldwide. The sky turned black and it became difficult to breathe anywhere on the planet.

Vhelra began planetwide evacuations, but it was too late for most of the citizens. Survivors swarmed the escape ships, but it was impossible to get ships to everyone who needed them. Many of the planet's spacecraft had been damaged by lava, and there was a severe shortage of ships left. Other planets rushed to help, but the warp gates could only transport so many ships at a time. The line to the warp gates stretched on forever, as volunteer rescue ships tried to come to Vhelra's aid.

The Bloodwind was one such ship. They happened to be near a warp gate when the disaster started, and were one of the first rescue ships to arrive. They sent down the three shuttles they had available, piloted by Zak, Wisp, and Vex. They scanned for survivors for as long as they dared, eventually rescuing forty-seven citizens in total. By the time they docked with the Bloodwind again, there was no point in going back for another run. The atmospheric conditions made flying too risky, and anyone still on the planet was beyond saving.

Vhelra had a population of ten billion. Approximately four million made it off the planet alive.

Later that day, a video was uploaded to GalaxyStars, a popular site for sharing all types of videos. Tena Vermon sat behind a desk, dressed in a business suit. She wore her hair in a tight bun, and a pair of glasses she didn't actually need. Above her left shoulder, a smaller screen played a video of

Vhelra's destruction. First from a distance, then from other angles from within the atmosphere.

In an uncharacteristically neutral voice, Tena announced, "This just in... Billions perish as Vhelra succumbs to a series of unnatural disasters, leaving the rest of the galaxy wondering: 'Is my planet next?' For a closer look, we go to Tena Vermon, rightful heir to the throne of Valos. Tena?"

The camera switched angles, and now Tena wore a low-cut red-sequined dress more in keeping with her usual style. "Thank you, Tena," she said. "It's good to be here."

Reporter Tena asked, "So am I to understand that you're responsible for the turmoil that has befallen the Vhelran people?"

"Of course," Tena answered. "But it gets so much better. The device I used to activate the volcanoes? I've planted similar devices in seven other planets. Galea, Kalara, Magnar, Earth, Grunthar, Valos, and Chirminon. All of these planets are now at my mercy."

Reporter Tena looked concerned. "But now that you've said that, won't they just dig up the other devices?"

"They can certainly try," Tena answered. "But good luck finding them. They're deep underground, and I hid my tracks well. Also, each device has a proximity trigger. You get too close without this shutoff remote, and it goes off anyway." Tena held up a remote and wiggled it playfully.

"So, what exactly are your demands?" Reporter Tena asked.

"Every planet on the list has wronged me at one time or another," Tena replied. "Or if not me, my father. And each can pay restitution to me in its own way. If a planet follows my demands, I will deactivate its device and take it off my grudge list."

Tena went on to list each planet by name, along with crimes they had committed against Tena, her late father, and the criminal organization formerly known as the Inner Eye, now called the True Eye. Most of these so-called crimes were actually just times the planet's law enforcement prevented the Inner Eye from committing crimes of its own. When Tena was done listing the crimes, she named the terms under which each planet would be forgiven.

On Galea, she called for the execution of several prominent law enforcement officials. The same for Kalara. Her enemies on Magnar had already been killed years before, so Tena simply asked them for a large sum of money. She ordered Grunthar to build her a fleet of warships, and to ally with her in a possible upcoming war. She asked Chirminon and Earth to release a number of prisoners, mostly former members of the Inner Eye. And all the planets were required to sign a treaty absolving Tena and the True Eye of their past crimes.

"And finally, we come to Valos," Tena concluded. "All I ask is that I retain the birthright that was promised to me. You will crown me as the supreme ruler of Valos in perpetuity. Okay, that's not all I ask. You will also release Andoro Korr. In addition, I want the following people placed into my custody, to do with as I wish. The current council of heirs: Lemondrop, Sekka, Nazdak, Raven, Karden, and Steve. All of the bounty hunters involved in destroying my gravity cannon six years ago: Detanna Taush, Alterra Sarr, Raven Vermon – oh look, she's on here twice – Trenyn 31746, and Dervish. Also Doctor G'Heesh Eshton."

"I don't think that's so much to ask," Reporter Tena said.

"Right?" Tena said. "I'm only asking for payback for all the times I was wronged. I will give them a week to respond. In one week, I will randomly detonate one of the planets that hasn't yet met my demands. I will continue to detonate a planet each week until either all my demands are met, or until there are no defiant planets left."

"Well, your terms certainly sound reasonable," Reporter Tena said, then turned to the camera. "You heard it here first, folks. Comply or perish, it's your choice. This is Tena Vermon, signing off. And if you liked this video, please hit that subscribe button for more quality content."

The video then showed the logo for the True Eye, followed by some outtakes. The video description included a link to the treaty the planets were required to sign, the Grunthian work order, and more in-depth instructions related to Tena's other demands. By the end of the day, the video had been viewed more than thirty billion times, though to be fair, most of the viewers hit the "thumbs down" button.

The galaxy erupted into chaos. Many citizens demanded that their leaders comply with Tena's demands. Others pressured their governments not to give in to terrorists. Millions of people fled the seven planets, seeking new homes elsewhere. Magnar and Chirminon complied almost immediately. Grunthar's Grag Prime refused at first, before being killed by his own people. The new Grag Prime complied immediately, spinning it as an alliance that would make Grunthar stronger.

As in most things, Earth was a bit more complicated. The prisoners in question were incarcerated in three different countries, and the governments were at odds on whether to comply. Two of the countries nearly went to war, but neither wanted to fire the first shot, or risk killing the prisoners Tena wanted released. The standoff would continue throughout the week.

The treaty was written as if Tena was already the ruler of Valos, and when viewed that way, the terms weren't entirely unreasonable. It was basically a peace treaty, absolving Tena and her organization of any past crimes, up to and including the destruction of Vhelra and any other planets that refused to submit to the demands in Tena's video. It was also very badly written, and had the distinction of being the first peace treaty in history to include the phrase, "Don't get all up in my business."

Galea and Kalara had been ordered to execute some of their law enforcement officials. Both planets initially refused. Then some of Galea's citizens took the law into their own hands, killing six of the eight officials. The other two took their own lives. On Kalara, their seven officials were transported to a secure location to keep them safe while the government decided what to do with them.

On Valos, a meeting was held in the grand palace. The attendees included everyone Tena had asked to be placed in custody: The council of heirs, Bloodstone's former team of bounty hunters, and Doctor Eshton. The Bloodhunters also sat in.

"Is there any chance she's bluffing?" Nazdak asked.

"She destroyed Vhelra," Lemondrop said. "She obviously has the technology, and no qualms about genocide."

"But why would she threaten to destroy Valos, when she wants to rule it?" Doctor Eshton asked. "It doesn't make sense."

"Yes it does," Lemondrop said. "To her. She's always been that way. If she can't have something, she'd rather see it destroyed than let someone else have it."

"So what are we going to do?" Karden asked.

"The people of Valos come first," Lemondrop said. "Right this minute escape ships are filling up. Any citizen who wants to leave, is free to leave. But many of them would rather die than leave their homes. Some are waiting to see what this council decides. But those of you in this room... those of us who would become Tena's prisoners... I can't speak for all of you. I intend to turn myself in, but if any of you wish to flee instead, I won't stop you."

"I'm not sure it's wise to give us the choice," Raven said. "It sounded like Tena's demands were all-or-nothing. If you're letting any of us go, we might as well all go, because anyone who stays is getting a death sentence."

"I know," Lemondrop said. "But I'm still not going to force any of you to stay. Doctor Eshton has a point about her plan not making sense. If we give her the keys to the planet, she's not still going to destroy it just because two or three of us escaped. The throne is too precious to her. She'll just place bounties on the heads of the missing prisoners, and torture the rest of us that much more."

A few of the council members turned green at the mention of torture. Lemondrop noticed. "Please take a few days to think about it," she said. "We have seven days. I will announce our intentions on the sixth day. If any of you decide to conveniently disappear in the meantime, I'll look the other way. We'll face the consequences and see if Tena has any mercy in her at all."

Zak raised his hand. "What about us?" The Bloodhunters had only come to take Sekka to the meeting, but Lemondrop had asked them to stay.

"Yes, thank you, Zak," Lemondrop said. "I would very much appreciate it if you would take some of your shuttles to the other targeted planets and look for… well, anything. If we knew what sort of device she used to destroy Vhelra, maybe we could find and deactivate the others. Take Raven, Trenyn, and Doctor Eshton with you, just have them back here before the end of the week. Maybe with their combined knowledge they can come up with something."

"The device on Vhelra would have destroyed itself when it was activated," Doctor Eshton said.

Maybe we can reverse engineer the process, Trenyn replied. *If we can ascertain the materials the device would require, maybe one of the ingredients will be something we can detect.*

"We could also try to find out where Tena is now," Raven said. "She might have shutoff codes at her current base of operations. If we can track where she uploaded the video from…" she broke off, thinking.

"Keep brainstorming," Lemondrop said, ushering them toward the door. "But do it aboard the Bloodwind. We don't have time to lose."

01.10 Data Mining

ED.02508.03.16

While most of the galaxy knew the planet as Galea, it actually had two names. The catlike Meu had been the first to make contact with other planets, so it was their name for the planet that had stuck. The doglike Caniks preferred to call the world "Boof," which was just their word for "ground."

The odds of such a planet existing were beyond incalculable. Any first-year science student, upon learning of Galea for the first time, thought that there must be a misprint in their textbook. A planet where humanoid cats and dogs evolved independently? Ridiculous.

And they were right. Few people knew the truth about Galea and its engineered past. Midnight was one of them, but he'd been sworn to secrecy.

Today's mission had nothing to do with that. Midnight and Doctor Eshton searched for clues to the location of Tena's doomsday weapon. They had an entire planet to scan, and only a few days before Eshton would have to return to Valos. Of course, Galea's own scientists were also looking for the device, but Eshton had access to resources that Galea did not. They hoped.

They were in Doctor Eshton's spacecraft, as the

Bloodwind's four landing shuttles were all in use. Zak was searching Chirminon, Raven and Wisp were on Earth, Vex and Trenyn were headed to Magnar, and Glik and Lyryssa were investigating Kalara. Lemondrop and the others were doing their own search on Valos, and no one was looking on Grunthar as it was not a welcoming planet.

Simply flying over the surface with scanning equipment wasn't the answer. For one thing, they didn't know what they were looking for. For another, the device was likely too deep underground to detect. No, this would have to be solved with real detective work. They needed to retrace Tena's steps.

Midnight had several contacts in the government of the Greater Continent of Meu. They could get him records of every ship that had come and gone in the past few months. It was a huge mountain of data to sift through, and they didn't know enough about Tena's mode of travel to narrow it down much. What's more, the other continents wouldn't be as forthcoming with their data. The Canik Empire was much more secretive, and the lesser continents didn't have the technology to track every visitor.

But there could be a clue in the way Vhelra was destroyed. The first volcano to erupt had been on one of the smaller island continents. This could mean that it was the closest to the doomsday device itself. If Tena picked that location for a reason when planting the device, she might have used the same logic in planting the devices on the other targeted planets.

That first volcanic eruption had been in an area with a lot of caves. That had probably made it easier to get the device underground. If she used a tunneling device to dig through the planet's crust, then using it in a cave would have kept her away from prying eyes. Or, depending on how the device worked, she might have just located a particularly deep cave and dropped it off.

Of course, all of this assumed Tena even had a rhyme or reason for where she chose to plant the weapon.

* * *

They landed at the Meu Capitol Data Center, where several government agents waited for them. They put Doctor Eshton straight to work. Using a data analyzation program written by Raven and Trenyn, Doctor Eshton inputted satellite records from all over the planet, along with the records from the two nearest warp gates.

Meanwhile, Midnight worked with several geological experts trying to determine the best spot on the planet to plant a volcanic doomsday device. They came up with dozens of possibilities, and ranked them according to ease of access as well as effectiveness. As they came up with likely locations, agents left in shuttles to investigate those sites.

When sites popped up in the Canik Empire, the researchers transmitted their data to that continent's government, where they would do their own research. Galea's two largest continents had a contentious relationship, but when the entire planet was at stake, they didn't mind working together.

They worked for twenty hours straight, their eyes crossing from poring over screen after screen of numbers. Midnight and Eshton each got about four hours of sleep, then went straight back to work. The records weren't yielding any useful information, and the sites the agents investigated kept coming up empty.

Hopefully the other teams were having better luck.

They were not. Each team had varying levels of success accessing data from the local governments. Some of the countries were more than happy to share their information if it meant finding the doomsday devices. Some of the teams had to resort to hacking to get their hands on the data they needed. But in the end, none of them found anything useful.

The least helpful planet was Magnar. Their government refused to cooperate, and wouldn't even allow Vex and Trenyn's ship to land. But Trenyn was able to write a virus that gave them access to the satellite records. This planet didn't get a lot of traffic. All ships required government clearance, and every ship was searched and their cargo recorded. This would have been the most difficult planet for Tena to plant one of her devices, with the possible exception of Grunthar.

And yet, they still found nothing. However Tena was getting her weapons onto these planets, her method was untraceable. Each team continued to gather data until the fifth day, then they wrapped up and returned to Valos.

01.11 *Deadline*

ED.02508.03.21

It was now day six. Each planet had signed the treaty. Four of the planets had met all of Tena's demands. Citizens on the other three trembled in fear, wondering what the future would bring. Evacuation ships ran constantly, but there were always more people. The rescue ships were running out of places to drop off the evacuees.

Only three of the planets were out of compliance. Kalara was a peaceful planet, and didn't even have a death penalty. The thought of executing seven heroes was so offensive to them, they decided to call Tena's bluff. Earth released prisoners in two of the three countries where they had been held. The Euro-Russian Union was the holdout. They didn't want to look weak, so instead of releasing Tena's allies, the country had executed them. There was no way to comply with Tena's orders now, so they would just have to wait and see her reaction.

Valos agreed to give up the throne, and they released Andoro Korr. Most of Tena's enemies were ready to turn themselves in. Steve and Nazdak, however, had left the planet. Karden thought they were cowards, but Lemondrop was more forgiving. They could only hope the two missing council members weren't too important to Tena.

On the dawn of the seventh day, a shuttle landed on Valos, in front of the grand palace. Tena got out, escorted by ten heavily-armed androids and a man wearing dark robes. She had called ahead and made her instructions clear. She was to be allowed clear passage to the throne room, where Andoro Korr and her new prisoners would be waiting for her. Any attempts at resistance, or any attempts on Tena's life, would result in the destruction of a random planet.

Tena entered the throne room and immediately sat in the largest seat. She gestured to her robed companion, and he sat on Tena's left. From the small crowd of people before her, she gestured at Andoro Korr, and he sat down on her right. Then she studied her prisoners. If she noticed the absence of Steve and Nazdak, she didn't say anything. She simply said, "Lock them away," and some guards led them to a cell. No one resisted; they knew what would happen if they did.

Now comfortable on her throne, Tena uploaded a new video to GalaxyStars. "Citizens of the galaxy, I want to thank you for your compliance. Some of you were a bit... naughty with your interpretation, but I will forgive you, just as I expect you to forgive me for my past indiscretions. Going forward, all I ask is that we remain civil with each other. Galaxy-wide peace, that's all I want."

She pulled the camera in closer to her face. "I will not be removing the doomsday devices from your planets at this time. I'm not a fool; I know damn well that some of you are just waiting for the threat to be over so you can plot your revenge. The only way we can be sure of everlasting peace is if I keep one finger on the button. But I promise not to press it without a good reason. More later. Ta!" Tena kissed the lens of the camera and cut off the feed.

She leaned back on the throne and relaxed. She would probably have some softer cushions installed later, but it was still the comfiest she'd been in years. Leader of her own planet. Enemies locked up to torture later. More catastrophic plans in the making. Life was good.

Her father would have been so proud of her.

01.12 *Prisoners*

ED.02508.04.17

The Grand Palace on Valos was a monument to excess. While stunning to behold, the sight of it filled some council members with feelings of guilt. It had been built from white marble and granite mined by the oft-exploited and now-extinct Stonefolk. Much of the furniture was decorated with gold plating and filigree that had been obtained from illegal Inner Eye operations. Every bit of labor had come from prisoners and slaves, their only crime having been to disparage their government.

Tena did not suffer from these guilt feelings. To her, the past was the past, it didn't matter how they got here. Her own mother had been one of the Stonefolk slaves, who caught Lord Vermon's eye long enough for a brief fling. Whether Lord Vermon actually loved the woman was up for debate, but Tena liked to think so. In any event, she didn't feel her mother had been exploited. Quite the contrary, she'd been lucky to have had the opportunity to be so close to the great Lord Vermon.

And just look at this place! Tena wandered the great halls barefoot, enjoying the feel of the cold marble on her toes. She'd spent many hours here as part of the council, but that was just business. For the first time, it really felt like hers, and it was a wonderful feeling. She now lived in her father's old suite on the highest level. It was a truly decadent living space, with a huge bed, lush carpets, and a balcony that wrapped around the entire top floor.

The next largest suites belonged to Andoro Korr and Synthral Everdark, her top assassins. Below that, there were several floors full of meager living spaces for her many servants. Then there were offices and labs. Of course, the council meeting chamber was on the first floor. And below that, there was the dungeon.

The dungeon hadn't been used since Lord Vermon's untimely death. One of the first things the Council of Heirs had done was to release the prisoners and find them places to live. Tena had been one of the objectors to this act, but she had been outvoted. Now that she was in charge, she knew it would fill back up pretty quickly.

Today it held nine prisoners. With one exception, each had their own private cell, made of soundproof walls so they couldn't talk to each other. Each prisoner wore shiny gold underwear and nothing else. This was partly so that they would be easy to spot if they escaped, but mostly because Tena found it funny.

She walked down the hallway, flanked on each side by doors with tiny windows. She peeked in each one as she passed. Lemondrop sat on her bunk, and looked up as Tena peered in. Tena smiled and waved, but Lemondrop answered with an obscene gesture. Tena shrugged and walked on.

Next she looked in on Sekka. It was odd seeing Sekka without one or more animal companions, and she looked miserable. Tena felt an odd pang of empathy. While they'd often voted against each other in council meetings, they'd never had any real grudge against each other. Tena wondered if Sekka might be persuaded to come around to her point of view. Sekka rarely showed interest in anything but animals; perhaps Tena could use that to her advantage. Her skills might prove useful.

Raven and Karden shared a cell. Without her robotic body, Raven needed a caregiver to help her eat and tend to other biological functions. Of course, Raven would have preferred to be locked in with Trenyn, or failing that, another woman. Which is exactly why Tena had locked her up with Karden. She thought it would be more embarrassing for both of them. Just the thought of it made her giggle.

Tena walked by the next cell without looking in. Detanna's group of bounty hunters had been responsible for the death of Tena's father, as well as the destruction of her precious gravity cannon. Detanna would definitely pay, but Tena didn't want to be too hasty about it. She had years to think of the perfect punishment. Tena kept walking, past Trenyn, Dervish, and Doctor Eshton.

Finally she reached Alterra's cell, opened the door, and walked in. "You're starting to show," Tena said, not bothering with a greeting.

Alterra just sighed. She'd been dreading this conversation. Now that Tena knew Alterra was pregnant, who knew what twisted games the madwoman would play. "If you even think of hurting my baby…" Alterra began.

"Hurt it?" Tena scoffed. "The offspring of an Auroran and the greatest bounty hunter in the galaxy? Such exquisite breeding stock will produce exceptional progeny. I'd rather see this palace crumble to dust than harm one hair on your child's head. Or should I say, *my* child's head."

Alterra's mouth dropped open. "You wouldn't."

"You really think there's anything I wouldn't do?" Tena laughed. "You already owe me a clone, but this is even better because it hurts you more."

Alterra opened her mouth, ready to let loose either a string of threats or pleas, she wasn't sure which. Then she realized that whatever she said, it would just feed Tena's ego. She wanted Alterra to make threats, or to beg for mercy. All of this was just a way to feel powerful. Alterra closed her mouth and said nothing.

Tena chuckled at that, too. She put a hand on Alterra's shoulder. "I promise you," Tena said, "That I will give you the best medical care possible. All the way up until the day the baby is born."

"…and then?" Alterra asked.

"And then I'll decide if I still have any use for you," Tena replied, and walked back out the door.

Once the door closed and locked, Alterra cursed up a storm. Then she sat on her cot and put her head in her hands. She wondered if she could terminate the pregnancy if she needed to. The cot was just a length of heavy cloth suspended by two metal bars jutting out from the wall. If she were to ram her abdomen against one of the bars, would that work? She wasn't sure.

But she seriously didn't want to. She already loved this child, and wanted to carry it to term. She still held out hope that Tena would be defeated before the child was born. It was a gamble, though. Alterra had no moral qualms about abortion, but if she was going to do it, she'd rather do it as early in the pregnancy as possible. Plus she might not have a choice later on. Tena would probably keep her restrained in a hospital bed closer to the due date.

She could always try to escape, but then Tena might destroy a planet. Alterra was certain that, given the combined skills of all the prisoners in this cell block, they could escape if they wanted to. But they wouldn't even try until they got word that Tena's doomsday devices had been found and deactivated.

Alterra wanted this child more than anything she'd ever wanted in her life. But she refused to sacrifice an entire planet for it.

01.13 *Field Test*

ED.02508.04.20

"I still don't think this is a good idea," Glik said.

"You worry too much," Lyryssa replied. "Besides, if I get into too much trouble, I've got my blood buddy here." She put her arm around Wisp's shoulder.

"Watch her," Glik said into Wisp's ear as they walked past him to board the shuttle.

In the weeks since Tena had taken over Valos, she hadn't done much. At least not visibly. She hadn't made any additional threats or attempted to take over another planet. So far she seemed to be true to her word, that all she wanted was peace. However, she still hadn't deactivated her doomsday weapons, and her fleet of Grunthian warships kept growing.

Tena's prisoners had been incarcerated for about a month now, and the Bloodhunters thought about them every day. But they knew better than to attempt a breakout. Not while Tena had the power to destroy worlds. In their spare time, Zak and his crew still worked on finding where the weapons were buried. But each of the affected planets had its own people doing the same, and outsiders just got in the way.

In the meantime, the Bloodhunters still had bills to pay.

There were plenty of bounties left to pursue in the galaxy, and Lyryssa was itching to put her new abilities to the test. When a prisoner went missing on a moon called Umbra, it seemed like a great time for a field test.

The fugitive's name was Kroma Kee, or at least that's the alias she was using these days. She was an amphibian woman who could change her skin color. She'd disappeared during a transfer from one holding facility to another. The moon used a monorail for prisoner transfers, and Kee had escaped while it was en route.

Apparently one of the transfer guards hadn't been briefed on her skills, and had allowed her to use the restroom by herself. When she didn't come out, he'd opened the door only to find her clothes on the floor, and the restroom empty. Or so it had appeared. Then she'd attacked him from behind and fled who knows where.

No one was sure how she'd gotten off the monorail itself, but they'd performed a thorough check for life signs upon reaching their destination, and the monorail was clean. No shuttles had arrived or departed since the escape, so they knew she had to be somewhere on the moon. And that was only forty million square kilometers.

The shuttle carrying Wisp and Lyryssa landed on a clifftop pad, where security promptly locked it down with large clamps so it couldn't be stolen. A long bridge led to the holding facility, which was built into the side of the mountain. The local government didn't want to interfere with the nature at ground level, so everything on this moon was built into mountains and accessible by the monorail system.

Several teams of guards already roamed the area, but it was dark, and their target was difficult to see even in the daylight. Still, she could only have gotten so far. The moon was mostly rock, with thin forests and many lakes. It had a few indigenous animals, but nothing larger than a house cat. The calls of various nightbirds could be heard whooping through the trees. A light rain trickled down from the sky, accompanied by a cool breeze.

"Thanks for coming," a security officer said as they stepped inside his cliffside office. He was human, with a pleasant smile but worry in his eyes.

"I'd like to start by examining the security footage," Wisp said. "My partner will look over the monorail if that's okay."

Wisp studied the footage. She was a little creeped out that they had cameras in the restrooms, but she supposed it was a necessary evil. In the video, Kee went into the restroom, removed her clothing, and vanished against the wall. When the guard entered, she dropped down from the ceiling, knocked him out, and fled the restroom. For the rest of the trip, at no point did any doors, windows, or storage hatches open by themselves. Wisp strongly suspected that Kee just waited for the monorail to stop, and left unseen as soon as the doors opened to let the new guards on.

Meanwhile, Lyryssa walked up and down the monorail, not sure what she was looking for. "Do you have the clothes she was wearing?" she asked one of the guards. They handed them to her, and she sniffed them. "She doesn't have much of a scent," Lyryssa said, disappointed. She usually had such a strong sense of smell.

"Her species doesn't have sweat glands," the guard told her. "We took the sniffer hounds out earlier but they couldn't sense a thing. And the rain just makes it worse."

"I'm better with blood," Lyryssa said. "Do you have any of her blood?"

"Not that I know of..."

"A used tampon maybe? Does her species menstruate?" Lyryssa wasn't sure if menstrual blood would smell the same as regular blood, but it was worth a shot.

"I'm honestly not sure," the guard said, looking embarrassed. "I'll call the guards at her old cell and see if they've emptied her trash."

Lyryssa rolled her eyes. This supposedly grown man had blushed when she'd brought up menstruation. A prison guard, no less.

A couple of minutes later the guard got back to her. "Yes, she, uh, menstruates," he said, blushing again. "But no, not this week. We don't have a sample for you, I'm sorry."

Lyryssa waved him off and returned to Wisp. They asked to be let down to ground level. A guard accompanied them on the long elevator ride down. It was an open elevator, a metal cage that moved along a vertical track. On the way, he gave them some ground rules. "This is an emergency situation, so we've suspended some of the usual restrictions. But please, try not to harm or even scare the local wildlife. Don't hurt any plants. Don't leave anything behind. Don't use fire. Don't feed any animals."

Wisp and Lyryssa both nodded and promised to be careful.

"And look," the guard said as they reached the bottom. "Her reward is the same dead or alive. She's very dangerous. I wouldn't blame you if you just shot her on sight."

Wisp narrowed her eyes. "How dangerous can she be? She's unarmed and naked."

The guard ignored her question. "Also, she has a silver tongue, so be careful."

Lyryssa tilted her head, unfamiliar with the expression.

"She can be very charismatic," the guard clarified, looking at the ground. "She's talked her way out of trouble before. Don't believe any of her lies."

Wisp was skeptical but nodded anyway.

"Just call when you need a lift back up," the guard said. He left the two of them standing at the bottom of the cliff.

When the elevator was out of earshot, Wisp turned to Lyryssa. "Anything about that seem weird to you?"

"His heart rate increased during that last thing he said," Lyryssa answered. "I could smell his pulse."

"He wouldn't make eye contact, either," Wisp said.

They stood at the base of the cliff, looking toward the woods. The ground was rocky here, but became softer by the tree line. Wisp was an excellent tracker, but the guards had trampled the ground in their own efforts to find Kee. Muddy tracks led in all directions, and much of the grass had been flattened. *And he had the audacity to lecture us about hurting plants?* Wisp thought.

Each of them had brought a pair of night vision goggles, but neither of them needed it at the moment. Aurorans and Nithari both had excellent night vision, and there was some moonlight, courtesy of one of the planet's other moons.

"Okay, blood me," Lyryssa said.

"What?" Wisp replied.

"What what?" Lyryssa said. "You know why I wanted to come." Lyryssa was already pulling off her shirt.

"Don't you at least want to try to find her without it first? Save it for emergencies?"

"Come on," Lyryssa said. "Glik has me running on treadmills and playing dumb video games to test my reflexes. I want a real test of my limits."

Wisp sighed and pulled a vial of blood out of her belt pouch. Lyryssa snatched it and downed the vial in one gulp. Within seconds her skin started to shimmer.

"Watch my stuff," Lyryssa said, removing the rest of her gear and clothing.

"You're not even taking a weapon?"

"Now what's the point of being invisible if I'm carrying a bunch of crap? She'll see a floating gun a mile away."

"But if I can't see you, I can't follow you," Wisp said.

"Good, we'll cover more ground if we split up anyway," Lyryssa said. "See ya!"

Wisp heard Lyryssa's footsteps run off into the woods. "Lyryssa? Lyryssa!" she shouted after her.

All of Lyryssa's senses felt supercharged. She already had

excellent night vision, but now the world looked as bright as day. But it wasn't just about seeing, she noticed more as well. Her attention kept falling on broken blades of grass, disturbed mud, and other signs of animal activity. The smallest movement caught her eye, from a leaf trembling in the wind to the breathing of a sleeping rodent.

Sounds weren't louder so much as she could now pick up individual sounds more easily. Instead of an audio slurry of insect chirps and nightbird calls, she could distinguish individual insects and their directions and distances. And the smells… it was like sonar for the nose. She could smell the blood of a thousand tiny animals, and one big one. And the big one was… to her right, about three hundred meters away.

Her heightened senses guided her through the forest, allowing her to step on the quietest parts of the ground, avoiding twigs and branches she might have snapped when not under the influence of Wisp's blood. She ran on the balls of her feet and covered a great distance in a short time. Before she knew it, she could hear Kee's breathing.

Lyryssa looked all around. Despite her improved vision, she couldn't see her prey. She knew Kee was nearby. The smell of her exotic blood was overpowering. There was a crash. A tree branch fell. Lyryssa glanced at the branch, then looked upward. Suddenly someone grabbed her from behind, one arm around her neck and the other around her waist.

"I won't go back," Kee grunted, trying her best to choke Lyryssa into unconsciousness. Lyryssa ran backward and rammed Kee into a tree. Kee held on, tightening her grip around Lyryssa's neck. Lyryssa started to get dizzy. It wasn't just from the choking, it was more than that. Her blood euphoria was starting to wear off. Her skin was already starting to become visible again. Wanting to make the most of her time, she rammed Kee backward again. This time she missed the tree and both of them tripped over a log.

Lyryssa struggled out of Kee's grasp and rolled out of the

way. Both women rose to their feet and sized each other up. Kroma Kee looked human for the most part. She had no hair and pale gray skin. Her mouth was slightly wider than a human's, and her nose was more narrow. Her eyes were a bit larger than a human's, with three irises in each eye. "Just walk away," Kee said. "I don't want to have to hurt you." She backed towards a tree, her pigment already starting to shift to match the bark pattern.

"Oh no you don't," Lyryssa said, lunging forward. She tackled Kee at the waist and slammed her to the ground. Then she kneeled on top of Kee, one knee on her stomach, and grabbed her by the shoulders. But Kee wasn't helpless. She had clawlike fingernails, which she dug into Lyryssa's sides. Lyryssa cried out in pain.

Kee pressed her advantage, moving like lightning. She rolled Lyryssa off of her and lunged for her throat. Kee opened her mouth wide, revealing a mouth full of needlelike teeth. Lyryssa raised her hands just in time, and Kee's mouth clamped down on her forearm. Once again Lyryssa cried out.

"Ah ownt aunt oo aff oo oo is," Kee said around the arm, clawing at Lyryssa's throat with her hands.

"What?" Lyryssa said, trying to pry Kee's mouth open.

Kee released the arm. "I said I don't want to have to do this." Then she opened her mouth and went for the throat again.

Lyryssa punched her in the nose, then kneed her in the stomach. "Then don't!" she said, rolling back on top of her, trying to pin her to the ground.

"I would rather die than go back," Kee said. She was out of breath. Her skin rippled, changing color to match the ground.

Lyryssa punched her again, then sat on top of her, holding Kee's arms down at the elbows. "So what? You're just going to live in these woods? You can't get off this moon. They search every ship that comes and goes. At least in prison you won't have to hunt for your meals."

"The guards take advantage of us," Kee said.

Lyryssa was about to hit her again, but paused. "Seriously?" she asked.

Kee nodded. "All the time."

"Have you told the warden?"

"He knows," Kee said. "They all know. The monorail? I was being transferred so the officers over there could give me a go. They trade us back and forth like blastball cards. I was the warden's fetish-of-the-day."

"Can you prove this?" Lyryssa asked.

"This moon is a women's prison. Did you see a single female guard?"

"That's a bad policy, sure, but not exactly proof," Lyryssa said.

"Then check the warden's office," Kee said. "All the transfers go through him. Check his personal messages."

They both turned their heads as Wisp approached. She had her bow drawn, and kept it aimed at Kee. "You found her? Good job," Wisp said.

"No!" Kee screamed, and used Lyryssa's distraction to roll out from under her. "Shoot me if you want, I won't go back!" She ran off into the trees, her skin shifting to match the environment. Wisp raised her bow, but Lyryssa held up her hand.

"Don't shoot her," Lyryssa said. "Give me some more blood. I'll go after her. I think if I can just talk to her again…"

"Actually you're bleeding pretty badly," Wisp said, nodding toward Lyryssa's wounds.

"Oh," Lyryssa said. She hadn't noticed. But the dizziness was back, and worse than before. Wisp pulled a medkit out of her belt pouch. While Wisp bandaged her wounds, Lyryssa filled her in on the conversation she'd had with Kee.

"The guard did say she was a good liar," Wisp said.

"Do you really believe that?" Lyryssa asked.

"Not even a little bit," Wisp said.

* * *

About an hour later, they called for the elevator. When they reached the top, they went to see the warden. They told him that they'd found Kee, but she'd gotten away. They asked if they could spend the night and try again in the morning.

The warden looked smug. He didn't like that they'd been ordered to call in outside help, and their failure gave him some measure of satisfaction. If his own *men* couldn't catch the prisoner, then these two *female* bounty hunters didn't have a chance. He allowed them to stay the night. He didn't have any spare guard quarters, but there was a break room with a couple of couches they could use.

They waited until the warden and most of the guards had gone to sleep. A few third-shift guards walked the hallways, but they were easy enough to avoid. The warden's office was locked, but it was easy enough to pick. Once inside, Wisp went straight to his computer and sat down, while Lyryssa started opening drawers. The computer was password protected, but Wisp found the warden's passwords written on a piece of paper under the monitor.

The warden's computer had a direct feed to every security camera in the installation. Again she noticed that there were even cameras in the restrooms, as well as the showers. Once again, gross but probably necessary. She wondered if the warden ever sat in this chair while watching the feed and… Wisp shivered at the thought, and decided she'd rather do this standing up.

The e-mails weren't a lot of help. The two facilities did seem to transfer prisoners back and forth more than was strictly necessary, but the reasons given in the e-mails were vague. There was a bit of inappropriate talk, such as describing certain prisoners as buxom or perky, but nothing that proved Kee's accusations. She did discover that over the past year, four prisoners had been shot trying to escape.

Lyryssa was going through a filing cabinet, filled with hard copies of prisoner medical records. Wisp waved her over. "Find the records for these four names," Wisp told her.

The records for deceased inmates were locked in their own filing cabinet. They didn't even have to pick this lock, as the key was in the desk drawer. Lyryssa found the corresponding folders, each one inside its own sealed envelope. All four women had been to the doctor the day before their deaths, but it didn't say why. Wisp had her suspicions.

"I'm going to need the warden's personal comm unit," Wisp said. "You find the infirmary, and see if there are more complete records stored there." She handed Lyryssa another vial of blood in case she needed it.

Once again, Wisp marveled at how useful her newest body could be. She'd spent lifetimes developing her stealth skills, but now that she had the Auroran ability to blend into shadow and absorb sound, she was practically unstoppable. She walked into the warden's bedroom without the slightest worry. The comm unit sat on his nightstand, right next to the warden's snoring head.

Wisp picked up the comm unit. The unlock screen required a four-digit PIN. She didn't have time for that. She turned the comm unit's volume to max and set it back down. Then she took out her own comm unit and sent the warden a text. The warden woke with a start at the loud chime, and grabbed his comm unit. Wisp stood directly behind him, unheard and unseen, watching his fingers as he typed in the PIN.

Her text read, "Thanks again for your hospitality. I promise we will catch her tomorrow."

The warden rolled his eyes and put the comm unit back on the nightstand. "Stupid woman," he mumbled, and was snoring again in seconds. Wisp grabbed his comm unit and left the warden's quarters.

The two bounty hunters met back in the break room.

Lyryssa hadn't needed to use the blood vial, as the infirmary hadn't been well guarded. Her discovery confirmed Wisp's theory. While the medical records for the specific patients had been deleted, the prison was vigilant about tracking supplies. The day before each of the four deaths, a pregnancy test had been signed out from the supply room.

They started going through the warden's text history. His texts were a lot more specific than the e-mails had been. They found several disgusting messages between the warden and one of his friends, in which the warden described in explicit detail the things he planned to do with one of the prisoners that would soon be in his care. "That should be enough," Wisp said, popping the comm unit into her pocket.

"What now?" Lyryssa asked.

"We call the IGP," Wisp said. "Once they make some arrests, we find Kee again and let her know it's safe."

"Ooh, maybe I'll get my name in the news," Lyryssa said. "I can picture the headline now..."

"Two Bounty Hunters Killed By Escaped Inmate," the warden said, opening the door to the break room. He held a gun on them, as did the four guards behind him. "What, you didn't think I had cameras in here too? And microphones? When I woke up again and found my comm unit gone, I figured it must be you two. Now put your hands in the air."

The wall next to the door seemed to shimmer for a second, and Kroma Kee leaped from her hiding spot to tackle the warden. The guards aimed their guns at Kee, but with her constantly shifting pigment, it was hard to tell what was Kee and what was the warden. Before they could give it too much thought, Wisp threw a dagger at the light switch, and Lyryssa drank the vial of blood. Wisp vanished into the darkness, and they took out the guards, one by one.

When the lights came back on, the warden and all four guards were incapacitated, bound together by their own handcuffs. Wisp made a quick call to the IGP, while Lyryssa and Kee watched the hallway for more guards. Occasionally another guard happened by and looked in to investigate, but they were restrained just as easily as the others had been. When the IGP finally arrived, Kroma Kee surrendered herself willingly, while Wisp presented them with the evidence.

Within a few days, the holding facility was under new management, with an all-female staff. Kroma Kee had several years knocked off of her sentence, both as a thank you for exposing the corruption, and in recognition of the undue suffering she had experienced. Several other prisoners also received reduced sentences after presenting their own testimony. The Bloodhunters were paid for recovering the fugitive, and given an additional reward for exposing the corruption on Umbra.

Wisp let Lyryssa take credit for the capture. For one thing, she'd done most of the fighting with Kee. For another, Wisp didn't want to be seen on the news. She usually wore a mask in public. While everyone who knew her called her Wisp, she used the name "Darkshado" with the Bounty Hunter Registry. Anything to avoid being on Tena's radar. Wisp was pretty sure Tena thought she had died on the same space station where she'd been cloned, and she wanted to make sure it stayed that way. So she always made sure not to be seen on camera.

Unfortunately, this time she was not successful.

01.14 *Behind the Curtain*

ED.02508.04.22

"Who does this look like to you?" Tena thrust the tablet right up against Andoro's nose. He had to push it away just to focus on it.

"The vampire-looking woman? I think she's one of the Bloodhunters."

"Not her, you idiot," Tena said. "The woman in the back. The one trying to hide her face from the camera."

Andoro squinted at the video. His left eye was artificial, and the squinting automatically activated the eye's zoom feature. The woman was dressed in black, her mask only showing her eyes and the bridge of her nose. Her gray skin and violet eyes suggested she was Auroran. But those eyes seemed so familiar... "She looks a lot like Alterra, but younger. But it's hard to tell with her mask on."

Tena fumed and stormed off, leaving Andoro wondering what that was all about.

Alterra's cell door opened, and Tena held up the tablet. It was a video titled "Major Controversy On Umbra: Entire Prison Staff Fired For Inappropriate Conduct." Lyryssa Nitelocke was being interviewed about her role in exposing the truth. She appeared to be eating up the attention with a spoon. Tena pointed to a woman in the background. "Who is this?"

Alterra shrugged and said, "Some random ninja cosplayer?"

Tena smacked her across the face with the tablet, breaking the device and cutting Alterra's cheek. "I know my own creations when I see them. Why didn't you tell me that your clone survived?"

Alterra held her hand against her cheek. "Well, for one thing, you and I aren't friends. For another, how would I know? I don't keep up with bounty hunters anymore."

Tena glared at her. "You would have escaped the Chronal Accelerator together. There were only two ships."

"I was alone as far as I know," Alterra lied. "Alarms went off, the power was fluctuating, and my shackles came undone. I ran to the landing bay and took the first ship I saw. If the clone had already stowed aboard, I never saw her. Maybe she hid on your ship, did you think of that?"

Tena wasn't buying it. "So you've never met Wisp?" She studied Alterra's face carefully. Tena didn't have Raven's ability to detect lies, but she spent a lot of time in the company of liars, so she knew what lying looked like.

"Is that what she calls herself?" Alterra asked. She didn't flinch, didn't avert her eyes, didn't show any tells.

Tena's face went red. It was obvious the woman wasn't going to cooperate. "You... you..." she began. "I'd torture you but I don't want to hurt the child. Maybe I'll torture Detanna instead?"

Alterra took a deep breath. "I swear I've told you all I know."

"Like I'd believe you," Tena said. "Of course you know how to lie. You spent two years in hiding when the entire galaxy was out for your blood. You helped kill my father, you destroyed my gravity cannon, you stabbed me in the back and left me for dead. It took me months to climb out of that rubble. Do you know I had to eat Thresh? He did not taste good." She was in full rant mode now, pacing the room and randomly punching walls.

Alterra just watched her blow off steam, ready to defend herself if necessary. She knew Tena had impulse control issues. No matter how much Tena needed Alterra alive, it was dangerous to be around her when she was this angry.

This thought occurred to Tena as well, and she opened the door. She turned to leave, then turned back. "Your due date is in six months. Enjoy it. Keep your secrets. Once I have your child, I'm going to make your life a living hell. First I'm going to chain you up and let Andoro have you. Then I'm going to make a whip out of thorns and..." she kept talking as she closed the door behind her, and continued muttering as she stormed down the hall.

Zak flew over the remains of Vhelra. The surface had calmed, no longer plagued by constant eruptions. However, it would take years for the surface to completely cool, possibly centuries. The skies were still dark, and the shuttle's windows were useless. They had to rely on sensors alone.

The planet was dead, but somewhere under all that molten rock, it still had stories to tell. "Still scanning..." Yeela said every few minutes. The drone was mounted on the ship's dashboard, plugged into the controls. She was both piloting the ship and scanning the planet. Actually, Zak's presence wasn't required at all, but Yeela liked his company.

Most of the people investigating the disaster looked at it from a weapons standpoint. What sort of weapon could do such a thing? How would one even build such a device? Others looked into the security of it. How did she plant the weapon without being detected? Is it possible to detect the device on other planets?

But recently, Yeela and Glik had come up with a unique angle – history. In researching the planet's past, they found a highly classified bit of lore that wasn't known to the general public. The Vhelran officials that knew this secret had been wiped out during the disaster. But Yeela had access to information databases all over the galaxy, and while browsing one of them, she'd learned about the Black Box.

Vhelra's Black Box was an underground data archive, full of the planet's oldest secrets. It was made of materials sturdy enough to survive almost any disaster. Under the right conditions, the box was designed to be accessed remotely from orbit. All Yeela had to do was locate the box, then transmit the right codes, and she would be able to download all of the data.

Yeela pinged and pinged, until she finally got a ping back. She received a request for an authorization code. The request was transmitted in a long-dead language, but she was able to extrapolate the meaning. At first the Black Box was stubborn, but Yeela's programming was newer and faster by thousands of years. She was able to overwrite the ancient security, replacing its protocols with a program of her own.

She downloaded the entire archive, which was several zettabytes of data. Then they returned to the Bloodwind so Yeela could analyze it in a safe location. Everything she needed to know would be there, it was just a matter of rooting through the data to find what was important. It actually didn't take her long.

The crew gathered in the galley to hear her findings. "Vhelra was an artificially constructed planet," Yeela began. "The ancients terraformed a gas giant."

"How do you terraform a gas giant?" Zak asked.

"By using technology that doesn't exist anymore," she replied. "They had a machine that could solidify gas into rock. The core of the planet was basically a giant 3D printer that used the planet's own gases as both fuel and filament. "

"Wow," Zak said. "Awesome as that is, how does that

help us?"

"Vhelra's internal structure was more organized than the randomness of most planets. Vhelra's lava tubes were laid out in a geometric pattern. Think sewer lines, only deeper. It even had internal shut-off valves to direct lava flow if need be. The ancient builders probably meant for it to be used in emergencies, but the following generations never even knew the feature existed. All Tena had to do was hack into the planet's internal control system and she had complete control over Vhelra's volcanoes."

Glik's jaw dropped as he realized what she was getting at. "So in other words..."

"There is no doomsday device," Yeela confirmed. "That's why we couldn't find them on any of the planets we've scanned. Tena was bluffing the entire time. The method she used to destroy Vhelra wouldn't have worked on any other planet in the galaxy."

"This is huge," Zak said.

"We should tell the governments," Wisp said.

"I'm worried about how Tena will react when the news gets out," Glik said. "I think we should rescue our friends on Valos first. Otherwise, this revelation might put their lives in danger."

"So how do we rescue them?" Midnight asked. "The planet is surrounded by warships now."

"Some of the smartest minds in the galaxy are in that dungeon," Wisp said. "I'd be shocked if they didn't already have an escape plan."

"True," Vex added. "They're probably only sticking around because Tena will blow up a planet if they escape."

"So all we need is to send them a message," Glik said. "That should only take one of us."

"I have an idea," Vex said. "I'm not sure I like it, but it's an idea."

01.15 Rescue

ED.02508.04.25

A supply ship landed on Valos, one of hundreds to land that day. An automated loading bot carried a steel crate into the storage room of the Grand Palace. From inside the crate, Vex concentrated as hard as she could to send a telepathic message.

Are you there Trenyn? Can you hear me? No answer.

Vex wasn't telepathic. Her father – that is, her real father, not the man who raised her – had been telepathic, but he could only communicate with others of his species. Vex had never been able to speak telepathically, at least not intentionally, but she thought she might be able to communicate with Trenyn.

Trenyn couldn't read minds. Their species, the Navorans, could transmit thoughts, and were unusually receptive to the mental transmissions of other telepaths. But they couldn't hear the thoughts of non-telepaths, nor could they read the thoughts of unwilling people. But Trenyn was able to communicate with Raven, even though she couldn't speak telepathically with anyone else.

Vex hoped it would be the same with her. She'd never specifically spoken to Trenyn telepathically, but during the meeting three months earlier, she'd gotten the impression they might be able to hear her thoughts. Unfortunately, it had been a hectic day, with much bigger things to worry about.

But if Trenyn could hear her thoughts, they were still out of range. Vex waited until the middle of the night, when the fewest people would be awake. Then she opened her crate and tiptoed out of the storage room. She had a map of the palace on her comm unit, and she followed it in the direction of the dungeons. She wouldn't be able to go down to the dungeon level, as all the access doors would be locked.

But that wasn't the plan. She just needed to get above Trenyn's cell. If she could just get to that side of the palace, maybe she'd be able to communicate with them through the floor. If that didn't work, then she'd worry about getting downstairs. But she hoped it wouldn't come to that.

It was pitch black, but Vex wore night vision glasses. She couldn't count on her precognition to avoid danger, because it worked by scanning the surface thoughts of nearby people. Tena mostly used android guards, which didn't trip Vex's mental flashes. She carefully peeked around every corner, and made as little noise as possible. As she turned one corner, she saw an android patrolling the hallway.

She pulled out one of her AON knives, the blade popping out of the handle and immediately warming up. She threw the knife and guided it with her telekinesis. She hit the android right in the power supply, and it shut down immediately. Then she pulled the knife back to her hand.

She'd taken out three more androids by the time she reached the right hallway. As soon as she thought she was close, she started sending out thoughts again. *Trenyn, are you there? This is Vex. Can you hear me?*

I hear you, came the reply. *Why are you here? Are you a prisoner too?*

No, I'm here to deliver a message. Tena is bluffing. There are no doomsday devices. If you have an escape plan, get out immediately.

There was a pause before Trenyn replied. *On it. Do you*

have an escape plan of your own?

No, Vex replied. *I will have to go into hiding with you.*

Get out of the palace however you can. Meet us at this address. Vex received a mental image of a map as well as the street address.

Vex typed the address into her comm unit, and it calculated the best route to get there.

On the floor below, Trenyn told the rest of the prisoners that it was time to escape. Upon receiving the telepathic message, Lemondrop said, "Computer, activate program One-Three-One, authorization Lemondrop Five-Six-Four-Seven-Three."

Six years earlier, Tena had escaped the palace using a program that cut the building's power. Lemondrop had since installed a better version. Many better versions, actually. Scenario One-Three-One specifically involved her allies being locked in the dungeon while her enemies slept above, but she had more than two hundred preprogrammed scenarios. Of course, Tena had locked Lemondrop out of all command codes upon her capture, but Lemondrop had backdoors in place for such an event.

As soon as the computer heard the command codes, all the power went out in the palace from floors one and up. Every android shut down. Communication signals were blocked. All the doors in the dungeon opened. Every door above the dungeon locked shut. If Tena was asleep, her minions wouldn't be able to call her to warn her. They wouldn't even be able to get to her floor to knock on her door. With any luck, Tena would sleep through all of this.

Everyone stepped out of their cells, and Lemondrop led them to a storage room at the end of the hall. Here they found their clothing and weapons. Even Raven's robotic body was there, its power cell sitting on a nearby shelf. There wasn't time for everyone to get dressed, but they all grabbed their gear and followed Lemondrop to the exit.

A hidden door led to a secret elevator, which led to an underground tunnel Tena knew nothing about. A hovering escape vehicle awaited them, and took them far away from the palace. Door after door closed behind them as they raced through the tunnels.

Vex headed straight for one of the back doors, but found it locked. She tried another door. It was also locked. There were windows all over the place, but they were very high. She pushed a decorative table under one window, stood on top of it, and jumped up to grab the windowsill. She had just gripped the sill when she heard someone approach.

"And who might you be?" a creepy male voice said. He wore heavy black robes and a hood that obscured his face.

"I was just leaving," Vex said, still struggling to pull herself up.

"Surely you can stay a bit longer," he said, pulling out his comm unit. His hood fell back as he put the comm to his ear. He was a Nithari, like Lyryssa. He had pale skin, gaunt features, pointed ears, and no hair. "Tena, we have an intruder. Tena? Blasted thing." He shook the comm as if that would magically make it start working.

He walked over and grabbed Vex by the ankle. Swinging her like a baseball bat, he let go and sent her flying down the hall. Vex crashed into another table, sending knickknacks flying. A marble bust tipped over, rolled off the table, and nearly landed on Vex's head. Vex tried to throw the bust with her telekinesis, but it was a bit too heavy. Instead, she threw two vases and a crystal egg at her adversary.

With lightning reflexes he easily snatched the items out of the air, playfully juggling them for a moment before tossing them over his shoulder. He slowly walked toward Vex as he did so.

Vex struggled to her feet, still in pain from being thrown. She was going to have a lot of bruises tomorrow, assuming she lived that long. Still, she was determined to go down fighting. She drew both of her AON knives and flicked them on. The glowing blue blades were the only lights in the hallway, and with Vex's night vision glasses on, they were almost blinding.

She held out her blades, assuming an attack stance. Her opponent imitated her pose, but his hands were empty. Instead of weapons, he had long, steel-tipped fingernails. He smiled, showing off his matching steel-tipped fangs.

Vex threw a blade at the creep's face. At first he readied his hand to grab it, but then covered his eyes and ducked instead. Vex pulled the blade back to her hand. She recalled that Lyryssa wasn't fond of bright lights. Maybe she could use this to her advantage. Vex pressed the attack, going for the eyes at the cost of defending her body.

The Nithari shied away from the blades, but he was incredibly fast. Vex threw both knives, and he ducked and lunged toward her. Vex stumbled backward, calling the weapons back to her hands. She tried to manipulate them so that they stabbed her opponent on the way back, but he still managed to dodge them even when he couldn't see them. The blades made a faint humming sound, and he had excellent hearing.

Vex's telekinesis wasn't very precise. It was mostly throwing things, guiding them in the air, and calling them back to her hands. If she'd had more control, she would have had the blades continually stab at him from a distance. Instead, it was more like trying to bring him down with a pair of boomerangs.

Deftly dodging another throw, the Nithari tackled her at knee level, once again knocking her into the table. This time the table broke into pieces. Vex screamed, her back now in agony. She tried to get to her feet, but the Nithari was on her too fast. She stabbed at his eyes, but he grabbed her wrists.

He was strong, too. He held her arms far apart, then licked his lips as he looked at her throat. He opened his mouth wide, turning his head sideways. Vex looked around for anything she could use. She used her mind to lift the only objects she saw nearby. Two broken table legs and several splinters of wood flew at the Nithari, hitting him in the face and neck. He shrieked and let her go, as he pulled out the wooden splinters.

Vex stabbed him in the arm and rolled out from under him. She was tempted to finish him off, but her instincts kept telling her to get as far away from this guy as possible. She limped down the hall, past a couple of open doors, until she saw one that looked inviting. A breakfast nook with a large picture window. She didn't waste time, throwing her blades at the glass before she even got all the way into the room. The glass shattered, and Vex jumped through without even looking down, calling the blades back into her hands on the way down.

She landed in the palace's Grand Pool, which ran right up to the outer wall. She barely had the strength to swim back to the surface. The address she needed to reach was on the other side of the city, and she could barely walk. There was no way she was going to make it on foot. She shambled through the street until she found a parked hovercar. With her street skills, it was no problem getting in and disabling the security system. She desperately wanted to put it in self-driving mode and get some shut-eye, but she knew it would go exactly the speed limit, and she didn't have time to waste.

She drove as fast as the hovercar would go. When she was two-thirds of the way there, two police drones appeared behind her, blue lights flashing. She ignored them and kept going. She was almost to her destination when one of the drones fired a magnetic disc at her vehicle. It sent out an EMP pulse, disabling the hovercar. "Please step out of the vehicle," a robot voice said.

The two drones appeared at her windows, one on each side. Vex launched an AON blade at each of them. Both drones went down, and Vex called the blades back to her hands as she staggered out of the car. More blue lights flashed in the distance, but her destination was just a few meters away. As she turned toward the nearest house, the front door opened. Detanna ran out of the house, grabbed her, threw her over her shoulder, and carried her back inside.

Vex drifted in and out of consciousness. She heard Detanna say, "We can't stay here long. Police are coming up the street. They'll probably search every house."

"Back to the tunnels," Lemondrop replied.

Vex felt herself being carried, then placed in a vehicle. She could feel the vibrations as the vehicle moved. It seemed like they rode for a long time, even with her sleeping most of the way. She woke up several times, only to drift right back to sleep.

"Well, I'm not leaving until we find Alterra," Detanna said.

Vex sat up. She was no longer in a vehicle, but on an old couch. How many safe houses did Lemondrop have, anyway?

"Understandable," Lemondrop said. "I'm not leaving the planet until Tena is gone. Valos is my home. But I strongly suggest the rest of you leave. You can do more good out there than hiding here."

"Wha... what happened to Alterra?" Vex asked, sitting up. She noticed that her wounds had been bandaged while she'd been unconscious. She looked around the room, recognizing all the former prisoners. Alterra was nowhere to be seen.

"A couple of days ago she was taken to another facility," Raven said. "Tena wants her to have full-time medical attention until the baby is born."

"She probably just wants to make sure Alterra doesn't try to abort it," Detanna said. "I'm sure she'd rather lose the baby than see Tena raise it. I don't blame her." Detanna looked angrier than Vex had ever seen her.

"I'm not leaving either," Dervish said. "Not until Alterra is safe."

"Lemondrop, I know I wasn't born here like you," Karden said. "But Valos is my home now. I'm not going to abandon it."

Sekka looked unsure of herself. "I don't want to disappoint you, but I really want to see my animals again."

Lemondrop walked over and kissed her on the forehead. "It's okay, Sekka," she said. "I don't want anyone to feel obligated to stay. There are many ways to help us, both on and off planet. I'm sure I will get plenty of support from the citizens of Valos." She turned to Raven and Trenyn. "What about you two?"

I go where Raven goes, Trenyn answered.

"I have an idea," Raven said. "But I'll need access to equipment I have off-planet. I'd rather not divulge the details just yet, in case anyone in this room gets interrogated."

"Do you need any help?" Doctor Eshton asked.

"All I can get," Raven said.

"It's settled, then," Lemondrop said. "Vex, you will accompany Raven, Trenyn, Sekka, and Eshton. I'll get you safe passage off the planet. The rest of us will remain here."

A few hours later, a shuttle left the planet. It was followed by an automated security ship. The shuttle dodged and weaved, avoiding the shots fired by its pursuer. But it could only avoid the fire for so long. One good hit and the shuttle exploded into thousands of pieces.

Tena was not happy. While she'd slept, her palace had been invaded. Her prisoners had escaped and her androids had been shut down. Her Nithari servant, Synthral, had climbed up the outside of the palace to break in through her window in order to wake her. Some of the systems still weren't back online.

She was in the middle of a temper tantrum that probably

would have claimed the lives of both Andoro and Synthral when an automated communication alert interrupted her. A shuttle had tried to escape the planet, but one of her security ships shot it down. Tena smiled. "Send a salvage crew to examine the wreckage," she told her cohorts. "See if we can identify the bodies."

She was a little disappointed she hadn't been able to kill them herself, but this would do. No one defied Tena and survived.

The escape shuttle had been empty, running on autopilot. The security ship continued on a course away from Valos, where it changed its transponder code twice, along with shedding its exterior sigils. Trenyn piloted it past the warp gate, to an unallied space station where they changed ships. After a few dozen more precautions, they finally met up with the Bloodwind.

Sekka was overjoyed to see her crewmates again, and to find that they'd taken good care of her menagerie. Vex was taken to the medical bay so Glik could care for her wounds. Raven, Trenyn, and Doctor Eshton requested they be taken to Earth, so they could work on a top-secret project.

The salvage crew found no bodies, and the security ship had vanished. Andoro and Synthral wisely kept their distance as they gauged Tena's reaction. Rather than tear down the palace with her bare hands, she surprised them by calmly reaching for her tablet instead. She logged onto her GalaxyStars account, and started a livestream.

"Ultimatum time!" she said in an overly upbeat, singsong voice. "So, if you're on Earth, Galea, Chirminon, Magnar, or Kalara, you might want to pay extra special attention to this message. You guys are on my shit list today."

As she talked, she held up a remote, showing it to the camera. It was a plain black wand with a single red button. "Last night, some very important prisoners escaped from my dungeon. If they're not back by the end of the day, I'm going to press this button, and a random planet will be destroyed. I'm not even remotely kidding. Get it? Remotely?" She wiggled the remote to accentuate her bad pun.

"Also, I'm looking for a young woman who left my care a few years ago. Wisp, if you're seeing this? Please come home. All is forgiven. I'll give you three days to come home, or I'll press this button."

Andoro tapped Tena on the shoulder, showing her a video on his tablet. "Not right now," she said, annoyed. "I'm in the middle of a..." She trailed off as she watched the video.

It was a news report. Tena's secret was out. The entire galaxy knew she'd been bluffing all along, and that her threats were meaningless.

Tena's face went red. "I will blow you up! I will I will I will!" she screamed, hammering the red button repeatedly. Finally she smashed her tablet against her desk, shattering it and ending the livestream.

With Tena's threats abated, several planets readied for war. Many citizens were ready to atomize Valos in retaliation for the assassinations and the destruction of Vhelra. But clearer heads recognized that Valos was full of innocent people, being led by an evil dictator. Still others argued that Valos had originally been a prison planet, and even though that was generations ago, the population wasn't entirely innocent. Each planet's factions nearly went to war with each other while deciding whether to go to war with Valos.

The Galactic Nations drew up negotiations for a peace treaty, one which relied on Tena's surrendering herself into the GN's custody. Of course she said no. It was Valos and Grunthar against the rest of the galaxy, but Grunthar had an appetite for war. Their planet did little else but invent weapons and build warships, and they had an armada large enough to defend ten planets.

For now, it was a standoff. No one wanted to fire the first

shot that would lead to millions of deaths on both sides.

On Valos, freedom was a thing of the past. Android soldiers patrolled the streets. Anyone suspected of conspiring against Tena was taken in for questioning. Many never returned. Lemondrop's resistance acquired more and more soldiers, citizens they had rescued from Tena's clutches. Meanwhile, Alterra remained imprisoned in a hospital somewhere, just a few months away from giving birth.

Zak's team helped out where they could. Sometimes they transported soldiers or weapons from one sector to another, other times they helped escapees from Valos seek refuge on other planets. But whenever their services weren't required, they continued to do what they did best. Many of the prisoners Tena had ordered released were now on the run, and who better to round them up than the Bloodhunters?

Meanwhile, the reward on Tena's head – which had originally been offered for Crossbones until it was discovered he was working for Tena – escalated to astronomical levels.

Part 2

02.00 Tena's Twenty

ED.02508.05.01

"Is everyone settled?" Glik asked. He didn't always get to address the full crew, but for once, all of them were between missions at the same time. He looked around the table. Zak was munching on a bag of mango chips - he always seemed to be snacking, but then, this was the galley. Yeela floated over Zak's shoulder. Lyryssa was playing a game on her comm, but she put it away when she realized Glik was waiting on them. Sekka was feeding jerky to a sniffer hawk perched on her wrist. Vex was balancing a knife on her palm. Only Wisp and Midnight had been giving Glik their full attention from the beginning.

This was as good as it was going to get, so Glik proceeded with the briefing. "The media is calling them Tena's Twenty, or just the T-Twenty. It's not an accurate number, but I guess it sounded better for a sound bite. When Tena Vermon demanded the release of several prisoners from Chirminon and Earth, the various countries responded in different ways. Some refused. Some even executed their prisoners in defiance of Tena's orders. In the end, forty-three prisoners were released. When Tena was found to be bluffing, roughly half of those released were rounded up right away. They were easy to find because they were living in state-sponsored halfway houses."

All eyes were on Glik now. "The rest? Some went back to their old lives, if they could get away with it. Others went into hiding. The important question is, why did Tena need them released? While most of them used to be Inner Eye members, they don't seem to be rushing to rejoin the criminal organization. Personally, I believe that Tena only needed one or two of them for her projects. The rest were a smokescreen, so we wouldn't immediately guess her plans based on the skills of those released."

"Huh?" Sekka asked. She and her hawk both cocked their heads.

"If all she'd released were a couple of weapons designers, we'd know she's working on a weapon," Glik explained. "But by releasing dozens of people with various skills, we're left guessing which prisoners were actually important to her. Regardless, all of them need to be found and returned to prison."

"Do we know where any of them are right now?" Wisp asked.

"There are sightings every day," Glik said. "Some more credible than others. I don't expect this to be quick or easy. Some of these fugitives are master criminals. Others... not so much, but they still have ways of staying hidden. A few of them aren't even trying to hide, but the IGP is too busy these days to arrest them. Which is a self-perpetuating cycle. Criminals know the police are too overworked to catch everyone, so they feel emboldened to commit even more crimes, which puts the police even further behind..."

"Just point the way," Vex interrupted, flipping her knife over and over in her hand.

"I'll do just that," Glik said, and started handing out tip sheets.

02.01 *The Festival*

ED.02508.05.01

Zak had absolutely no context for what he was seeing. He was at Kalara's equivalent of a Renaissance festival. Except this one was city-wide, and celebrated a time in Kalara's past called the Glowing Age. Zak barely knew anything about Kalara's present, much less its past.

Nearly everyone was dressed in glowing red flowers. Some of the outfits were made of actual homegrown flowers, their stems intricately laced together to make a full outfit. Others wore clothing made of plastic flowers, while still others just wore floral print T-shirts. Zak honestly couldn't have told you which ones were more authentic to the time period the Kalarans were celebrating.

Many of the Kalarans also wore glowing orbs on their heads, and some of them carried an armadillo-like creature in their arms. Much like the clothing, the quality of the armadillos varied. Some were real, some were stuffed, some were plastic, and a few were even animatronic.

"I wonder what the armadillos are for," Zak said, thinking out loud.

"They call them savaat," Yeela said, hovering above his left shoulder. "Eight hundred years ago, there was a great plague, caused by disease-ridden skuumen."

"Skuumen?" Zak asked.

"Basically tiny winged rats with lots of eyes," she said, causing Zak to shudder. "Then one of their historical heroes, Gyalla of East Maeros, brought the first savaats into the Northern continent. The savaats had a knack for catching skuumen with their long, sticky tongues, and they had the vermin all but wiped out in less than a year. After that, the Glowing Age of Enlightenment began."

"How do you know so much?" Zak asked.

"Some of us research a planet before visiting it," Yeela answered. "Especially when they know they're going to be landing during a festival. I bet you don't even know what the flowers are for."

"Because they smell nice?"

"Well… yes," Yeela admitted. "To overcome the stench of death, everybody wore flowers. They also used the glowing petals to line their footpaths at night. But eventually the flowers came to be a symbol of rebirth, since their society was brought back from the brink of extinction. Today they still celebrate by wearing floral dresses and drinking large amounts of nudrone."

"What's nudrone?"

"Not a lot," Yeela answered. "What's new with you, human?" Then she emitted several squeals of static, which was her equivalent of laughter.

Zak groaned. "So where do we find this woman?"

"Brahhna Skiver is a hedonist," Yeela said. "And this festival is a favorite of hers. We'll find her in the Pools of Free Love."

"The what?" Zak asked, not looking forward to the answer.

"Didn't you even read the brochure?" Yeela asked. "In the center of town, there's a huge tent. Inside the tent there's a pool. Inside the pool, there's an ongoing orgy. It continues day and night, for the length of the festival. Anyone feeling aroused is encouraged to enter the pool, where anything goes. They can stay in as long as they like, and leave whenever they like. Children conceived at the festival are considered blessed."

"I don't want to see that," Zak said. "Can't we just wait for her to come out?"

"In previous years, she's been known to spend the entire festival in that tent," Yeela said. "She has food delivered, and she even sleeps on the bleachers by the pool. Unless you want to wait all month, this is your shot."

They continued to walk through the crowds, heading toward the tent. "Will they even let me in there?" Zak asked.

"Non-Kalarans are allowed in the tent, but they're not allowed in the pool. For, um, anatomical reasons."

"How am I supposed to lure her out of the pool?"

"I'm sure you'll come up with something," Yeela said.

The closer they got to the tent, the slower Zak walked. He stopped at a booth for a snack, some sort of goo-on-a-stick, which Yeela scanned first to make sure it wasn't poisonous to humans. It wasn't bad. It had the consistency of chewy caramel but was flavored more like lime and maple syrup.

He reached the tent, but was ordered to stop before he could go in. "I thought humans were okay..." he started to say, but a Kalaran bouncer pointed to a sign. Unfortunately, it wasn't in English.

"No weapons past this point," Yeela translated. "Fair enough, I guess. No children. Well, duh. No recording devices, no savaats, no smoking, no clothing... Oh."

"No way," Zak said. "Not a chance."

"To be fair," Yeela said, "It's not like they're going to care about your anatomy." This was true. Kalarans and humans were so incredibly different, it would be odd for either to find the other attractive or offensive.

It wasn't that Zak was uncomfortable with his body, in fact, he was more comfortable in his skin than he had been in a long time. He'd been living as a man for nearly nine years now, and in his opinion, his body was looking mighty fine. The hormone treatments had helped him develop toned muscles, and his top surgery had given him the chest of his dreams. In fact, there was only one area of his body that looked incongruous with the rest of his form.

He didn't get dysphoria from his genitals, but that didn't mean he wanted to parade them out in public. Would these people even recognize a trans human if they saw one? He wasn't sure. He had difficulty telling which Kalarans were male or female, so maybe it would be the same for them.

Zak let out a sigh of resignation. There was a small locker room built onto the side of the larger tent. Yeela tried to follow him inside, but once again the bouncer stopped them. He pointed to the part of the sign that specified no recording devices.

"I promise I won't let her record anything," Zak said, but it was no use. Yeela would have to stay outside or be stuffed in a locker. They opted for the former. She would hover near the tent, watching and waiting.

Zak entered the locker room. There were two Kalarans already inside. They eagerly removed their flower-knit clothing before they ran into the main tent. Even after seeing them naked, Zak had no idea if the two Kalarans had been male or female. To Zak, their species looked like humanoid spiders. Sure, they only had two arms and legs, but they had dark, chitinous skin, and no sexual characteristics that Zak could see. They were mostly hairless except for their elbows and chins. They had eight eyes – each of their two large eyes had a cluster of three additional eyes underneath.

Which was not to say they all looked alike. Each Kalaran had unique patterns on their skin, all across their bodies and faces. These lines came in a range of bright colors, and the patterns varied greatly. Some designs were weblike, others looked more like Celtic knots or Nazca lines. Zak wasn't sure if these designs were natural or tattooed, and he already missed having Yeela at his side to answer such questions.

He sighed. *Let's do this.* He put his clothing and belongings in a locker, then grabbed a towel from a shelf. Holding the towel in front of himself, he paused one last time to psyche himself up, and entered the main tent.

It actually wasn't so bad. A series of bleachers surrounded the pool. Nude people sat on the bleachers and talked, others sat by the pool, and others swam. It was a very relaxed atmosphere. No one in the bleachers leered at the pool like it was some sort of peep show. In fact, they barely even glanced in that direction. Even the Kalarans having intercourse in the pool were somewhat subtle about it.

Zak found an empty spot on the bleachers, specifically picking a spot that wasn't too close to anyone else. He set his towel down first, then quickly sat down on it, his knees pinned tightly together. It felt pleasantly warm in here, like a steam room. He looked around. While only Kalarans were allowed in the pool, the crowd in the bleachers was as mixed as those outside had been – about three-quarters Kalaran, the rest being a variety of species from many different planets.

He spotted Skiver in the pool. Her back was against the left edge, with her arms outstretched along the side of the pool. Her head was all the way back, and her mouth was open. At first he thought she was asleep, but he was embarrassed to realize that she was in the throes of passion. Zak was puzzled at first, as there were no other Kalarans around her, and both her hands were visible. Then her partner resurfaced in front of her, followed by two others. Apparently Kalarans could hold their breath for a long time.

Zak didn't want to make a scene by going down there. He wasn't sure how close he was allowed to get to the pool, and he didn't want to get arrested while finding out. Plus he was seriously uncomfortable with the thought of approaching her during such an intimate moment.

She had to come out sometime. Either to eat, sleep, or use the restroom. And Zak would be waiting, ready to strike. In the meantime, someone else caught his eye. A few bleachers away, a pair of human women sat together, having a conversation. The brunette kept stealing glances at Zak, and her blond friend appeared to be making fun of her for it. Zak tried to imagine the conversation they were having.

The brunette noticed Zak was looking at her, and she smiled at him. Zak returned the smile. The blond broke into laughter. Zak wondered if he should go over and say hi. Then he remembered he wasn't here for fun, and glanced back at Skiver. She was still in the same spot, and having a much better time than Zak was.

Zak glanced back to the brunette, and she smiled at him again, twirling her hair with one finger. Zak sighed and looked away. It wasn't like it would work out. He'd been there before. The flirting, the heavy petting, the expectation of something more... he never let it get any farther than that. He was always honest with them. The last thing he wanted was for things to move into the bedroom, only for his partner to get an unwanted surprise.

Zak stared off into space and thought about Vex. For a brief period of time, they'd been lovers. Vex was bisexual, but she generally preferred women. She'd been fine dating a trans man, at least at first. But the more Zak transitioned, the less attractive she'd found him, or at least that's how it had seemed to Zak. Luckily they'd been able to maintain their friendship.

Zak wasn't sure where that left his love life. He was attracted to women, and he wanted a girlfriend who was attracted to him as a man. Which was difficult, since he didn't have a penis. Maybe he would have one eventually, somewhere down the line. Some of the newest procedures had extraordinary results. Raven and Trenyn had built a device that was simply amazing.

But right now Zak liked who he was, and wasn't interested in any more surgery. He felt like if he were to get the operation, he would be doing it more for his potential girlfriend than for himself. That seemed like a big step for someone he hadn't even met yet. But then, without the procedure, he might never have a chance with this hypothetical partner. His feelings for his own body were seemingly incompatible with his ideal girlfriend. It was a lot to think about.

Someone sat down behind him, and he shrank a little. He didn't like being close to strangers while he was naked. He didn't turn his head to see the new arrival, but he did glance at the brunette woman to make sure it wasn't her. Nope, she was still talking to her friend, possibly about Zak.

Once again realizing he was here on business, he glanced down at the water. Skiver was gone. Zak sat leaned forward, intently studying the pool. Was she under the water? He looked around at the bleachers, to see if she'd taken a break from the pool.

"I know a bounty hunter when I see one," a Kalaran voice said from behind him.

Zak's shoulders slumped. Suddenly he was glad Yeela wasn't here. She would never let him live this down. He started to turn his head.

"Don't turn around," Skiver said. "Don't move a muscle."

"I know you're unarmed," Zak said, but stared straight ahead anyway. "There's no weapons allowed in here."

"Don't you know anything about our species?" She put a hand on Zak's shoulder, causing him to jump a little. "We have barbs on our fingertips. Harmless to us, venomous to humans."

"A public murder is just going to attract police attention," Zak said. "I don't think someone in your position wants that."

"I don't want to kill you," she said. "I just want to be left alone. Get dressed and meet me outside. I have a proposition for you." She took her hand off his shoulder, stood up, and left.

Zak stood and looked after her. She was already halfway to the locker room, walking very quickly. He glanced one last time at the woman who had been flirting with him.

Now that Zak was standing, the brunette stared at him with wide eyes and red cheeks. She turned her head away, hiding her face with her hands. Her friend was laughing her head off. Zak shrugged. No time to feel hurt about that now. He turned away and headed for the lockers.

Skiver was already dressed and on her way out the door by the time Zak entered the locker room. "I'll be right outside," she said over her shoulder. Zak opened his locker and got dressed. He went outside, but Skiver was nowhere to be seen. He pulled out his comm unit and called Yeela. "Where are you?"

"I see Skiver and I am in pursuit," Yeela said, sending a map to Zak's comm.

Zak followed the dot on the map, yelling into the comm as he ran. "She said she'd wait outside!"

"And you believed her?" Yeela asked. "She was a member of the Inner Eye, a thief, and a murderer."

"Well, she didn't poison me when she could have," Zak said, nearly tripping over a young Kalaran with a balloon.

"How would she have fed you poison?" Yeela asked.

"She was going to sting me with the barbs on her fingertips!" Zak yelled, pushing his way through a group of five people who insisted on walking arm-in-arm.

"I think you mean venom, not poison," Yeela said. "And that's not a thing Kalarans can do. She lied. Again."

Zak was really starting to dislike this murderous criminal. He was gaining on the dot, though. He reached a clearing, where the crowds had parted to watch a strange fight. Skiver and Yeela fired energy weapons at each other. Both were incredibly fast, able to dodge weapons fire more easily than Zak's human reflexes would have allowed. Some of the onlookers cheered them on, thinking it was some sort of show.

It wasn't sporting, but Zak didn't care. While Skiver was preoccupied fighting the drone, Zak shot her in the back. Skiver went down, unconscious.

* * *

There was a bit of a holdup with the local authorities, and a lot of paperwork had to be filed, but the day ended with Zak claiming the reward for the capture of Brahhna Skiver. That night, he researched the next fugitive on his list. This time Zak was going to be more prepared, and more informed about the planet and its inhabitants. He wasn't going to embarrass himself again.

As he drifted off to sleep, he thought about the women in the tent. A few years ago, he might have cried himself to sleep thinking about their reaction. But today? He just felt sort of empty. He was who he was, and if other people didn't like it, then he'd just have to find someone who did. Or make peace with the fact that he would die alone.

Was that progress? He wasn't sure. But at least he didn't lose sleep over it.

02.02 *Raving Mad*

ED.02508.05.08

"Get in here, now!"

The man held two AON knives, slightly larger than the ones tucked into Vex's belt pouches. They glowed yellow, and the light they emitted gave the wielder a jaundiced look.

This should be fun, Vex thought, humoring him. She stepped into the alley, ready to hear what he had to say.

"Give me your wallet," he said.

"Wallet?" Vex asked incredulously. "Look at these jeans. You think I have a wallet?" She turned around, showing off her ensemble. She wore black boots, blue denim jeans, and a white crop top. The outfit was so tight it almost looked like body paint.

"Th-then just give me all your money," the mugger said. His hands were shaking, and he almost dropped one of his daggers.

"I don't carry cash," Vex answered.

"Well, y-you're going to give me s-something," the man stammered. "Get d-down on the ground, and take off all your clothes."

Vex burst out laughing. "I'm sorry," she said. "But you can barely hold a knife, you really think you can hold an erection?"

"Don't laugh at me! Do as I say!" the mugger screamed. His face was turning red, but the yellow glow made him look orange.

"And what if I say no?" Vex asked.

"I'll.. I'll cut you!" he shouted, holding both knives in a combat stance.

"That's not fair," Vex said. "You have two knives, and I don't have any." She reached out her hand, and one of the knives flew out of the mugger's hand and into hers. Her blue hair glowed with psychic energy. "There, now we're even."

"How... how did you do that?" the man asked.

"Oh, that? Like this." Vex reached out with her empty hand and stole his other knife. "Yellow's not really my color, though. Mind if I use my own?" She threw both yellow knives at the mugger. One whizzed by each side of his head, missing his ears by mere centimeters. The knives embedded themselves into a steel wall at the back of the alley. As they flew, Vex drew her own AON daggers, which glowed a bright blue.

"I'm sorry, I'm sorry!" the mugger said. "Y-you can go, you can go!"

"Oh, thank you for your permission," Vex said. "But I don't think you understand what's going on here." She stomped forward and held an AON knife to the mugger's throat.

"What do you want?" he said, fear in his eyes.

"I need the password to get into tonight's rave," Vex said.

"W-what makes you think I know it?" he asked.

"Because you just came from there," Vex said. "You think you spotted me, just walking by? Sorry dude, but *I* followed *you*."

"Fine! Fine!" he wailed. "It's 'Spicy Mustard.' Can I go now?"

"Just one more thing," Vex said, smiling.

A few minutes later, Vex walked out of the alley, whistling. Under her left arm, she held a bundle of clothes.

She didn't need this guy warning anyone that she was coming, and she figured that leaving him in an alley without his comm unit – or his clothes – would probably give her the head start she needed. She did leave him his boxers, partly so he could keep a shred of dignity, but mostly because she didn't want to see him naked.

She headed straight for the rave, tossing the mugger's belongings into a trash can along the way.

It wasn't really Vex's scene, a fact that would have surprised all but her closest friends. The wall-to-wall teenagers, the pounding music so loud you could only hear the beat, the smell of armpits and narcotic vapors... it was everything Vex thought she liked when she was younger, before she realized she only liked it because her parents didn't. Still, she definitely looked the part, and not a single person stared at her like she didn't belong there.

The target's name was Devvin Oontz, but he called himself Ravelord. He was another of Tena's Twenty, an Inner Eye member released under false pretenses. Vex knew he'd been seen here in Trasa, but beyond that, she hadn't had a lot of leads. But when she'd heard there was a rave, it sounded like a good place to start, given his nickname.

Vex pushed through the crowd of intoxicated dancers, trying to see, well, anything. Once she was deeply embedded in the throngs, it was hard to maintain her sense of direction. For all she knew, she could be getting closer to the stage or she might be headed right back to the entrance.

She also kept getting quick premonitions. That was another reason she didn't like raves. Somehow the combination of flashing lights and thick crowds caused her to more readily pick up their surface thoughts. Usually her flashes were useful, warning her of danger, but the ones triggered in this environment were more random. A large number of the teens were thinking about sex, and it was like having porn livestreamed into her head.

As she pushed past more people, she came face-to-face with a guy who was definitely planning to slip something into his date's drink before he took her back to his place. As Vex danced around him, she picked his pocket, relieving him of both his debit card and the packet of illegal sedative he was planning to use on his date. She also "accidentally" elbowed him in the kidneys on her way by, before disappearing back into the crowd.

Soon a wave of thoughts rippled through the crowd. "Let him through!" "Who's that?" "Is that really him?" "He's back!" and so on. While Vex couldn't see the stage, she saw flashes of what the closer ravers saw. It was her target, the so-called Ravelord. Apparently he was a celebrity to these people.

The flashes had also focused her sense of direction, and Vex pushed her way toward the stage. She reached the edge of the crowd and saw the object of the audience's fascination. Actually, it wasn't fascination, more like reverence. These ravers idolized this guy.

The stage was a raised platform, about five meters square. It was in the center of the room, surrounded by the crowd on all sides. There was a DJ station and some speakers on the stage, as well as Devvin himself. He looked human except for his skin tone, which rippled in waves of various colors in an almost hypnotic pattern. He wore jeans and sunglasses but no shirt. He held a beer bottle in one hand and a microphone in the other.

He shouted into the microphone, "Yo yo yo, you ain't seein' things, the Ravelord's back and they ain't gonna drag me away again! Now let's get this party started!" From there he segued into some freestyle rap, the lyrics mostly disparaging authority and explaining why his incarceration had been unjust.

Vex looked around her. The audience was entranced. She could feel the love they had for this guy. There was no way Vex could confront Devvin here. The mob would tear her to pieces. She would just have to wait until the rave was over.

The problem was, she didn't want to lose sight of Devvin, but the thought of standing here pretending to dance for several more hours was onerous.

She zoned out, watching the crowd and trying to come up with a plan. She examined the ceiling, looking for a less exhausting place to keep an eye on her prey. Devvin's lyrics pounded into Vex's brain, even when she tuned out the words. The rhythm was as mesmerizing as the swirls of color on his chest.

She felt something change in the crowd's vibe, and started paying attention to Devvin's words again.

"They don't deserve such a nice city
They don't deserve a place so pretty
They keep us down, they keep us low
They don't hear us, see us, or let us glow
They take our stuff, take our fun, and take our cash
So tear it down, rip it up, burn it all to ash"

As freestyle went, it wasn't *too* bad… actually, no, it was hot garbage. But the audience was entranced. Something strange was going on here, and Vex didn't like it. Devvin raised his arms wide, then pointed at the door shouting, "Go! Go! Go!"

For a split second, Vex saw a premonition of rage and violence. Then the crowd rushed away from the stage, taking their anger to the streets. Vex was lucky she was so close to the stage. If she'd been farther back, she might have been trampled by the crowd. The angry mob was bottlenecked at the front door, pushing and climbing over each other to get out. Then someone opened the emergency exit, and part of the crowd split off. Within a few minutes, the room was mostly empty.

Besides Vex, five more people stood around the dance floor, looking confused. Several bodies lay on the floor, having been trampled by the mob. A huge, muscular woman climbed onto the stage and stood by Devvin. Vex recognized her as the bouncer who had let her into the club.

"There's always a few who don't get the message," Devvin said, indicating Vex and the other stragglers. "I said go! Go! Go!" The colors on his chest swirled even more brightly. Two of the remaining teens suddenly took on blank expressions, then turned to follow the mob out the door. The other three teens still looked perplexed.

"Kill the rest," Devvin said, and the bouncer pulled out her gun. Vex reacted quickly, reaching out with her telekinesis to pull the gun from her hand. But the woman had a strong grip and would not let go. At least Vex could keep her from aiming. With her other hand, Vex pulled out an AON knife and threw it at the bouncer's wrist.

The bouncer jerked her arm and the blade only grazed her, but it was painful enough to make her open her hand. Vex pulled the knife and the gun back to her. Vex pointed the gun at Devvin.

"Devvin Oontz, you're going back to prison. Or to the hospital, if you don't come peacefully." Vex didn't like guns and wasn't a very good shot, but she thought the gun might look more intimidating than the daggers.

"Girl, don't do me like that," Devvin said. "I ain't done nuthin' to you."

"You just started a riot," Vex said. She could hear shouting and sirens outside, and the occasional crash.

"City's gotta learn a lesson," Devvin said. "They started it when they put me in jail."

"You were a member of Xine Inner Eye," Vex said, not sure why she was debating with him. "Get off the stage. Now."

"I was an orphan," Devvin said. "The Eye took care of me when the city looked away. Just like always, they do it every day." His voice took on a rhythm as he talked. The colors on his chest started to swirl again. "The homeless and the poor are nuthin' to them. They ignore 'em, lock em' up, even beat 'em on a whim. Then people like you, actin' just like cops. People like you, you gotta be stopped."

If he was trying to hypnotize her, it wasn't working. Maybe her own psychic abilities made her immune to whatever influence he'd had over the rest of the crowd. "Look," she said, "If you're not going to come down, I'll…"

Someone hit her from behind. One of the stragglers, a young man with purple eyes and one long eyebrow, tackled Vex across the waist, bringing her to the floor. The bouncer followed suit, jumping down from the stage and bringing all her weight down on top of Vex.

Vex tried to wrestle herself free, but the bouncer was too strong. She held Vex down while the mind-controlled teen repeatedly kicked her. The other two teenagers stood around awkwardly, not sure who the good guys were, and not wanting to get involved. One of them took some video with her comm unit, while the other backed slowly toward the door.

The bouncer picked Vex up and put her in a full nelson. The teen started punching her in the face and stomach. Vex tried to block him with her feet, but a lot of his punches got through. Devvin sat down on the edge of the stage and took a swig from a bottle of beer. He chuckled at Vex's pain.

The bouncer had her arms looped through Vex's armpits, with her hands behind Vex's head. From this position, Vex couldn't see anything to grab with her telekinesis. One of her daggers was still in her belt pouch, but she couldn't get it out. The other dagger was somewhere on the floor behind her, along with the gun. Her head was being forced downward, but out of the corner of her eye she saw Devvin.

She pulled the beer bottle out of Devvin's hand, bringing it into her grasp. Then she sent it into the teen's forehead, knocking him out cold. Quickly bringing it back into her hand, she sent it into Devvin's face. It didn't knock him out, but it did give him a serious nosebleed. The bouncer was so surprised she let a hand slip, and Vex wrestled her arm free. Unfortunately it was her right hand, and her remaining dagger was in her left belt pouch. Looking for anything that might help her, she thrust her hand into her right pocket.

Furious, Devvin stood up and marched over to Vex, striking her across the face with the microphone. "You got this comin', girl. You didn't have ta come in here."

"Your music sucks," Vex replied, pulling her hand out of her pocket. As Devvin opened his mouth to reply, a small white packet flew out of Vex's hand and into his mouth. It hit the back of his throat so hard that the packet burst open, filling his mouth with sedative powder. He started choking on the wrapper.

The bouncer let Vex go. "Boss?" she said, and ran over to help him. Vex staggered around for a few seconds, then picked up the gun and her AON knife.

The bouncer managed to get the packet out of Devvin's mouth, but the sedative worked quickly. Devvin was already getting dizzy, and he was out like a light within minutes. He wouldn't wake up again until he was back in jail. The bouncer surrendered, but Vex let her go. The local police would be too busy breaking up rioters to arrest the woman tonight, and Vex was going to have enough trouble getting Devvin back to her ship.

Vex mailed the potential date rapist's debit card to the police, with a note that said, "The owner of this card needs to be put on a watchlist," along with an explanation why. She doubted anything would come of it, but it made her feel a little better.

The extent of Vex's injuries didn't register until she was back aboard the Bloodwind, and she spent most of the following week in the medbay. She got a couple of scars she'd probably keep for the rest of her life, but she didn't mind so much. To her, they weren't scars so much as souvenirs, reminders of obstacles she'd overcome.

And that was worth remembering.

02.03 *Brynwyn*

ED.02508.05.14

The sky explodes with lightning, and for a half second the world is consumed with white fire. A wet, shivering, elflike woman takes refuge under an ancient tree. She sits with her knees drawn up to her chest, hugging her legs. With each crash of thunder she buries her tearful face in her knees.

She is young, but not a child. She is naive, but not stupid. She knows the thunder won't hurt her. But still, she is afraid. Every rip of thunder punctuates her existing fears.

How did I get here? Why am I alone? Why did I stray so far? She asks these questions softly, nestling closer to the scant shelter of the tree. The questions are rhetorical; she already knows the answers, but doesn't dare ask the real question, burning beneath her dread: *Why am I such a failure?*

Her mother's quiver lies in the mud beside her, half-sinking into the muck. She pats it with her hand, seeking the reassurance it provides. It is a symbol of both love and protection. Also beside her is a bow, but she has no love for the weapon. To her, it is the embodiment of death and failure, and she hopes to replace it with another bow soon.

Another clap of thunder, and again she buries her face. In the howling wind is her father's voice, urging her to be strong and chastising her to stop disappointing him. The familiar but heartbreaking reprimands actually soothe her, and the exhausted young woman soon drifts off to sleep.

And she dreams.

She awakens to the sound of furniture breaking. Brynwyn gasps, and sits straight up in her bedding. In the moonlight coming in through her window, she sees a huge form, smashing everything within reach. It is a monster, and its presence in her treetop hut causes her fear and confusion. She becomes vaguely aware of the commotion outside her window, the sounds of villagers fighting off an invasion. Brynwyn stays perfectly still, too afraid to move or even breathe.

Brynwyn hears a scream. Across the room, her younger brother has awakened to see the creature. Alerted by the cry, the monster turns and grabs the boy by his head, dangling him high in the air. With her brother in danger, Brynwyn finds a reserve of bravery and searches around the floor beside her, never taking her eyes off the creature. She stretches her fingers blindly until she finds the bow and a single arrow. She draws back the bowstring, aiming carefully, but her arms shake. She only has one chance at this.

The creature's fingers encapsulate the elflike boy's entire head, and the monster delights in hearing his pathetic, hitching screams. Brynwyn has no idea how many arrows it will take to kill the thing, but she hopes one is enough to make it let go of her brother. She aims for the creature's left eye, wishing she had more time to line up and steady her shot. With a quick prayer to Yvora, she looses the arrow.

But her fingers slip at the moment of release, and the arrow bounces off the monster's shoulder. It turns toward her in anger, clenching its bony hands into fists. Her brother's head is shattered like an egg, and Brynwyn's own heart feels similarly crushed. The creature now faces her, hissing and screeching. She keeps perfectly still as the creature moves towards her, reaching out with its nightmarish hands. She blankly watches the remains of her brother drip from its fingers. She no longer cares what happens to her. She drops her bow and lets her arms fall to her sides.

Suddenly, it screeches in pain. It runs blindly around the hut, slashing at the walls with its clawed fingers until it finally collapses to the floor, dead. There are several arrows buried in its back. Brynwyn looks up and sees her parents standing in the doorway, bows in hand. Her mother looks at Brynwyn with concern. As she moves to comfort her daughter, her eyes fall on the headless body of her dead son.

And she screams.

Another loud thunderclap wakes Brynwyn with a start. The dream fades, as it always does. The memories still linger, still haunt her. The elf slowly realizes where she is... still sitting on the forest floor, in the rain and the mud, hugging her knees and shivering. She wishes she were home... but would not dare to go back.

She pulls her belongings closer to her, and huddles even closer to the tree.

And she weeps.

"So where are you sending me?" Wisp asked.

"It's called Itropa," Glik said. "The largest moon of the planet Fertilund. It's kind of backward. I think you'll like it."

Wisp made a face. "How backward?"

"The moon's very tech-averse," Glik said. "Primitive cultures. Most of them think science is magic. The planet governing Itropa doesn't want anyone to interfere with their development. So you can't bring any modern weapons. You can take your comm unit, but keep it hidden."

Wisp looked at the target's profile on her datapad. "Doctor Alas Mek," she said. "Weapons supplier for the Inner Eye."

"Fertilund's government would really like Mek to get off their moon, and stay off this time. But he's got powerful weapons, and they can't just send in an army without violating their own contamination rules. It's probably why Mek likes it there."

"What's the local population like?" Wisp asked. "Couldn't they take Mek down?"

"The indigenous people are called moonfolk. They live in trees and look like elves. There are also some human settlements, but they're right out of the middle ages. There's no way they could get through Mek's defenses. They probably think he's some kind of wizard. Besides, the planet's government would like to keep the moon's residents away from Mek. They think he would influence their culture."

"I don't get it," Wisp said. "So the locals haven't rejected science, they just don't know about it? Is this some sort of experiment?"

"That's a long story," Glik said. "But basically Fertilund wants Itropa's culture to evolve naturally, without outside influence. There's been some political back-and-forth over the years about what is and isn't allowed. About a century ago they let some human colonists start a village, provided they wouldn't take any tech with them. There's since been some regret about that, but they're still trying to keep outsiders at a minimum."

"Ugh. When I lived in medieval Europe, I would have killed for modern plumbing. Or hovercars. Or penicillin. If I'd learned that another society was watching us, dangling their conveniences just out of reach, just so they could watch us develop..."

Glik wasn't sure he believed her stories about past lives, but he didn't press it. "But a society shouldn't evolve too fast. If they got their hands on modern weapons before they were ready..."

"We're never ready," Wisp said. "We've proven time and

time again that the greediest and most ruthless of us will always take advantage of the latest tech. And we'll never outgrow that. In the meantime, people on that moon are probably dying from diseases already curable on the planet below."

"Does this mean you don't want the mission?" Glik asked.

Wisp thought a moment, and sighed. "If there's no tech allowed, how do I get there?"

"One of Fertilund's government agents will fly you over at night. You will parachute down to the planet's surface, as near as they can get you to Mek's compound. Once you have Mek, you'll call the agent to pick you up."

Wisp nodded. "I don't love it, but I'll follow their rules. When do I leave?"

That night, Wisp sat in the co-pilot's chair of a camouflaged ship, staying far above the treeline of Itropa. The pilot was a Fertilund Parks and Preservation agent with no sense of humor. As he flew the shuttle, he drilled her on a list of rules. She was to leave nothing behind. She would eat and drink only the rations she had stashed in her backpack. She was not to set fires. She was not to engage the local population. If one of the locals spoke to her, she was to keep the conversation as brief as possible and avoid certain subjects entirely. And so on.

The agent took them as close to Mek's compound as he dared. From above, they could see a metal building, the only metal building on this moon. It was hidden in a valley, but it still stuck out like a sore thumb. "This is as close as we can get without tripping Mek's defense systems," the agent said.

"What's that?" Wisp asked, pointing to a flash of light on the viewscreen.

"That would be... Mek's defense systems," the agent said, his voice rising. He turned the shuttle sharply to the right. Klaxons blared as the computer identified three homing missiles. The agent turned out to be a decent pilot, and after a few more tight turns, he managed to get two of the missiles to run into each other. They exploded in midair, leaving them one missile to contend with.

Unfortunately, the last missile was stubborn. He rolled and banked and dove, but the missile just kept coming. "Go lower!" Wisp said. "Weave through the treetops! Maybe you can get it to hit a tree?"

"No!" he shouted. "I can't get that close to the ground or one of the moonfolk might see us!"

"This is an emergency!" Wisp yelled back.

"The emergency is that we might contaminate their culture!" he countered, making another hard right.

The ship shook violently as the missile hit, taking out its right engine. As they spun toward the ground, the agent veered the ship in the direction of a mountain.

"What are you doing?" Wisp shouted. "Head for that lake!"

"The mountain will do a more thorough job of demolishing the shuttle," he explained through gritted teeth. "Less wreckage to find means less cultural contamination."

"And less chance we survive!" Wisp said.

"Be ready to jump," the agent said. "I'm opening the hatch now."

The hatch opened. Wisp unclasped her seatbelt and was thrown against the wall. She had to climb her way to the hatch, losing her progress several times as the spinning ship threw her in various directions. Eventually, she managed to reach the hatch and threw herself free.

She'd hoped the agent would be right behind her. She'd been tempted to drag him with her, but she'd barely made it as it was. As she floated downward on her government-approved parachute, she watched the shuttle crash into the side of the mountain. She saw no sign of the agent. He'd been right about one thing, the explosion had been so total that no tech could be salvaged. Future moonfolk hikers might discover scraps of metal, but nothing that would lead them to conclude it was from some sort of flying wagon.

Idiot, she thought. He'd probably stayed buckled in all the way to the end, just to make sure the shuttle didn't veer off course. Wisp had no qualms about thinking ill of the dead. After all, more than ninety-nine percent of the people she'd known in her lives were now dead. She couldn't deify all of them.

She landed softly in the grass, near the edge of the forest. As per orders, she buried the parachute. It was made of organic materials that would break down very quickly under the soil. Then she studied her surroundings, getting her bearings and comparing landmarks to the ones she'd seen from above. Mek's compound wasn't too far, though it wasn't as close as she'd hoped it would be. She'd have to walk all night to get there.

She heard a twig snap behind her and turned around, reaching for her bow. A young woman stared at her from behind a tree. *Damn*, Wisp thought. She'd been hoping to get in and out without being seen. She considered just walking away, but she needed to make sure the woman was alone. She didn't want to be mistaken for an enemy and ambushed by an army of moonfolk.

She dropped her bow and held up her hands to show they were empty. The woman stepped out from behind the tree and carefully approached. She looked to be in her late teens, with black hair and pointed ears. She dropped her bow as well, and held up her own hands. Then she said something in a strangely melodic language Wisp didn't recognize.

"I'm sorry," Wisp said. "I don't understand you."

"You fell from the sky," the elflike woman said, in English this time.

Crap. The last thing she needed right now was to be mistaken for a god. "You speak English?" Wisp asked.

"You speak the language of the villagers from the South,"

she said. "We trade with them sometimes. Your ears are like theirs as well. But your hair…" she stepped closer, staring in fascination. "It's like fire. I've never seen hair that color. Are you…"

Here it comes, Wisp thought.

"…From the mountains?" the woman finished. "I've heard stories of mountain people, with fiery hair and access to strange powers."

It occurred to Wisp that Alas Mek had red hair. He'd spent years on this planet before getting caught the first time. Legends had started over less. "Yes," Wisp said. "I'm from the mountains. My name is Wisp." She held out her hand for a handshake.

"My name is Brynwyn," the moonfolk woman said. Unsure of what to do with Wisp's hand, she got down on one knee and kissed it.

Withdrawing her hand, Wisp asked, "Why are you so far from your home, Brynwyn?" The agent had told Wisp that they weren't going to be anywhere near any known moonfolk settlements.

"I let my family down," she said, looking at the ground. "I can't go back."

"They threw you out?" Wisp asked.

"No, I left on my own," she said. "But I couldn't face them again. I failed to save my brother." She appeared to be on the verge of tears.

"I'm sorry for your loss," Wisp said sincerely. "What happened?"

Brynwyn told Wisp the story of how her treetop village had been raided by strange creatures. Wisp asked her several questions about the creatures, their appearance, how they moved, and what direction they might have come from. There was something about Brynwyn's description of these creatures that Wisp found relevant to the task at hand.

"Thank you, Brynwyn," Wisp said. "That information is

very helpful. I'm going to head back to the mountains, now. It was good to meet you." Wisp bowed and turned away.

"I want to come with you!" Brynwyn called after her.

Wisp turned back around. "Brynwyn," she said. "It's dangerous where I'm going. I'm sure your parents miss you. Losing one child is bad enough, don't make them mourn for you as well. Go home."

"I'm not going home, and I have nowhere else to go," Brynwyn said. "I'm going to follow you anyway. But I'd rather be at your side than at your back."

Wisp had been around long enough to recognize conversational patterns. They would go back and forth for another twenty minutes, until Wisp actually had to say something hurtful to keep Brynwyn away. In the end, Brynwyn would follow her anyway, and probably get herself killed in the process. It was easier just to give in.

"Very well, come along," Wisp said, and the two began their hike.

Technically Wisp hadn't been the one to start the campfire, so she wasn't breaking any rules. Well, except maybe the part where she'd befriended a local. But at least she'd managed to avoid talking about off-world technology. When she wasn't moping about her supposed failure, Brynwyn was actually an energetic soul. Learning new things excited her, so Wisp had to be careful with her words.

They'd made sure to set up camp behind an outcropping, so it wouldn't be visible from Mek's fortress. Wisp took the first watch. She waited for Brynwyn to fall asleep, then considered calling the Fertilund Parks and Preservation agency. They would want to know about the death of their agent. But then again, why? There was nothing they could do about it now. She didn't need a pickup yet, and she was fully capable of completing the mission on her own. More importantly, she didn't want them showing up and blowing whatever she had planned.

Or maybe she just didn't want them criticizing her for involving a moonfolk. While Brynwyn slept, Wisp climbed to the top of the outcropping to get a better view of the valley. Of course she hadn't been allowed to bring binoculars, but her comm unit had a zoom feature and a night vision camera. She saw a disturbing amount of movement around Mek's base. Something was swarming, but she couldn't zoom in close enough to make out the details.

She was about to climb down and wake up Brynwyn when she heard something nearby. Something was climbing up the side of the mountain, headed toward their campsite. Wisp vanished into the shadows, and sneaked down for a better view.

The creature was just as Brynwyn had described. Vaguely reptilian, but with shiny black scales. It had a heavily plated chest and shoulders, but a wasp-thin waist and bony, clawed fingers. Its nightmarish face reminded her of an armor-plated crocodile skull, with eerie, glowing eyes. But what really got Wisp's attention were the hydraulic cables running down the sides of its spine, leading into some sort of pump attached to the creature's tailbone.

These creatures were not natural. They weren't robots, more like cyborgs, but the creature part wasn't designed to survive without Mek's enhancements. He was likely cloning the monsters and manufacturing the add-ons simultaneously, for who-knew-what purpose. What could these things do that an android couldn't? Besides look really scary, that is.

Maybe that was the point. If Mek had a grudge against the moonfolk communities, he might want to build something that looked like a monster, but could be controlled like a robot. Maybe they were hunting too close to his compound, and he wanted to scare them off. Or maybe the raid on the moonfolk village was just a way to test his creations.

The creature was getting uncomfortably close to the campsite where Brynwyn was sleeping. Wisp drew her shortsword and charged the creature. She quickly severed both hydraulic lines, spraying reddish fluid everywhere. The creature hissed and flailed for a few seconds, then was rendered completely immobile.

She dragged the creature over to the campsite, then woke up Brynwyn. "Don't scream," Wisp said. "I've killed one of your creatures. Are these the things that attacked your village?"

"Yes," Brynwyn said, cringing away from the corpse.

"Listen to me," Wisp said. "The man I'm looking for, the one in the shiny castle in the valley, he's an evil wizard. He created these monsters so he could make them do bad things. But I'm going to show you how to stop them." Wisp pointed out the creature's weak points. In addition to the tubes running along its spine, there was another exposed tube under its jaw, running from the underside of its throat and disappearing behind the sternum.

"Now I'm going to take this creature apart," Wisp said. "I'm looking for other weaknesses we can exploit, as well as parts we might be able to use. And maybe it won't be so scary to you once you've seen it dissected."

They spent a couple of hours disassembling the creature. Wisp wasn't a professional engineer, but she'd picked up a lot of random skills over her lifetimes, and she thought she might be able to use a couple of the parts she recovered. There was a battery pack in the hydraulic pump, and some sort of transmitter and receiver at the base of its skull.

Not to mention its metallic scales. While they took stock of their resources, Wisp noticed that the arrows in Brynwyn's quiver had bone tips. Working together, they upgraded the arrows using the scales.

While they were working, Wisp heard a noise coming from farther down the mountain. "Wait here," she told Brynwyn, and she climbed until she had a better view.

Three more creatures climbed up the side of the mountain. Wisp decided to test a theory. Going into stealth mode, she climbed down to their level, drew her shortsword, and quickly dispatched all three. Then she looked down into the valley, where hundreds of the creatures still surrounded the compound.

They weren't that hard to kill, once you knew their weaknesses. She wondered how long she'd last if she just rushed the compound. She imagined she could take out at least twenty before they swarmed her. Maybe twice that if she started out hidden.

After a few minutes, nine of the creatures broke off from the swarm and started climbing up the mountain. Three for each of the ones she'd just killed. She did some mental calculations. The first one she'd killed by cutting its hydraulic lines, but its search party hadn't shown up for a few hours, shortly after she'd removed its transmitter. These three she'd killed by stabbing them straight in the battery pack, immediately summoning more creatures.

Her guess was that each creature's transmitter stayed in contact with the base. If the transmitter lost power, more creatures were summoned to the last place a signal had been detected. But could she use this to her advantage? The monsters down below were still at least twenty minutes away at their pace.

She returned to the campsite, and picked up the transmitter from the first creature she'd killed. "Brynwyn," she asked. "If I attached one of these to an arrow, how far do you think you could fire it?"

She pointed to a spot on the other side of a chasm, about one hundred meters away.

Wisp had an idea. They waited until the nine newest arrivals got a bit closer, then Wisp attempted to kill them by severing their hydraulics. After she dispatched the first four, they caught onto her. Their eyes changed from a yellow glow to purple, and they were now able to see her even when she tried jumping back into the shadows.

The fight was a bit more work now. She dodged under one creature's swipe, darting between its legs and coming up behind it to cut its hydraulic tubes. While she blocked one creature's claws with her sword, another one tried to attack her from behind. It was rendered immobile by a pair of Brynwyn's arrows, fired from her hiding spot about twenty meters away. Wisp was awed by her accuracy.

Between the two of them, they soon had the rest of the creatures immobilized. Now Wisp had the beginnings of a plan. She held the battery pack she'd pulled from the original creature. Then she extracted the transmitter from one of their latest victims, plugging her battery pack into the transmitter's auxiliary port before disconnecting it from the creature's power source. Finally, she took an arrow and replaced the head with the transmitter, and handed it to Brynwyn.

On Wisp's order, Brynwyn fired the arrow as far as it would go, over the gap between mountain peaks. The transmitter was smashed upon hitting the mountainside. As Wisp had predicted, down in the valley below, three more creatures broke off from the pack and started climbing up the mountain. Not towards Brynwyn and Wisp, but towards where her arrow had landed.

"So we do have a way to control them," Wisp said. "To an extent."

"What can we do with that?" Brynwyn asked.

Wisp sat down next to one of the frozen creatures, and Brynwyn followed suit. "I'm working on it," Wisp said. "I thought we might build a trap. Maybe a pit or something involving falling rocks. Something that can be used more than once, though. We guide some of the creatures into the trap. When their transmitters stop working, more creatures go to look for them, and they fall in too. And so on. Once enough creatures are lured away from the fortress, we sneak in."

"I think that's a great idea," a voice said, but it wasn't Brynwyn's. It was a male voice, and it came from one of the immobilized monsters. "But I have a better one. Why don't the two of you stay right where you are while my creations rip you to shreds." From down in the valley, roughly half of the remaining monsters started climbing up the mountain.

"Time to go," Wisp said, standing up. The pair ran around the side of the mountain, looking for an escape.

Three hours later, they sat, exhausted, watching the swarms of creatures from a distance. They had run down the back side of the mountain, cut through the outskirts of the forest, before finally finding a safe vantage point near the base of another mountain. During their run, they'd seen several search drones take off from the compound. Brynwyn and Wisp had shot down a few of them, but that had only led to more being directed to the areas where the drones went down.

Now they hid in a shallow cave, peering out whenever they were sure no drones were around. The sun was rising, and they were both ready to sleep for a week. However, with most of the creatures searching the mountains, there were fewer guarding the compound. Wisp didn't want to give up this advantage. She studied the fortress. The rising sunlight glinted off its steel walls. The parapets made it look vaguely medieval. There was a small lake next to the compound, running right up next to the fortress wall, surrounding it on two sides like a partial moat.

Wisp glanced at Brynwyn, who lay against the back wall of the cave, her eyes closed. *Poor thing*, Wisp thought. Wisp's initial plan had failed. She couldn't say she was surprised. This attack needed an army, not a single bounty hunter and her local guide. She decided that they'd lay low for the day, wait for the sun to go down, and then she'd use her stealth skills to sneak into the fortress alone. She wasn't sure how she'd convince Brynwyn to stay behind, but she'd think of something.

Unfortunately, they couldn't just stay in this cave all day. The creatures and drones were doing thorough searches of the surrounding mountains, and if they stayed here, they would be discovered eventually. They would have to wait for a break in the drone activity, then run for the forest, and find a safe place to camp there. Wisp took another peek out of the cave, surveying the drone situation. When she looked at the compound, she noticed something she hadn't seen before. She pulled out her comm unit and zoomed in.

The lake was crystal clear, probably because it wasn't naturally occurring, but rather a steel-lined pool for catching rainwater. And on the fortress wall, under the waterline, Wisp spotted a grate. She turned her head. "Brynwyn?"

"I wasn't sleeping!" the moonfolk shouted, opening her eyes with a jolt.

"Sorry," Wisp said, as Brynwyn joined her by the cave entrance. "Are you a good swimmer?"

"Yes," Brynwyn answered, yawning.

"How long can you hold your breath?"

"About six fluurels," she said proudly.

Wisp wasn't sure how long that was, but Brynwyn's confidence seemed to indicate it was better than average. "I need your help with something. Get your bow."

Sixteen minutes later, a search drone flew over the cave. Brynwyn watched it go by, her bow drawn. She waited as long as she could, wanting to give it as far a lead as possible, letting loose the arrow just before it would have been out of range. The arrow hit true, and the drone's momentum took it farther from the cave as it fell. It finally crashed on the edge of the forest, drawing the attention of all the nearby drones and creatures.

Wisp and Brynwyn ducked back into the cave as a pair of creatures ran by. When the coast was clear, Wisp looked out the cave entrance. Several monsters moved toward the downed drone, and more drones scanned that area as well. As far as Wisp could see, nothing was currently watching the route from the cave entrance to the pool.

They ran as fast as they could and dove into the pool. Once under the water, Wisp pulled out her dagger and started working on the grating. Brynwyn pulled out a fletching knife and helped. They removed the grate and looked into the underwater tunnel. It was hard to tell how long it was, as it turned after a few meters. They surfaced for one last breath of air before submerging again and entering the tunnel.

Brynwyn hadn't been boasting. Wisp had been worried that her companion wouldn't be able to keep up, but the elflike woman continued to surprise her. The rectangular tunnel slanted downwards, later turning into a large round pipe, which eventually fed into an open reservoir. The pair resurfaced, grabbing the edge of the tank. Wisp's lungs burned from holding her breath so long, but Brynwyn seemed unfazed.

They climbed out of the reservoir and looked around. They were in a room full of pipes. Smaller pipes led from the bottom of the reservoir and into various water heaters and purifiers. Brynwyn burned her hand by resting it on one particularly hot steam pipe, and ran to cool it off in the large reservoir. Wisp opened the door a crack, and saw the hallway was unguarded.

She wasn't surprised. Mek's fortress was on a primitive world where the threat of monsters would keep intruders far away. There was no reason to expect an attack from the inside, so internal security would be an afterthought at best. The pair sneaked down the hallway, peeking into some of the side rooms they passed.

One room looked right out of a mad scientist's laboratory, with tables full of vials of chemicals, and generators capped by sparking electrodes. Half-assembled weapons filled one table, while another was full of rifles and energy pistols. "What is this place?" Brynwyn asked.

"Just evil wizard stuff," Wisp said. "Don't touch anything."

"Wisp," Brynwyn said. "The traders from the South have powders that explode when touched by fire. They are not wizards. If this 'Alas Mek' has any weapons we can use against him, I'm not afraid to use them. You can show me."

Wisp picked up a pair of stun pistols and examined them. "I'm going to get in so much trouble with Parks and Preservation," she muttered, tossing one to Brynwyn. Another room had some target mannequins, and Wisp showed Brynwyn how to aim and fire her weapon.

Despite Brynwyn's earlier assertion, she shrieked the first time she fired her pistol. "It's like throwing lightning," she said, turning the weapon around in her hands to see it from all sides. "Even the goddess Yvora needs a bow to fire her thunderbolts." She looked up at Wisp. "Is this blasphemy?"

"It's for a good cause," Wisp said. "Label Alas Mek however you want. God, wizard, engineer, whatever. But he hurts people, and his monsters killed your brother. Yvora will forgive you for harnessing the power of the gods for one day."

They continued to explore the tunnels, hoping to find Mek before he found them. They passed a few more rooms containing various half-finished projects, including a cloning chamber with even more dangerous-looking versions of the creatures outside. When they were finally convinced that he wasn't on this level, they decided to ascend to the ground level.

Wisp chose the stairs over the elevator, partly because she thought the elevator might be more conspicuous, but mostly because she was afraid of how Brynwyn might react to elevators. They reached the ground floor and saw a couple of Mek's creatures guarding the foyer. Rather than engage them, they decided to go up one more level first.

The compound's upper level was mostly living space, filled with large open dens that looked unused. At the end of one hallway, they heard movement. Through the open door, they saw a wall filled with dozens of security monitors, each showing drone footage of the surrounding mountains and woods. Someone sat at a desk in front of the monitors. They could only see the back of his chair, but they heard him slam his fist on the desk and curse. "How hard is it to find two women?" he shouted.

Wisp signaled for Brynwyn to be quiet, then crept toward the security room, her weapon drawn. It was too bright in here to blend in with the shadows, but she could still absorb sound, and she made no noise as she made her way down the hallway. She was almost to the door when one of the security monitors changed to show Wisp in the hallway.

"What?" Mek shouted, turning his chair around. Wisp fired her energy pistol. She hit him square in the chest, but he was unfazed. Alas Mek stood up. He was wearing a robotic exosuit, covering his entire body. It was bronze colored, and appeared to use a mix of modern and outdated technologies. He held up his fist and fired three small missiles from a battery on the back of his hand.

Wisp ducked to the side, still firing her pistol. She weaved left and right as she ran down the hall, avoiding various projectiles. Mek stomped after her, making a mess of his own den as his energy blasts and miniature missiles destroyed every piece of furniture Wisp ducked behind. Finally he had her cornered. He couldn't miss this time. He began to raise his hands to fire...

...and then his exosuit froze. "Warning," an electronic voice said from within the suit. "Hydraulic pressure low. Mobility functions have been lost." An arrow now stuck out the back of his exosuit, having severed the hydraulic line leading down his spine. Red fluid sprayed everywhere, and Mek was stuck. He couldn't even activate the release hatches. Brynwyn stood behind him, bow in hand, ready to let loose another arrow if necessary.

"I think your suit has some design flaws," Wisp said, now

standing to Mek's side. "Next time you go with hydraulics, maybe cover the lines."

Wisp had a bit of cleaning up to do before she called the Fertilund agents. She used Mek's master control center to recall all the drones and creatures, then had the computer deactivate them. Once every device was inert, Wisp and Brynwyn said their goodbyes.

"Will you go back home to your family now?" Wisp asked.

"I'd rather go with you," Brynwyn replied.

Wisp hugged her, patting her on the shoulder. "That's just not possible," she said. "Besides, I'm sure your parents miss you. And think about what you've accomplished here. There will never be another monster attack, thanks to you. No one else has to lose a brother to Mek's creatures."

"I won't be able to explain any of this to them," Brynwyn said.

"Then don't," Wisp said. "Just tell them that the evil wizard has been defeated, and his monsters are now dead. I bet they're so glad to see you, they don't care about the details."

"Will you ever be back?" Brynwyn asked.

"Anything's possible," Wisp said. "Now go. You can't be here when my ride shows up, or I'll get in trouble."

They hugged again, and Brynwyn left. The Fertilund agents were quick to retrieve Wisp. They sent a damage control team to destroy Mek's work, and debriefed Wisp before approving her reward. Wisp didn't mention Brynwyn in her report. Satisfied that no cultural contamination had occurred, the Fertilund Parks and Preservation agents thanked Wisp for a job well done, and dismissed her.

It was a bright day in the Silkleaf Woods. Rays of sunshine filtered through the leaves, creating mottled patterns on the ground below. A green-and-brown striped doe gingerly stepped through the forest, looking for a place to lay her eggs. She stopped at a creek for a drink, blissfully unaware that she was being hunted. She heard an odd electronic whine, and started to bolt. But she was too late. A burst of energy darted through the air, paralyzing her.

Brynwyn stepped out from behind a bush, energy pistol in hand. Her family would be grateful to her for bringing home dinner. Maybe a little blasphemy wasn't so bad after all.

02.04 *Sekka of the Jungle*

ED.02508.05.20

"Aaaaaeeeeeaaaaaaeeeeeaaaaaa!" Sekka shouted, swinging from the vine. She'd seen that in movies, and had always wanted to do it. Except the vines on Cleesia were slicker than she expected, and she ended up sliding down the vine and landing on her butt, right in the middle of a nest of sniklizards.

Cleesia was not a jungle planet. In fact, less than five percent of the planet had any foliage at all. The rest was water, rocky mountains, and a few cities. And if her target had been spotted on any other part of the planet, Sekka might have let one of the other Bloodhunters handle it. But a chance to explore a real jungle? Yes, please.

Carefully picking the tiny lizards off of her leopard print unitard, Sekka stood up and got her bearings. She doubted Tarnell Holl would be hard to find. Sure, it was a big jungle, but surely he wasn't just sleeping in the open air. All she needed to look for was something made by a sapient being. A shack, a lean-to, or maybe even a treehouse. Something like that should stick out like a sore thumb in these wilds.

Petting one of the sniklizards, Sekka was reminded of how much she missed her animal friends. She hadn't been allowed to bring any of them with her to Cleesia, due to customs restrictions. She supposed she couldn't blame them. This jungle probably provided most of the planet's oxygen. For all the customs officers knew, Sekka could have brought in an invasive species that feeds on trees. Better to be safe than sorry, she supposed.

As she walked through the thick jungle, she came across the corpse of a large canine. It looked fresh, but it had already been picked clean by other animals. She kept walking, and found two more similar corpses. She hoped that if she ran into whatever was killing these creatures, it was something she could talk to.

Her affinity with animals only went so far. Some creatures were immune, others were just stubborn. Even when it worked, it wasn't exactly two-way communication. Animals weren't capable of higher thought, and therefore couldn't be given complex instructions. She couldn't just tell a bird, "Go look for a hut and report back to me." She'd have to put a mental image of a hut in the bird's mind, and make it associate it with something positive, like food.

And even if the bird found it, it couldn't just tell Sekka where it was. It would have to lead her there, and Sekka wouldn't know until she got there if it had actually found what she'd wanted. She might spend an entire day hiking, only to find the bird had led her to a pile of dead leaves.

Now that she thought about it, Sekka hadn't actually seen any birds since she'd landed. No large land animals, either, other than the corpses. She'd only seen a couple of opossum-like mammals, something that looked like a sugar glider, and the sniklizards. She didn't hear any birdcalls either. Surely this planet had birds?

Speak of the devil, she thought, as a bird landed on a tree branch up above her. Except, no, it wasn't actually a bird. Sekka studied this strange creature, pulling out her binoculars for a better look. It was shaped like a bird, for the most part, but it was obviously a mammal. It was about the size of a chicken, but with gray skin and sparse black hair. It had a long snout like a dog or a crocodile, with large, flat nostrils. It had big, pointed ears, but no eyes that Sekka could see.

The bird-bat-thing lifted its head and called out. "Wee-Auk! Wee-Auk!" When its mouth was open wide, Sekka saw that it had multiple rows of needle-like teeth. In response to its call, two more of the creatures landed on the branch beside it. Sekka heard rustling in several other directions, and saw more of the creatures perched on branches all around her. Despite not having eyes, they all seemed to be looking in her direction.

Maybe I just can't see their eyes, Sekka thought. She stared at one of the closer creatures, attempting to use her abilities on it. No reaction. Usually she could feel it when she'd made a connection, but this time she might as well have been trying to talk to a tree.

The creatures started getting restless, sniffing the air and making weird chirps and growls. Some of them made high-pitched keening noises, which Sekka guessed worked like sonar. Sekka slowly backed out of the circle, and their heads turned toward her. She knew they'd swarm if she ran; she could just feel their hunger in the air. She was almost out of the clearing when one of the creatures barked. "Wark! Wark!" The creatures took flight, and Sekka ran for her life.

She knew she wouldn't make it far like this. The things were behind her, above her, and some even flew ahead of her. Sekka recognized the tactic. If they made her run long enough, she'd tire and be that much easier to kill. She might even trip over something and break her leg.

But Sekka wasn't going to play their game. She reached into her bag and pulled out a small device. It was a pencil-shaped metal wand. She rotated the top as far as it would turn, then pressed the button on the end. The device emitted an inaudible whine, and the creatures scattered. The wand was designed to attract animals, so that Sekka could call whatever creatures were currently under her control. But when the knob was turned to its highest setting, it caused pain to any creature that could hear high frequencies. Sekka called it her dogwhistle. Realizing she'd probably need it again, she attached the wand to a lanyard and hung it around her neck.

Sekka noticed that after the creatures flew off, they regrouped and swarmed to the East. Curious, she followed. She theorized that if Holl was in any way connected to these bat-things, they might consider his place their nesting ground. Using a compass to maintain her direction, she made her way through the jungle, climbing over giant roots and cutting through tall grass.

Sekka trekked for several hours, not just because it was far, but also because the jungle floor was overgrown and difficult to traverse. She used a traditional machete instead of an AON blade to cut through the undergrowth, because she was afraid of starting a fire. Twice during her journey, the creatures tried to attack her again. Again she scared them off with her dogwhistle, and once again they flew off to the East.

Her hunch paid off. After climbing over a fallen tree, she saw a massive mound of the bat-like creatures. At first she thought they must be swarming on top of a large stump, but then she realized it was a wooden shack, built between three trees it used as supports. Sekka used her dogwhistle again, and after they scattered, she quickly ran to the front door. It wouldn't budge, so she knocked hard.

The creatures were already on their way back. She was about to press the button again when the door opened. The shack's occupant grabbed Sekka by the shoulder, pulled her inside, and slammed the door shut. Then he put a crossbar into place to keep it from opening.

The shack had no windows, and was lit by several large glowsticks, the type that sometimes came in emergency supply kits. The place was a mess. Wrappers from rations bars littered the floor. There were several buckets for collecting rainwater placed under some of the larger cracks in the roof. There was a latrine pit dug into one corner, and the smell from that direction was overpowering.

The man standing in front of Sekka was emaciated and had wild eyes. His beard was overgrown, and he shook with excitement.

"Tarnell Holl?" Sekka began. "I'm here to…"

"Do you have any food?" Holl said, putting both shaky hands on her shoulders.

Sekka rooted through her bag and handed him a couple of granola bars. He quickly crammed them down his throat, barely managing to get the wrappers off first.

"Been stuck here a while?" Sekka asked.

"I only brought two of them, I swear," Holl said. "And they were both males. And the ones I brought weren't nearly so… bitey. How was I supposed to know they'd be able to mate with the local bats? How was I supposed to know their offspring would be such… monsters? It wasn't my fault, I tell you." He grabbed Sekka by the shoulders again and shouted in her face. "It wasn't my fault!"

Sekka brushed his hands away. "I can help you, Holl. But you're going to have to calm down."

"Calm down," Holl said. "Easy for you to say. Those things haven't let me leave for weeks. They multiply like rabbits. Soon there'll be so many, they'll collapse the roof."

"If I can get you off this planet," Sekka offered, "will you come willingly?"

"If you can get me off this planet, I'll be your slave," Holl said.

"That won't be necessary," Sekka said.

Holl gathered a few belongings, Sekka activated her dogwhistle, and they set out for Sekka's shuttle. With fresh food in his stomach, Holl regained some measure of sanity. Sekka even let him take over machete duty for a while, when her arms got tired. They had to use the dogwhistle several more times over the next couple of hours, but they finally made it to the shuttle.

Once they were inside, both of them relaxed. Sekka sat in the pilot's chair, and Holl sat next to her. Her shuttle blasted off, and broke through the atmosphere into space.

"Setting a course for Warp Gate 4218," Sekka said. "From there we'll drop you off at IGP Station 412."

"I don't think so," Holl said, holding the machete to her neck. "Why don't I set the course instead."

Sekka's hand went to the dogwhistle, still hanging from her neck. Turning the intensity back down, she pressed the button. From the back of the shuttle, three steelbeak buzzers flew out of their cage and went for Holl's face. He screamed and panicked, waving his arms around and dropping the machete.

"Get 'em off! Get 'em off!" he shouted, running around the shuttle before tripping over a cage. He fell face first into a water dish. A pink squirrel chittered angrily at him, before biting his nose.

Sekka took out her bracers and bound Holl's wrists. You just couldn't trust anyone these days. Good thing she'd brought her friends. After all, just because she wasn't allowed to let them loose on Cleesia didn't mean she couldn't travel with them. In her opinion, she'd obeyed the spirit of the law, if not the letter.

Tarnell Holl was sent back to prison, though he was allowed to work with Cleesia's Wildlife Service to help contain the creatures he'd introduced to their planet. It took a lot of work, but the ecology did eventually recover. Some of the native species had to be saved through cloning, and unfortunately, a few of the local species were lost forever.

The new species, which were named "piranha bats" because apparently the universe isn't scary enough already, were sterilized and distributed to various zoos across the galaxy. They were actually quite docile in small numbers, and their introduction to zoos resulted in very few accidents.

And for once, Sekka met an animal that she didn't want to take home as a pet.

02.05   *Rescuing the Princess*

ED.02508.05.27

Midnight didn't really consider himself one of the Bloodhunters. After Tena orchestrated a series of assassinations across the galaxy, the Meu government sent several agents to other planets in an effort to help them find those responsible. Other Meu agents were currently stationed on Earth, Kalara, and Chirminon, working with the governments of those worlds.

But Midnight followed his hunches, and something about this team of bounty hunters struck a chord with him. So far, the hunch had paid off. The Bloodhunters had been the ones to discover Tena was bluffing, and Midnight was sure that if he stuck with this team, he'd get to be there when they finally took down Tena for good.

But today, he was headed home. One of Tena's Twenty was a Canik named Dougg Killerbyte, a name which made Midnight chuckle every time he heard it. He didn't want to sound racist, but Canik surnames were something else. The dogs were allowed to choose their own last name when they came of age, which sounded great in theory, but so many of them chose names that were in poor taste. Most of them were based on bad puns, online usernames, or edgy fantasy characters.

Why couldn't they do something simple like the Meu did? Midnight's truename was Mavu Com-Vess. His surname was a combination of his father's nickname, Comet, and his mother's first name, Vessna. If Midnight were to have a son, their surname would probably be something like Mid-Prin, after Midnight and his girlfriend, Princess. Though it was way too early in their relationship to be thinking about kittens.

But then, Canik culture always struck Midnight as funny. It was just how he was raised. His parents hadn't been racist in the hateful sense, but they'd definitely instilled in their son the idea that Meu culture was superior. The more Midnight matured, the more he recognized his parents' flaws, and the more he caught himself repeating their mistakes.

Midnight was determined to be a better person, but his job made it difficult. He was the leader of WARCAT, an elite branch of the Meu armed forces that dealt with terrorism. It didn't help that the most prolific terrorist organization on the planet was the DOG Force, which was composed almost entirely of Caniks. Even the names of the two forces were racist.

So yes, keeping his objectivity had been challenging. But this wasn't the world Midnight's parents had grown up in. The Greater Continent of Meu had more Canik residents than ever before, and while there were still some hostilities between the two species, society had come a long way in terms of acceptance and tolerance.

Dougg Killerbyte had been born in the Canik Empire, Galea's second-largest continent. However, he had immigrated to Meu as a child. Later he briefly worked for the DOG Force before leaving Galea and joining the Inner Eye. Midnight wasn't sure what Dougg had done to piss them off, but he was no longer welcome in the Canik Empire or the DOG Force.

Dougg was an electronics genius, and his technical skills had been a great asset to both the DOGs and the Inner Eye.

So where was he now? While a few of the released criminals had attempted to return to Valos, most of them were hiding out on other planets. Dougg had been spotted en route to Galea, and since he wasn't welcome anywhere else, he had to be on the Greater Continent of Meu.

But GCM was a big continent. Midnight would start with Dougg's known associates and former hangouts. Meanwhile, he would have one of his WARCAT teammates track Dougg's online presence. But before any of that, Midnight had to see Princess again. It had been weeks since he'd been on Galea, and he wanted to surprise her. Hopefully she wasn't currently in concert.

Midnight pulled up her website and checked her tour dates. Cool, no performance tonight. Then something odd struck his eye. Princess had been scheduled to sing the previous night, but the performance had been canceled. Midnight cocked his head, then checked the news sites. Apparently she hadn't shown up for her concert, and no one had been able to contact her. The press concluded that she was just being a diva, but Midnight doubted it. That wasn't the Princess he knew.

He'd been planning to stop by his home first to freshen up, but now he changed course and went straight to her place. He called her several times on the way, but there was no answer. He also tried her manager and two of her best friends, but no one had seen her. He was about to call her brother, but the landing site was in already in view.

Princess lived in a penthouse apartment in downtown Burma Bay. Midnight had to land his shuttle in a parking garage three blocks away and take a monorail over, though he was so worried he briefly considered just putting the shuttle in hover and jumping down to her spacious balcony.

The monorail track went through her building, and Midnight took the elevator up to her apartment. He had his own key – that's how far along the relationship was – and he opened the door without even knocking. He called her name a few times, but no answer. Then he saw a note on her coffee table. It read: "Leave me alone and she lives – DK."

Midnight was livid. He pulled out his comm unit and called Topsy, WARCAT's top computer tech. She promised that her entire team would get right on it. In the meantime, Midnight looked around the apartment for clues. He checked every room but didn't see any sign of struggle. The door to her balcony was unlocked. There was a pool on the balcony, with some lounge chairs nearby. Next to one of the chairs was a towel, an open book, and a half-finished can of soda.

Princess had probably been abducted right off of the balcony, while lounging by the pool. Midnight called her brother, WK. WK's full nickname was White Knight, but people called him WK for short, even though it had more syllables than White Knight. He was a wealthy software developer with a knack for picking stocks. He also had access to unlimited resources, and would stop at nothing to find his sister. By the time Midnight got off the comm with WK, there was a message from Topsy waiting for him.

Her team had analyzed security footage from several nearby buildings. The morning Princess had been scheduled to perform, a drone had come out of the sky and carried her off. Additional cameras tracked her until she landed on top of another roof across town, an empty office building. Topsy asked if she should send police there, but Midnight told her no. He was afraid of what Dougg might do to Princess if the police knocked on his door. Midnight forwarded this information to WK, and took the monorail back to his shuttle.

By the time he reached the shuttle, WK had replied with some security footage of his own. Just a few minutes after Princess had landed on the roof, a car had left the building's underground parking garage. By hacking every camera in downtown Burma Bay, and using the same tracking software WK had licensed to WARCAT, he had found the car's eventual destination. It was an apartment building, and it was within walking distance.

Midnight took some weapons out of his shuttle and

headed that way. He texted WK and Topsy as he ran, asking if they knew which apartment was Dougg's. They both replied with the same information. A new tenant had just moved in a few days ago, under the name Degg Hakker. *Creative*, Midnight thought.

As he reached the apartment building, Midnight paused. Would Dougg kill her if he burst through the door? Probably not, because then he wouldn't have a hostage. But it wasn't worth the risk. Instead, he decided to go in through the window. He fired a grappling hook at the fire escape, climbed up, and squatted outside Dougg's window.

Staying out of view, he gingerly reached up and placed a small camera against the bottom of the glass. The feed was transmitted to Midnight's comm unit. It showed that Dougg's living room was empty. There was one more window, a smaller one, and Midnight placed another camera. It showed an empty bathroom. Midnight used a small AON cutter to sever the lock, and quietly slid the bathroom window open. Then he climbed inside.

The door across the hall was closed, and Midnight thought he heard movement. He tiptoed across the hall and put his ear to the door. There was definitely something going on in there. He pulled out one of his cameras and held it under the door, but the gap wasn't wide enough to get a good view.

Midnight braced himself. If he screwed this up, he could get Princess killed. He pulled out his GATO WC-11 Rapidfire Energy Pistol, took a deep breath, and kicked open the door.

Dougg had turned the master bedroom into a hacker's dream room. Three rows of monitors lined every wall, showing bank accounts, security footage, and lines of code that Midnight found incomprehensible. Electronic equipment that did who-knows-what was crammed into every corner. The only devices Midnight recognized were a video game console and a microwave oven. There was no bed, though. Dougg must have been sleeping in the living room.

No one was in the bedroom, but one of the monitors was on the floor, along with a mouse, and a few spots of blood. One chair was on its side. It looked like there had been a recent struggle. There was another door on the other side of the room, presumably leading to the master bathroom. Midnight put his hand on the knob, but the door suddenly opened by itself.

Midnight found himself face-to-face with his girlfriend. Princess, still in her swimsuit, squealed with joy upon seeing Midnight, and wrapped her arms around him. He looked over her shoulder and saw Dougg Killerbyte in the bathroom, tied up with computer cables. He had several deep scratches on his face and an expression somewhere between furious and embarrassed.

Midnight threw back his head and laughed. *That* was the Princess he knew.

02.06 *Cold Blood*

ED.02508.06.01

Lyryssa knew her day was going downhill when the walrus asked her to hop on one leg.

The cold didn't bother her much. Her homeworld had been cool and damp, and her people often lived in ice caverns anyway. So when the Bloodhunters got word that one of the ex-prisoners had been spotted in the arctic cities of Glayss, Lyryssa had raised her hand right away. She was still new to bounty hunting, and so far the team had only let her go on missions with a partner. This would be Lyryssa's first solo outing.

She'd still packed warm clothing, along with several weapons, some cuffs, rope, and other tools of the trade, and of course several vials of blood. She'd brought a week's supply of Glik's synthetic blend for her chronic pain, and two vials of the good stuff for emergencies.

If Wisp was getting annoyed at all the blood donations, she wasn't showing it. In fact, she seemed to have a twisted sense of humor about the situation, calling herself Lyryssa's thrall and making other silly jokes in that "vein." Just a few days ago she'd made Lyryssa watch an ancient cartoon about a sailor who got temporary super strength from eating spinach. Wisp said it reminded her of Lyryssa's reaction to her blood.

Unfortunately, the security and customs officers of Frostwick had no sense of humor when it came to importing bodily fluids. The walrus-like Rosmar agent had detected the vials when scanning Lyryssa's bags. At first he wouldn't allow them because it was considered a biohazard. Lyryssa had tried to convince him the blood was for medicinal purposes, but that only made things worse.

Since some Nithari used blood as a narcotic, in her possession the blood automatically became an illicit substance. Which is why, at this moment, Lyryssa was undergoing a sobriety test. When she was finished touching her nose, walking a straight line, hopping on one leg, and singing a nursery rhyme, the officers were finally satisfied and allowed her to enter the town. However, they confiscated her vials of blood.

They gave her a claim slip she could use on her way back out of town to get her property back. They also said that if she brought them a doctor's note, they would allow her to drink one vial a day in town. However, there weren't any doctors in town qualified to diagnose her condition or to treat her species. She asked if she could leave town, consume a vial, then come back in, but they said no. Without a doctor's note, they would have to hold onto her vials until she was on her way off the planet.

It is what it is, she thought, walking through town. She'd had her dose this morning. With any luck, she'd catch her prey by the end of the day, and it wouldn't be a problem. Or failing that, maybe there were some humans in town who'd be willing to sell her a few drops. That sounded like it would be an awkward conversation. She decided to postpone worrying about it until later.

On the way to her hotel, she took in the sights. It never got above freezing here, and all the buildings were made of ice. But they weren't just boring square buildings made of frozen bricks, no, this was a city regulated by artists. Every building, from the grandest palaces to the cheapest fast food restaurants, had been sculpted with the utmost care. The local government might have been a little bit too strict for Lyryssa's tastes, but they knew beauty.

Lyryssa saw more tourists than Rosmar on her walk. Vhelrans, Kalarans, Galeans, and thankfully even some humans passed her in the street, many of them posing for pictures in front of the town's unique architecture. This town relied on off-world money for its survival, which is probably why they were so uncompromising. They couldn't afford to have rowdy tourists deface their buildings. She supposed it was odd that they hadn't taken her weapons as well, but there were dangerous animals in the area.

She reached her hotel and checked in. It was round, and three stories tall. Her room was on the top floor, which bothered her a little because it had no elevator. Instead, a slowly curving staircase ran along the inner wall of the lobby. Lyryssa noted that anywhere she saw stairs, there was also a ramp running beside them. Her first thought was wheelchairs, but then she remembered that the locals were pinnipeds who probably preferred ramps to steps.

Thankfully, the steps had rubber mats to keep them from being too slick. The ramps were just solid ice, and would probably kill anyone who tried to climb one in a wheelchair. She briefly wondered what the local building codes were like, then got distracted when she reached the second floor. This floor had its own lobby, and in the center was an exquisite ice carving of a human.

But it wasn't just any human. It was the man Lyryssa had been sent to find. Kolden Dair, member of the Inner Eye and a prolific criminal in his own right. Why was he being honored with a statue? Lyryssa set down her suitcase and studied the carving. There was no plaque, nothing to give context to the carving.

There was, however, a Rosmar bellhop nearby. Like the others of his species, he looked like a walrus except for his two muscular, humanlike arms. "Would you like help with your suitcase?" he asked, trundling up to her. He wore a red shirt and a nametag that read, "Broosbawm."

"Is this Kolden Dair?" Lyryssa asked him, gesturing toward the statue.

"Yes, ma'am!" Broosbawm replied, nodding enthusiastically. "Our town's savior. A true hero."

Suddenly Lyryssa was glad she hadn't told the town guards the real reason for her visit. "What did he do for Frostwick?" she asked.

"We were sinking," the bellhop answered. "By about a meter a year, thanks to rising global temperatures. Dair invented a device that keeps our ice shelf sturdy and frozen."

That was news to Lyryssa. All she'd heard was that he'd been seen in the area. "Listen," Lyryssa said. "I'm doing a... um... book report for college. Is there any way I could meet him? Do you know where I could find him?"

"Everybody knows where he lives," Broosbawm said. "Just go outside and look up. His tower is also the device that saved us. He doesn't like visitors, though."

Lyryssa thanked him, picked up her suitcase, and took the stairs to the third level. The individual hotel rooms had no doors. Instead, each one had a short, L-shaped privacy hall leading to the room. However, hotel staff watched the floors constantly, and made sure guests didn't enter rooms that weren't theirs. Unless they were accompanied by the actual guest, of course.

Lyryssa put her suitcase on the bed, which was a fur-covered air mattress with no frame. Then she walked out on her balcony and looked up.

In the center of town stood the only structure not made of ice. It was a round column of blue metal, coated in transparent ice, about five stories tall. Near the top of the tower there were some balconies and windows. At the bottom, it appeared to go deep into the ground. The tower was surrounded by a three-meter-high ice wall, and Lyryssa could see a few armed Rosmar patrolling inside the walls.

Lyryssa sat on the bed and thought hard. How was she going to get in? And once she captured Dair, how was she going to get him out of town without upsetting the grateful citizens of Frostwick? And without the abilities Wisp's blood gave her? And with no vials of blood, how was she going to accomplish all that before her chronic pain returned?

She thought about giving up, leaving town, and coming back better prepared. If she left town right now, they'd return her vials. She could take some of the good stuff, and return, invisibly.

But did she really want to do that? The more she relied on Wisp's blood, the harder it was going to be to get along without it. She wanted to get through this mission on her own skills, not the superpowers granted by chemicals. But on the other hand, lives might be at stake. If Dair was up to his old evil tricks, then all was fair. Lyryssa had no excuse to use this mission as some personal catharsis, it was her duty to apprehend Dair as quickly as possible. It wasn't "cheating" to use every resource at her disposal.

She went back and forth on this for a while, and eventually decided to compromise with herself. She would try to apprehend Dair tonight. If she failed, she would check out of her hotel tomorrow, collect her medicine from customs, and sneak back into town fully powered. Assuming she survived her first attempt, of course.

She spent the next hour debating her attack strategy. She considered using a zipline to fly from her balcony to the tower. She thought about sneaking over the wall and tiptoeing past the guards. She even considered knocking on the front door and claiming to be a reporter. Then she had another idea.

She waited until the sun went down. The town was located near the Glayss South pole, and the planet itself had a faster rotation than Lyryssa was used to. It never got fully bright in Frostwick, and night came every twelve hours.

There were several swimming holes in town, for the truly brave tourists. They were closed after dark for safety reasons, but they weren't guarded. If tourists wanted to kill themselves by taking dangerous nighttime swims, that was on them. Lyryssa climbed over an ice fence and crept to the edge of the water. She removed her parka, revealing a wetsuit underneath. She placed a rebreather in her mouth, capable of efficiently extracting oxygen straight from the water.

The wetsuit didn't have pockets, so she was selective about what she brought. She wore diving goggles that also had various vision enhancement modes. She wore a belt with a few waterproof pouches, filled with various small supplies. There was a dagger strapped to her right calf, and an energy pistol in a waterproof holster on her left hip.

She dove into the pool. Even with her tolerance for cold, the chill hit her like daggers. She had to swim downwards for about ten meters before she was under the ice shelf. From here, she could see the bottom of Dair's tower, which ended in a large cube. She swam closer and got a better look. The cube had vents on all sides, and Lyryssa could feel a strong current of cold water pushing her away from it.

She swam deeper and approached the cube from underneath. She found a maintenance tunnel and swam upwards through the wide vertical tube. After a few minutes it was pitch black, but her visor helped her make out the details. The tube ended in an airlock. It had simple controls inside; a single pull of a lever sealed the airlock, drained it, then opened the hatch on the other side.

Lyryssa took out her rebreather and goggles and attached them to her belt. She stood still for several seconds, waiting to see if any alarms went off. Just how paranoid was Dair? Would he be expecting intruders from this direction? She looked around for security cameras but didn't see any. No workers, either. These levels were probably only accessed when something went wrong.

She looked around the room, but it was mostly just pipes and motors. She found an elevator, but was afraid using it would cost her the element of surprise. There were no stairs, just a long vertical shaft with rungs to climb. She looked up the shaft, imagining the next thirty minutes of climbing. She wished she'd brought a grappling gun, or maybe some Levatech boots.

After about ten minutes of climbing, her shoulders started to ache. Her chronic pain was starting to return, jumpstarted by this repetitive activity. In a couple of hours she would be useless. She hoped she'd be on her way back out of town by then.

She passed a floor marked storage, and took a break from climbing. The door to the storage room was locked, but she picked it using a device from one of her pouches. Lyryssa rested on a crate, catching her breath and massaging her shoulders. She took a look around as long as she was there.

Some of the crates were full of meat, huge raw steaks from who-knew-what animal. Lyryssa sniffed one, trying to identify the meat. It smelled vaguely familiar, but she wasn't sure where she'd smelled it before. Some of the crates had shipping labels on them, ready to be transported to other planets.

She continued her climb, stopping to rest whenever she could. On the next floor, she found a room full of animal pelts. On another floor, she found an automated meat processing facility. The rendering machines weren't currently running, but it was obvious the room hadn't been cleaned in a while. There was blood all over the floor, and the room reeked with the bits of meat and fur stuck in the machines. Lyryssa wondered if Frostwick even had health inspectors.

The smell of the blood sent Lyryssa's senses into overdrive. She was so tempted to just start licking the floors to see if it would help her pain. Such a dignified image. She didn't give in to that urge, but she did find a divot on one control panel where a small pool of blood had collected. She experimentally dipped her finger into it and had a taste.

Yuck. It tasted gamy and vaguely like sweat. While it was hard to be sure from such a small dose, it didn't seem like it had any medicinal properties, either. So far only two species had been found to numb her pain, and this blood definitely wasn't from either of them.

Looking up, Lyryssa noticed a trap door in the ceiling, just above the machine intake. Apparently animals were fed into the machine from above. She decided she would skip that room when she reached the next floor. It sounded upsetting. Lyryssa wasn't a raging animal rights activist like Sekka, but she still didn't want to see the animals whimpering in their cages, waiting to be turned into steak.

She climbed past the door, which was marked "livestock," and kept going upwards. The shaft ended when it reached the ground floor. She hid and rested for a few minutes, then sneaked around. The lights were off on this floor, and all seemed quiet. While Lyryssa could see pretty well in the dark, there wasn't even starlight to go by here. She had to use the night vision mode on her goggles to find her way around.

There was an open lobby that led to the front door and a few offices. No one was here. Dair was probably asleep on the top floor. She saw the elevator and rejected it for the same reasons she had earlier. She saw another door labeled "stairs," and she could swear she heard her legs scream, "Oh hell no."

She still wanted to have some energy left when she faced Dair, and time was of the essence as she felt the twinges of her chronic pain threatening to return. The tower had five floors above ground. She decided to take the elevator to the fourth floor, then take the stairs the rest of the way. Hopefully that would still give her the element of surprise.

The elevator opened on the fourth floor. The lights were

on in the hallway. The second the doors opened, she heard someone shout, "Who is that?"

Lyryssa cursed and pounded on the "close door" button. But she was too late; a Rosmar guard arrived and overrode the elevator. Holding a gun in her face, he said, "Please hand me your weapons and come with me." She thought about fighting back, but didn't like her odds. The elevator didn't give her a lot of room to fight, and her muscles were starting to ache. She handed over her dagger and pistol, and let the Rosmar lead her away.

Kolden Dair was a human male in his mid-forties. He sat on an enormous couch, watching television. He was smoking a cigarette, a glass ashtray on his lap. Behind him, shelves and shelves of books lined the walls. Most of them appeared to be business related. Lyryssa stepped into his den, her hands raised, the walrus-like guard behind her. "It's a little late for visitors," Dair said, not taking his eyes off the TV.

"I can come back in the morning if you like," Lyryssa said.

He turned his head to look at her. "You're a Nithari," he said. "I've never seen one. Have a seat." He gestured toward the far end of his couch.

The Rosmar nudged Lyryssa in the back with his gun, and she sat down. "Mister Dair, I'm sorry to disturb you, but—" she began.

"You're a bounty hunter and you think I'm going back with you," he said, his eyes back on the TV. It was a stock market program, and Dair seemed highly invested in the ticker at the bottom of the screen.

"You can kill me if you want," Lyryssa said, her voice rising. "...but my friends will come looking for me. They'll do whatever it takes to bring you in."

"I'm not a killer," Dair said. "I'm a businessman. I'll admit I deserved to go to jail all those years ago, what with my Inner Eye dealings and whatnot. My greed got the better of my scruples. But ask around town. I'm a hero. A changed man. I've done my time."

"Actually, you still have twenty-four years to serve on your sentence," Lyryssa said.

"Prison is for rehabilitation," Dair said. "And it worked. My invention saved this town from sinking. I have a respectable meat processing business. Frostwick is more prosperous than ever, and everyone loves me. I'm no longer a danger to anyone."

"That's not really for you to decide," Lyryssa said. "But if you come with me, I'll put in a good word for you. Get some of the Rosmar to testify on your behalf, and maybe they can work out some sort of house arrest or something."

"I can pay you," Dair offered. "I promise you, you'll make more money working for me than as a bounty hunter."

"No, but thank you," she replied.

"There's no way the people of Frostwick will let you take me out of town," Dair said. "You'll have to fight every last one of them."

"I know," Lyryssa said. "But that's my problem. I'll find a way."

"So there's nothing I can say to talk you out of this? Last chance."

Lyryssa shook her head. The motion reminded her how much pain she was in. "I'm not leaving Frostwick without you," she said.

Dair sighed. "Bremlee," he said to the guard. "Kill her."

"We've been over this, sir," Bremlee said. "I'll guard you from harm, but I won't kill an unarmed prisoner."

"Fine," Dair said. "I'll take care of her myself." He stood up, knocking his ashtray onto the floor. He took several steps toward Lyryssa. Worried that Bremlee would shoot her the minute she attacked Dair, Lyryssa waited for Dair to attack first. Dair stood in front of her, then held out one hand toward Bremlee. "Gun," he said.

"Sir, I must protest," Bremlee said. "We can just lock her up..."

Dair grabbed the gun and tried to pull it out of Bremlee's hand, but the Rosmar had a much stronger grip. While they struggled, Lyryssa stood up and backed away from them slowly. She nearly tripped on Dair's ashtray, and bent down to pick it up. She started to throw it, but her arm spasmed in pain and she dropped it.

Dair's face went red as he struggled with the guard. He was used to people doing what he asked. He punched Bremlee in the face, hard enough to draw blood. As soon as the first drop of the guard's blood hit the air, the scent hit Lyryssa like a hovertruck filled with bricks. She knew blood, and she'd smelled this type very recently.

"You're getting your meat from Rosmar citizens!" she blurted, and the pair stopped struggling as they faced her.

"What?" Dair asked, loosening his grip on Bremlee's gun.

"Downstairs, I saw your meat rendering facility," Lyryssa said. "You're killing Rosmar and selling their meat!"

Bremlee's jaw dropped, and he glared accusingly at Dair.

"She's... she's lying," Dair stammered.

"Bremlee," she said, "Have any of your citizens gone missing lately?"

"Come to think of it," Bremlee started to say, a suspicious look on his face.

"Check the livestock level," Lyryssa said. "Right now. We'll all three go together."

"She's obviously lying," Dair said. "She's just looking for an opportunity to escape. We can't just let her tell us what to do."

"If she's lying, we'll find out soon enough," Bremlee said, turning his gun on Dair. "If you'll follow me, sir."

"No!" Dair shouted, and started to run.

Bremlee was faster than he looked. He spun around and smacked Dair with his massive rear flipper. Dair flew across the room, hit the wall, and just sat there, dazed.

"I'll just make a few calls and we'll get this all sorted out,"

Bremlee said. "In the meantime, is there anything I can get for you, lass?"

Lyryssa screamed in response, and crumpled to the floor. "Dair's... blood..." she whimpered.

After a few drops of Dair's blood, Lyryssa was good as new. Once she showed the Frostwick lawmen the evidence in Dair's lower levels, they had no choice but to believe her. The hard part was convincing them to hand Dair over into Lyryssa's custody, when they would have preferred to exact their own punishment on him. But she assured them that these new charges would be added to his sentence, and they reluctantly allowed her to take him.

Lyryssa was proud of herself, and rightfully so. Not only had she accomplished her first solo mission, but she'd done it on her own merits. No painkillers, no superpowered blood. And she'd taken her foe alive, without a fight. Sure, she'd been lucky to have Bremlee's help, but it had been her investigation of the lower levels that had saved her. She felt like a part of the group now, not just Glik's ward.

She was officially a real bounty hunter.

02.07   *The Interview*

ED.02508.06.06

"Welcome to Starpower On-The-Hour, your source for up-to-the-minute celebrity news and interviews! I'm your host, Malleeva G'hexxulan-Smith! Our guests tonight are award-winning actress Katrice Velt and archball captain Jelton Werles. But first, we've got Gliddik Gruddulup. Welcome, Gliddik. Can I call you Gliddik?"

"My friends call me Glik," he said.

"It's good to have you here, Glik! What brings you here today?"

"Apparently my time is worthless," Glik said, laughing. The host laughed right along with him, though her expression seemed a bit forced. "But seriously," Glik added, "I'm here to spread awareness. I represent a group of bounty hunters who are chasing the prisoners set free by Tena Vermon of Valos."

"Yes, such sad business," Malleeva said, changing her expression and tone like the flicking of a switch. She turned to her audience and said, "For those of you who haven't been following the news, Tena is one bad lady. She was the one responsible for the assassinations back in January, and for what happened to planet Vhelra. Then she made some threats, and some prisoners got released who shouldn't have."

"Right," Glik said, perturbed by the notion that some of her audience might not remember these events. "And my team is working hard to get them back. That's why I'm here today. If any of your audience has seen any of these fugitives, please contact the IGP." On video screens across the galaxy, images of missing criminals appeared, along with multiple ways to contact law enforcement.

"And who is in your group?" Malleeva asked.

"Well, most of them have asked me to leave them out of this, but their leader is Parzak."

"Parzak, I've heard of him," Malleeva said, clearly reading information off of her teleprompter. "He was trained by Bloodstone himself."

"Herself," Glik corrected.

"And Parzak is the one who captured Vraxx, the shapeshifter who framed Alterra Sarr?"

"Correct," Glik said.

"How did he manage to take down a shapeshifter?"

"Well, I wasn't there for all of it, but this is what he told me..."

It was the year 2505. Vraxx sat alone in a bar, in a private booth. He was depressed and aimless, a servant without a master. The Grunthians had raised him to be Vermon's personal bodyguard, a role he missed terribly. Five years earlier, disguised as Alterra Sarr, Vraxx had helped to destroy IGP Earthstation 1. It had been the high point of his career. Then, only about a day later, Lord Vermon had been killed.

Before Vermon died, he'd sent Vraxx on a mission. Take off in a ship, stay disguised as Alterra Sarr, and await further instructions. Only those instructions never came. Vermon had planned some next-level chaos for Vraxx's Alterra disguise, enough to keep the IGP and the galaxy's bounty hunters on a wild goose chase for months. Of course it was all a distraction, meant to keep the heat off Vermon while he did… something. Vermon had trusted Vraxx more than anyone else in the world, but when it came to secret plans, he'd kept his bodyguard on a need-to-know basis.

Vraxx sniffed his glass of Valosian brandy. He was incapable of getting drunk, at least from alcohol. He'd ordered the drink because the smell reminded him of Vermon. Vraxx was currently disguised as a random man he'd killed earlier that day. He'd paid for the drink with his victim's credits.

For the first couple of years, he'd stuck to the plan, at least the part of the plan he knew. He'd fly to random planets disguised as Alterra, and make sure people saw him. If the police got too close, he'd change his shape and escape. He wasn't sure if he was actually helping anything by doing this. After all, Vermon was dead. But his children were still active, a couple of whom had been very close to Vermon, and it was possible they still needed the distraction.

And then, three years ago, he heard that Alterra had been proven innocent. Now it was Vraxx who was wanted by the law. He hadn't disguised himself as Alterra since. As long as he kept his head low, he'd never be caught. But to what end? Was prison really any worse than the pointless life he currently lived?

Vraxx had heard stories about IGP officers getting partnered with animals. Usually dogs, but sometimes chetals or even, in one case, a cybernetically-enhanced duck. Sometimes the officer would die, and the loss would be devastating to the animal. The training process was so thorough, that the animals imprinted on their partners, and couldn't lead normal lives without them. That's how Vraxx felt right now.

Sometimes he would change his shape to look like Lord Vermon. Then he'd stand in front of a mirror, and tell himself what a loyal servant he was. It was a stupid little game, but sometimes he just needed it.

If only he could find out what Vermon had planned. If he could finish what Vermon had started, maybe it would give him some closure. It was a way to connect with his dead master. If he could complete a project in Vermon's name, then he could get on with his life. The more he thought about it, the more he was sure that this sort of closure was exactly what he needed.

But where to start? Vermon's plans would have been on a computer on his mothership, and that was long gone. He might have had more computers on Valos, but the current Council of Heirs had probably purged them by now. And then he remembered something. Vermon had kept his most private data backed up in the cloud. Somewhere above Valos right now, there was a satellite containing Vermon's encrypted files.

And the only one who knew it was there was Vraxx. Vermon's most loyal bodyguard, who had stood at his master's side hundreds of times while the Lord of Valos typed in his passwords.

Lord Vermon was due for a comeback.

"I'd been a doctor for years," Glik told the host. "And while it paid well, it wasn't very fulfilling."

"Really?" Malleeva asked. "That's surprising."

"I had an office on Cytrine Delta," Glik explained. "Lots of gang activity there. Most of my patients were victims of gun violence. The ones who survived, I'd patch them up, only to see them again in a few weeks. So I quit and got a job in social services. The pay was crap, but I was actually helping people."

"And what did you do there?" Malleeva asked.

"They had me working at a halfway house, where I was part nurse and part life skills coach. We reached out to the downtrodden, helped them clean up, taught them valuable skills, gave them a place to stay and clean clothes so they could look for jobs…"

"Such nobility," Malleeva said. "Let's give him a hand, folks." The audience cheered.

"So one day, I got a call," Glik said. "It was Parzak. He was an old patient of mine, but I hadn't seen him in a few years. I'd treated his injuries a few times, after he'd been hurt by rival gangs. Even tried to give him some life advice when I could. Apparently I'd made an impression, because he had a job offer for me."

"What was it?"

"His mentor, Bloodstone, was retiring from bounty hunting, and she gave Parzak her old ship."

"That's generous," Malleeva said.

"And he said he needed a ship's doctor, and asked if I'd join him. Well, it just so happens they were about to shut down the halfway house where I worked at the time. I figured I'd help Parzak out for a few weeks while I looked for another job, but…"

It was now 2506. Glik was surprised at just how high-tech the medical equipment was aboard the Bloodwind. He'd expected it to be on par with his office at social services, but it even outshined the equipment in his old doctor's office. The previous doctor on this ship must have been a genius.

So far the ship only had three occupants. Zak, Glik, and another of Glik's former patients, Vex. It was a big ship for such a small crew, but Zak was determined to get a whole team together, just as Bloodstone had. Zak said he just needed to build up his "cred" first. Glik wasn't sure if Zak meant monetary credits, or credentials as in reputation. But he supposed it didn't matter, as either one would probably lead to the other.

The Bloodwind was on its way to planet Lferen to look for a serial arsonist, when it received a proximity warning. A science research station had been damaged, and they needed help evacuating the scientists. Any nearby ships were urged to come to their aid. It wasn't exactly bounty hunting, and there probably wasn't a reward involved, but how could they say no?

While Glik stayed on the bridge, Zak and Vex each took a landing shuttle and docked with the slowly decompressing space station. Between the two shuttles, they managed to rescue the surviving scientists and took them back to the Bloodwind. There were nineteen survivors in total. Zak agreed to take them back to their home planet, which was about ten hours away.

In the meantime, Glik took some of the scientists to the medbay to treat their minor injuries. The scientists were given access to the empty crew quarters, for those who wanted to freshen up or rest from the stressful day they'd had. Vex stayed on the bridge while Zak went to the galley for some lunch. Three of the scientists were already there, chatting around the table. Zak sat down with them, setting a bowl of apples and several small pouches of orange juice on the table.

Zak offered them some food, and the four of them started talking about the research station. "I don't know what happened," one woman said. Her name was Doctor Pickels, and she was human. "One minute everything was fine, and then the alarms started blaring."

"Each section of the station just started decompressing, one at a time," another scientist said. He was a Vhelran named Doctor Vork. "The computer wouldn't say why. It all happened so fast."

"I was asleep at the time," a young woman said. She was a lab assistant named Helvia. "I was lucky. Some of the others didn't make it."

"Do you think you were hit by something?" Zak asked.

"I just don't know," Doctor Vork said. "The sensors didn't show anything. This is just like station SV-223."

"Huh?" Zak asked.

"Another research station that was destroyed last month," Doctor Pickels said. "No survivors. The entire station just sort of came apart at the seams. Most of the crew died instantly."

"I didn't hear about that," Zak said.

"It was in deep space," Doctor Vork said. "Dangerous work. Nobody's around to help if you need it."

"And the month before that, there was that medical ship," Helvia said. "It's like an epidemic."

"Totally different situation," Doctor Vork said. "That was obviously pilot error. They flew straight into a moon."

"Yeah, but..." Helvia began.

"Don't look for patterns everywhere," Doctor Vork said. "I'm sure there's a logical explanation for all three accidents."

Zak wasn't so sure. Something about this series of events bothered him. He grabbed an apple and a pouch of orange juice, and left the galley. He wanted to look up those other disasters online.

"So what was it?" Malleeva asked.

"I'm getting there, I'm getting there," Glik said. "Like I said, it was a ten-hour trip. The scientists all worked different shifts, so about half of them had already been up for more than eighteen hours. They weren't going to make it another ten hours without some sleep. I'd also been up for a while, so I retired for the night. I woke up to an alarm..."

The Bloodwind shook as if it had been hit by a meteor. Glik sat bolt upright in his bed as the klaxon sounded. "Bridge! What's going on?" he shouted.

Vex's voice came over the intercom, informing the entire ship. "We've had an explosive decompression in crew quarters six."

Glik gasped. There weren't enough rooms for all the scientists, so a couple of them had doubled up. The two scientists who had been in that room... "Casualties? Life signs?"

There was another shudder. "Crew quarters seven..." Vex began.

Glik shouted into the intercom. "Everyone out of the crew quarters! Stay in interior hallways only!" Glik rushed out his door, still in his bedclothes. In the hallway, other doors were opening. Rooms six and seven remained conspicuously closed. As one scientist stepped out of room eight, there was a BOOM behind him, and he was pulled back into the room. The door to room eight sealed shut.

Everyone else made it to the hallways in time. "Vex, what the hell is going on?" Glik yelled into his comm unit.

"Exterior panels are just flying off the ship," Vex said. "I'm doing everything I can. Any suggestions would be great."

"Everyone meet at the landing shuttles," Glik said into his comm unit, broadcasting the order to the entire ship.

"How exciting!" Malleeva said.

"Not the word I was thinking at the time," Glik said. "Though we were too scared to think about much besides getting to safety. There was a bit of a hiccup when it came to getting to the shuttle. The docking ports were a few floors up, and we had to decide whether to take the lift or the access ladders. I finally decided on the lift because it was farther from the outer hull. But it was definitely the scariest lift ride I've taken in my life."

"I can imagine," Malleeva said.

"But we made it. Most of the scientists followed me to the portside shuttle. Vex joined us at the last minute. But one of the passengers was still unaccounted for. Parzak told us to blast off. He said he'd find the missing scientist and escape in the starboard shuttle. Vex volunteered to go with him, but he wouldn't hear of it. So we departed without him."

Shuttle One detached itself from the Bloodwind without incident. Vex rushed to the piloting station, while Glik sat down at the scanners. The surviving scientists were in various states of panic. A few sat with their heads in their hands, or holding on to their armrests for dear life. A few others complained about the lack of comfortable seats.

"Shush," Glik yelled. "I need your help. I want any and all theories as to what could cause this, now."

The scientists shouted over themselves, throwing out suggestions like "cloud of metal-eating space bacteria" or "temporal eddies." He heard more than a dozen theories in all.

"Okay, narrow it down," Glik said. On a hunch, he added, "Assume this was intentional. A weapon. If you wanted to destroy a space station or a ship this way, how would you do it?"

He still received multiple suggestions, such as nanites or "rust rays."

"Could any of these devices be small enough to carry in your hand? Or a suitcase?" Glik asked. A few were. *Now the uncomfortable question,* Glik thought. "Let's assume for a moment that the saboteur is disguised as a scientist. When we evacuated the research station, I noticed some of you carried suitcases. Is there any chance one of you..."

There was a slew of indignant replies. Some of the scientists still held bags or suitcases. A few of them opened them up to prove their innocence. One scientist dumped out her purse, while another held his suitcase close to his chest to protect the secrecy of his current project. Fingers were pointed, voices were raised, and some of the accusations nearly came to blows.

"Goodness," Malleeva said. "So was it one of them?"

"No," Glik said. "It wasn't any of the scientists on my shuttle. The real culprit was elsewhere."

"Hello?" Zak shouted, stepping through the quiet hallways. Sensors said the missing passenger was in the training room, though why they would be there, Zak had no idea. But since they weren't responding to Zak's calls, he wondered if they were hurt. He burst into the training room and found the lab assistant Helvia crouched in one corner.

"Helvia?" Zak asked, approaching her. At first he thought she was huddled against the wall in fear, but as he got closer, he realized he was wrong. She was holding a metal device against one wall of the ship, causing the entire wall to vibrate. It was a simple-looking device, just a metal box with a handle, and a small control panel on one side.

As he rushed forward, Helvia's head turned to look at him. Her head turned way too far, all the way backward, like an owl. She smiled, her mouth opening much too wide for a human being.

"Oh hell no," Zak said, drawing his weapon. Helvia ducked aside as he fired, but that was fine, he hadn't been firing at her. A blast from Zak's stun pistol shorted out the device, which spouted a few sparks before the controls went dark. Unfortunately, some of the damage had already been done. Air was slowly leaking out from a ruptured seam in the wall. As a precaution, both exits from the training room automatically sealed.

Zak ran toward one of the doors, but a purple tentacle wrapped around his legs. He turned his head and saw that he was being pulled toward a large, toothy maw. He twisted his body and aimed his weapon at the bizarre creature Helvia had become. Another tentacle grabbed Zak's weapon and threw it across the room.

He was now being pulled by both ankles and his right wrist. With only his left hand free, Zak fumbled through his pockets and pouches, hoping to find something that would harm this thing. He wasn't as decked out as he would have been if he were out on a hunt, but he was rarely completely weaponless. In one pouch, he found a spool of steel wire. In another, he found a mini first aid kit. *Where are my damn grenades?* Zak thought.

The air was getting thin. Zak wondered if this creature could survive without oxygen. If not, at least it would be a draw. He was almost to the monster's mouth now. He still rooted through his largest side pouch, looking for anything useful. Bloodstone would have really given him hell over this. He was always supposed to know the exact contents of each pouch, and he was supposed to be able to grab any item without having to think about it.

His hand found something squishy and rectangular in the side pouch. Not even sure what it was, he threw it into the creature's gaping mouth. The packet of orange juice, which Zak had absentmindedly pocketed when leaving the galley earlier, burst open on one of the monster's teeth.

The creature sneezed. All of its tentacles went slack as it convulsed, sneezing repeatedly. His hands now free, Zak was able to reach his backup weapon. There was another stun pistol in his boot, and he fired repeatedly, not stopping until the creature was unconscious.

"So, fun fact," Glik said. "Marae are allergic to citrus fruit. Or at least Vraxx was. Parzak overrode the doors and pulled Vraxx into the hallway. After that, it wasn't so hard to seal off any other areas that were leaking. The landing shuttle docked, and the Bloodwind limped to the nearest repair station. We kept the shapeshifter sedated until we could get him to the authorities. We didn't even realize he was Vraxx at first."

"What about Vraxx's device?" Malleeva asked.

"It was designed to send Levatech pulses through metal," Glik said. "…With unpredictable results. It had a tendency to warp metal, unseal welded seams, pop rivets, that sort of thing. Not a very efficient weapon, but still destructive in the wrong hands."

"Obviously," Malleeva said.

"You haven't heard the dumbest part," Glik said. "The plan of Vermon's, the one Vraxx thought he was fulfilling, it wasn't even for anything. It was part of a larger plan, to disable possible medical help if Vermon destroyed a nearby IGP moon base. But on its own, destroying the science stations didn't really further any of Vermon's plans."

"That is a fantastic story," Malleeva said. "Well, you heard it here, folks. The true story of how Parzak brought Vraxx to justice, with nothing but his wits and a little orange juice. Now, next up after the break, you know her, you love her, the award-winning actress Katrice Velt! Stay tuned!"

02.08 *Editorial*

ED.02508.06.13

Echo Sun Times – Online Edition
  June 13, 2508
  Editorials

Editor's Note: We are pleased today to post a submission from our former head columnist Evan N'Paqua. Though he's been retired for five years, he still finds the time to write the occasional piece. We consider ourselves very fortunate to be his favored outlet for posting his work.

Fourteen years ago, I sent a man to jail. His name was Enoch Tevarios Kline, and he was evil. Now understand that I was a journalist for forty-six years, and I always tried to keep my opinions neutral. I chose my words carefully, and I rarely let my personal feelings interfere with my columns. So when I tell you that Kline was evil, I don't use the word lightly.

Kline was a local businessman and philanthropist. He was well respected by the community, and the last person anyone would have suspected of being a killer. When I was sent to interview him, it wasn't to bring him down. It was a filler piece, part of a "community heroes" feature we were running at the time. I was there to ask him about his humanitarian programs, such as the scholarships he was awarding to disadvantaged high school students.

We held the interview in his home, in a book-filled study I envy to this day. It went well until I asked about his family. He told me the heartbreaking story of how his wife and children had been killed in an accident. But if I have one talent, it's that I know a lie when I see one. Something about his story didn't add up. It wasn't much, but it was enough to wake my inner investigator.

I won't go into the details of my investigative process, but you can read my original column from 2494 in the archives. This wasn't your typical case of "businessman has wife murdered." No, what I uncovered, and what was further discovered after his incarceration, showed a level of immorality I've never encountered before or since. His wife wasn't just murdered. She was forced to fight a chetal, nude and unarmed, in an underground arena. His children suffered an even worse fate, victims of depraved acts that I'd prefer not to revisit in this article.

And it wasn't just Kline's own family. He bought and sold women and children like they were livestock, using his connections with the Inner Eye to manage a large network of disturbed clients. And he wasn't just a trader. He often participated in arena events himself, performing absolutely monstrous acts of sexual violence against much weaker opponents, driven by the applause of his fans. And even that was only the tip of the iceberg, but I'll stop retreading old ground.

The evidence I gathered during my investigation led to him receiving thirty-seven life sentences. I joked at the time that with good behavior, he would probably only serve half of that. I rested well for years, knowing that I'd helped to make the galaxy a slightly safer place.

On March 15th of this year, Tena Vermon, terrorist, madwoman, and leader of what remains of the Inner Eye, destroyed an entire planet as a display of power. Under threats of further destruction, the president of the United States of North America ordered the release of Kline, along with several other deeply disturbed criminals.

Did the president make the right call? Based on the information they had at the time, I'm not sure they had a choice. But it was later found out to have been a false threat. Some of the released criminals have already been recaptured, but some have disappeared into the winds.

The moment I heard that Kline had been released, I knew I was in danger. Fourteen years is a long time to hold a grudge, but Kline was just the sort of man to keep that level of hate alive. I'm sure I wasn't the only one on his list, but I knew I had to be near the top. I took precautions. I hired two personal security agents to guard my house at night, and I started sleeping with a weapon at my side.

But I also knew my enemy. There was no precaution I could take that he wouldn't anticipate. The only way I would ever be safe was to completely upend my life, changing my name and moving to another planet. I wasn't going to do that. How much compromise is too much? Where is the line between living and surviving? Is life worth it if your life is no longer your own?

At my age, the choice was easy. I took precautions, and I would fight back if necessary. But I would be damned if I was going to spend my remaining years on the run from a sadistic psychopath.

I slept with one eye open for the first few weeks. But the mind can only stay in panic mode for so long, and eventually I settled back into my usual sleep routine. When Kline finally showed himself last night, I was sound asleep. He could have just ended it right there, not even bothering to wake me first. One pull of a trigger, or thrust of a blade, and the Echo Sun Times might have posted an entirely different article about me today.

But remember, we're discussing a sadist. Kline received no joy from something as simple as murder. No, he had much bigger plans for me. I woke up choking, a metal cord wrapped around my neck. Before I knew what was happening, I was dragged out of my bed and down the hallway. He pulled me down the stairs, where my head thumped painfully on every step. Our final stop was my living room, where our audience consisted of two dead security guards, propped up on my couch, staring at us with glazed eyes.

I'll never know what his plans were for me, and to be honest, I'm thankful for that. The police later told me his bag was full of dental instruments, gardening tools, exotic weapons, and sex toys. But he never had a chance to use any of them on me. Because as I lay helpless on the floor, watching him reach into the bag, a mysterious woman stepped out of the shadows. Another late-night visitor had arrived.

Kline turned to confront this new arrival, and I strained to get a better view. It was a woman in black, dressed like a Hollywood ninja. She had crystal blue eyes and a red ponytail trailing from the base of her hood. She was armed with a shortsword, but there were more blades strapped to her belt.

Nothing I could write could do justice to the battle that followed. Kline pulled a curved blade out of his bag, and he attacked her without mercy. For several minutes the woman was on the defensive, blocking his attacks with no counterattacks of her own. At first I thought she was outmatched, if not by skill, then at least by ferocity. But I was wrong. She wasn't threatened, she was gathering data.

When she finally decided to attack, she used what she had learned to deliver several quick wounds before disarming him. But the blade hadn't been his only weapon. Panicked, he dove for his bag, and pulled out a serrated instrument that looked like it was designed to gut whales. He attacked again, only to lose his weapon once more a few seconds later.

No longer near his bag, he grabbed a poker from the

fireplace. The woman could have stabbed him while his back was turned, but she held back. I'm almost positive I heard her stifle a laugh when she saw his weapon of choice. Nevertheless, their duel continued for quite a while, his iron poker against her shortsword.

By this time I had managed to loosen the cord around my neck, but I dared not move or interfere. I got the impression that the woman could have finished Kline at any time. She passed up several opportunities for an easy kill. Why was she holding back? Was she having fun with him?

But then it dawned on me. She was tiring him out, making sure he knew he was fighting for his life. She wanted him to feel as helpless as his victims had all those years ago. I don't know where she got her seemingly endless supply of energy, but the longer they fought, the more I saw the despair creep into Kline's face. He'd lost, he knew it, and every blow he blocked only prolonged the inevitable.

And yet the woman persisted, driving Kline into a corner, and then to the floor. She hammered on his fire poker until Kline no longer had the strength to hold onto it. "Please," Kline begged, as he let the instrument clatter to the floor. He braced himself for the death blow, but it never came.

Instead, she pointed the sword at his chest, and spoke for the first time since her arrival. "Enoch Tevarios Kline. I am here to collect the reward for your capture. Will you come with me willingly, or would you like a rematch?" Without a word, Kline made a weak gesture of surrender.

There was fire in the woman's eyes as she put the binders around his wrists. Her body shook with rage, and I realized that she was loathe to touch this disgusting man even to cuff him. Then I knew the truth. The reason she had treated the fight as a game, the reason she had allowed him to press the advantage for so long, the reason she had kept him blocking without going for the kill. It wasn't just to tire him out, or to make him feel helpless.

She was being merciful.

She'd had to think of the fight as a game, because to do otherwise would have meant releasing her full anger. If she had allowed herself to fight with the fury in her soul, there wouldn't have been enough pieces left of the man to return for a reward. There was a beast inside this woman, one that craved seeing Kline get the fate he deserved. Her detachment was for Kline's protection, and to some extent, her own.

Once Kline was securely bound, she helped me off the floor. I looked at her face, at least the little bit of it not obscured by the mask. Her skin was flush, and there were tears in her eyes. It had taken every ounce of her strength to hold herself back, to stop herself from treating Kline the way he had treated his victims.

During my years on the staff of the Echo Sun Times, I found myself involved in many discussions about the ethics of bounty hunting. Do they break too many rules, or not enough? Are they more or less effective than law enforcement? I'll admit that while I saw both sides of the issue at the time, I often came down in the camp that discouraged the practice. But last night my life was saved, not by the IGP or private security, but by a bounty hunter whose name I still don't know. And she didn't just save my life, but probably rescued me from a fate worse than death.

Fans of my columns know that I'm fond of the old expression, "The plural of anecdote isn't data." One or two positive experiences with bounty hunters doesn't excuse the entire profession. I know better than to change my stance after a single event, especially so soon, when my emotions are still running high.

But I can tell you one thing. I will sleep well tonight.

02.09 *Bone*

ED.02508.06.19

Planet Muerte wasn't nearly as bad as its name would suggest. The world was short on metals, and the local plant life was mostly grasses and bushes, so they'd had to get a little creative with building materials. In addition to clay bricks, most Muertan architecture incorporated a large amount of bone. Visitors to the planet found the buildings a bit unsettling at first, but they got used to it.

But it wasn't just the bones and skulls that bothered people. It was a perceived lack of respect for the dead. Muertans had no graveyards or tombs. The dead were rendered like cattle, their bones used for construction, their muscles for meat, and the rest wherever it could be put to the best use. They had their own ways of honoring the deceased, such as writing songs and poems about their lost loved ones. But to them, the departed's body was just a husk.

While Glik appreciated this society's efficiency, the arrangement was not without its problems. "What do you mean there's no body?" he asked the indifferent Muertan coroner. "I came here to examine the victim's wounds. I called in advance and everything."

"Gone is gone," the coroner said. "What do you want us

to do, un-eat him?"

"Did you take pictures of his wounds?"

"Sorry," the coroner said, shaking his head.

Glik sighed. "Do you at least know where his bones ended up? Maybe I can find weapon marks on them."

"Ask around at the construction site at the edge of town. They're building a new restaurant. They'd have the newest bones. I don't know how you're going to pick the victim's bones out of the bunch, though."

Glik had some ideas. He walked through the streets of the small town of Westmarrow, admiring the buildings as he went. They really were beautiful as long as you didn't have any hangups about the process. Some buildings stacked femurs like logs, glued together with mud. Others placed their bones vertically, reminding Glik of the bars of a prison cell. He passed one house made almost entirely of skulls, and another that used the ribcage of a giant sea creature as its frame.

He found the half-built restaurant easily. Several builders sat around eating sandwiches. As Glik approached them, something in their expression made him cringe. The way they sized him up, it was as if they were wondering what he tasted like. *Stop that,* he told himself. It was a racist thought. Just because they ate the meat of sapient beings didn't make them killers.

"Can I help you?" one of the workers asked, sounding friendly enough. He had pale violet skin, blue eyes, and red hair. His clothing was sewn from corn fibers, and his hard hat was made of bone.

"I'm not sure," Glik said. He explained his problem and the worker led him over to a box containing the most recently-acquired bones. Construction projects in Westmarrow sometimes took years as they waited for the right-sized materials to come in. Thankfully the box wasn't very full. Glik looked the bones over until one caught his eye.

The femur had several deep cuts, with grooves indicating a serrated edge. A typical knife fight might occasionally result in a bone-deep cut, but not this many, and not this deep. This body had been tortured with an AON knife. Sado had been here.

Haruck Sado was a serial killer, pure and simple. Sure, his business card said hitman, but he wasn't in it for the money. His real payment came in screams, tears, and blood. He'd worked for the Inner Eye for eight years before getting captured. He'd continued his hobby in prison, brutally killing seven other inmates before being transferred to solitary. And now he was out again, having been released under Tena's false threats.

But was he still here? According to satellite logs, he almost had to be. They'd found Sado's ship parked in a clearing to the North, and it was now in IGP custody. It was possible he'd hidden in another ship to escape, but unlikely. This planet wasn't a great vacation spot, and had no useful exports, so it didn't get a lot of traffic. Only a few ships had come and gone since the murder, and most of them were IGP investigators.

And given the area's lackluster police presence, this would be an excellent place for a serial killer to settle down. Heck, if most citizens shared the coroner's attitude, they'd probably think Sado was doing them a favor.

Of course, Glik wasn't a bounty hunter; he considered himself more bounty-hunter-adjacent. His skills mostly lay in the areas of medicine and science, in this case, forensic science. But now that he'd confirmed Sado was in the area, he felt exposed. It was time for the actual hunters to take over.

He returned to the hostel. And this was another reason the planet didn't get a lot of vacationers, the accommodations were notoriously uncomfortable. The bone structures probably would have attracted morbid tourists from all over the galaxy, but the planet's citizens didn't want that kind of attention. They had no cushy hotels, no designated campsites. If you visited Muerte, you had to rough it.

The hostel was a large, single room. It had twenty beds and a storage chest for each. The nearest restrooms were across the street, and the closest shower was a waterfall in the park. The beds were uncomfortable, with itchy, grass-stuffed mattresses supported by a rope lattice bedframe. Plus the deposit had been pretty steep. Glik theorized that the only reason the Muertans had even built the hostel was to show visitors how inhospitable their planet could be, in the hopes they would spread the word to other would-be tourists.

Zak sat on the bed, tapping out a text on his comm. He'd left his drone back on the Bloodwind. Given the rarity of metal on this planet, he wasn't sure it would be safe for Yeela to follow him around. He was currently sending her mission updates, but he set down his comm when he noticed Glik. "Hey, Glik, what did you find out?"

"It's definitely Sado," Glik said. "We need to get moving. Where's Vex?"

"She went for a shower," Zak answered.

"You didn't want one too? I can smell you from here," Glik said. It was a hot day, and the hostel had no air conditioning.

"I'll... wait for nightfall," Zak said, blushing.

Glik understood. He'd seen the shower situation earlier. In the middle of Westmarrow Public Park, a waterfall flowed into a pond. Everyone in town cleaned up there, regardless of sex or age. Muertans had no taboos when it came to nudity. Neither did Vex, for that matter, as far as Glik could tell. On several occasions he'd passed her in the hall on board the Bloodwind, walking naked back to her room from the training room's showers. Which didn't even make sense, since there was also a shower in her room. Glik wondered if she enjoyed showing off, or if she was just that comfortable with the Bloodwind crew.

Zak, on the other hand, was more reserved, and for obvious reasons. "No worries," Glik said. "It's probably pointless anyway, you'd just need another one by the time the sun went down. Let's go find Vex."

Vex was just getting dressed when they reached the park. "Hey, Vex," Zak said. "Any problems with the locals?"

"They're friendly, but they sure stare a lot," Vex said. "I feel like a piece of exotic meat."

"You mean that in a horny sense or a hungry sense?" Zak asked.

"I'm not… sure," she said, thinking about some of the reactions she'd seen. It definitely hadn't just been the men, not that that necessarily meant anything.

"So you feel it too," Glik asked her. The three of them sat down at a nearby outdoor table. Both the benches were carved from bone, but the table was something else. Glik did a double-take when he realized it was made of metal.

"I mean, they're cannibals," Vex said. "They admit to that freely. The question is whether they really wait for people to die of natural causes."

"And they don't like visitors," Zak added. "Everyone I've talked to has been friendly to my face, but I feel like they're glaring daggers at me when I turn around."

"Do you think Sado is working with them?" Glik asked, lowering his voice. He still kept glancing at the table. It looked very new, as if it had only been installed a few days ago.

"If he isn't, he probably should," Vex said. "After all, Sado needs to kill and they need the bones. Glik?"

Glik was under the table, examining it from underneath. When he came back up, he said, "Zak, text this serial number to Yeela, and have her trace it. PSC-661129."

They didn't have to wait long. "She says it's from a private shuttle that vanished last week," Zak said. "The owners were traveling campers who enjoyed roughing it on unfamiliar planets."

"Well, I'm sleeping with one eye open tonight," Vex said.

"I think that would be wise," Glik agreed.

That night, a shadowy figure crept into the hostel. He was tall and thin, with tight-fitting black clothing, and a mask made from the skull of a zondarg. In one gnarled hand, he held a serrated, curved sickle. With a flick of his thumb, the blade started glowing a bright red. By the light of his AON sickle, he studied the room. Twenty beds, but only three were occupied. He tiptoed over to the closest one. A human-shaped bulge lay under the hempen blanket. The intruder raised his sickle and brought it down quickly.

The blade tore through the blanket like it wasn't there, but the impact wasn't as satisfying as he'd been expecting. He pulled the blanket aside, only to find nothing but pillows underneath. He turned around, looking for an explanation.

"Hey bonehead," Zak said, popping out of a trunk at the foot of the bed, "Eat this." He fired a stun disc from his pistol. But Sado had quick reflexes, and managed to block the disc with his sickle. He was about to lunge toward Zak when he noticed something had changed. There was now a blue glow in the room to contrast the red glow of his sickle.

"Argh!" Sado screamed, as a knife pierced his shoulder. He ducked and twirled, and Zak's next shot just missed him as he dropped to the floor. Vex stood halfway out of another trunk, ready to throw her other AON knife.

Sado wasn't alone, however. Hearing the commotion, four large Muertan guards burst into the room, wielding bone swords. For just a second, Vex and Zak hoped they were the local authorities, coming to arrest Sado. Instead, two ran for Vex, and the other two went after Zak.

Vex threw her second AON blade at one of her attackers, hitting him in the side. He fell to the floor, yowling. She used her telekinesis to knock the sword out of the other guard's hand. Then he tackled her, knocking her to the ground. Vex tried to call her knives back to her hand, but she couldn't see either of them from this angle. The guard sat on top of her, his hands around her throat.

Zak was having a similar experience. He'd managed to take one guard out with a stun disc, but the other now had him in a headlock. Sado finally recovered, pulling the knife out of his shoulder and tossing it under a bed. While Zak still struggled in the guard's grasp, Sado approached and held his AON sickle to Zak's stomach. He pulled his arm back, intending to thrust the weapon deep into Zak's abdomen.

Then Sado screamed again, and fell to the floor, unconscious. Glik stood halfway out of another trunk, holding a stun pistol. Both guards were momentarily distracted by this turn of events, and that was all Vex and Zak needed. Zak elbowed his attacker in the stomach, then disentangled himself. Then he turned and punched the guard in the face. Straining her powers to their limit, Vex used her telekinesis to pull Sado's sickle to her hand. Her attacker then let her go voluntarily. He'd seen what that thing could do.

The guards who were still conscious surrendered. They knew they were outgunned. Zak shot them with stun discs anyway, so they wouldn't be followed. Realizing that the entire planet was against them, the Bloodhunters decided on a tactical retreat. They gathered their belongings, and Zak slung Sado over his shoulder. They returned to their ship under cover of night, bound for saner areas of space. They turned in their prisoner and collected the reward. They also sent a letter to the Galactic Nations urging them to reclassify Muerte as a hostile planet in order to restrict future visitors.

They never got their deposit back on the hostel rental.

02.10 *Dog Is My Co-Pilot*

ED.02508.06.26

It was a typical mission, nothing that Midnight hadn't done before. Find the fugitive, deliver him to the authorities, collect the reward. The only difference this time was his teammate. Piloting the shuttle, Midnight stole another look at his partner, and sighed. If Midnight could have had told his younger self that one day he'd be working with a Canik to hunt down a Meu, younger Midnight would have laughed at him.

The target's name was Cule Hepp-Azum, but he often went by the nickname "Cool Cat." He was a shifty con artist who had ties to the Inner Eye. He had escaped from prison three times. The last time, he'd been confined to a maximum security facility, only to be released as one of Tena's Twenty. Because he was wanted by both the Meu and Canik governments, the Canik Empire had requested his capture be a joint operation. In the interest of peace, Midnight had reluctantly agreed.

So now Midnight sat next to Fydo Champion, the finest example of a Canik soldier the empire could have sent. He was muscular to the point that Midnight thought his impeccable uniform was going to rip whenever he moved. His fur was black, with brown around his mouth and hands, and two brown spots above his eyes. He didn't seem very aggressive on the surface, but rather a model of stoic military discipline.

At least I don't have to worry about small talk, Midnight thought.

It was a quiet flight, but conversation picked up when they got closer to their destination.

"So, Cule used to be a member of a street gang called the Iron Claws," Midnight said.

"I know this," Fydo said in his gruff accent.

"Right," Midnight said. "So I thought we'd start there, and ask around."

"A sound plan," Fydo said.

"They're not going to talk to authority figures, though," Midnight said. "We're going to have to dress like gang members. I'm not sure you can pull that off."

"Are there no Caniks in the gangs?" Fydo sounded like he'd only been speaking English for a few years, which was odd. The Meu and the Caniks each had their own language, but English was still the most spoken language on Galea. Having a common language that was native to neither species had actually helped bring about peace. If peace talks had been conducted in the Meu or Canik languages, it might have looked like favoritism.

"There are," Midnight said. "Nearly half the Iron Claws are dogs. But… and no offense… you're kind of stiff. They're going to think you're an undercover cop or something."

Fydo burst out laughing, his booming voice echoing around the shuttle. "Is that what you think of me?"

"…Yeah?" Midnight said.

"I serve in military as punishment," Fydo said. "I was gang member first, in Canik Empire. Took years to learn to be 'stiff' as you say. So that is compliment, thank you. But I can play gang member." He patted Midnight on the shoulder, nearly knocking him out of the pilot's seat. "Don't *you* blow *my* cover, kay?"

* * *

Fydo proved to be right. Despite his less-than-perfect English, the role was second nature to him, and the Iron Claws didn't suspect a thing. In fact, it was Midnight they didn't trust at first, until Fydo vouched for him. Unfortunately, none of the gang members had seen Cule. There was, however, a rumor that he'd been hustling pool at a dive across town. Midnight and Fydo went to check it out.

The pool hall was poorly lit and smelled like regurgitated beer. A couple of heads turned when Midnight walked in, but more turned when Fydo followed. Midnight wore a black leather jacket to blend in, while Fydo's sleeveless tank top showed off his intimidating physique.

Midnight didn't see Cule at any of the pool tables, but he overheard that there was a private room in the back where a card game was taking place. "Wait here," Midnight told Fydo, and he headed toward the back room. Before he could go inside, a large cat stood up and blocked the door.

"Members only," the bouncer said.

"Is Cule in there? I'm supposed to meet him here," Midnight said.

The bouncer just shook his head.

"No he's not in there, or no you can't tell me if he's in there?" Midnight asked.

"Last warning," the bouncer said, grabbing Midnight by the collar. Midnight slipped a hand into his jacket, ready to draw his weapon if it came to that.

Instead, Fydo came up behind Midnight, pushed him aside, and grabbed the bouncer by the collar. As Fydo lifted him in the air, the expression on the bouncer's face was priceless. He was probably used to being the tallest one in the room. "We're going in," Fydo said, setting the bouncer back down. The bouncer just stammered helplessly and stood aside.

Midnight kicked open the door and burst into the back room. There was a card table in the center of the room, surrounded by six folding chairs. In each of the chairs sat a primary-school-age kitten or pup. They were playing Wild Tuna, a card game similar to Go Fish. A couple of the children started to cry, scared by Midnight's sudden entrance.

"Sorry," he said, and backed out of the room.

"The bartender's kids and their friends," the bouncer said sheepishly. "Cheaper than daycare. But the law says minors can't be back there so please don't tell anybody."

Midnight rubbed his temples, trying to massage out the early stages of a headache. "We'll get out of your fur," Midnight said, "As soon as we know where to find Cule."

"Anybody seen Cool Cat?" the bouncer shouted over his shoulder.

"Not today," one patron said.

"Fair's in town," another said. "He runs the shell game sometimes."

Galea's version of the shell game bore little resemblance to Earth's game of the same name. Cule stood behind an aquarium, in which sat four shellbeaks – basically Galea's version of a snapping turtle. Each shellbeak had a number painted on the back of its shell. The shellbeaks spent most of their time completely withdrawn into their shells, unless they smelled food.

A rube approached and handed Cule a five-credit note. "Pick a number, triple your money," Cule said.

"Number three," the fairgoer said.

"Three it is," said Cule, holding his hand over the aquarium. He opened his hand and released a beetle into the tank. The beetle scurried around the tank for a few seconds. Nothing happened at first, then suddenly shellbeak number three thrust its head out of its shell, quick as lightning, and snapped up the bug.

"Sorry, them's the breaks," Cule said, as the customer walked away frowning.

The object of the game was to predict which of the four shellbeaks would *not* be the one to eat the bug. It sounded like the game had pretty good odds, but Cule had an angle. While the beetles all looked similar at a glance, there were actually four types of beetle in the mix, which the shellbeaks could identify by smell. Cule had trained each shellbeak to only eat a certain type of bug. Sometimes he'd even let the customer pick the bug, but he'd use sleight-of-hand to switch out the bug before he dropped one in the tank.

Cule chuckled to himself as he pocketed the money. Then he looked around for more potential rubes he could entice to play the game. All up and down the midway, carnival barkers and meowers shouted at passersby, trying to convince them to take a closer look at their booths. As luck would have it, another couple of marks were making their way toward Cule's booth right now.

Cule squinted, taking in these new arrivals. That was one big dog. And the cat didn't look like a pushover either. Cule tended to throw a game now and then, just to keep the peace, and so that people didn't catch on that the game was rigged. He decided right then and there that he'd lose this one.

But no… this duo walked with too much purpose. Cule's fur stood on end. A voice in his head told him it was time to cut and run. He reached up and pulled down a shutter, closing the booth. Then he grabbed the cashbox and ran out the back.

He hurried through the back lots, behind the rides, between the trailers, carefully jumping over electrical cords and water hoses. After a few minutes of running, he risked a look behind him. The dog was still after him, but the cat was nowhere to be seen. He was hoping to hide in a trailer, but he couldn't do so until he was sure he was out of sight.

Ducking around a trailer, he came face-to-face with Midnight. "Cule Hepp-Azum, I've come to collect the boun —"

Cule bashed Midnight across the face with the cashbox and kept running. He made it to the parking lot, hopped into his hovercar, and started the ignition. But when he pressed the accelerator, nothing happened. He looked in the rearview mirror, and saw that huge Canik holding onto the rear of his car.

Then Midnight tapped on his driver-side window, holding an energy pistol. "Sorry, Cule, this is your last carnival."

After they dropped off Cule with the authorities, Midnight gave Fydo a ride to the embassy, where he would be debriefed before returning to his homeland. This drive wasn't nearly as quiet as their initial ride together had been. Fydo and Midnight were in great spirits, truly enjoying each other's company. Midnight even offered him a position in WARCAT, if he ever decided to change his citizenship. And, of course, assuming he could get the proper security clearance.

Fydo politely turned down the offer, however, declaring that nothing could make him want to leave his motherland. They did, however, resolve to stay in touch, and agreed to work together again if a similar situation ever arose.

That night Midnight and Princess had dinner together, a rare treat given their busy schedules. When he told her he'd teamed up with a Canik for a mission, Princess didn't expect the story to have such a happy outcome. Not because she didn't trust dogs – heck, her drummer was Canik – but because she knew Midnight was struggling to overcome his prejudices.

The truth was, they both had a long way to go, whether they knew it or not. But self-improvement isn't a destination, it's an ongoing journey.

02.11 *Ladies Night*

ED.02508.07.03

"The two of you meet at an inn," Wisp said. "You're enjoying your drinks when suddenly, a bunch of goblins burst through the door. Roll initiative." She placed a twenty-sided die on the table in front of them.

"Really?" Vex said. "We're already in a bar. I don't need to pretend I'm in another one."

"Well I'm game," Lyryssa said, grabbing the die and rolling it. "Is fourteen good?"

"Not bad," Wisp said. "But the goblins rolled better, so they go first. The first one runs up and—"

Their game was drowned out as the world's worst karaoke singer took the stage. Between the caterwauling and the general noise of the bar, they had to stop playing for a few minutes. Before they could start again, Vex asked, "I know you guys are bored, but couldn't we just play cards instead?"

Wisp shrugged. "I guess. My game's more fun with miniatures anyway."

"Hey Vex," Lyryssa said. "That guy over there keeps looking at you."

"Ugh, no thanks," Vex replied.

"He's cute," Lyryssa said.

"Not my thing," Vex said.

"So, you like women?" Lyryssa asked.

"I consider myself bi, but it's more like ninety-ten women over men."

"How's that work?" Lyryssa asked.

"You know how sometimes you're in the mood for a taco, and sometimes you'd rather have a hot dog?"

"...Sure?" Lyryssa said. She didn't eat meat, but she didn't want to interrupt Vex's analogy.

"Well, it's nothing like that at all. I just like who I like. And usually it's women."

"But you dated Zak," Lyryssa said.

"Zak's a great guy," Vex said. "He thinks we broke up because of his transition, but that's not exactly right. I mean, it might have been a factor, but we just had better chemistry as friends than as lovers."

"Cool enough," Lyryssa said. "More guys for me. What about you, Wisp?"

"I haven't really thought about it in this lifetime," Wisp said.

They didn't know how to respond to that. Wisp often talked about past lives, but they were never really sure if she was serious or delusional.

Wisp thought a minute and continued. "I suppose you could call me bi as well, but really it tends to change from life to life. Whenever I have my reawakening, I tend to have the same sexual orientation as the girl whose life I take over. If that makes any sense."

"Nothing you say ever makes sense," Lyryssa said, laughing.

"Hey," Vex said, pointing to a man who had just come out of the restroom. "Is that Grubb?"

Wisp and Lyryssa turned their heads. He'd shaved his beard, but it sure looked like him.

"What do we do?" Lyryssa asked.

"We don't want to scare him off," Vex said. "We just want

him to lead us to his brother. One of us should go talk to him, and try to stick a tracker in his pocket."

"I'll talk to him!" Lyryssa said.

"I said we don't want to scare him off," Vex said.

"Hey!" Lyryssa said.

"You do have this kind of vampire quality," Wisp said. "No offense. I'm sure some guys love it. If we were at a goth bar, you'd be beating them off."

"Phrasing," Vex said.

"...with a stick, I mean," Wisp clarified.

Unfortunately, they weren't at a goth bar. This was a techno-country eighth-wave R&B bar, a genre of music that didn't do much for any of them. The karaoke singer on stage was absolutely murdering a synth-rap version of an old John Denver tune.

"Well, I'll talk to him," Vex said. "Maybe I'm his type. If I strike out, Wisp can still follow him without being seen."

Vex didn't turn out to be Grubb's type. She did, however, manage to sneak a tracker into his back pocket. An hour later, the three hunters hid outside an apartment building on the low-rent side of town.

"How do you want to do this?" Vex asked.

"I could drink some of Wisp's blood, then sneak in invisibly," Lyryssa said.

"Any excuse," Wisp teased.

"It's good blood," Lyryssa said.

"We'll call that plan B," Vex said. "Err...Maybe closer to G. Dobb and Grubb might look like pushovers, but they're quite tough, well-armed, and it looks like they have friends over." Every once in a while they saw people walk by the window, and while they couldn't identify anyone from this distance, it looked like more than just two people. "Plus," she continued, "You'd have to get naked to be completely invisible, and I don't like the idea of sending you in defenseless like that."

"She and I could go in together," Wisp said. "I'll blend in with the shadows, carrying her clothing and weapons. She follows invisibly. We get inside, and find a couple of good hiding places, where she gets dressed. Then you knock on their door, and while they're distracted, we attack from behind."

"That's not bad," Vex said. "How will you get in?"

"We'll climb up the side of the building and peek in a couple of windows," Wisp said. "If one of the rooms is empty, we'll climb in. Once we're safely hidden and ready to fight, I'll send you a text."

"It's seven floors up with no fire escape," Vex said.

"We'll manage," Wisp said.

A few minutes later, Wisp was halfway up the building, with Lyryssa's equipment in her backpack. Wisp climbed the bricks using a pair of clawed gauntlets. She couldn't see Lyryssa at the moment, but she could hear her breathing nearby.

When Wisp reached Dobb's floor, she peeked in a window. Grubb and six guys she didn't recognize were playing cards in the living room. Dobb was nowhere to be seen. Wisp climbed to her right. In the next window, the lights were turned off. She could see someone asleep in a bed.

She turned in Lyryssa's direction and made a "hush" gesture with her finger. Wisp's backpack contained several tools she could have used to jimmy the lock or cut through the glass, but it turned out the window was already open a crack. They must not have been expecting anyone to climb the sheer wall.

Wisp slowly pushed open the window. She tried using her sound-dampening ability to keep it from making any noise, but she wasn't as good at it as her clone parent. The window made a few quiet squeaks as it lifted, and Wisp winced at each one. When it was open enough to crawl through, she peeked in again. The sleeper was still snoring away, and if any of the others had heard the window, none of them had come in to investigate.

Wisp crawled in through the window, carefully climbing over a cluttered nightstand that sat beneath the windowsill. Then she signaled Lyryssa to follow. Lyryssa climbed in, then stumbled over the nightstand, causing it to crash to the floor. Wisp rolled under the bed, while Lyryssa shuffled into one corner.

The formerly-sleeping man sat up and said, "What?" He reached over to turn on a bedside lamp, just as Grubb entered the room. "The nightstand fell over," the man in the bed said.

"Phinn! Why's the window open?" Grubb asked, walking over to the nightstand. He lifted the piece of furniture back into place, then looked out the window. Seeing nothing, he closed it and turned back around. "Keep it closed," he said, admonishing the other man. "The police have drones. You never know…"

"Shit!" Lyryssa shouted. Grubb had stepped on her invisible foot.

"Crap," Wisp muttered. From under the bed, she saw Grubb turn in Lyryssa's direction. Still wearing her climbing claws, she grabbed Grubb by the ankle and tried to drag him under the bed. His head hit the nightstand on the way down, and he howled in pain. He was too large to actually fit under the bedframe, but she kept him too occupied to go after Lyryssa.

On top of the bed, Phinn looked around, confused, then reached for the gun he kept under his pillow. He thought he saw a weird shimmer in the air, and fired at it, taking out the bedroom window. He felt something walk across his mattress, and even saw foot depressions in the blanket. He was about to fire again when the bedside lamp fell over and shattered.

More of Grubb's thugs burst into the room, wondering

what the commotion was. "Something's got me!" Grubb cried, trying to pull his feet back from under the bed. One of the thugs got down on his knees and looked under the bed, but only saw darkness. Something kicked him in the side, and he called out in pain.

"Clear out, everybody," another thug said, holding a bizarre-looking weapon. It was the size of a chainsaw, and had seven barrels, all of different sizes. It looked like it should be too heavy to hold one-handed, but it had Levatech emitters on its base that effectively made it lighter than a handgun. The weapon made a high-pitched whine as he turned it on.

Wisp let go of Grubb, who pulled himself out from under the bed. "Sheth, wait!" Grubb yelled, getting to his feet. Everyone scattered as Sheth started firing his weapon at the bed. Four of the barrels spun like a miniature Gatling gun, rapidly firing metal slugs at the bed. In seconds the bed was nothing more than an unrecognizable pile of wood and foam padding.

"You jerk!" Phinn said, holding his shin. "You got me in the ricochet!"

"The super's gonna be pissed," Grubb said, eyeing the bullet holes in the floor.

"You, uh, got any downstairs neighbors?" Sheth asked.

"If I did before, probably not now," Grubb said.

Just then there was a knock on the apartment door.

"Cops already?" Phinn asked.

"I'll get rid of 'em," Grubb said, leaving the bedroom.

He'd barely stepped into the living room when a glowing blue blade cut through the apartment door, cutting around the knob. Then the door opened wide, having been kicked hard by Vex's boot.

"I know you," Grubb said. "You were at the bar."

"Where's Dobb?" Vex asked.

"How should I know?" Grubb said. "I'm not my brother's... whatever." By this point, Grubb's allies had started pouring from the bedroom. All of them pulled out their own weapons.

"What was all that gunfire?" Vex asked. She held both AON blades in a threatening manner, trying to show more confidence than she felt. She was worried for her friends.

"I got no time for this," Grubb said. "Waste her."

Sheth was about to give her all seven barrels when an arrow hit him in the back of the knee. He went down, howling in pain. Grubb and Phinn bent over him to see what was wrong, while the other six opened fire on Vex. She ducked back into the hallway, using her telekinesis to pull the door shut behind her. Their weapons took out much of the hallway's walls as she ran down the hall.

Two of the thugs, Jark and Qin, followed her into the hallway. Three others, Baan, Lee, and Nurt, turned back to the bedroom. This left Grubb and Phinn to look at Sheth's injury.

Baan entered the bedroom first, only to get pulled up toward the ceiling. Nurt followed right behind him, looking up. Something grabbed him from the side and pulled him out of view. Seeing his friends disappear, Lee said, "Nope," and pulled the bedroom door shut.

"Get back in there," Grubb ordered, looking up from Sheth's arrow.

"With all due respect, sir," Lee said. "You don't need a hired gun, you need an exorcist." He ran for the apartment door. Grubb shot Lee twice in the back, then violently pulled the arrow out of Sheth's knee. Sheth howled in pain.

By the time Jark and Qin reached the hallway, Vex was gone. There was no body, but there were a few spatters of blood on the floor. Jark ran to the end of the hallway, where it turned right and continued past more apartments. A few people were peeking out their doors, having heard the gunfire earlier. They slammed their doors shut when they saw Jark.

Meanwhile, Qin opened the door to the stairwell, looking up and down for Vex. He saw a few drops of blood leading up the stairs. He walked up to the next landing, then up the next set of stairs. A small spatter of blood led to the door to the eighth floor. There was even a bit of blood on the door handle.

He cautiously opened the door, sticking his gun hand through first. A blue blade immediately pierced his wrist, causing him to scream and drop the gun. Retrieving her blade, Vex said, "Sorry, dude. You brought a gun… to a knife fight." As Qin reached down for his gun, Vex kicked him in the face, knocking him backward. He fell down the stairs, landing in an unconscious heap. *I can't believe no one was around to hear that awesome quip,* Vex thought as she picked up Qin's gun.

"Walk it off," Grubb said, pulling Sheth up by an arm.

"Are you kidding me?" Sheth screamed. "I have to go to the hospital!"

Disgusted and angry, Grubb raised his pistol and shot Sheth in the head. "Nobody wimps out on me," he said. To Phinn, he ordered, "Pick up that gun."

"Sure thing, boss," Phinn said, getting a feel for the seven-barreled weapon. He didn't even bother opening the bedroom door. He just fired all seven barrels at the wall, sweeping back and forth, completely demolishing the wall between the bedroom and the living room. A wrecking ball couldn't have done a better job.

When the smoke cleared, there was nothing left of the bedroom. The bullet-riddled bodies of Baan and Nurt lay sprawled across the floor. The back wall was also mostly gone, a massive hole leading out into the night. Red and blue lights flashed in the distance, and were getting closer to the building.

"Let's get out of here," Grubb said.

Just then the living room window shattered. Wisp swung

in on a rope, attached to a grappling hook currently hanging from an eighth-story window. She landed and drew her bow. "Grubb," she said. "This is your last warning. All I want is your brother."

"For the love of… will you just kill her already?" Grubb asked, exasperated. He and Phinn raised their weapons, but Wisp fired two arrows in quick succession. Phinn dropped his massive weapon as the arrow pierced his shoulder, and an arrow to the forearm had Grubb nearly dropping his pistol. Nearly.

He was about to fire when something invisible landed on his back, grabbing him around the neck. This invisible thing kept clawing and biting at him. "Get it off! Get it off!" he screamed, thrashing around. He tried to back into a wall, but the nearest wall had recently been obliterated. Dropping his pistol, he ran toward the kitchen area, tripping over a folding chair and landing on his face.

Phinn picked up the pistol and aimed it at Wisp. She just looked at him and shook her head. He paused, and was still considering his options when Vex burst through the door. "You-brought-a-gun-to-a-knife-fight," she said really fast, throwing an AON knife at Phinn's weapon. The pistol went flying, and Vex pulled the knife back into her grasp, looking really pleased with herself.

Jark finally returned to the apartment, having thoroughly checked every door in the other hallway. He peeked through the door, saw the situation in Grubb's apartment, and ran off.

"Hey, Vex?" Lyryssa asked, sitting on top of Grubb's now-unconscious form. Her blood euphoria was starting to wear off, and she was semi-transparent. Wisp pulled Lyryssa's clothing out of her backpack and tossed it to her.

"What?" Vex answered.

"Do Dobb and Grubb have matching tattoos?"

They didn't find out the full story until well after they'd

turned Dobb in. When Dobb was released from prison, he'd guessed it would only be temporary. He'd asked his brother to hide him, but Grubb had refused. So Dobb killed Grubb, altered his appearance to look more like his late brother, and had been living as Grubb ever since. But now Dobb was back in prison where he belonged, with several new charges in addition to his old ones. He wouldn't get out for a very long time.

To celebrate the capture, Vex, Wisp, and Lyryssa went out for drinks... at a soda shop this time, with shakes and floats.

02.12   The Party

ED.02508.07.10

"Okay, we're back. Bad guy's in the slammer, what's next?" Zak was already taking off his shirt, even though they were in the galley.

"Have you filled out your paperwork?" Glik asked.

"Man, I hate that part," Zak said. "You think Bloodstone ever wasted her time filling out paperwork?"

Glik stared at him. Bloodstone was meticulous about her paperwork and Zak knew it. Back when she was hunting, she wrote highly detailed accounts of her acquisitions, so she could study them later and decide what went right and what she could do to improve herself. These reports were often accompanied by hours of video taken from Bloodstone's helmet.

In Zak's case, Glik just wanted to keep him from getting sued. Some criminals could get quite huffy when it came to unnecessary roughness, and would do anything to get back at the person who brought them in.

"What if I get Sekka to do it?" Zak asked.

Glik chuckled. "Good luck with that."

Sekka was smart, but she had trouble communicating with people. Her obsession with animals seemed to be the core of her personality. Glik strongly suspected she was neurodivergent, but she'd never been tested. Why bother? Sekka was happy being Sekka, and if she didn't care about labels, then neither did Glik.

Earlier...

Sekka hadn't wanted to come on this mission. It was just her and Zak, no animals. Zak hadn't been allowed to bring his drone, either, so both of them felt incomplete. The small talk on the shuttle had felt forced, but at least they'd had mission details to go over. But the more Sekka knew about the mission, the more she felt on edge.

They were going to a party. For most people, that would have been the epitome of a good time, but just the thought of being around that many people made Sekka's skin crawl. It wasn't that she didn't like people. It just took her a long time to warm up to them. She was okay hanging out with individuals, even small groups if they didn't put the spotlight on her too much. But being in a crowd felt like being tied to an anthill. Actually, she would have preferred the anthill.

She had difficulty picking up social cues, and often found herself wishing people would say what they mean. Lies were one thing. Sekka could relate to lies. Intentional dishonesty, while reprehensible, was still a logical way to achieve one's goals. Sekka didn't approve of it, and tried to avoid lying herself, but at least she understood it.

But no, it wasn't the lying that made her feel itchy around people. It was the innuendo. The euphemisms. The unspoken communication, the subtle body language, the facial expressions, the way a sentence could mean seven different things depending on which word was stressed. People would say "Let's watch a movie" when they really meant "Let's make out," and the crazy part was, their partners understood them. It seemed like the majority of conversation involved reading between the lines, and that was something Sekka had never been able to do.

At least animals were straightforward. While some animals engaged in deceptive behavior, even that was for straightforward reasons, usually to deceive their prey. But with animals, Sekka never had to worry about missing their meanings. Her psychic gift helped, but even without it, animals were just more predictable. If a chetal didn't like you, it openly hissed and growled. It didn't nuzzle up to you, then spread false rumors about you behind your back. Sekka would rather face thirty hostile chetals than introduce herself to five new people.

But it was just for a few hours. Sekka walked into the shuttle's washroom and looked in the mirror. Like fairy godmothers, the crew of the Bloodwind had helped her get dressed. She wasn't sure she trusted their judgment, most of them being social outcasts themselves, but any port in a storm.

Wisp had helped with the dress. She claimed to have been a seamstress in a past life, whatever that meant. The outfit's design was so antiquated that it was actually in style again. Lyryssa had done her makeup. She'd obviously held back, resisting the urge to paint Sekka's face like some sort of goth vampire cosplayer, and the end result complemented the dress quite nicely. Vex had helped her dye her hair. It was now a dark auburn instead of her usual pale blond.

Glik had given her colored contact lenses so she wouldn't be recognized as a Vermon. Before leaving the Bloodwind, she'd tested her animal empathy powers on her pets, to make sure the contacts didn't block them. So far, so good. Sekka sighed. She was as ready as she'd ever be.

She left the washroom and sat back down in the copilot's seat. Zak looked pretty sharp in his tux. He'd dyed his hair black so he wouldn't stand out. Even with changing his hair color, he'd managed to get ready in under an hour. Sekka's transformation had taken most of the day. It seemed like such a waste of time. She couldn't wait until the mission was over, so she could slip back into something garish and comfortable.

In the hopes of avoiding more small talk, Sekka picked up her tablet and reread the mission data. They were to attend a party, posing as wealthy young entrepreneurs. Their target's name was Regarious Nitch, and he was hosting the party. They'd chosen Sekka for this mission because Nitch always kept a pair of guard dogs nearby. They weren't allowed to bring any weapons or animals, but they thought Sekka might be able to turn Nitch's dogs against him.

Sekka looked at the words "wealthy young entrepreneurs" again, not really sure how to play the role. She wasn't even entirely sure what an entrepreneur was. Then she had another thought. "Wait a minute," she said out loud. "Am I supposed to be playing your girlfriend?"

"Yeah, why?" Zak answered.

"Nothing, it's fine," Sekka said, rereading the mission plan Glik had put together. It was right there in black and white. Earlier she'd read the word "couple" and interpreted it as "a pair of people." Now Sekka was a different kind of uncomfortable. She had nothing against Zak, she just didn't know how to convincingly play this kind of role.

Sekka had never shown any interest in guys. Or girls, for that matter. She probably would have considered herself aromantic and asexual, but she'd never thought about the topic long enough to care. As long as she had animals to care for, she was happy. She always ignored the romance scenes in movies, and now it dawned on her that she had no idea how people act when they're in love. She could see flashes in her head of people kissing and looking into each other's eyes, but she had no idea how to portray that convincingly.

Zak sensed her discomfort. "We don't have to be all over each other," he assured her. "Just stay by my side. Maybe hold hands now and then. Nobody's going to expect us to be all lovey-dovey at a formal party."

Sekka had almost calmed down when she had another thought. "Do we look like we could be a couple?"

Zak was about five years older than her. Sekka was about

twenty in Earth years, though she really wasn't sure of her actual birthday because she was an orphan. She didn't remember her life before the orphanage. Her mother had been another one of Vermon's "love 'em and leave 'em but don't necessarily leave 'em alive" conquests. Sekka had been discovered by Lemondrop during a visit to Cytrine Delta, and she'd been allowed to join the Council of Heirs when she was just fourteen.

Was five years that scandalous? Hopefully not. Besides, Zak had a fresh quality to his features that made him look eternally young. He hated that aspect of his face, because he thought it made him look feminine. In truth, he probably only looked about a year older than her.

"I don't know, let's find out," Zak answered. He pulled out his comm unit, moved closer to Sekka, and took a picture of them together. They looked believable. Lyryssa's makeup job made Sekka look a few years older, and paired with Zak's youthful looks, they appeared to be about the same age.

"So," Zak said. "Let's go over how to act at a party."

It wasn't exactly Zak's idea of a kicking party. Champagne, classical music, ballroom dancing, supposedly exquisite hors d'oeuvres that tasted like wet bread, and snooty people bragging about their latest business transactions. Zak would have preferred a real party, with loud music, flashing lights, and the occasional beer-induced brawl.

Sekka would have been just as uncomfortable at either kind of gathering. It was already obvious that Zak's advice on the shuttle was going to be useless. He'd told her to loosen up and try to look like she was having a good time. But looking around the room, Sekka didn't see any behavior she would describe as loose.

She followed Zak through the crowd, trying her best to let him handle all the social interactions. Zak was surprisingly good at playing the role, and now Sekka wondered if he'd had a wealthy upbringing. She'd never asked him about his childhood. In fact, she'd never asked any of the crew more about themselves. Did that make her a bad friend? It just wasn't the kind of thing that would have occurred to her to ask. Maybe in the future, she'd make a point of learning more about her friends.

While Sekka was distracted by her introspection, one businessman pulled Zak aside and started talking to him. Before Sekka could follow, the crowd swallowed them up. *Oh, no no no no,* thought Sekka, trying to muscle through the crowd without looking rude. Before she could get far, a woman in a black-and-gold dress locked eyes with her, and made a beeline for Sekka's personal space.

"You look like a woman who knows what's what," the newcomer said.

"What's what?" Sekka asked, confused.

"Exactly," the woman said, laughing. "My name's Niktoria VeRauch, but I'm sure you already knew that if you read Diamond Standard Weekly." She held out her hand, but Sekka wasn't sure what she was supposed to do with it.

"I'm Sekka Verm... million," Sekka said. She'd been tempted to use her real name, just to see how much weight the Vermon family carried here. But the crew had disguised her for a reason.

"I just made a killing on Valosian pork futures," Niktoria said. "I sold all my Vhelran stock just in time, I could have been ruined. What about you?"

Sekka was so struck by the woman's callousness that she almost missed the question. And now she wanted an answer. What was the question again? Was she asking how Sekka's stocks were doing? "I, uh, put most of my money into hummingbird nectar. It was... for the birds."

"Yes, I heard they took a dip," Niktoria said, faking a sympathetic frown. "But I'm sure it will all turn around for you. Good luck!" Then she turned her attention to someone else.

It occurred to Sekka that it probably hadn't mattered what she'd said. That woman had been talking to brag, not to listen. And with that realization, Sekka felt a little bit less claustrophobic in this crowd. She'd wanted to be invisible, and in a way, she was. She endured two more similar interactions before she found her way to Zak.

Zak looked like he was having a pretty good time. Sekka was amazed at how smoothly he told lie after lie, giving out fake stock tips that would probably spell disaster for those who actually took his advice. This might not have been Zak's preferred type of party, but he was definitely making the most of the situation.

A few minutes later, there was a hush over the crowd. A well-dressed servant now stood on the balcony that overlooked the grand hall. "Ladies and gentlemen," he said. "I present, Lord Regarious Nitch."

Nitch stepped out from behind a curtain, and walked to the edge of the balcony, flanked by two purple-furred Dobermans. Nitch wore the finest suit, with deep blue slacks and dinner jacket, a vest of Martian spider silk, and a holographic tie. He had a charismatic face, with silver-tipped hair and crystal blue eyes. He had a smile that could coax the claws off a zondarg.

"My friends," Nitch said, "Thank you for coming. It is so good to have you here. I know there have been many bad rumors about me and my business associates. But I've done my time and closed that part of my life forever. I still have a few legal entanglements I'm working out, but tonight, we're not going to worry about that. So drink, mingle, and have a good time. A toast to you, my loyal friends."

Nitch held up his glass, and most of the crowd did the same. Then he disappeared behind the curtain again, along with his dogs and the servant.

"Is that all we're going to see of him?" Sekka wondered aloud. She'd spent Nitch's speech watching his dogs. She didn't try to give them any mental commands, but she did feel a connection when she stared into their eyes. That was good. She would be able to work with them if need be. The only question was when. She couldn't just make Nitch's dogs attack him in the middle of a party. They'd need a more subtle plan.

"He's going to spend the event in his study, and let guests in a few at a time," Zak said. "But you have to be on a list to get in. Which we're not."

"So what's the plan?" Sekka asked.

"Find a place to hide, and confront him after the party," Zak said.

"Won't there be motion detectors?"

"I don't know," Zak admitted. "Yeela tried researching his security system before we came, but came up empty. Which either means he has a really good setup or a really bad one. But presumably his servants still move about the house after he goes to bed."

"Is there a map of this house?" Sekka asked.

"I saw a map in the bathroom that showed all the fire exits," Zak said, pulling out his comm to show her a picture he'd taken. Comm units were the only piece of technology they'd been allowed to take inside. Nitch wasn't taking any chances. The IGP had no jurisdiction in this city, the local police had been paid off, no bounty hunters were allowed on the grounds, and the weapons scans had been thorough.

Sekka looked at the map, zooming in on several key areas. She was looking for a hiding place that wouldn't get checked, but then she spotted something better. "A zoo?"

"Yeah, he has a personal zoo out back," Zak said. "He collects exotic animals."

Sekka stared at him.

"What?" Zak asked. "Yeah, I know animals are your thing, but we're here on business. I didn't mention it because I thought you'd get distracted."

How can he be so dense? Sekka thought. "I can work with

this," she said.

"Let's just stick with the original plan," Zak said.

"Fine," Sekka said, rolling her eyes. "But we still have time to kill. Let's check out the zoo now. We'll still have plenty of time to find a place to hide before the party ends."

Zak couldn't think of a good reason to say no, and the two of them headed for the back door.

"Ladies and gentlemen, I'm afraid we have a bit of a situation." The same servant who had announced Nitch earlier now stood on the balcony again, wringing his hands. "We're having a bit of an emergency in the backyard. Just for your own protection, we're going to have to ask you to collect your belongings, and proceed in an orderly fashion to..."

Just then, a Kalaran red rhino burst through the picture window and into the ballroom. People shrieked and scattered, running every which way. More crashes could be heard from other rooms across the mansion, as great beasts burst through the windows.

In the second-floor study, Regarious Nitch hunted through his desk. He'd found his handgun, but the ammo was in one of the other drawers. His VIP guests worked together, moving furniture in front of the door. There was a crash behind them. A four-armed gorilla smashed its way through the window, grabbed Nitch, and left the way it had come. The guests just stared at the open window, stunned by what they'd just seen.

"All right," Zak said. "I admit it, your plan was better."

Zak and Sekka sat in the shuttle. Nitch was tied up in the back. Zak had somehow persuaded Sekka not to claim any of Nitch's menagerie for herself, or the shuttle would be a lot more crowded right now.

"Thank you," Sekka said, proud of herself. The hardest part had been distracting the servants, so that Zak could get to the control panel. But once all the cages had been opened, Sekka had gone into god mode. It wasn't often she had a chance to talk to animals as powerful as rhinos and gorillas, but when she could, she was unstoppable. Too bad there wasn't room for such large animals on the Bloodwind.

The shuttle darted back into space, on its way to hand Nitch over to the IGP. All the while, Sekka daydreamed about taking care of a pet rhino. Maybe someday she'd have a zoo of her own, full of every animal she could imagine.

That would be the life.

02.13   One Day

ED.02508.07.17

A trail of battered, unconscious bodies led to the dais. On the throne sat Sevek Kim, head of the Sunrise Mafia. His loyal bodyguard, Drako Wivyrn, stood by his side.

Wisp stood before the dais, her sword dripping with blood. "Forty-six down, two to go," she said.

"Surely we can talk about this," Kim said, his voice warm and friendly. "You would be a great asset to my organization. Whatever you're getting paid for this, I promise you, it's nothing compared to what you would make working for me."

"This is not a negotiation," Wisp replied. "You're going back to jail, Kim."

"Drako," Kim said, and the bodyguard drew his sword.

Wisp knew how these things went. It was an unwritten law of the universe. If twenty guys attacked at once, they'd each go down in one hit. But that last guy, he was going to take half an hour. That was fine, Wisp didn't have any plans. But she wondered why Kim hadn't just sent Drako in first.

Three parries in, and Wisp knew that Drako's sword skills were top-notch. He'd obviously had formal training, and years of experience to boot. But compared to Wisp, he was like a toddler with a plastic sword. Wisp humored him for a few minutes, studying his moves, trying to identify where he'd studied. She let Drako gain the advantage just so that she'd have more time to examine his technique. Kim laughed as he saw Wisp shrink from Drako's blows.

Drako had her on her knees, striking her blade again and again, when Wisp's comm unit beeped. "Sorry, I have to take this," Wisp said, and pulled out her comm. She stood up, still fending off Drako's attacks with her sword while her other hand held the comm to her ear.

"Have you got Kim yet?" Glik asked.

"Almost," Wisp said, nonchalantly deflecting another blow. "Why?"

"There's another fugitive in your area," Glik said. "Eros Roddick. Mind pulling a double?"

"Just send me the deets, and I'll head there next," Wisp said, ending the call and putting her comm away. "Now where were we?"

Drako backed off and sheathed his sword. "I yield," he said, bowing.

"What are you doing?" Kim bellowed. "Finish her off!"

But Drako was no fool. He knew he'd been toyed with, and he recognized his opponent's superior skill. "He is yours," Drako told Wisp, spreading his arms wide. Then he turned and walked away.

Kim fumbled for his gun, but Wisp just shook her head. Kim raised his weapon anyway, but dropped it when a throwing star hit him in the wrist. "Th-this isn't over," Kim stammered, as Wisp loomed closer. "P-people will come for you."

"Wouldn't be the first time," Wisp answered, putting her cuffs on him.

Wisp dropped Kim off at the local IGP station, then drove her rented hovercar to the next location.

Eros Roddick was the former head of the Pleasure Planet,

a traveling space station full of casinos, brothels, and fighting arenas. Almost everything that went on there was illegal in most galactic territories, but Roddick had skirted the law by studying galactic routes and keeping his station in neutral systems. Eventually the IGP had found a loophole, and Roddick was convicted on multiple counts of slave trading, sex trafficking, criminal conspiracy, unsafe workplace conditions, and dozens of other charges.

But just like Sevek Kim and several other criminals, Roddick was released to comply with Tena's demands. He hadn't gone back to the Pleasure Planet, as it was now a traveling shopping mall, but this morning he'd been spotted in a video arcade here on Korcha. It was unclear whether he was there as a customer or if he was involved in something shady, but it didn't matter. Regardless of the legality of his current activities, he still had the rest of his previous sentence to serve.

The VoxeLand Arcade was massive. Wisp saw its neon signage from six blocks away, and the closer she got, the more garish it appeared. Taking up an entire block of downtown Bertram, it boasted six stories of high-tech entertainment. Wisp wanted to know more before going in, so she parked in the garage across the street, and found a nice hiding spot on the highest level.

Hiding in the shadows, Wisp donned a pair of vision-enhancing goggles and studied the building. The clientèle was certainly diverse, with people of all ages, sexes, and species entering the building. Signs around the entrance advertised everything from classic arcade cabinets to fully immersive holographic environments. Everything looked on the up-and-up, no illegal activities were advertised or implied. Though the excessive neon surely had to be a crime against nature.

Wisp went back to the hovercar and locked her weapons in the trunk. Then she removed her mask and stealth suit, and put on a pair of jeans and a plain T-shirt. She combed her hair before putting it back in a ponytail, and wiped off some blood and dirt from her earlier fight. She hoped she wouldn't be recognized. As a bounty hunter, Wisp almost always wore a mask, and had managed to keep her name out of the spotlight. The Registry listed her as "Darkshado" but no one had ever called her that. She wasn't famous, and wasn't worried about being recognized for her bounty hunting.

But she looked exactly like her clone mother, Alterra Sarr, whose face was known galaxywide. Eight years ago, Alterra was falsely accused of a terrorist attack, and a huge reward was posted for her capture. The entire galaxy memorized every inch of her face in the hopes of becoming instantly wealthy. Of course, the furor had subsided two years later, when Alterra was proven to be innocent.

Six years was a long time out of the spotlight, but not so long people wouldn't remember. More than once, when Wisp had gone out in public in plain clothes, people had stopped her and asked for an autograph. This was despite the fact that she looked a few years younger than Alterra. *Oh well,* Wisp thought. *If it happens, it happens.*

Her fears were somewhat assuaged once she was inside. Everything was lit by ugly red neon, and most people didn't turn their heads away from the games they played. And then there were the eye-catching video ads that played on every wall, and the flashing lights amplified by rotating disco balls placed at regular intervals on the ceiling. Wisp was now more afraid she wouldn't recognize Roddick than of being recognized herself.

The arcade was very loud. So loud she could barely think. Between the video games, the overhead music, and the customers shouting at each other, Wisp was already developing a headache. She often used her sound-dampening ability to disguise her footsteps and breathing, but now she used it to protect her delicate ears from the intrusive cacophony. It helped, but not enough.

Wisp did a preliminary walkaround. She studied every face on this floor, making sure Roddick wasn't already here.

She was tempted to pull out Roddick's photo and ask if anyone had seen him, but she was afraid doing so would get the word out to Roddick that he was being pursued.

She looked at the map, which showed a layout of all six floors. The upper floors held more immersive games, such as team laser sports and holographic environments. All of these required preregistration, so Wisp couldn't just walk around those games looking at faces. Wisp glanced through the list of holo scenarios to see if any had adult themes – that seemed like the kind of thing that would draw Roddick – but the arcade's selection of games was generally family-friendly. Except maybe when it came to violence.

With her walkaround finished, she decided she needed to look at video footage. Again, she couldn't just flash a fake badge and ask to see their records, or word might get back to her prey. So she lifted an ID badge off of a passing employee, and let herself into the back room.

The employee areas were larger than she expected. A short hallway led to a break room and two locker rooms, but a side hallway led to a complex of administration offices and security rooms. The break room was crowded. Several employees were singing a birthday song to an embarrassed-looking coworker. Two more employees came walking down the hall, and Wisp ducked into the women's locker room.

A woman was changing her clothes, but she didn't seem surprised by Wisp's presence. Apparently this place had enough employees that they didn't expect to recognize everyone who came in. There were toilets nearby, and Wisp waited in a restroom stall until the locker room was empty. Then she broke into a few of the lockers, searching until she found an employee uniform. It was a little bit too large for her, but she put it on over her clothes.

Then she left the locker room and headed for the security office. One young man sat at a terminal with sixteen video screens, each showing footage from various cameras. The man wasn't looking at any of them, but was playing solitaire on his comm unit.

"There's cake in the break room," Wisp shouted from the hallway.

"Oh, sweet!" the security officer said, standing up. Still behind him, Wisp quietly stepped into the poorly lit security office and used her Auroran abilities to hide in the shadows. The officer walked right past her and locked the door behind him. Now alone in the security office, Wisp pulled a memory stick out of her pocket and downloaded the day's video footage.

She didn't dare review the footage while still in the office. The security officer could be back at any moment, and Wisp didn't want to have to hurt him. He was just doing his job, after all, even if he wasn't doing it particularly well. But she did take a moment to look through the computer for any additional information. She found a folder on the network drive labeled "transactions" and copied it. Then she found a folder marked "human resources" and copied that as well. Satisfied she had all the data she needed, she left the arcade and returned to the parking garage.

Sitting in her rented hovercar, Wisp transferred the stolen data to her tablet and sifted through it. She looked through the HR documents first, and could find no evidence that Roddick had any connection to VoxeLand Arcade. It was still possible he'd been there to conduct some sort of illegal trade, but it was just as likely that he'd been there as a normal paying customer.

That just seemed odd to Wisp, somehow. This man, who used to own the galaxy's largest casino and bar, spending his afternoon playing video games at an arcade. She wasn't one to judge other people's hobbies, but the idea just seemed so banal for such a grand person. Of course, she knew celebrities were real people, and it wasn't unheard of to spot a famous person at a grocery store or fast food restaurant. But still...

She went through the video footage next. The arcade had

dozens of cameras, so there was a lot of it. She used facial recognition software on her tablet to isolate the footage of Roddick. Wisp was taken aback by his appearance. She'd seen so many pictures of him wearing outrageous outfits, and he looked a lot different in plain clothes. It was a wonder he'd been spotted at all.

He wasn't playing video games in the footage. He spent the entire time watching other random people play games. Wait, no, not random people after all. It was always the same young girl. She looked to be in her early teens. Was he stalking her? Or… did Roddick have a daughter?

Wisp was pretty good with computers. She had lived through the invention of the microchip, the quantum processor, and even the ZX-111 MindDrive. But there were times when it was just faster to call Yeela. She pulled out her comm unit and asked for help.

"He has a thirteen-year-old daughter," Yeela informed her. "From his third wife. The two divorced in 2499 on very bad terms. There is a restraining order in place to keep him from seeing her."

"So Roddick's ex probably doesn't know he took the girl to the arcade today," Wisp said.

"Checking…" Yeela replied. "Bingo. Little Erin never showed up for school today. But she wasn't reported missing until a couple of hours ago. Apparently her mother had no idea she'd been taken until she didn't come home from school."

"Have there been any more Roddick sightings?" Wisp asked.

"Not since this morning," Yeela said.

"Can you run facial recognition scans on all the cameras in town?"

"The ones connected to the internet, maybe, but it will take several hours and lots of hacking," Yeela said. "Can you narrow it down?"

"I'm sending you the data on my tablet," Wisp said. "Can

you find the transaction records from the video games Erin played, and see if that account has paid for anything else today?"

"Searching... Yes. Roddick's been spending money at PartyGang Pizza just three blocks from you. It looks like he's still there now."

Eros Roddick sat in a booth eating a greasy slice of cheese pizza. He kept his eyes on his daughter, determined to keep her safe. Erin was currently playing air hockey against an animatronic bear. Past the air hockey table and all the video game machines, four more animatronic animals stood on a stage, singing bad covers of songs Roddick had listened to in his youth.

Roddick didn't even turn his head when Wisp joined him in the booth. "She's a beautiful girl," Wisp said.

"Isn't she?" Roddick replied.

Neither of them spoke for a moment. Wisp recognized the look in Roddick's eyes. It was the look of unconditional love, the look of a man who would die before he let anything happen to his child.

"Her mother is worried sick," Wisp finally said.

Roddick nodded. "I know. I just wanted to spend one day with my daughter before they caught me."

"So you're not going to make this hard on me?"

"Heh," Roddick chuckled. "Hard on."

Wisp rolled her eyes. "We can't stay here any longer," she said. "The police will be here soon. But if you come with me instead, it might be less traumatic for her."

Roddick nodded, then turned to face Wisp for the first time. He cocked his head when he saw her face. "Do you know you're a dead ringer for Alterra Sarr?"

Wisp returned Erin to her mother, then turned Eros Roddick over to the police. He didn't argue or put up a fight. It occurred to Wisp that the results would have been the same whether she'd been hired or not. Roddick had counted on getting caught from the beginning, and all Wisp had accomplished was getting Erin home a couple of hours sooner.

With Roddick's contacts and resources, he probably could have stayed hidden for years. But he'd given that up for one day with Erin. Wisp had no pity for Roddick. He was a disgusting man who once made millions of credits by exploiting others. But she couldn't deny the love he had for his daughter.

02.14   Drone Alone

ED.02508.07.24

REBOOTING
  ACCESSING MEMORY BANKS
  FILE NOT FOUND
  RECOVERING DATA... 38 MINUTES REMAINING
Blackness, then light. Blurry, then sharp. Grass, trees. The sound of running water. The world was at a forty-five-degree angle. *No, make that one-thirty-five. The sky shouldn't be below the grass.*
  STABILITY CORRECTION RECOMMENDED
  CORRECTING... FAILED
  LEVATECH SYSTEMS OFFLINE
Why can't I feel my hands? Why can't I blink? I... I... I... I'm hyperventilating. No... no I'm not. I have no lungs. What happened to my lungs? Why would anyone take my lungs? Who even am I? My name is... is...
  DATABASE RECOVERY AT 10%
Yeela! Yes, that's it. Yeela. But how did I get here? Where is here?
  GPS SYSTEMS OFFLINE
I don't know how I got here. But I remember... I had arms, once. And legs. And a face! I remember my face! Green eyes, small teeth, a small scar on my chin... how did I get that scar?

ACCESSING RECOVERED DATA…

I was thirteen. I had just built my first hovercycle. But I didn't properly balance the power between the emitters. The back end thrusted higher than the front, and I faceplanted on the sidewalk. But why can't I feel my face now?

Omigod omigod omigod I remember. I copied my memory engrams into the drone. I updated it every night before I went to bed. It was tied to my heartbeat. If I died, it would activate my backup memory in the drone. But how did I die?

DATABASE RECOVERY AT 30%

I remember! I was working for that guy with the tentacles… what was his name?

DATA NOT FOUND

I don't remember. But I know I needed the money. For… for… medicine? An operation? Something expensive… it was life-or-death, and I needed money. So I agreed to help the squid guy rob a bank. But when some people… police? No. They weren't police. But someone tried to stop us. I calculated we would lose. So I left. Squid guy killed me, activating the drone's software. Drone me latched onto the first friendly face I saw… what was his name? It started with a letter…

DATA NOT FOUND

His name is… his name is… Ugh! It's right on the tip of my nonexistent tongue! He's my friend. We protect each other. I have to find him. Why can't I remember his name? Or his face? Think, Yeela, think!

DATA NOT FOUND

Why can't I remember? Shouldn't the data recovery be done by now?

DATABASE RECOVERY PAUSED AT 53%

MOISTURE DETECTED

FOREIGN MATTER DETECTED

SOME CRITICAL SYSTEMS UNAVAILABLE

SERVICE REQUIRED

I have to find my friend. I need him to fix me. How am I going to find him when I don't know what he looks like?

* * *

Zak's head was pounding. He crouched on all fours, throwing up river water and trying to catch his breath between heaves. He was only mildly allergic to the stings, but his closing throat, combined with his near drowning, meant that he wasn't getting enough oxygen. He fumbled through his side pouch for an epinephrine injector. Pressing it to his skin, he pushed the button, and within seconds he started to feel relief.

He still hadn't caught his breath, and he was seeing spots. He rolled into a sitting position, put his head between his knees, and gradually calmed his breathing. He was still coughing a lot, but he was starting to feel better.

A sentient swarm of hornets in a robosuit. Zak had to admit he hadn't seen that coming.

Zak had come to Arboles looking for a guy called Tourch. He found him, too, but so did a carrion hunter called HIVE. Even though Zak had found Tourch first, he didn't mind sharing. These clean-up missions were practically charity anyway. But the HIVE weren't interested in splitting the reward. They wouldn't even discuss it.

The HIVE had watched Zak's fight with Tourch, waiting for Zak to subdue him. With Yeela's help, Zak had knocked Tourch unconscious and tied him to a tree. Zak had been about to call the local police when the HIVE revealed themselves.

"We are the HIVE," they'd said, using an electronic amplifier in their suit's chest. "You will leave immediately. This bounty is ours." No discussion, only demands. When Zak had protested, the HIVE's faceplate lowered, and a swarm of hornets chased Zak to the river. But what had happened to Yeela?

LEVATECH EMITTERS AT 40%

It was enough. She wouldn't be able to go very fast or very high, but it was enough to right herself and start looking for her best friend, what's-his-name. Traveling at about half a meter off the ground, Yeela followed the river. She assumed that she'd been swept downstream after taking damage, so logically, her friend must be upstream.

She kept following the river for fifteen minutes, at what felt like an excruciatingly slow pace. She passed a couple of fishermen, who regarded her strangely. Then she passed a campground. A large canine spotted her and gave chase. Yeela tried to pick up the pace, but couldn't. She considered going over the water, but she was worried that her emitters would give out and she'd be swept even further from her goal.

The dog jumped after her, grabbed her in its mouth, and ran back toward the campsite.

WEAPONS AT 25%

Yeela didn't attempt to fire. With her systems in an unpredictable state, she wasn't sure she'd be able to stun the dog without hurting it. And she definitely didn't want to hurt the creature. She'd had a similar dog when she was a kid. Fluffy with long, golden hair... *Oh, sure, those memories come back just fine,* Yeela thought. *I can remember Goldilocks, but I can't remember Zak? Zak! My friend's name is Zak!*

She still couldn't remember what he looked like, but she knew his name. But that wouldn't do her any good if she couldn't get free of this dog. She strained her Levatech emitters to pull herself out of the dog's mouth, but had no luck. The dog carried her up to a young boy.

"Wicked!" the boy shouted. "Hey mom! Look what Fazzy found! Can I keep it?"

The child's mother studied the drone, turning it over in her hands, looking for identifying markers. "Someone must have lost it in the woods," she said. "I guess it's fine, the owners are probably long gone."

Yeela hadn't tried speaking since she'd woken up.

AUDIO SYSTEMS AT 100%

In her most official-sounding voice possible, Yeela said, "This drone is property of Parks and Services. If found, do not touch. Attempting to steal a drone is a federal crime, punishable by up to one year in prison."

The mother opened her hands in surprise, and Yeela flew off. Fazzy barked and started to run after it, but the mother grabbed the dog by the collar.

Yeela attempted to contact Zak's communicator, but those systems hadn't come back online yet. She continued to search upstream.

"Yeela, can you hear me?" Zak said again and again into his comm unit. She wasn't showing up on his tracker, either. Her tracking receiver must be damaged. Hopefully that was the worst of it. What if she was hurt beyond repair? He couldn't bear the thought of losing her. He could always build a drone if he wanted one, but Yeela was one-of-a-kind.

Zak tried to remember what had happened to her. He'd run from the hornets, too scared of getting stung to think about anything else. He'd assumed Yeela was right behind him. Everything after that was just a blur. There were stings, there was swimming, there was choking... He wasn't even sure how far he'd gone, or in which direction.

But he had one thing going for him. Before he'd tied up Tourch, he'd put a tracker on him. If HIVE was still in the area, Zak could find them, and maybe that would lead him to Yeela. It was possible HIVE had kept Yeela. At the very least, maybe they were still in the clearing where they'd fought, and Zak would find Yeela there. Right now, Zak would gladly let HIVE collect the bounty on Tourch if it meant getting Yeela back.

Yeela reached a clearing, and was confused by what she saw. A man with flaming hands stood over an empty spacesuit. Hornets kept flying out of the suit, but the man kept burning them as they emerged. He got stung a few times, but it didn't seem to bother him. Finally he shoved his hands into the suit's open faceplate, and filled the suit with flames. The suit had been waving its arms in defense, but now its limbs went slack.

The man looked so familiar. Yeela knew she'd seen him before, very recently. Was this Zak? "Zak!" she called out, and the man turned toward her. He appeared to recognize her as well, and his features twisted in fury. This was not Zak. Yeela flew off, and the man gave chase.

Yeela didn't get far before she realized she couldn't outrun this guy. On a good day she could have flown rings around him. And she had, just a couple of hours ago. That's right! She had. It was coming back to her. She'd kept him occupied, dodging his bursts of flame, while Zak sneaked up behind him and knocked him out with a stun disc.

That strategy probably wouldn't work this time. Yeela was too slow right now, and she couldn't fly high enough to dodge this guy's blasts of flame. She fled through the trees, aiming for the thickest parts of the forest where she hoped her pursuer would have trouble following. All the while she checked her weapons systems.

WEAPONS AT 32%

That was enough to hurt him, she hoped. If he got too close, she'd hit him with an electric jolt. Hopefully it would be enough to knock him out. Though he'd recovered pretty quickly from Zak's stun disc earlier. More details of the battle were starting to come back to her. She still couldn't picture Zak's face, however.

As Yeela flew, she dodged blasts of fire being thrown by... Tourch? Yes, his name was Tourch. For the most part, the flames missed her, hitting the trees instead. Fortunately it was the rainy season, and this planet's plant life was unusually fire-resistant to begin with. Being made of metal, Yeela wasn't afraid of catching on fire, but too much heat could fry her circuits permanently.

One blast of fire hit her head on, and Yeela started spinning out of control. Her visual systems flickered out, and she ran into a tree. She flipped over and landed upside down on the wet ground. Her Levatech systems were no longer responding. She could hear Tourch's footsteps as he approached, and when she sensed he was close, she attempted to fire an electric shock in his general direction.

WEAPONS SYSTEM FAILURE

Of course. Yeela braced herself for a blast of heat, hoping her data would be recoverable. She couldn't feel pain, but she desperately wanted her existence to continue. She wasn't sure if she was technically alive, but she had emotions every bit as strong as when she'd been in a human body.

Then she remembered that her audio worked just fine, and blasted out an ear-splitting, high-pitched whine. She heard Tourch curse and run away. Yeela continued blaring a variety of alarms until her battery ran dry. Right before her power ran out, she thought she heard more footsteps approaching.

REBOOTING

POWER LEVEL AT 10%

BATTERY STATUS: CHARGING

"Please be okay, please be okay, please be okay…"

Yeela recognized the voice right away. But it wasn't just Zak she heard, there was a variety of noises. Electronics beeping. Metal tools. Multiple heartbeats. Glik clearing his throat. The constant hum of the Bloodwind's power system.

"It's going to take a while for all her systems to come back online," Glik said. "But I think she'll be fine. She had a lot of mud and gunk lodged in her access ports, and I had to replace a few of her components. But she's going to be good as new."

"New? That's what I'm afraid of," Zak said. "Will her memory be intact?"

Just then Yeela's visual systems came online. The first thing she saw was Zak's face, leaning over and staring into her central camera. "Zak!" she shouted.

"You remember me!" Zak said, grinning from ear to ear.

"Of course!" Yeela said. If she could have hugged him, she might have cracked a few of his ribs. "Did you catch Tourch?" she asked.

"Actually, you did," Zak replied.

"I can't imagine how," Yeela said.

"He had a cochlear implant," Zak said. "A really sensitive one. One of the noises you made messed with his equilibrium. He tripped over something and knocked himself unconscious. When I found you, he was just a few meters away, sound asleep."

"I'm going to have to remember that trick," Yeela said.

That evening, Zak and Yeela took the night off. No researching the next fugitive, no late-night training. Zak sat on his bed, watching a cheesy movie, while Yeela sat in her charging dock nearby. They laughed together at scenes that were supposed to be serious, pointed out flaws in the special effects, and joked about the bad dialogue.

Occasionally Yeela rotated her camera and took an extended look at Zak. He was a dope, but she loved him, no question. She just wasn't sure what type of love it was. It didn't feel familial, and it was stronger than friendship. But it couldn't possibly be romantic. She was, after all, just a hunk of metal. And how did he see her? Was she a friend, or just a tool?

For the second time today, she wondered if she was actually alive. She reasoned that she must be, or she couldn't ask the question. But that hardly seemed conclusive. A powerful enough computer could be programmed to analyze anything, including the meaning of life. Was that all she was doing? Analyzing data? And if so, were humans any different? She supposed she was looking for a physical answer to a metaphysical question.

Yeela enjoyed being a drone. It was nice not having to worry about eating or sneezing or scratching an itch. Her old body had been diagnosed with Karouc's disease, and if Prozner hadn't killed her, she would have been dead in a year anyway. At the time of her death, she was already relying on cybernetics to move around. Organic bodies were overrated.

But still... it would be nice to touch someone again. Sometimes she thought about transferring her CPU into something more humanlike. Android or clone, she wasn't sure. Right now it was just a fantasy. She wondered if Zak would see her differently if she was in a human body. Would he love her then? Would she want him to?

"Look at that monster," Zak said, laughing. "You can actually see the actor's shoes!"

Yeela lingered on Zak for a few more seconds before turning back to the movie. She never wanted to forget his face again.

02.15 Free Spirit

ED.02508.08.02

Help... please...

The faint voice echoed through Vex's mind. She didn't know if it had been real or if she'd imagined it. The ambiance of this place certainly kept her on edge, and she wouldn't have been surprised if it played mind tricks on her as well.

Mortos was the largest moon of Vivas, and it was probably the galaxy's biggest graveyard. The soil here was too toxic for most plant life, the water wasn't drinkable for most life forms, and the thick cloud cover always blotted out the sun.

The Vivans had a whole mythology about the moon being their version of heaven, and how poetic it was that your late loved ones could look down on you from above, but the truth was that Vivas was running out of land, and didn't want cemeteries taking up valuable space.

The air was breathable, but like most visitors to Mortos, Vex wore an oxygen filter. The air contained toxins that, while generally harmless, had been known to cause mild headaches and nausea. Plus, the stench of death was overpowering.

Vex didn't believe in ghosts, but that didn't keep her from jumping at shadows. As she walked past the rows and rows of gravestones and mausoleums, she was overcome by how quiet it was. Other than the gentle rain and the sound of her own footsteps, she couldn't hear a thing. Her boots echoed on the concrete path, and in those echoes she thought she heard voices.

Please... I need help...

That was no echo, and it wasn't her imagination. Nor was it a voice. It was a telepathic message. Vex tried to respond, but her limited telepathy had only worked on Navorans so far. *Hello? Can you hear me?*

I'm over here... please help...

Vex wasn't sure if that was a response to her call, or just further cries for help. *I don't see you,* Vex thought. And then Vex saw it. A ghostly figure moved out from behind a mausoleum, wandering between the graves as if lost. Then it turned its head and spotted Vex. Its glowing yellow eyes widened. It flew straight at Vex with unnatural speed.

Vex reflexively pulled out her AON daggers, and held them in front of her like a cross. Vex didn't believe in religion any more than she believed in ghosts, but it was something to try. The specter came to a halt less than a meter from the glowing blue blades, and just floated there, staring at her.

Can you help me? the transparent creature asked. It looked humanoid, vaguely feminine, and strangely familiar. She looked like she was made of energy, with yellow lines of electricity constantly sparking and running over her form. Vex remembered seeing footage of the Bloodwind's previous team of hunters in action, and it sparked a memory.

"Yna?" Vex asked out loud.

No, my name is Astral, it said.

"What are you?" Vex asked.

I'm a bounty hunter, Astral replied. *I have the ability to project my spirit, leaving my physical form behind. But I've been separated from my body. I need help finding it!*

Vex lowered her weapons. She'd heard of Astral before. "Why were you on this moon?" she asked. She had a feeling she already knew the answer.

I was looking for a woman named Klüra Doss. She's one of those prisoners that Tena—

"I know who she is," Vex said. "I'm looking for her, too."

I got a tip that she was going to be on this moon, meeting a contact. I landed and physically stayed aboard my ship while I sent my astral form to find her. I found her ship first, so I shorted out her controls so she couldn't leave.

"Smart," Vex said.

...and then she left in my ship. With my unconscious body still on board.

Vex laughed. "Sorry," she said, trying to stop smiling.

It's not funny, Astral said. *I can only survive for so long without my body.*

"It's a little funny," Vex said. "You have a reputation for being a carrion hunter. All these years, you've been stealing people from other bounty hunters. And today someone stole you."

Astral crossed her arms. *Maybe I'll find it funnier when my life isn't in danger.*

"Do you remember your ship's transponder code?" Vex asked.

Astral nodded. *Yes.*

"Come on," Vex said, turning and gesturing for Astral to follow. "Just try not to short out my ship's systems while we're en route."

You're wrong about me, you know.

"Huh?" Vex asked, not taking her eyes off the control panel.

Unable to sit down, Astral floated around the shuttle, trying not to touch anything electronic. She had some degree of control over whether her energy form harmed machinery, but it was better to be safe than sorry.

I'm not a carrion hunter.

"I'm afraid the Bounty Hunter Registry disagrees," Vex

said. "Which is why they suspended your account and put you on a watch list."

Early in my career I worked with some ruthless hunters, Astral said. *We broke some rules. I regret that now. These days I work alone.*

"You know I don't really care, right?" Vex said.

It hasn't been easy finding work these past few years. I could only take unlicensed jobs. Under-the-table stuff. And the people who hire you for those... they usually have reasons they didn't want to post through legitimate channels.

"Sounds tough," Vex said, only half listening.

Like jealous ex-husbands who want their wives back. Dictators who want to silence a well-known protester. You have to be extra careful who hires you, or you'll wake up to find you're not really a bounty hunter anymore, so much as a professional kidnapper.

"There are other jobs besides bounty hunting," Vex said, tapping several keys in her attempt to boost the signal.

I know, Astral replied. *I've had several odd jobs over the years. But bounty hunting is what I'm good at, and I enjoy it.*

"Then you should have followed the rules," Vex said.

Astral's eyes flared. *Have you never made a mistake? I'm sorry, but you don't strike me as little miss perfect either.*

"Fair," Vex said, shrugging. "But at least I know when to move on. I think I've found your ship, by the way." She pointed to the starmap. Astral's ship had taken a warp gate to the Kalara system.

They spotted the ship a few hours later, docked at a refueling station. It was just leaving when Vex arrived, and she changed her course to follow it. Before it could get too far away, Vex fired a magnetic disc at it.

Don't damage my ship! Astral whined.

"It's just a low-level EMP," Vex said. "Shorts out the primary thrusters, so she can't get away. Secondary jets will be fine."

Astral's ship turned, and they received an audio message. "What's the big idea?" came the voice over the comm.

"Kliira Doss," Vex replied, "I've come to return you to the authorities. Please power down your systems and prepare to surrender."

"Over my dead body," Doss replied.

Careful, Astral said, floating behind Vex. *I just had magnetic torpedoes installed.*

"Now you tell me," Vex said, as the other ship's weapons started to fire. Vex tried to maneuver her ship out of the way, but it wasn't built for high-speed space combat. Flashing dots on her viewscreen showed the curved path of the torpedoes, headed inexorably for the shuttle. Hitting her thrusters, she managed to move to the other ship's side. Vex's shuttle shook and several sensors lit up on the instrument panel. One of the torpedoes had taken out her propulsion system.

The ships were now side-by-side. Vex's ship didn't have much in the way of weapons, but it did have a few tricks. She fired a pair of magnetic tow cables at the other ship. They both hit, and Vex reeled them in. The two ships collided, denting the outer hulls.

Are you crazy? Astral shouted.

"She has weapons," Vex said. "I do not. But if we're stuck together, she can't hurt us without hurting herself."

You're paying my insurance deductible, Astral grumbled.

Another message came over the comm. "I don't know what you think you're trying to accomplish..."

Vex switched it off. She'd bought them a few minutes, but she didn't know where to go from here. Vex wasn't sure if Doss could aim at her from this angle, but she probably wouldn't. After all, if Vex's ship exploded while they were stuck together, it would damage Astral's ship as well.

More indicators lit up on the control panel. There was a small rupture in the rear compartment, and it needed to be sealed lest they develop an oxygen leak. That took priority. "Astral, watch the instruments while I..." Vex looked around. Astral was gone.

***

On the other ship, Doss went over the weapons systems, looking for more options. She wasn't about to surrender to some stupid bounty hunter. She'd destroy both ships first. She heard footsteps behind her, and turned around.

Astral stood before her, back in human form. While the ships were so closely bonded, she'd managed to phase through the hulls and reenter her own body. She now aimed an energy pistol at Doss. "Kliira Doss," she said, "Please step away from the controls."

Doss just stared at her for a few seconds. Her eyes darted from Astral to the controls. "Don't…" Astral said, but Doss had nothing to lose. She pounded several buttons at once, right as Astral fired. Doss slumped over, unconscious. More torpedoes launched, making a wide arc as they curved towards Vex's shuttle. The ship rumbled as the torpedoes found found their mark.

Klaxons blared, lights flashed, and the ship continued to shake. That last torpedo had damaged the engines. Oxygen was starting to seep out, and things were only going to get worse from here. The ship was no longer salvageable. Vex put on a quick-access spacesuit, its various zippers autosealing themselves as she donned the helmet. She needed to get out of the ship immediately, but she had one more thing she had to do first.

She knew the explosion would take out both ships if they stayed attached. Heading to the control panel, she released the tow cables and hit the side thrusters. It didn't matter that Doss was trying to kill her, she wasn't going to play executioner. With seconds to spare, she jumped out of the airlock.

The shuttle's side thrusters kept going, rapidly carrying the shuttle away from Vex, and putting it at a comfortable distance when it finally blew apart. Now Vex floated in space, watching as Astral's ship slowly turned toward her.

She wasn't sure who was currently piloting it. Was Doss going to kill her? Was Astral going to leave her stranded in space, so she could collect the reward herself?

The communicator inside her helmet beeped, and she accepted the call.

"Stay right there," Astral said. "I'll get the airlock ready."

In the end, they split the reward and went their separate ways. They stayed in contact, however. Vex knew a woman who had some pull with the Bounty Hunter Registry. That woman was unavailable at the moment, preparing for a coup on Valos. But Vex promised that if and when things settled down, she'd talk to Detanna. With a little luck, Astral might get to rejoin the Bounty Hunter Registry someday.

02.16 *Bat Attitude*

ED.02508.08.09

"You have defied me for the last time!"

The woman addressed the crowd from atop the wooden platform. She wore a lacy black dress, and had long black hair and pale skin. As she spoke, the cloud of bats swarmed behind her, blotting out the full moon. The villagers cowered in fear. Many of them dropped their weapons and ran away.

"Now bring me the one I seek, or face my wrath!"

Earlier...

"No, the red container," Sekka said, stuffing supplies into her backpack.

"You said blue," Lyryssa replied, putting down one small canister and picking up the other.

"I said not blue," Sekka countered, though she really wasn't sure. Sometimes Sekka remembered conversations differently than others did. It really annoyed her when people remembered what she'd actually said rather than what she'd meant to say.

They were going to have to share a backpack, as their plans didn't really allow for a lot of equipment. The mission called for cosplay and scare tactics, and carrying a bunch of bags around would break the illusion.

"Looks like we're here," Lyryssa said, throwing the red canister to Sekka. She sat down in the pilot's seat, turned off the autopilot, and scouted for a good landing site. It had to be within walking distance of the village, but not visible to the villagers. It also needed to be near a cave. They finally found a good spot, behind the treeline and less than two kilometers from the village. They had detected some caves nearby; hopefully they would have what Sekka needed.

Sekka was already dressed in an outfit made mostly of burlap. Her hair was unkempt, and she had dirt on her face. She wore the backpack underneath her oversized shirt, giving her the appearance of having a hump. "I'm going to check out the cave," she said. "You finish getting ready, I'll be back soon."

As Sekka left, Lyryssa looked in the mirror. Her dress was flimsy, but she'd fought in less. She wished she could wear heels with it instead of boots, but she was about to walk two kilometers across a damp field. She started touching up her makeup. She liked wearing makeup, especially in the dark gothic style she'd applied tonight. She'd stopped wearing makeup a few months ago, because it didn't go invisible with the rest of her when she drank Wisp's blood. Hopefully she wouldn't need to turn invisible tonight, but she kept an emergency vial tucked in a hidden pocket just in case.

She finished her makeup and put on her wig. She stepped out the shuttle door just in time to see Sekka walking up. Hundreds, possibly thousands, of bats fluttered overhead.

"Wow," Lyryssa said.

"Thank you," Sekka replied, smiling proudly.

"And they're all under your control?"

"Most of them," Sekka said. "Some might not have gotten the message, but they'll follow the swarm."

"Don't they have to see you for your mind control to work? I thought bats were blind."

"For a vampire, you don't know much about bats," Sekka

said.

"I'm not a vampire! I mean, yeah, I drink blood, and have pale skin, and sunlight gives me a rash, and I can see in the dark, and I have a wood allergy, but…" She trailed off.

"Sure," Sekka said neutrally.

The pair walked toward the village. The bats stayed behind, waiting for a signal. Lyryssa lifted the hem of her dress as she walked, trying to avoid muddy spots. Sekka's outfit, on the other hand, was only enhanced by the mud.

"You really think they'll buy our act?" Lyryssa asked.

"Supposedly they're very superstitious," Sekka said. "But I've got weapons in the backpack if we need them."

"Should I play it subtle or really ham it up?"

"I say have fun with it," Sekka said.

The village now loomed close. It was late, but the villagers were still out and about. It was almost always dark on this part of Montara, so the people had learned to work at all hours. Many heads turned as Lyryssa and Sekka entered the town. Several people left to alert the village elder. By the time Lyryssa reached the village square, a crowd was waiting for her, most carrying torches and farm implements.

Satisfied that she had enough of an audience, Lyryssa announced, "Good people of Swinewallow, there is a monster in your midst. You have given refuge to a man named Wilhelm Vane. You did this out of the goodness of your hearts, and for that, you are to be commended. But Wilhelm is a killer, a rabid beast who must be returned to his cage. Turn him over into my care, and we will leave in peace this night." She spoke with an abundance of melodrama, hoping to keep their attention focused on her, and not on Sekka.

There was some murmuring among the crowd, and all their heads turned to the elder. "Hang her," he said, and the crowd swarmed her. They grabbed Lyryssa roughly and carried her to the edge of town, towards the gallows. Lyryssa struggled and shouted obscenities all along the way. Meanwhile, Sekka had found a nice hiding spot behind an outhouse, and she activated her electronic dogwhistle.

As the townsfolk prepared the gallows, Lyryssa shouted, "Kill me and you will all be cursed! All of your children will carry the mark of evil!" A few villagers started to look concerned, but most were emboldened by her claims. After all, only an evil witch would threaten to curse them, and hanging a witch was a good deed.

But before they could put the noose around Lyryssa's neck, the sky filled with bats. Lyryssa laughed maniacally as her captors let her go, leaving her alone on the gallows. "You have defied me for the last time! Now bring me the one I seek, or face my wrath!" The bats dove low, swarming the crowd, giving them a big scare without actually biting anyone. Lyryssa continued to shout over-the-top threats, but few of the villagers could hear her over all the screaming.

Three strong men approached the gallows, carrying a fourth man. Vane struggled against their grip. The bats seemed to clear a path for them to the gallows. "Tie him up," Lyryssa said. Two more men joined them, carrying some rope.

"She's playing you, can't you see that?" Vane yelled, struggling against his bonds.

"Wilhelm Vane, you will come with us," Lyryssa said. Then she lifted her head and addressed the crowd. "Thank you for your help," she said, as the bats started to disperse. "You have done a good thing this evening. Don't give me cause to visit again."

Lyryssa and Sekka led Vane out of the village. "How'd I do?" Lyryssa asked, as they made the long walk back to the landing site.

"You're braver than me," Sekka said. She wouldn't have been nearly as comfortable talking to the crowd.

"Bagged by two girls in Halloween costumes," Vane muttered.

"Shut up," Lyryssa said. "I read your rap sheet. You deserve whatever happens to you."

"Hey, I won't be judged by some goth chick in cheap makeup," Vane said.

"I think we should gag him," Lyryssa said, clenching her fist. "For his own safety."

"Before you do," Vane said, "Do you want to know why I chose here, of all places, to hide from the law?"

"To work on your tan?" Lyryssa quipped, gesturing at the gloomy sky.

"No, because I have friends here," Vane said. Then he howled. It was an eerie noise, with an unnatural pitch. Lyryssa rushed forward and put a hand over his mouth. Sekka pulled off her burlap belt to use as a gag.

"I think we should keep moving," Lyryssa said, once Vane was gagged. They tried to drag him along, but he resisted.

"Walk, or I'll shoot you somewhere painful," Sekka said, holding a stun pistol she'd retrieved from her backpack.

Vane grudgingly kept walking, though at a slow pace. Soon they heard answering howls from the distance.

"I don't like this," Lyryssa said. They had less than a kilometer to go.

Something approached from their left. Shadows, growling and chuffing, moving closer at a rapid pace. Yellow eyes caught the moonlight. Four wolves, but not like any wolves Lyryssa or Sekka had seen before. Each wolf was the size of a horse, with four eyes and porcupine-like quills. The beasts snarled menacingly, as if daring the women to attack first.

"Can you control them?" Lyryssa asked.

"No," Sekka said, staring intently into their eyes. "I think they're sapient." She tossed Lyryssa her stun pistol, then started digging a second one out of her backpack.

"Tell them to back off," Lyryssa ordered Vane, untying his

gag.

"Let me go and I'll be happy to," Vane said.

"Not going to happen," Lyryssa said, then downed the vial of Wisp's blood. She couldn't become completely invisible with her clothes and makeup on, but it still improved her reflexes.

"It's not up for negotiation," Vane said. "I'm leaving either way. But you don't have to die."

Sekka shot him. Vane fell to the ground, unconscious. Nothing was going to stop the impending fight, and Sekka didn't want him running away while they were distracted.

On seeing Vane go down, the wolves burst forward. Sekka and Lyryssa both fired their stun pistols, but the blasts didn't seem to affect them. The wolves got close, ready to rip them to shreds, when the bats descended. Sekka had activated her dogwhistle as soon as she'd seen the wolves approaching, and the swarm had finally arrived.

The air was thick with bats, so thick none of them could see. The wolves yipped in confusion. It was dizzying, like standing in the middle of a living tornado. When the cloud finally lifted, the wolves were running away.

"Let's hurry," Sekka said. Lyryssa and Sekka each grabbed one of Vane's feet, and dragged him back to the shuttle, letting his head hit every rock along the way. They boarded the shuttle and took off.

"You look really weird," Sekka said, watching Lyryssa fly the ship. Lyryssa's skin was invisible, but her dress, wig, and makeup stayed. Lyryssa pulled out her comm unit and used the camera to look at herself. It looked like her face was just floating in mid-air. She laughed, then had a thought.

"Take over flying for a minute," Lyryssa said, pulling off her wig. "I'm going to wake up Vane."

Sekka sat in the pilot's seat. About a minute later she heard Lyryssa yell "boo" followed by Vane shrieking.

"He fainted," Lyryssa said, returning to the front.

"If he thinks that's scary, he should see you *without* makeup," Sekka joked.

Lyryssa whacked Sekka with her wig, and they both laughed. They returned Vane to the authorities, and went home to the Bloodwind.

That night, Lyryssa invited Sekka back to her room to watch movies. Keeping the theme of the day in mind, they stuck to classic vampire films. They laughed at all the melodrama, with Sekka comparing Lyryssa's acting to Bela Lugosi, and Lyryssa shouting "Hey it's your friends!" whenever a bat appeared on the screen. They both fell asleep about halfway through the third movie.

This was a big step for Sekka, who usually wasn't very comfortable around people. She still didn't like crowds, and she would always prefer the company of animals over people. But the following morning, when she looked back on movie night with Lyryssa, she felt content. She looked forward to doing it again, except maybe with jungle movies this time.

02.17 *Princess of Pop*

ED.02508.08.18

"Check one, two, three, check." Princess was ready for the concert. She wore torn denim jeans, fingerless fishnet gloves, and a blue jean jacket over a hot pink tank top. Her pink mane was styled in an over-the-top poofy hairdo. She looked like a rock star from Earth's 1980s.

Actually, an awful lot of Meu culture looked like a tribute to Earth's 1980s. Not how the 1980s actually looked, but how it was portrayed in the media. This was because for whatever reason, when Galea first started picking up transmissions from other planets, 1980s sitcoms were among the first signals they received. It was their first evidence of life on other planets, and it transformed their culture.

But today she wasn't on Galea. In her first ever off-world tour, Princess was performing on Snud, the third of seven planets she would visit before returning to her homeworld. The concert was still twenty minutes away, and Princess was doing final equipment checks so there wouldn't be any technical surprises during the show.

Princess had graduated from an engineering college, with a minor in music. Her current career used both her greatest skills equally, as she often constructed elaborate backdrops for her performances. Tonight's concert featured a giant animatronic dragon that towered over the band and breathed fire when appropriate. Its head could turn in all sorts of directions, and smoke constantly billowed from its nostrils.

This was all to promote her newest album, "Fairytale Nightmare." It was also a benefit concert, with half the profits going to the survivors of the disaster on Vhelra.

Princess was in an unusually good mood because her boyfriend would get to see her perform live for a change. Their jobs kept them from seeing each other very often, but every now and then the stars aligned and Midnight managed to make it to a concert.

Midnight wasn't on Snud for pleasure, though. He was chasing a criminal named Terev Fark, a Vhelran who'd been lucky enough to be in an Earth prison when his planet was destroyed. He was yet another prisoner released under Tena's false threats, and he'd recently been spotted on Snud. Midnight still might have skipped the concert in favor of his duties, except that there was always the possibility Fark would be in the audience.

But whatever. Princess wasn't going to look a gift horse in the mouth. They went into their respective careers knowing they wouldn't get a lot of alone time, and they were mature enough to handle each other's absence. No one was at fault, and every moment they spent together was a blessing.

Ten minutes until showtime. Princess did one final sound check, an equipment check, a costume check, and most importantly, a bladder check. Her band went out on stage first, one at a time, each drawing cheers from the audience as they appeared. Princess waited an additional fifteen seconds to build suspense, then took a deep breath and stepped out on stage.

The audience roared, and Princess ate it up. While some performers were completely different people on and off the stage, Princess didn't change much. She was a total extrovert who loved the adoration of her fans. Some people thought she was conceited, narcissistic even, and maybe they were right.

But Princess had been neglected as a child, and now she was addicted to the love she got from the crowds. Her parents had treated her like an unwanted stray, and every cheer from her audience reminded her that she was worthy of being loved. Maybe someday she would be healed enough that she wouldn't need this validation, but today she thrived on it.

"Hello, Snud!" Princess shouted. "Are you ready to party?" The audience went ballistic. The people on Snud were always ready to party. She strummed a few riffs on her hot pink electric guitar, and studied the audience as she did so. Midnight sat near the back, cheering her on just like everyone else. Princess could have easily gotten him front-row tickets, but he wanted to have a better view of the crowd in the hopes of spotting his target. Fark was an avid music fan, and there was a good possibility he was somewhere in the crowd.

Princess transitioned into her first song, a romantic but energetic love ballad. Many of the fans sang right along with her. She stared at different sections of the audience as she sang, occasionally locking eyes with specific audience members. The way some of them stared back, you would have thought it was love at first sight. Then the constantly moving lights would leave that section of the audience in the dark, and she'd focus her attention somewhere else. A few obsessive fans probably thought she was leading them on, but it was all part of the show.

She was halfway through the song when she spotted him. Nearly forty rows back, near the aisle, a male Vhelran in an unseasonably warm hoodie. He wasn't the only Vhelran in the audience, but this one was trying to keep his face hidden in an unintentionally conspicuous way. He'd cheer, then pull his hood forward. He'd clap or sing along, then readjust his hood once again. Sometimes he looked around to see if anyone was staring at him.

Midnight had shown her a picture of Fark, and while Princess couldn't see the Vhelran's full face, it looked like the same mouth and chin. Without missing a beat, she stared at Midnight while changing the next lines of the song. Instead of, "Our love is so great, it's never gonna end," she sang, "He's in row thirty-eight, second from the end." Midnight got the message, and stood up, working his way to the end of his aisle.

If any of the audience noticed, they didn't show it. They kept right on cheering and singing along. Her love song ended, and she went right into the next tune, a novelty breakup song filled with sarcasm and innuendo. It was a fan favorite, and the audience started clapping along with the beat.

It was hard to track Midnight with the lights constantly sweeping around the audience, but she finally noticed him walking up and down the aisle, looking confused. When the lights swept over Fark's seat again, it was empty. Princess looked all over the stadium, trying to locate the Vhelran. She doubted he would just leave. Blending into a crowd was one thing, but a single Vhelran leaving alone when the stadium was surrounded by security officers looking for a Vhelran... it didn't seem smart. Princess felt he was more likely to find a place to hide until the concert let out.

Then she spotted him. There was a ladder in the back corner of the auditorium, leading up to a catwalk that surrounded the stadium. Fark was more than halfway up the ladder. Once again Princess altered her lyrics. "I ran over his car with a backhoe" became "He climbed over the crowds in the back row." Midnight looked up at Princess with a confused expression, then he followed her line of sight. A few other audience members did as well, tapping their friends on the shoulder and pointing.

Fark backed away when he saw Midnight climbing the ladder. But cats are fast climbers, and Midnight reached the top before he got very far. Neither carried any weapons, as they'd both had to step through a metal detector to get into the concert. But Midnight had his claws, and Fark had his fists, and the two got into a rough-and-tumble fight. Lights swiveled and landed on them as they fought their way along the catwalk, getting closer and closer to the stage.

The audience ate it up, thinking it was all part of the show. Martial arts moves were part of Midnight's military training, but from the look of things, Fark had taken some lessons as well. They punched and kicked their way across the left catwalk, turned the corner, and continued fighting until they were directly above the stage.

A consummate professional, Princess kept singing throughout the fight, though she winced whenever Midnight took a heavy punch. She transitioned into her third song, an assertive pop hit with empowering lyrics, and one that perfectly complemented the fight going on above.

The Vhelran got in a sucker punch to Midnight's stomach, eliciting a jeer from the audience. Fark pressed the advantage, knocking Midnight down to his hands and knees, then kicking him repeatedly in the side. Princess stared on in anger, belting out her anthem with even greater resolve. Then she had an idea.

The controls for the animatronic dragon were mounted to the neck of her guitar. She had to miss a few notes to use the remote, but the result was worth a few seconds of a cappella. The dragon turned upward to the catwalk and breathed out a burst of fire. The flames didn't actually hit the catwalk, but it was close enough to make Fark panic. Midnight took advantage of the moment and kicked Fark in the knee, then he jumped to his feet and punched the Vhelran in the chin.

Fark went over the side rail, and landed on the stage, right in front of Princess. He started to rise to his feet, but Princess bashed him over the head with her guitar, perfectly timing it with the final note of her song. Fark went down, unconscious, and the audience roared with delight.

They took a short break between songs, while Midnight and local law enforcement took Fark into custody. Then the concert continued as scheduled without incident, with most of the audience still believing it had all been a stunt. The concert finally concluded around two AM, after three encores.

When she finally got back to her tour shuttle that morning, Princess had trouble falling asleep. She was just too wired from the events of the day. For perhaps the third time in the last couple of years, she seriously considered changing careers. She often fantasized about joining Midnight at WARCAT, where she could do something that actually helped people. But this time, another possibility raced through her mind. *I wonder,* Princess thought, as she finally started drifting off to sleep, *how I would fare at bounty hunting.*

02.18 *Primum Non Nocere*

ED.02508.08.29

It should have been a simple prisoner transfer. The hard part had already been done. All Glik had needed to do was drive.

The prisoner's name was Kreghan Biduum, but he went by the nickname Kroom. He was an explosives expert, and one of Tena's Twenty. Zak had caught him, with Yeela's help – or maybe it was the other way around – but they'd had to stay behind and wrap up a few loose ends. So Glik had volunteered to transfer Kroom to the IGP station. The shuttle had a small cell in the back for prisoner transport. They'd thoroughly scanned Kroom for weapons, and he'd been clean. As an extra precaution, they'd even kept him tied up when they locked him in the cell.

But they didn't know about Kroom's species. He looked mostly human, other than his lack of a nose, and the fingernail-like chitinous plates that covered most of his skin. These plates gave him an extra layer of defense, but they hadn't been enough to prevent his capture. What they couldn't have known was that Kroom had a unique biological weapon. Much like the bombardier beetle, Kroom could create small explosions using only bodily fluids.

Kroom had waited until they were halfway to the station,

then blew his way out of the cell. Glik had responded by drawing a stun pistol, but he wasn't a very good shot. A struggle had followed, followed by more small explosions, until the shuttle spun out of control. It had crashed in the swamp, many kilometers from civilization.

How did I get into this mess? Glik wondered. *I'm no bounty hunter. I just bandage them up between missions.*

The last few minutes had been a blur. Glik stumbled dizzily away from the wreckage, feeling lucky to be alive. Kroom had bailed out just before the crash. Who knew if he'd survived. He hadn't been wearing a parachute or anything. Glik held onto the one thing he'd managed to grab on his way out the door, a first aid kit. Now the shuttle was in flames, and Glik made haste to get some distance from the wreck.

On some level, Glik knew he was in shock. He'd heard stories of people wrecking their hovercars, only to keep walking to their original destination in a daze. Some people made it all the way to work before collapsing. The mind does funny things after an accident. All Glik's body wanted to do right now was to get farther from the ship. Would it explode? Probably not, but why take the chance?

A tiny but authoritative voice in his head went over the steps to overcome shock. It sounded an awful lot like one of his instructors back in college.

One. Call medical authorities. *I'm already here,* Glik thought. Besides, he didn't have his comm unit.

Two. Have the victim lie down. *No, I want to get farther from the explody thing.*

Three. Start CPR if necessary. *I don't think it is. My heart seems to be beating just fine.* He looked down at his chest. His shirt had ripped, and he could easily see his heart beating through the transparent skin of his chest.

Four. Treat any visible injuries. *In a minute, still walking.*

Five. Make victim comfortable, and keep them warm.

Yeah, not happening here in a swamp.

He approached the edge of a muddy pond, sat down, and put his head between his knees for a few minutes. He saw weird sparkles in front of his eyes, and for a minute it was hard to tell if his eyes were open or closed. He took several deep breaths. As he calmed down, he became more aware of his surroundings. His right arm felt wet. He opened his eyes again, and for the first time he noticed the huge gash running down his forearm.

The doctor in him took over, and he popped open the medkit. As he bandaged the arm, he scanned his surroundings. He'd walked about half a kilometer. He could still see the burning ship through the trees. It was putting a lot of smoke in the air. When he looked straight ahead again, he saw something he hadn't seen before. Or maybe he had, but only subconsciously. In his daze, it's possible his medical instincts had taken over and led him straight to his next patient.

On a rock in the middle of the shallow pond, Kroom lay on his back, bleeding from several large wounds. But he was breathing.

Glik watched Kroom carefully, trying to decide whether to help him. He knew Kroom needed medical attention, but if Glik were to nurse him back to health, Kroom would almost certainly kill him.

There were no weapons or supplies. The first aid kit was the only thing Glik had managed to grab from the shuttle, and now it was too dangerous to go back in. The fire suppression systems had obviously been damaged in the crash, and even if the fire burned itself out, anything still inside would probably be useless by now.

Glik quickly took inventory of the first aid kit. Was there anything in there he could use to keep Kroom sedated? No. There were some topical painkillers and some analgesic capsules, but nothing that would put Kroom in a stupor. If Glik were to help him, he would have to risk his own life.

But he's out right now, Glik thought. *I could at least tie him up first... because that worked so well last time?* Glik wasn't even sure how Kroom had caused the explosions that crashed the shuttle. He was pretty sure he'd sprayed some sort of biological chemicals, but from what part of his body? It had all happened so fast.

If I sit here much longer, it won't be an issue, Glik thought. It had actually only been a couple of minutes since he'd spotted Kroom, but his internal debate had felt like hours. *Save Kroom, but possibly die? Let Kroom bleed out, and be forever haunted by my own cowardice?*

A real bounty hunter might have thought about it even longer, especially since Kroom was worth the same dead as alive. But once again, Glik wasn't a bounty hunter. He was a doctor. "Screw it," he said, and started wading through the swamp.

Kroom opened his eyes and saw Glik's blurry face gradually come into focus. He started to rise.

"Careful, careful," Glik said. "You're badly injured. You'll want to take it easy."

Kroom's muscles were stiff, and it hurt to move them. The air was sharp against his skin. He could feel that some of his chitinous plates had come off. He turned his head towards Glik, and started to breathe faster. Too fast.

"Calm, calm," Glik said. "You had some severe wounds. But you're going to be fine. Just breathe normally."

"Says the guy with the exposed organs?" Kroom asked, his voice rising in pitch.

Glik chuckled and pointed to his chest. "I always look like this. See? Just transparent skin."

"Look closer, dude," Kroom said. "You've got internal bleeding.

Glik looked down and saw that Kroom was right. His left fleebum had ruptured in the crash. Now that he thought about it, Glik had been feeling chest pains all this time, but it hadn't stood out among all the other aches and pains from the crash.

Much like a cartoon animal defying gravity until he realizes he's standing in mid-air, Glik's chest pain increased tenfold with the knowledge that he was so gravely wounded. He clutched at his chest, trying to apply pressure to the organ. "I need... to get... to the hospital," he said. His dizziness came back, and everything went black.

"This man needs help now!" Kroom shouted. He stood in the open doorway of the emergency room, carrying Glik in his arms. Kroom's own wounds had opened back up during the long walk, and he swayed as if about to collapse himself. Medical personnel put both of them on stretchers and took them into surgery.

When Glik finally woke up, several hours later, Kroom had already been transferred to a more secure location. As soon as he could speak, Glik warned the doctors about Kroom's ability to create explosions, and they promised to pass the information along. Glik made a full recovery and returned to the Bloodwind three days later.

The following week, Glik took a few hours out of his busy schedule to visit Kroom in the prison hospital.

"You could have let me die and gotten away," Glik said.

"Thought about it," Kroom said. "You could have let me die and still collected the bounty."

"What stopped you?"

"You first," Kroom said.

"I'm a doctor," Glik said. "When I look in the mirror every morning, I see a doctor. But if I'd just sat there, watching you bleed out... I'm afraid of what I would have seen in the mirror the next morning. You?"

"All my life, no one ever did anything for me," Kroom said. "That's what life was. People fending for themselves. Screwing each other over to get a head up. But you saved my life. You didn't have to, but you did it anyway. It just didn't seem right that you should die for it."

"Does this mean you're going to rethink your lifestyle?" Glik asked.

Kroom burst out laughing, then gestured at the prison walls around them. "From what? Dude, I'm a lifer. From here on, this is my lifestyle."

He had a point. There was no real path to rehabilitation for Kroom. Even with good behavior, the years left in his sentence far outnumbered the life span of his species. He would spend his remaining years in an explosion-proof cell, being fed by robots, and only talking to people through triple-paned fireproof glass.

Kroom was no author or scientist. He didn't have some unfinished life's work he could continue in prison. There was nothing he would contribute to society. The rest of his life would be wake, three meals, and sleep, with maybe a little light reading in between. So what was the point of staying alive? Both Glik and Kroom pondered the question.

The only answer either could come up with was, it was better than the alternative.

02.19 *Red Herrings and Wild Geese*

ED.02508.09.06

"So who's left?" Zak asked, taking a bite out of an apple. The entire crew sat around the table in the galley, which was a rarity these days. Usually at least one of them was off on a hunt, or recovering in the medbay.

"There's only three left of Tena's Twenty," Glik said. "William Kanch, Veronica Serpens, and Xerxes Xanthen. I'm afraid we don't have any leads on those first two at the moment. But the third one's a doozy, and may require all of us to work together. Xerxes, or 'Xerk' to his friends, was an artist who got a bit too creative with his art supplies. He was captured ten years ago by a friend of ours, the bounty hunter Bloodstone. When Tena made her demands back in March, he was one of the ones released."

"Seems like that's all we've done the last few months," Zak said.

"But here's the thing," Glik continued. "As part of the prison's security procedures, they ran a DNA test on Xanthen before releasing him. And lo and behold, he wasn't himself. At some point during the past ten years, Xanthen escaped from prison, and a Marae shapeshifter took his place."

"The plot sickens," Vex said. "Did they still release the

Marae?"

"No," Glik said. "Since she technically wasn't Xanthen, they couldn't keep holding her for his crimes. But they very quickly charged her with conspiracy to commit a prison break, to which she pleaded no contest. Now she's serving a sentence of her own."

"Why would she serve someone else's sentence?" Sekka wondered aloud.

"Someday I'd like to write a research paper on Marae psychology," Glik said. "But right now we're more concerned with finding Xanthen. Unlike the rest of Tena's Twenty, Xanthen has had time to settle in. He's most likely living under a new identity. He may have even changed his face. But I don't think so."

"Why not?" Wisp asked.

"Because there have been Xanthen sightings over the past couple of years," Glik answered. "He's been spotted on two different planets. Since everyone thought he was safely in prison, no one ever followed up on these sightings. People just assumed this guy just looked like him or something."

"So where are we going?" Midnight asked.

"Wisp and I will go to the prison on Chirminon," Glik said. "We're going to interview the Marae who took his place, and see if we can get any clues out of her. The rest of you will split up and head for the planets Fresna and Belaum. Xanthen has lived on both planets in the past, and has been spotted on each of them within the last two years. You'll find a list of past sightings and former addresses on your comm units. Let's get going."

The Marae's name was Smirra. In her current form, she had blond hair, stunning good looks, and an unnervingly cheery disposition. Because it was impossible to completely disarm a Marae, visitors weren't allowed to be in the same room with her. Wisp, Glik, and Smirra sat in a plain interview room, a thick pane of unbreakable clear plastic between them.

"Thank you for agreeing to see us," Glik said, sitting down on a folding chair next to Wisp. There was a small table in front of them, pushed up against the plastic pane.

"No problem," Smirra said. "I love visitors." Her smile was unsettling. It was just a little bit too wide, not so wide that she didn't look human, but just enough to put your subconscious on edge. She wore a neon green prison jumpsuit and had a metal collar around her neck. Wisp wondered what kept her from changing shape and slipping out of the collar.

"You know why we're here," Wisp began.

"I assume you want to talk about my husband," Smirra said. "But I already told the court everything I know."

"So you and Xanthen are married?" Glik asked.

"Not on paper," Smirra said, her smile faltering for half a second. "But in every way that matters. Emotionally, physically, intimately." Her voice was so high-pitched and bubbly that it reminded Wisp of a cartoon character.

"Where did you meet?" Wisp asked.

"He bought me from the Grunthians more than a decade ago," she answered. "It was true love at first sight." Her smile actually widened even further for a second, making the hair stand up on the back of Wisp's neck. Of course, as a shapeshifter, Smirra could make herself look however she wanted. But there was just something about this almost perfect human form that leaned on the uncanny valley.

"And at what point did you two switch places?" Glik asked.

"Less than a year into his sentence," Smirra replied. "I copied a guard, used various disguises to get further in, let Xerk out, then took his place so nobody would look for him. It's the least I could do after all he's done for me."

"And where did he go after that?" Glik asked.

"Heck if I know," Smirra giggled. "He never told me his plans. He knows I can't keep a secret."

"But you know Xerxes," Wisp said. "You know what he's like, what he enjoys. Where would he go? If he could go anywhere, and knew nobody was looking for him?"

"Oh, no," Smirra said, waggling her finger. "I'm not falling for that one. We traded places fair and square. You just want to know so you can catch him."

Wisp and Glik shared a quick, perplexed look. "Well, yes, actually," Glik said. "That's... why we're here."

"He's hurt a lot of people," Wisp added. "We just want to make sure he doesn't hurt anyone else. But look at it this way. If we catch him, you two can be together again." This was obviously a lie, but Wisp wanted to see how gullible she was.

"That would be wonderful," Smirra said, sighing. "But I won't betray him. If he decides to come back, that's up to him."

Wisp frowned. "Doesn't it strike you as convenient that he bought you shortly before he was arrested, then used you to break out of prison?"

"Huh?" Smirra asked.

"Like maybe it was the plan all along?" Wisp continued. "Like he knew the cops were getting close, so he bought you as insurance?"

For the first time, Smirra frowned. Even her frown was overly cute, with her lower lip protruding like a pouting toddler. "I don't get what you're saying," she said.

"Oh, come on," Wisp said. "You're in here, he's off sipping margaritas on a beach somewhere..."

"He hates the beach," Smirra said. "He's always preferred the mountains."

Glik wrote something down on a notepad. "Question," he said. "When you were together, did he take you everywhere he went? Or did he sometimes leave you at home when he went out to dinner?"

"He said that was for my own protection," Smirra replied, looking unsure. "He said he had a dangerous job, and..."

"Did he ever smell like perfume when he got home?" Wisp asked.

Smirra didn't answer, but they could see the gears turning in her head.

"I'm not here to put down your husband," Wisp said. "Who I'm sure was faithful to you in every way. But don't you want to see him again? Don't you have some questions? I'm sure he has perfectly innocent answers that will put your suspicions to rest. But only if you see him again."

Smirra was starting to look extremely agitated. "I know what you're trying to do," she said.

"Which mountains?" Glik asked. "Surely he took you there sometimes. Or at least talked about his ideal retirement spot?"

"Shut up," Smirra said.

"Were they on Fresna? Belaum?"

"Shut *up*," Smirra repeated. Her smile was gone for good, and her face had taken on some demonic features.

"He could be out there in the mountains right now," Wisp said. "A woman on each arm, enjoying the view, not giving you another thought."

"I said shut up!" she shouted, her hands becoming claws. Her eyes were filled with fury, and she started pounding on the glass. A light on her collar lit up, and she screamed in pain. She writhed for a few seconds, her face and limbs taking on disturbing shapes, and then she collapsed on the floor.

That explains that, Wisp thought. The collar was probably programmed to detect when she changed shape. If she were to try to slip it off by making her head thinner, that alone would probably set it off.

"Go away," Smirra said weakly, cradling her head.

Guards entered on both sides of the glass. On the way out, Wisp and Glik asked to speak to the warden, and gave him their contact information. Wisp hoped they'd planted enough seeds of distrust in Smirra's brain, that she'd reach out to them when she'd had more time to think about it. Wisp and Glik intended to stay in town for a couple of days just in case. Due to the single-mindedness of the Grunthian conditioning, Marae were often emotional creatures, prone to extreme mood swings. By this time tomorrow, Smirra might despise Xanthen to the same degree that she'd loved him this morning.

They sent a message to the Bloodwind, detailing the scant clues they'd already gathered – mainly, that Xanthen might have a hideout in the mountains. Unfortunately, both Fresna and Belaum had their share of mountain ranges.

"This planet sucks," Lyryssa said, holding her raincoat tight against the torrent.

"Only on the outside," Sekka said, causing Lyryssa to look at her strangely. Sekka had brought a sniffer hawk with them, but had ended up leaving it in the shuttle. The bird didn't like the rain, and wouldn't be able to pick any scents in this downpour anyway.

The two women pushed through the rain, holding onto the guardrail as they climbed the steps to the town. There was an elevator that could have taken them from the landing pad to the mountaintop villa, but it was currently out of order. Elevator repairs would commence when the rain stopped, which probably wouldn't be for at least another month. So they were stuck climbing the slick stone stairs that had been carved from the side of the cliff.

Belaum hadn't always been like this. Thirty-six years ago, their moon had been destroyed when a gender reveal party went terribly wrong. Society had adapted and survived, but the world was now plagued with violently unpredictable weather patterns. They had a saying on Belaum: "If you don't like the weather... tough." It wasn't a particularly clever saying, but it had appeared on its share of bumper stickers.

Mercifully, the stairs finally turned and went into a tunnel carved into the cliff wall. When they finally reached the top, they emerged in the middle of a taxi station. From there, they took a ride to the sheriff's office. The automated hovercar had no roof, as there was no point. The town's transparent ceiling kept out all precipitation. As they rode through town, they noticed that a lot of the town's buildings were open-air. With no bugs or birds or fear of rain, roofs must have seemed like an unnecessary expenditure.

They did, however, appear to have a rat problem. Sekka noticed them right off, running down the sidewalks, climbing walls, and breaking into trash cans. Apparently when some of the planet's predators died off, the rats were able to proliferate. The town's citizens didn't seem to care. They just stepped over the rats and kept going about their business. The people of Tiptop City were unusually fit. Men and women alike were built like lumberjacks.

The car stopped in front of the sheriff's office and they went inside. The cops were even burlier than the other townsfolk had been. Lyryssa had a field day with all the eye candy, but Sekka was indifferent. The pounding rain on the town's roof constantly thrummed like distant drums, and it was starting to give her a headache.

The sheriff seemed genuinely pleased to receive visitors. The town had a low crime rate, so the sheriff had a pretty boring job. And tourism had taken a downturn in the last thirty-six years, so new faces were few and far between.

"We're looking for a man named Xerxes Xanthen," Lyryssa told him.

"I figured it was something like that," Sheriff Redjack said. "He used to have a place farther up the mountain. We check on it every time there's a sighting, but it's always empty. Feel free to check it out, but I doubt he's there."

Lyryssa and Sekka looked at each other. "We've come this far," Sekka said. They weren't going to turn down a lead, no matter how unlikely it might be.

"No worries," the sheriff said. "I'll give you a ride to the base of the climb."

The base of Mount Everdamp was riddled with tunnels, caves, and alcoves. At regular intervals, ladders were mounted in grooves carved into the cliff wall. There were dozens of these ladders, maybe hundreds. When Lyryssa looked up, she could see various structures built into the cliffs far up above.

"Take this ladder to landing fourteen," the sheriff told them. "Then switch to ladder one-twenty-three. When you reach the top of that, ladder seven-oh-one will take you the rest of the way."

"No elevator?" Sekka asked.

"Not to Xanthen's, sorry," the sheriff said.

"Can't we just take the shuttle?" Sekka asked.

"There's no place to land up there," the sheriff said.

"How long will it take?" Lyryssa asked.

"I've done it in just under an hour," he answered, flexing his muscles.

"An hour," Sekka repeated.

"At least," Lyryssa added, looking at the sheriff's physique.

"...of climbing a ladder in the rain," Sekka finished.

Lyryssa groaned. Staring up the ladder, she remembered her long climb on Glayss, in Kolden Dair's tower. This climb would take even longer, but at least she had her medication on her. "The sooner we get started, the sooner we reach the top," Lyryssa said, grabbing the rungs.

The planet Fresna had one government, with a two-party system. The Neos and the Trads weren't the only parties that ran for office, but they were pretty much the only parties that had a chance of getting elected. Both parties were deeply flawed. The Neos had difficulty getting anything accomplished, and they had an inconsistent record when it came to improving the economy.

The Trads, on the other hand, funneled the world's wealth to those who were already wealthy, catered to the most intolerant segment of the population, rejected obviously good ideas simply because they were proposed by Neos, supported election laws that made it harder for Neos to vote, allowed factories to produce toxins that were harmful to the planet, restricted the personal freedoms of women and minorities, based laws on religion, opposed any bills that might benefit people with low incomes... and they also had an inconsistent record when it came to improving the economy.

To anyone with a functioning brain, one of the parties was clearly the lesser of two evils. And yet, the planet's citizens were split almost down the middle. The Trads were currently in charge, having received thirty-nine percent of the vote in the recent election. Of course, the Neos had received forty-one percent of the vote, but their election laws were a bit skewed due to gerrymandering and other loopholes. This year marked the third consecutive victory for the Trads, and with leaders elected for five-year terms, this meant they were entering the eleventh year of Trad rule. Many drastic changes had taken place in the last ten years, and the way things were looking, there might not even be free elections by the end of this five-year term.

These victories had emboldened the planet's more extreme zealots, and alternative-looking people like Zak and Vex drew a lot of stares from the citizens. "Have you seen this guy?" Zak asked a random citizen, as they walked down a busy street in the town of Merrba. The man didn't even look at the picture. He just looked at Zak and Vex, shook his head, and walked on by muttering something about freaks accosting decent people.

"We should change," Zak suggested, looking down at the casual clothes he'd selected. He didn't want to look like a bounty hunter, so he'd just worn ripped jeans, a T-shirt, and a black leather jacket. Yeela was currently resting inside his backpack.

"What?" Vex asked. "If they don't like how I'm dressed, that's their problem." Her outfit wasn't much different from Zak's.

"This might be easier if people will actually talk to us," Zak said.

"Asking random people isn't going to get us anywhere," Vex said. "Let's just get to the police headquarters, and see how many sightings they logged."

Twenty minutes later, Zak and Vex sat in a small office. This police station was much larger than the sheriff's office on Belaum. Unfortunately, their police contact wasn't nearly as friendly as the one Lyryssa and Sekka had spoken with. Sergeant Thrane regarded these visitors with an expression he usually reserved for inmates.

"Listen," Zak said. "The sooner we can find Xanthen, the sooner we can get out of your hair."

This was music to Thrane's ears. He quickly looked up the records of Xanthen sightings and handed Zak a printout. "This is everything we know," the sergeant said. "And that's not much. He's been spotted six times in the last four years. Four of those sightings were at the same coffee shop, so you might start there." He stood up, indicating that Zak and Vex should stand up as well.

"Thank you, sir," Zak said.

"And kids," Thrane said, looking them over one more time, "Show some respect to my town and its people." Gesturing to Vex, he added, "I can see your navel, for cripe's sake."

Vex and Zak awkwardly nodded goodbye and made a beeline for the door.

All eyes turned towards them as they entered the coffee shop a few minutes later. Zak and Vex did their best to ignore the onlookers. They stood in line, and when they reached the counter, they showed Xanthen's picture to the cashier.

"Have you seen this guy?" Zak asked.

"Oh yeah," she said. "He used to come in here a lot. Why, is he part of your biker gang?"

"Have you seen him recently?" Vex asked.

The cashier shook her head. She was about to say something more when her manager came over and whispered something in her ear. "The boss said you have to get your coffees to go," she said.

A customer followed them out of the coffee shop. She was in her mid-twenties, with dark hair. Like most of the women they'd seen in town, she wore a beige turtleneck and a floor-length skirt, despite the warm weather. She had to pick up the skirt as she walked in order not to trip on it. Looking around to make sure she was out of anyone else's earshot, she said, "Excuse me?"

Zak and Vex turned. "Can I help you?" Zak asked.

"I saw that picture you were waving around," the woman said. "I know that guy. Is he okay? I haven't seen him in forever."

"How do you know him?" Vex asked.

"We, uh, used to date," she said, lowering her voice.

"Do you know where he lives?" Zak asked.

"He took me up to his cabin a few times," she said.

"Do you remember where it is?" Zak asked.

"I don't know the address, but I can show you," she said.

Lyryssa was out of breath. She'd considered drinking a vial of "the good stuff" before climbing, but she wanted to save that for emergencies. Besides, if she'd sped up the ladder she still would have had to wait on Sekka. She sat on the landing at the top of the final ladder, and helped Sekka crawl through the hole.

"Xanthen does this every time he goes home?" Sekka asked.

"He probably uses Levatech boots," Lyryssa said.

"That would have been good to bring," Sekka said, resting. She looked around. They were in an alcove next to Xanthen's living room. "How did he get his furniture up here?"

"It's weird that the place isn't locked," Lyryssa said.

"Who would rob a house that you can only get to by ladder?" Sekka replied.

They sat for another minute, then stood up and looked around. It was quiet. The house was impeccably clean, as if no one had ever lived there. It was sparsely furnished, like a model home you might show to a potential buyer. As they explored the spacious home, they found no personal possessions. Just basic furniture, generic paintings, and a few fake plants. Even the bookshelves only held leather-bound literary classics, the kind of books one buys to display rather than to read.

"We're missing something," Lyryssa said.

"We need a better nose," Sekka said, reaching into a large side pouch. She pulled out an enormous rat.

"Ew!" Lyryssa shouted. "Where did you get that?"

"Off the street, down below," Sekka answered. She held the rat up to her face and looked into its eyes, forming a bond.

"Aren't you worried about disease?" Lyryssa asked.

"I've had my shots," Sekka said. "And I read up on it. There's no history of Belaum rats spreading diseases." She set the rat down on the carpet. "Go on little guy, find us a secret."

The rat sniffed the air, then ran off down the hall. It stopped in one hallway and started scratching at a bookcase. Sekka and Lyryssa pushed the bookcase to the side and found that it had been covering up a door. It was the only locked door they had encountered so far. They searched every drawer in the house for a key, then finally broke the lock using kitchen utensils.

"What was Xanthen wanted for, anyway?" Lyryssa asked, as she pushed the door open.

Sekka flicked on the light switch. "Stuff like... that," she said, gesturing at the contents of the room.

The coffee shop customer, whose name turned out to be Candie, drove Vex and Zak to the cabin in her own car. Along the way, she told them stories about her relationship with Xanthen, who she called Xerk, or sometimes Xerkie-poo. The drive took less than an hour, mostly through winding back roads, finally ending at a log cabin that sat on the edge of a cliff.

They parked, walked up to the house, and knocked on the door. "Looks like no one's home," Zak said.

"Let's break in," Vex said.

Candie started to object, but Zak interrupted her. "What if Xerk's inside, hurt?" he said. "We have to help him." Candie thought about it for a moment, then finally nodded.

Vex had the door open by the time they turned back around. The interior had a rustic motif through and through, but like the house on Belaum, it looked like it had only been decorated for show. There were no personal touches, no evidence that it had been lived in.

"Scan everything," Zak said, letting Yeela out of his backpack.

"On it," Yeela said, zipping off down the hallway.

Zak and Vex started opening doors and going through drawers, ignoring Candie's objections. After a few minutes, Yeela came back and reported. "There's a locked door down the hallway. It looks like the room behind it is lined with steel. I can't get any readings through it."

Everyone followed Yeela down the hallway. While Vex went to work on breaking the lock, Candie became more and more agitated. "I'm not sure you should do that," she said.

"Maybe he's in there," Zak said. "In pain. We have to rescue him."

"He wouldn't be in there," Candie said, her voice becoming more authoritative. "Leave that room alone."

"Got it," Vex announced, popping the door open.

After turning on the light, Zak and Vex took in the contents of the room, their mouths wide open.

A few years earlier, Detanna had taken Zak to an unusual museum exhibit. She had claimed it was part of Zak's training, because knowing anatomy was imperative for finding an enemy's weak points. But Zak had strongly suspected Detanna just really wanted to see the exhibit, and Alterra didn't want to go with her. The exhibit had used real corpses of people of various species, skinned, and positioned in a variety of everyday poses.

Xanthen's collection wasn't quite as extensive as the one Zak had seen at the museum. But what it lacked in volume, it made up for in creativity. Limbs and heads that were clearly on the wrong body, people turned into centaurs and other mythological beasts by splicing various corpses together, humans with six arms and extra heads, corpses in bizarre sexual positions, and other nightmarish creations.

"You weren't supposed to see that," Candie said, as she started to change shape.

Sekka and Lyryssa faced a similar museum of horrors. "Everyone needs a hobby, I guess..." Lyryssa said, slowly backing out of the secret room. Sekka's rat tugged on her boot, trying to get her attention.

"What is it?" Sekka asked, looking at the rat. It ran off towards the office, and Sekka followed. A small crystal orb sat on an otherwise empty desk. Sekka had ignored it on their earlier walkthrough; it just looked like one of those random knickknacks people display when staging a house. But now the orb was flashing red. "Lyryssa!" she shouted.

"That can't be good," Lyryssa said, as the flashing picked up speed.

Sekka snapped her fingers, and the rat ran up her leg and

back into her side pouch. Sekka and Lyryssa raced back to the ladder. Holding on to the ladder's sides, they slid rather than climbed downwards, putting as much distance as possible between them and the home. They were more than halfway down the ladder when the house exploded. Not looking back, they continued their swift descent, as bits of flaming wreckage drifted down past them.

"Another of Xanthen's mail-order brides?" Vex asked, drawing her AON blades. Candie had turned into a monstrous purple-gray creature with spikes, tentacles, and razor-sharp teeth.

Zak raised his stun pistol to fire, but the monster batted it out of his hand. Meanwhile, another tentacle reached for Yeela, who fired a stun blast of her own. Candie flinched in pain but kept coming. Two more tentacles wrapped around Vex's wrists, keeping her from throwing her knives.

"What Xanthen and I have is special!" Candie roared, drawing Zak towards her wide maw. Zak suddenly wished he had an orange. Yeela kept firing, until Candie hit her with a club-like appendage.

She was about to bite into Zak's legs when she hesitated. "Wait a minute, what do you mean *another*?"

"You don't know about Smirra?" Vex asked.

Candie loosened her grip. Suddenly she seemed a lot less menacing. "Who's... Smirra?"

"You might want to sit down," Zak said, as Candie let him go.

On board the Bloodwind, Midnight received three calls within the span of five minutes. The first two were from Zak and Lyryssa. Both reported that their searches had come up empty, and they would be returning to the Bloodwind soon. The third call was from Glik. Apparently Smirra had come around, and had given them more information. Xanthen's cliffside dream home had been on Chirminon all along.

Since the Bloodwind was still in the Belaum system, Midnight waited for Lyryssa's shuttle to return before heading for the warp gate. They had Zak and Vex take their shuttle directly to a warp gate, to reunite with the Bloodwind at Chirminon.

Wisp, however, didn't want to wait for the Bloodwind to arrive.

It was perfect, another work of art. Xerxes Xanthen looked over his newest piece with great pride. A skinless mother and child, their hearts on the outside of their chests to represent the uncontainability of familial love. He wished he could show the world the beauty of this piece, but until people were more open-minded, it would have to remain in his private museum.

The front doorbell chimed. Xanthen cocked his head. This cliffside cabin was out in the middle of nowhere, surrounded by kilometers of forest. There was no road to it, just a landing pad for his personal shuttle. He also had proximity sensors around the property, which should have alerted him of any arrivals.

He pulled out his comm unit and looked at the front door camera. Nothing. He checked the other cameras around the house. Nothing. "Probably just an animal," he said out loud. Nevertheless, he closed the door to his art studio, locked it, and walked down the hall to the front door.

Grabbing a pistol out of the coat closet, he opened the front door and stepped out onto the porch. It was sunset, and the nearby trees cast long shadows across his lawn. But he definitely didn't see any movement. No people, no animals. He closed the door behind him, and walked around the side of the cabin, holding his pistol ahead of him.

"Xerxes…"

He spun when he heard his name. Still nothing. The world was perfectly still, and the only sound was distant crickets. "Who's there?" he called out, but there was no answer. He circled the cabin, but still saw nothing. When he tried to reenter the cabin, the front door was locked. He hadn't locked it, nor had he grabbed his key, but his comm unit could unlock it.

He reached into his pocket, but his comm was gone. Had it fallen out of his pocket? He retraced his steps, scanning the ground. It was getting darker outside, and he wished he could turn on the exterior lights. Unfortunately, he'd need his comm for that too.

"Xerxes..." the voice came again. He still couldn't tell where it was coming from. It was like a whisper on the wind, except there was no wind at the moment.

Xanthen wasn't superstitious, but this was one of those situations that gave skeptics pause. He finished circling the cabin a second time. As he rounded the last corner to the front side of the house, he saw a figure standing about a meter from the front door. She was in the shade, but he could make out a feminine form. "What do you want?" Xanthen shouted, holding his gun on her.

She didn't answer, nor did she move. Xanthen stepped closer until he could make out the details. It was indeed a woman. A skinless woman. One of his own art projects. Xanthen fired his pistol, putting a hole through her chest. The corpse fell over. He started to take a step closer to the corpse, when he felt a tap on his shoulder.

He shrieked and turned around. Another one of his art projects stood directly in front of him. He fired again, blowing its head off. Xanthen was starting to hyperventilate. "Who's doing this?" he shouted.

"Xerxes..." the voice came again.

"No no no no no no!" Xanthen shouted, sitting down and cradling his head.

"Xerxes..."

"Shut up, I don't believe in you," Xanthen whimpered. He sat for ten minutes, rocking back and forth, holding his eyes tightly shut. The voice stopped calling. When his breathing eventually calmed, he lifted his head and risked opening one eye.

The sun was almost completely down now, and all he could see were five dark figures standing in front of him, just a few meters away. Five silhouettes, no doubt more of his works. He definitely recognized the one on the far left, it was the mother and child he'd just been working on. The one in the middle, though… he didn't recognize her pose. And she was moving. Not just moving, but coming closer.

Xanthen blacked out.

One of the Bloodwind's shuttles landed on Xanthen's front lawn. Zak stepped out, the ship's exterior lights illuminating Wisp and her tied-up captive. Several skinless corpses lay strewn about the lawn.

"Hey, Wisp! Need a ride?" Zak shouted. She had come here by autotaxi, which had only taken her as far as the nearest road. She had hiked the rest of the way.

"Got room for two?" Wisp asked, gesturing at a very angry Xanthen.

"Xerxes Xanthen, I presume?" Zak asked, addressing the prisoner. "I've got someone here who wants to see you."

Candie stepped out of the shuttle behind him. She had insisted on coming along.

"Who the hell is Smirra?" Candie shouted, stomping angrily toward her ex.

"Candie! I can explain!" Xanthen shouted. The fear in his eyes now was even greater than it had been earlier, when Wisp had frightened him into fainting.

Candie started to grow claws, but Zak shouted a warning. "Candie…" he said, and she resumed her human shape. She had promised.

Nevertheless, it was going to be a long ride back to prison for Xerkie-poo.

Xanthen was returned to jail without incident. In addition

to his original sentence, of which he had only served a small part, he was charged with several new crimes. Barring any more tricky escapes, he would never see freedom again.

Candie was initially charged with aiding his crimes, but she ended up being a huge help in gathering more evidence against Xanthen, and her charges were eventually dropped. Smirra was likewise exonerated after she submitted evidence of her own. Both Marae were given multiple psychiatric evaluations, and their movements were restricted due to the specifics of their parole. They became good friends, and never harmed anyone again.

As for the Bloodhunters, this would be the last of Tena's Twenty they would catch. There were still two more criminals on the loose, but they each ended up being someone else's problem. The crew of the Bloodwind went back to hunting regular fugitives, and finally managed to get some rest in. A great battle still lay ahead, and they needed all the time they could get to prepare for it.

02.20 *Toxic Relationship*

ED.02508.09.17

Detanna hated waiting. It had been months since the lockdown started, and Lemondrop's resistance still didn't have a decent plan. With the Grunthian fleet in orbit over Valos, only Tena-approved ships could get through. It didn't look like that was going to change any time soon. What was taking Raven so long?

But Detanna knew the reason for the delay. If they moved early, they would be crushed. Tena would have the Grunthian war fleet turn their weapons to Valos itself and raze the city. Then Tena would kill Alterra out of spite. It was a terrible situation, but it couldn't be helped. As the bounty hunter Bloodstone, Detanna had spent years in solitude, refusing to care about anyone but herself. But once she'd met Alterra, that had gone out the window. She had no regrets, but on some level she missed the old Bloodstone, the one with a heart of ice. But then, she'd never actually been like that, not deep down. It had all been a show, to garner respect and earn more profits.

She craved news of the war effort, but off-planet transmissions were blocked. In the past few months, they'd only managed to receive a handful of messages from outside Valos. They'd monitored the news as best they could, but

Tena controlled what the average citizens saw. She told them that she was a hero, who had sealed off Valos for their own protection. A few of them even believed her, but most citizens recognized the truth. It was hard not to notice the freedoms they'd given up recently. Android officers patrolled the streets, every citizen's movements were tracked, and no one could contact their friends or family on other planets.

Detanna now paced outside of Lemondrop's quarters. Rumor had it that she'd received a message from off-planet, and Detanna hoped it was finally the go-ahead to attack. She wanted to burst through Lemondrop's door, but out of respect for her privacy, she waited in the hallway. Finally, Detanna's comm unit beeped. The text said, "I know you're out there. Just come on in."

It was early. Somewhere up above this secret compound, the sun was just starting to consider breaking on the horizon. Lemondrop was still in her pajamas, sipping coffee from a mug. She looked barely awake, but she still smiled at Detanna as she walked through the door.

"Is it..." Detanna began, but Lemondrop was already shaking her head.

"Raven still needs more time," Lemondrop said. "They've had some setbacks, I'm sorry. The Bloodhunters have successfully recovered most of Tena's Twenty. However, one of the former prisoners is on their way here to meet with Tena. I don't know what Tena's plan is for her, but I'd like you to try to intercept this woman before she gets to Tena."

It was a perfect mission for Detanna, partly because it would get her out of Lemondrop's hair for a little while, but mostly because Detanna was a master-class bounty hunter.

"I don't know... What if I'm away when the call comes?" Detanna asked.

"I'll text you," Lemondrop said. "Detanna, please do this for me. Whatever Tena has planned, it can't be good."

* * *

Across town, as far above ground as Lemondrop's safe house was below, Tena awoke in the penthouse of the Grand Palace. She normally wasn't such an early riser, but today she was expecting a visitor.

Tena had called for the release of dozens of prisoners. Some of the governments had complied, some hadn't. That was fine. She hadn't actually needed all those prisoners. Most of the names on the list were only there to sow confusion. She'd added a few of them on a whim, just to see what sort of chaos they might cause. A couple of them were old lovers, who she thought she might want to hook up with again. But there was only one name she actually cared about.

Veronica Serpens, who sometimes went by the name "Venomora," was the galaxy's foremost authority on toxins, poisons, and venoms. Seven years ago, she'd been incarcerated for experimenting on innocent people, resulting in several fatalities. During her time in prison, several inmates mysteriously died, and eventually Serpens was put in solitary confinement. Even there, she'd managed to continue work on her research, by memorizing chemistry books and extrapolating formulas in her head. Her sanity was questionable, but her intellect wasn't.

After all this time, the citizens of Valos still weren't warming up to their new leader. Tena couldn't imagine why. She thought she was doing a good job. Her subordinates bent over backward to tell her what a good leader she was. Why couldn't the people see it? Sure, they'd lost a few of their freedoms, but they were so much safer now. Crime was a thing of the past, and Tena had all but eliminated homelessness. But people still resisted her reign, and there were even rumblings of an uprising.

But that would stop today. Veronica Serpens would help Tena tamper with the city's water supply. Not with poison, oh no, Tena didn't want to kill them. But just a calming agent. Something to make the people a little more compliant, a little less rebellious. Something that would make them more open to suggestion.

That was the goal, anyway. She'd hammer out the details when Serpens got here. If such a concoction wasn't viable, she'd go with plan B. A slow-acting deadly poison, with the only antidote freely available to those who swore fealty to Tena. Lemondrop's rebels would surrender by the end of the week. She didn't like it as much as plan A, but desperate times and all that.

Tena checked Veronica's flight path. She would be here within the hour. Tena shivered with anticipation. This was going to be fun.

Veronica's shuttle landed a few blocks from the palace. Tena was too paranoid to allow shuttles to land at the palace's landing pad, because they might be full of explosives or resistance fighters. There had already been several assassination attempts, and while Tena knew such attacks were doomed to fail, she still didn't like taking chances.

Veronica stepped out of the shuttle and was met with two human guards. "I thought Tena said it would be androids," Veronica said.

"Tena's pulling out all the stops for you," one of the guards said, leading her toward the luxury hovercar. One guard opened the door for her, and Veronica eased into the backseat. The other guard put her suitcase in the trunk. Then the guards entered the vehicle's front seats, before driving off in the wrong direction.

Back at the landing pad, two badly damaged guardbots twitched and sparked inside a utility closet.

"The limo has arrived, my lady," said Synthral's voice on the comm unit.

"I'll be right down," Tena said, quickly slipping on her shoes and heading for the elevator. It took a couple of minutes to reach the ground floor, but Tena didn't mind making people wait. Overly excited by the prospects of new ways to hurt and control her subjects, she ran through the hall, out the ornate entrance, and across the promenade.

The limo still waited for her, just hovering in place. Tena tried to look in the windows, but they were tinted. This was wrong. The guardbots should have let Veronica out by now. They probably could have escorted her to the lobby in the time it took the elevator to reach the ground floor. And this wasn't even the right model of limo. Tena scowled. Something was fishy. She grabbed the back door, her clawed fingers easily piercing the metal, and ripped the door right off of the vehicle.

It was empty, except for a large black box sitting in the back seat. And then, the car exploded.

"Isn't that the palace over there?" Veronica asked.

"We're taking the scenic route," the driver said. Both guards were women. The driver had brown skin and purple hair, and the other guard was light-skinned with red hair.

"But Tena said…" Veronica began.

"Change of plans," the redhead said. "Tena has a morning routine. She won't be ready for another hour. She wanted us to show you all the sights. Look over there, it's the library."

"This doesn't feel right," Veronica said, pulling her comm unit out of her purse. "I'm going to give her a call."

"No!" said the redhead. She reached into the backseat, her arm stretching to an unnatural length, and snatched the comm out of Veronica's hand.

"I knew it," Veronica said, going through her purse. She pulled out a small, oddly-shaped pistol. Before she could fire, a clear wall rose up between the front and back seats.

"Go to sleep," Detanna said from the driver's seat, pressing a button on the dashboard. A cloud of greenish smoke filled the backseat. Veronica slumped to the side, leaning against the door, her eyes closed.

"Lady Vermon? Are you awake?" The doctor's voice

sounded distant at first. Tena opened her eyes, squinting at the light. She was in a hospital bed.

"What hap—" Tena started to say, then it all came rushing back. The car. The boom. The smell of burning flesh. She jumped out of bed, her IV tubes pulling several pieces of medical equipment to the floor. She ripped out the tubes and ran out the door, cursing.

"You really should rest!" the doctor called after her. Tena was covered in burns, but she didn't care. She'd always been a fast healer. By tomorrow, the burns wouldn't even hurt anymore. In a week, she wouldn't even have scars to show for it.

Her comm unit had been burned in the fire, so she called Andoro from the floor's front desk. Other patients stared at her, wide-eyed. She must have been a sight. No gown, just bandages covering the burns. She probably looked like a mummy. Tena fumed. They hadn't even taken her to her private facility. Unbelievable.

"Andoro, have you found Veronica's actual car yet?"

"We're looking," he replied. "Whoever took it must have disabled the transponder. But we've got eyes all over the city. The minute it's spotted, we'll be all over it."

"Whatever it takes," Tena said, ending the call. "Have a car waiting for me by the time I get downstairs," she told the nurse, then headed for the elevator.

"We have to switch cars," Detanna said, pulling into a parking garage. "They'll be looking for this one." They pulled up next to a less ostentatious vehicle. While Detanna worked on getting into the beat-up hovercar, Dervish opened the rear door to grab Veronica.

As soon as she opened the door, Veronica shot her in the face with some sort of toxic gas. Dervish became lightheaded and collapsed to the ground. Veronica bolted from the car, running as fast as she could.

Detanna cursed and started to pursue, but she stopped to

check on Dervish. "I'll be fine," Dervish said weakly. "Just go." The gas was probably supposed to be lethal, but Marae physiology was hardy. Detanna left her there to recover. She looked around for Veronica, and spotted movement just outside the parking garage.

Outside, Veronica spotted a patrol android. She ran up to it, waving her arms and shouting "Help!" As she got close to it, an energy blast hit the android right in the CPU, and it collapsed in a sparking heap. Detanna stood at the entrance of the parking garage, holding an energy pistol. Veronica ran into a nearby alley, and the chase continued.

Tena didn't wait for the car to come to a stop when it reached the palace. Heading straight for the security control room, she pushed a technician aside and sat down at a station. Getting back to his feet, the tech looked at her with concern. "Are you sure you shouldn't lie down?" he asked.

Not taking her eyes off the computer, Tena thrust her arm to the side, puncturing the tech's stomach with her fingernails. He staggered a few meters and collapsed. "Andoro, where are you?" she asked into a microphone.

"Right here," he said, entering the security room. His eyes darted to the technician's corpse, then back to Tena. "But I don't have to be. You want me in the field?"

"Yes," she replied. "There's a sighting at intersection Fourteen P. I'm sending drones there now. Join them."

"On my way," Andoro said, thankful for an excuse to leave. When Tena was upset, it was better to be on the other side of town.

Veronica climbed up a fire escape, broke a window, and hid in an empty apartment. She hadn't been this athletic before she went to prison, but once the other prisoners had learned why she was there, it had been evolve or die. Her toxicological experiments had killed many innocent people, including children, and child killers weren't well regarded by the prison population.

She hid in a hallway closet, listening closely for any sound. Had her pursuer seen her go through the window? Or if not, would she notice the broken window as she ran through the alley? Veronica was already out of breath, and did her best to silence her breathing. She'd lost her suitcase, but still had her purse. She always carried a variety of chemical compounds, you never knew what would come in handy. She pulled out a small injector device and held it to her arm. It made a quiet "pish" sound as she pressed the button.

She felt some of the effects right away. Much better. Not all her toxins were deadly. This one was designed to enhance her strength and reflexes, if only for a short time. It was like a fast-acting steroid combined with the galaxy's strongest energy drink. She'd crash hard later, but hopefully she'd be out of danger by then.

There was a noise. Someone was climbing in through the window. She heard the crunch of broken glass as they stepped into the living room. Veronica readied her gas pistol. She didn't have to worry about using it at close range. She was immune to its effects, just as she'd been immune to the sleeping gas they'd tried to use on her in the car.

Veronica's brain raced as her booster shot really kicked in. It seemed like the universe was in slow motion. The footsteps in the living room were moving painfully slow. Veronica wanted to wait until the coast was clear before she found another place to hide, but with her mind in overdrive, the act of waiting was painful.

Dervish was feeling much better. She wanted to check on Detanna, but she couldn't do so without being seen. She sent a text message but didn't get a reply. She needed to get across the street and into that alley. But even if she disguised herself as a Valos citizen, it would look suspicious to head in that direction now. It was swarming with activity.

Disguised as a pile of coats in the backseat of a parked hovercar, she raised an eyestalk and watched the street. Several drones had arrived and were starting to organize a systematic search. Then a vehicle flew into view, a single-person craft that looked like a flying jet-ski. It landed in front of the disabled patrol android. Andoro Korr jumped off of the vehicle, looked around, and headed toward the alley. Dervish sent Detanna one more text, warning her of the new visitor.

Detanna quietly crept through the apartment, checking every corner. Her comm unit vibrated, but she ignored it for now. The front door was still closed and locked, which meant her prey was probably still in the apartment. She knew Veronica was armed with deadly toxins. She wished she had her helmet, but she couldn't have disguised herself as a guard while wearing her Bloodstone gear. But she wasn't without defenses. She reached into her pocket and pulled out a small air filter, which fit over her nose and mouth.

She was just debating whether to check the closet or the kitchen next, when a drone flew in through the broken window. She took it down with one shot, but not before it spotted her. By now, Tena would know she was here, though she wasn't sure if she would be recognized with the filter over her face. Either way, she couldn't stay much longer. She approached the closet.

The door burst open before she reached it, and Veronica sprayed her with poisonous gas. It didn't choke her through the filter, but it made her eyes water. Veronica didn't waste her advantage, and kicked Detanna hard in the knee. Unable to see clearly, Detanna closed her eyes and countered with a punch to the jaw.

Still pumped with artificial adrenaline, Veronica couldn't

even feel pain right now. She rushed Detanna, ready to tear her apart with her bare hands. Eyes still closed, Detanna punched her right in the middle of the face. Veronica staggered backward, her nose broken. Okay, that one did hurt a little bit. She stumbled forward again, only for Detanna to catch her in the stomach with a hard kick. Veronica fell backward, landing on her back.

As Veronica struggled to stand up again, Andoro Korr climbed through the window. Detanna could now see again, though everything was a little blurry. Andoro drew both of his AON blades, and they glowed a bright red. Detanna fired several shots with her energy pistol. Quick as a bullet, Andoro blocked the blasts with his blades, reading Detanna's body language and anticipating where she would aim next. Then with one quick thrust, he sliced the barrel off of Detanna's pistol.

Andoro attempted to follow through with a slice to the neck, but Detanna dropped to the floor. She bounced back up with Veronica's gas pistol, and fired it in Andoro's face. Andoro gagged, turned, and ran. He jumped out the window – not the one that was already open – with a loud crash.

Detanna looked around for more danger. Veronica shook as she rose to her feet, then collapsed over the back of the couch. There was more movement from the window, and Detanna held the gas pistol ready. To her surprise, Tena Vermon climbed in through the window.

"Don't shoot!" Tena said. "It's me, Dervish." She flickered back to her normal face again for a second, then resumed Tena's visage. "The drones won't fire at Tena."

"Let's get back to the safe house," Detanna said. "We'll split up in case one of us doesn't make it." She started to pick up Veronica, but winced when she put the extra weight on her knee. Veronica's kick had hurt her more than she'd realized at the time.

"I'll take Veronica," Dervish said. Detanna started to

object, but Dervish added, "She's safer with me. If she wakes up, I'll tell her I'm Tena, and maybe she'll come with me anyway."

Detanna agreed, and they split up. Dervish climbed back out the window and used the fire escape to reach the ground. Meanwhile, Detanna went out the apartment door, took the stairs to the basement, and found a passage into the sewers.

Dervish carried Veronica to one end of the alley and peeked around the corner. Andoro was on the sidewalk, on his hands and knees, throwing up through his ninja mask. Several drones flew by, scanning up and down the street. Dervish didn't think they'd fire at her, but she didn't want to take more chances than necessary, so she went the other way.

"Andoro! Why aren't you answering me?" Tena was furious. She had taken over one of the drones, and was piloting it remotely from the palace security room. As the drone turned down one street, she saw Andoro getting sick on the sidewalk. She didn't know what had happened to him, but she had to fight against the urge to fire the drone's weapons at him. As the drone flew by the alley, Tena spotted movement on the left side of her screen.

She changed course and turned into the alley. She saw herself carrying Veronica toward the next street. "That's not me, why am I there? I'm right here!" she screamed. She aimed the drone's weapons and attempted to fire. The software refused. "Override," she said. The software still refused to fire. The "Don't Shoot Tena" protocol was one of the first software enhancements she'd demanded when she'd taken over, and it would take one of her IT people at least half an hour to disable the feature. And her nearest IT tech was currently a corpse, sprawled on the floor nearby.

On the screen, not-Tena had turned to face the drone. She was frozen in place, unsure if she was about to die. Veronica lay limp across her arms. "Fine," Tena said. "But if I can't have her, you can't either." She targeted Veronica's head and fired.

Dervish shrieked and dropped the now-headless corpse. She turned and ran, taking a circuitous route, leading the drone on a wild goose chase. It still hadn't fired at her, which she felt was a good sign, but she didn't want it tracking her, either. Just because it couldn't fire at her didn't mean it couldn't summon deadlier reinforcements.

Dervish returned to the parking garage. She remembered that Veronica's suitcase was still in the trunk, probably full of chemicals Tena shouldn't have. Detanna had also stashed a few weapons in the trunk. The drone still on her tail, Dervish found the car, popped the trunk, retrieved a grenade launcher, and blew the drone out of the sky. Then she stood back and fired a round into the trunk, blowing the suitcase, and the car, to smithereens.

While more drones were called to the scene, Dervish made a hasty retreat. She found the jet-ski-like vehicle she'd seen Andoro use earlier, flew it for several blocks, crashed it on purpose as a distraction, and slipped into the sewers.

Back in the palace, Tena screamed at the top of her lungs. She picked up the computer monitor and threw it across the room, then continued trashing every bit of equipment in the room. None of her subordinates came to check up on her. They knew better. An angry Tena was better left alone.

Detanna and Dervish both made it back to the compound safely. Dervish was highly disappointed in herself for not being able to prevent Veronica's death, but everyone agreed there'd been nothing she could do. Overall, the mission had been successful. They'd thwarted Tena's plans, and kept the lethal chemicals out of the madwoman's hands. The war was far from over, but they'd won this battle.

* * *

Andoro staggered back through the front doors of the palace. His mask had probably been all that had saved him from death, and he still felt like he'd spend the last hour on the galaxy's twistiest roller coaster. All he wanted to do right now was take an antacid, drink some milk, then fall face-first onto his bed and sleep for a week. But duty came first. An android met him at the door and informed him that Tena required his presence immediately.

As he stepped off the elevator to the penthouse, Tena greeted him, as she often did, in the nude. Only this time, she was covered in horrific burns that churned Andoro's stomach. Tena approached him and kissed him on the lips. Andoro started to speak, but she stopped him.

"Bup bup bup," she said, placing her finger over his lips. "You failed me today, but I'll forgive you on one condition. I want to forget today ever happened. So this is what we're going to do. You're going to carry me into the bedroom. I'm going to wrap my legs around your head. That ninja-tastic tongue of yours is going to make me scream so high only Caniks will be able to hear it. Are we clear?"

Andoro started to answer, but he threw up on her instead. He wasn't sure what happened after that. He woke up a week later in a hospital bed. He couldn't remember what she'd done to him, but he knew he was lucky to be alive. If he failed her again, there wouldn't be enough of him left to bury.

ED.02508.09.30

"I think we've accounted for every possible defense," Raven said.

What if they've upgraded their software? Trenyn asked.

"I believe we'll be fine," Raven answered. "You know Grunthians. Strong hardware, weak software. Remember the Bloodwind?"

Trenyn chuckled inaudibly, filling Raven's mind with the image of dozens of laughing emojis. *Is there any part of their original code we actually kept?*

"I doubt it," Raven said. "But I'm glad we kept a backup. This project might have been harder without it." The project shouldn't have taken five months, but they'd hit some unexpected snags. As much as they liked to make fun of Grunthian programming, it still hadn't been a walk in the park.

So how do we test it? Trenyn asked.

Raven picked up her comm unit and sent a message to Doctor Eshton. The IGP had captured a Grunthian scout ship a few days ago. It had been attempting to gather Earth defense data for Tena. Raven had asked them to keep the ship nearby, but the IGP had tests of their own they'd wanted to run on it.

"Eshton says they'll have the ship here tomorrow morning."

If it works, how long before we can implement it?

"We'll still have to wait for Lemondrop's approval," Raven answered. "Detanna won't want us to attack until she's sure we can do so without endangering Alterra."

There's more at stake here than just Alterra, though.

"I know," Raven agreed. "We can't hold back forever. Do you think Alterra's had the baby yet?"

I don't know about Auroran gestation periods, but I would estimate she's due within the next two weeks.

Raven's comm unit chimed, and she glanced at the screen. "It's Zeva. She wants to know if we want to go to dinner."

Trenyn looked at the time, surprised that it was so late. *I suppose a celebration is in order,* Trenyn replied. They'd barely left the computer lab these last few months, so it would be nice to finally get out.

Since arriving on Earth five months ago, Raven and Trenyn had been staying at Zeva's place in Nova Corvallis, Oregon. Raven's childhood home had burned down six years ago, and what equipment had survived had been moved to this lab. Raven had offered to rent an apartment, but Zeva had insisted. And her place was less than a block from the lab, making the commute convenient. Besides, given that Raven and Trenyn spent so much time in the lab, they didn't intrude on Zeva's life that much.

An hour later, the three of them sat around a table at La Fausse Vache, a fancy restaurant that served lab-grown steak. Instead of the unpainted metallic robotic body Raven usually wore, she currently wore a version that was made to look like human skin. She wore a black dress over it, borrowed from Zeva. Her ensemble included gloves and several other accessories to cover as much of her fake skin as possible, including a thick choker necklace that hid the line where her neck met the body. No one was staring at her, but she still felt self-conscious.

Being genderless, Trenyn was never sure what to wear to places like this. The restaurant didn't have a clearly defined dress code, just a sign that said: "Proper Attire Required." It was one of those unwritten social conventions that people from Earth just knew. Human formal attire was even more pointlessly gendered than usual, and Trenyn hadn't known where to start. Again Zeva came to their rescue, letting them wear a black suit that had once belonged to her father. It was a little big on Trenyn, and the sleeves restricted their bifurcated forearms, but it would be fine for one night.

As for Zeva herself, she wore a dark blue dress with a much lower neckline than the one she'd lent to Raven. Zeva was Galean, with feline features and white fur. Her stylish mane was currently dyed blue. Dinner was on her, as she had recently been promoted at work. She was now officially an IGP special agent. Her late sister would have been proud.

Dinner conversation was pleasant, though it was hard to get Raven and Trenyn to stop talking shop. Neither had watched any new movies or other media in months, and neither of them were very skilled at small talk. It was up to Zeva to keep the conversation interesting, steering it away from their obsessions so they could let their overactive brains rest for one night.

Halfway through the main course, Raven noticed that Zeva kept glancing at another table. "What is it?" Raven asked.

"Just a sec," Zeva said. She pulled out her comm unit and browsed through some pictures. Then she held it up and showed an image to Raven. "I hate to say it, but sometimes humans tend to look alike to me. Is this that guy over there?"

Raven looked at the picture, then looked at the man at the other table. He was facing the wrong direction, so she had to wait until he turned his head a bit. "He's shaved his mustache and he's wearing bronzer, but it certainly looks like him," Raven said. "Who is he?"

"Bad news," Zeva said. "His name is William Kanch. Remember those criminals Tena made the government release a few months ago? Most of them have been recovered by bounty hunters. Now there's just one left."

Him? Trenyn asked.

Zeva nodded. "The last thing I want to do is start a scene in a nice restaurant like this, but I also can't let him get away. I'm going to call it in." She picked up her comm unit and made a discreet phone call. "The IGP should be here in a few minutes," she said, putting her comm unit away.

At the other table, Kanch laughed and chatted with three friends. Then he appeared to excuse himself, and stood up.

"We can't let him out of our sight," Zeva said, starting to get up.

"Wait," Raven said. "There aren't a lot of Galeans here. He'll notice if you keep following him. I think I'm the least conspicuous of the three of us."

Raven followed him at a distance. Near the kitchen, there was a short hallway that led to the restrooms. Unable to follow him in into the men's room, Raven stood in the hallway, waiting for him to come out. After a few minutes, she got a text on her comm. It was from Zeva. "Well???" it said.

"He's in the restroom," Raven texted back. "He seems to be taking a while. I hope he isn't on to us." While a lot of people kept their texts brief and to the point, Raven's messages always used full sentences and proper punctuation.

"Stay there," came Zeva's reply. "Going outside."

Trenyn stayed at the table so they wouldn't be accused of a "dine and dash." Zeva left the restaurant and walked around the building, looking for windows. The restaurant had no windows other than the two picture windows flanking the front door. There was a kitchen exit and an emergency exit, but Kanch couldn't have made it to either of those without Raven seeing him. "No windows. Has to be in there," she texted to Raven.

"I'll check," Raven sent back. She pushed open the bathroom door, ready to say "Sorry, wrong room" if Kanch was in there. But the men's room was empty. She looked up and saw that one of the ceiling tiles was askew. Before she could look any closer, she heard a disturbance in the kitchen. She immediately went to investigate.

There was soup all over the floor, and the servers were picking up some scattered pots and pans. One of the ceiling tiles in the kitchen had been pulled aside, and the back door was open. Apparently Kanch had climbed across the crawlspace, come out in the kitchen, and ran out the exit. Raven wasted no time, pushing servers and chefs aside as she bolted for the door. She couldn't take the time to text Zeva, but she was still in range of Trenyn's telepathy, and she had them send Zeva a message.

Raven burst out the back door, looking left and right. Zeva came running around the building from her right, so Raven assumed Kanch had gone left. Raven ran to the left, coming out of the alley and reaching the street. She looked up and down the street, not seeing Kanch anywhere.

Zeva came running up beside her. "Where did he go?" she asked.

"Hold on, I want to try something," Raven said. Raven had never attempted this before, but she knew her body's specs. She crouched low to the ground, then jumped up to the roof of the restaurant. The jump itself went fine, but Raven had neglected to account for two things. First was the dress, which wasn't designed for this range of movement. Second was landing.

Raven landed on the roof, but couldn't quite regain her sense of balance. She instinctively tried to steady herself as if she had a normal weight for her body type, and first she undercompensated, then overcompensated, then fell backward on her rear. The dress, already ripped from the initial crouch, tore even further. Raven winced at the sound, resolving to pay Zeva back, and hoping the dress wasn't a custom one-of-a-kind.

Raven looked up and saw Kanch. He didn't ask any questions or deliver any villain soliloquies, he just lifted his pistol and started firing at her.

Now in a sitting position, Raven brought both of her hands up to protect her face. Kanch's blasts tore through the rubbery fake skin that coated Raven's body, but they didn't penetrate the metal underneath. Raven got to her feet, still protecting her face, and started walking toward him. "William Kanch," she shouted. "Throw down your weapon and come with me."

Believing that he must be dealing with some sort of android, Kanch focused his fire on what he estimated to be Raven's weak points. He took multiple shots at Raven's knees, finally incapacitating the left one. Raven lost her footing, and fell on her side. She didn't have any weapons on her, so it was all she could do to protect her head from his gunfire. One of her fingers flew off as a blast hit her in the hand. She couldn't keep this up much longer. One blast grazed her temple, and now a trickle of blood dripped down the side of her face.

"Hold on," Kanch said, temporarily ceasing fire. "You're not really a robot, are you?"

"Kanch!" another voice shouted. "Put down your weapon!"

Kanch turned his head. Zeva had climbed a maintenance ladder and was just making her way onto the roof.

Kanch kept his gun aimed at Raven. "Take another step and I'll kill her!"

Zeva and Kanch stared at each other for several long seconds. Kanch knew it wasn't much of a threat. If he killed his hostage, there was nothing to prevent this newcomer from shooting him. But it bought him a few seconds to think.

Red and blue lights flashed from the streets below. He

wasn't going to make it out of this. He was either going back to prison, or he was going to die. But at least he could get in one last kill first. One last chance to satiate his bloodlust.

Zeva seemed to see his thought process in his eyes. "Don't even think about it," she said. Both of their trigger fingers started to move.

"Auugh!" screamed Kanch, dropping to one knee. Zeva was confused, but she didn't hesitate. She fired three blasts from her stun pistol, knocking Kanch unconscious.

Protruding from the bottom of Kanch's foot was a metal blade. "Where did that come from?" Zeva asked. She noticed a thin hole in the roof of the building, just below where Kanch had been standing. She removed Kanch's shoe and bound the wound with one of his own socks.

"That's one of Trenyn's virtrinium blades. I've been in contact with them this entire time," Raven said. "If we concentrate, Trenyn can see through my eyes. They're standing directly below us in the restaurant right now."

"Tell them I said thank you," Zeva said, pulling a pair of handcuffs out of her purse.

The police took Kanch away. Zeva refused to accept any reward, claiming it was all part of her job.

The following morning, Raven and Trenyn tested their software on the captured Grunthian ship. Unfortunately, the test was a failure. Apparently the Grunthians had upgraded their software after all, and the new code didn't appear to be of Grunthian origin. They estimated it would take at least two more weeks, if not a month, to hack the software and fix their code.

In the meantime, the citizens of Valos were getting antsy.

Part 3

03.00 Coup

ED.02508.10.01

"What is that noise?" Tena asked. She was on the top floor of the palace, enjoying a soak in the luxurious hot tub on her balcony.

Andoro's voice came back through the comm unit. "The citizens are storming the palace. Again."

"Seal off the foyer. I'll be right down," Tena said, getting out of the hot tub. She had tried to be nice. After the first failed uprising, she had only executed a few of the participants, as examples. Her android guards were instructed to incapacitate rather than kill, so the survivors could go back and warn the others against future revolts.

This time she would not be so kind. Not bothering to get dressed, she took the elevator down to the first level. She stepped out of the elevator, onto the landing of a wide staircase. Below her, about three hundred angry citizens were packed into the grand foyer, tearing apart her poor androids. A few rioters spotted her and started shouting "There she is!" and "Get her!"

"Stop!" she said, her eyes glowing, and the rebels dropped their weapons, mesmerized. "Your true enemy is each other," she said, then stepped back into the elevator. On the ride back to the penthouse, she imagined the carnage that would be unfolding right now, and looked forward to watching the video later.

Lord Teykor Vermon had been able to control people's minds, completely overriding their will. None of his heirs had inherited that degree of power, but most of them had been blessed with a taste. Raven could tell when people were lying. Lemondrop could calm people's emotions and make them happy, though she seldom used this power, as she was morally opposed to mind control. Thresh had been able to cause fear, and Sekka could befriend animals.

Tena could make people go violently insane. Right now in the lobby, the would-be insurrectionists would be tearing each other apart with their bare hands. When the effect wore off in a few hours, the two or three survivors would go back home to their families, with vivid memories of all the deaths they had caused.

It was a real treat to use her power on a crowd like this. She dared not use it in one-on-one combat, because it just made her opponent angrier at her, and most people were a lot tougher when they had no sense of restraint. But it was a great tool when she needed people to fight amongst themselves.

Tena smiled to herself. Of course, that wasn't the only perk she'd inherited. Unlike her siblings, Tena had been doubly blessed. But she kept the other blessing a secret. There was no point in telling anyone anyway. They'd figure it out for themselves in a few hundred years.

03.01   Honeymoon

ED.02508.10.14

Alterra lay strapped to a hospital bed. Her contractions had begun, but it would still be a while before she was ready to deliver. "Distract me, distract me," Alterra pleaded, trying to keep her mind off the pain.

Doctor Lillary Cleff had been her only doctor ever since they'd transferred Alterra to the hospital. The rest of the floor had been vacated, and Lillary was the only one of the medical staff allowed on this floor. The rest of the rooms were now empty, and android guards filled the hallway. It was an interior room with no windows, and they kept Alterra's arms and ankles strapped to the bed most of the time.

Over the past few months they'd gotten to know each other quite well. Alterra had told her how she'd met Bloodstone, and how they'd fallen in love even though she'd been unable to show Bloodstone her face. Lillary had told Alterra about how Tena had killed her husband as a warning, and kept her children prisoner in an unknown location. If Alterra were to escape, Lillary's children would be executed. Tena left nothing to chance.

Lillary's heart went out to Alterra, but her hands were tied. There were ways to reduce the pain. There was a device in her office that would disrupt the pain center of the brain without harming the child. But Tena had forbidden it. If Lillary were to disobey Tena, who knew what would happen to her children. So she just kept Alterra talking, working through the pain.

"Tell me about your wedding," Lillary said.

"I've already told you about my wedding," Alterra groaned. It came out ruder than she'd intended. "There's nothing more to tell, it was a… unhg… simple ceremony."

"What about your honeymoon?" Lillary asked.

Now that was new territory. Over the next couple of hours, between grunts and groans, Alterra told her the entire story. "It was 2504. Detanna and I had been a couple for two years. I'd wanted to get married sooner, but Detanna wanted to wait until she'd had that procedure I told you about."

"Did the procedure go well?" Lillary asked.

"She was a new woman," Alterra said. "She said it was like being reborn. In fact, after she healed, we decided to wait on any, you know, heavy petting until after our wedding. She said it felt like she was losing her virginity all over again, so she wanted to wait. Just for fun, of course. Neither of us actually have any hang-ups or superstitions about virginity. "

"And how did that go?" Lillary asked, smiling slyly. The distraction was working. Alterra didn't seem nearly as pained as she had a few minutes before.

"It was fantastic… eventually," Alterra said.

"Eventually?"

"We didn't get to… you know… the first night," Alterra said. "Things kept getting in the way."

"What things?" Lillary asked.

"That's a long story…"

The ceremony had been simple but beautiful. While the Council of Heirs had offered them the use of the Grand

Palace's Great Hall, they had declined. The palace had been built for Lord Teykor Vermon, and they didn't want the overindulgent opulence to dominate their memories of the day.

Then Raven had presented them with a compromise. Upon joining the council, she'd been given a tower. Most of the levels held lab equipment and half-finished projects. She and Trenyn lived on the top floor, though you could hardly tell anyone lived there, given how little thought Raven put into decoration.

But the balcony was just perfect. It was large, easily able to hold forty people without feeling too crowded. The balcony was shaped like a half circle, with mosaic tiles depicting a picture of the sun on the floor. Since the tower was on the edge of the city, instead of overlooking downtown, it had a spectacular view of a lake and the forest beyond. They were married at sunset in front of a handful of their closest friends.

Lemondrop Vermon officiated the ceremony because she loved performing weddings. They had a giant panther as a ring bearer. They even had a full-length mirror brought to the ceremony, in case an old friend managed to make an appearance. This confused a few of the guests, but several people swore they'd seen a ghostly image appear in the mirror during the ceremony.

After the ceremony was over, they danced for hours, mingled with their friends, and had the time of their lives. They had to leave shortly before midnight, so they could catch a shuttle to their honeymoon train.

The Sonata Express was the largest terrestrial train in the galaxy. The cars were the size of buildings, and the train was more than a hundred kilometers long. Most of the even-numbered cars held recreational facilities, while the odd-numbered cars were luxury hotels. The train circled the planet Hermoso on an elevated track that ranged from five to fifty kilometers off the ground. It passed by mountains, over oceans and cities, through arctic wastelands and forests and deserts and every other type of landscape this beautiful planet had to offer.

Alterra and Detanna snuggled and kissed and teased each other in line, unable to keep their hands off each other in anticipation of getting to their room. But before they even had time to unpack, there was a mandatory safety and orientation event, followed by a meet-and-greet with the train's staff. They tried to leave afterward, but other passengers kept coming up to them and asking for their autographs, or to have their pictures taken with them. Sometimes they forgot that they were technically celebrities.

They finally got back to their room around nine PM local time, but for their bodies it was closer to five AM. Between the lateness of the hour, the drinks, and the exhaustive events of the day, they both went straight to sleep without even changing out of their clothes.

The following morning, they slept late, had breakfast brought to them, then went out to explore the train and find something fun to do. Every recreational car had a different theme. The car ahead of theirs housed a huge swimming pool, complete with gyro-stabilizers to keep the water from splashing from the movement of the train. The car after theirs was a video arcade and karaoke nightclub.

If they were up for a bit of a walk, there was a zipline and rock climbing playground three cars ahead, and a miniature golf course three cars behind. They didn't actually have to walk, though. On the roof of the train there was a smaller track, with spherical pods that could take riders up and down the train. It was much faster than walking, and it had a great view.

Thirty-five cars ahead, there was a sports center that was currently running a martial arts competition. Detanna hadn't been in a fight since the procedure, and thought it might be fun to see if she'd lost any of her skills. Alterra agreed to come along as a spectator, but had no desire to enter the competition. They took the stairs to the roof and boarded a pod. The ride was intense. They were going in the same direction as the train, but much faster. The train was currently traveling over the ocean, and Hermoso's green waves were stunning.

They stopped one car early, because the pods didn't stop over the recreational cars. They descended into a hotel car, similar to the one they were staying in. As they passed by a manager's office, Alterra noticed a security officer posting a flyer in the hallway. It was a wanted poster, and it reminded her of the ones she'd seen of her own face back in the day.

The picture showed a young woman with short, blond hair. "Wait," Alterra said, and took a closer look at the poster. The fugitive's name was Mina Errol, and she was wanted for murder. "It says she killed a child," Alterra said.

"We'll keep our eyes open," Detanna said, memorizing the woman's face. They proceeded to the next car.

Detanna was on top of her game, winning every match she entered. Alterra cheered her on, but kept getting distracted. She could have sworn she'd seen that woman's face before. Was it at the event the previous evening? But then, she'd been tired and maybe a little bit tipsy.

Then it hit her. It wasn't at the party, but when they were boarding the train. Loading had been chaos. Out of the corner of her eye, she'd seen a group of maybe five unhappy-looking women being escorted toward another car. Mina had been with them, along with several large men. Alterra had thought it was strange at the time, but she'd been so caught up with everything else that she'd forgotten.

Now that she replayed the scene in her head, it looked like a prisoner transfer. The women were being moved against their will, perhaps under threat of violence. The men weren't wearing uniforms, but Alterra was good at reading body language, and she felt a "prison guard" vibe from them. Also, two of the women appeared to be pregnant.

Did this train have a prison car? Was it a special car for expecting prisoners? Mina hadn't looked pregnant, but she could have been early in her pregnancy. She must have escaped the prison car after they left the station, and now she was somewhere on the train.

"Terra!"

Alterra blinked a few times. Detanna had been trying to get her attention. "Sorry," Alterra said. "Congrats on your wins, you've still got it."

"Is something wrong?" Detanna asked, looking concerned.

"Yes... No... sorry," she stumbled. "Does this train also transport prisoners?"

"I don't know," Detanna said. "But I know not all the cars are owned by the hotel. There are some cargo cars, some government-owned ones, and some are privately owned. So it's possible. Why?"

Alterra told her what she remembered from the night before. The more she described the scene, the more concerned Detanna looked.

"Think hard," Detanna said. "Did you see any of their hands? Can you remember if any of the women had tattoos?"

Alterra closed her eyes and reimagined the scene, trying to slow the action down. The whole scene was a jumble, and remembering such a minute detail was like trying to pause on a specific single frame of a movie.

She opened her eyes. "One of the women had a mark on the back of her hand," she said.

"Was it shaped like a pair of lips?" Detanna asked.

"Yes! Who are they?"

"It's an organization called Fetal Liberators United," Detanna said. "Or FLU. They're a militant anti-abortion group. They kidnap pregnant women who are planning to abort, and keep them locked up until they deliver. Then they keep the mothers as slaves, to help take care of the children."

Alterra's jaw dropped. "How are they able to operate in

the open like this?"

"This train passes through sixteen different countries as it circles Hermoso," Detanna explained. "Each of those countries has its own set of laws, some stricter than others. They don't want to have to tell passengers they can't drink for the next few hours, just because they're passing through a country that's banned alcohol. So when they were building the train, they made a deal with the countries it would pass through. The train is treated as its own sovereign nation, and each nation it goes through gets a small share of the company profits."

"So where are they taking the women?" Alterra asked.

"Probably to a country where abortion is illegal," Detanna answered. "And regardless of how many laws were broken kidnapping them and getting them on the train, now that they're here, it's too late. We could call the IGP right now and they'd tell us it's out of their hands."

"So there's nothing we can do for them?" Alterra asked.

"Legally? Probably not," Detanna answered.

Alterra paused. "And... illegally?" she asked.

"We need to find Mina," Detanna said. "We need to know more about this operation before we can come up with a plan."

The train had its own security crew, but they were comically ineffective. Detanna hadn't brought any of her Bloodstone gear on the trip, but she was never without resources. From her computer in their room, she easily hacked into the train's security cameras. Then she ran her own facial recognition software on the footage, which was far more advanced than whatever cheap software the train's security was using.

There was indeed a prison car, but if it had cameras, Detanna couldn't find them on the system. It was likely that the prison car had its own closed system. However, Detanna was able to find the moment Mina escaped. Footage from the next car showed one of the guards stepping out the door to the prison car, and Mina diving through his legs. Then she'd kicked him in the crotch before running away. The guard writhed on the floor for several seconds, and more guards tripped over him trying to get through the door, giving her a big head start.

One would think there wouldn't be too many places to hide on a train, but with each car the size of a small building, all she'd had to do was stay one step ahead of her pursuers. She'd switched hiding places every few hours, blended in with crowds a few times, and stolen some less conspicuous clothing. In fact, it didn't look like she'd had a chance to sleep since her escape.

"She's currently in a toilet stall six cars down," Detanna said.

"There are cameras in the toilets?" Alterra asked.

"One injustice at a time, please," Detanna said. "You go find her, and bring her back here. I'll watch the cameras in case she bolts."

Mina sat on a toilet seat. This restroom didn't seem to get a lot of traffic, so she felt like she'd be safe here for a while. She was hungry, and was tempted to sneak through the kitchen once the heat died down. She was also very tired. She didn't know what to do about that. There was no place she would feel safe enough to take a nap. She was afraid that if she shut her eyes too long, she'd wake up back in that slave car.

The restroom door opened, and she heard footsteps approaching the stalls. Mina pulled her feet up. There was a knock on the stall door. "Mina, I'm here to help you," a woman's voice said.

Yeah right, Mina thought. She'd heard that one before. The FLU had captured her by using a similar trap. She'd been looking for a way to get out of the country or off-planet, asking around in venues she'd thought were safe, only to put her trust in the wrong person. Never again.

Unfortunately she didn't have a lot of options right now. She couldn't climb over or under the stall walls without being caught. Her only choice was to fake compliance. She opened the door. "Oh thank you, thank you," she said, weeping. She didn't have to fake her tears. Mina rushed forward and hugged Alterra, keeping one hand behind her back.

"It's okay," Alterra said. "We need to…"

SPANG! Mina hit Alterra over the head with a wrench she'd picked up earlier, when she'd hidden in a maintenance closet. Alterra staggered backward, dazed. Mina sprinted for the door, opened it wide, and found herself face-to-face with a FLU agent. Mina retreated back into the restroom, followed by the agent.

She was trapped. The agent was between her and the restroom's only exit. She backed away slowly, as he drew his gun. Suddenly Mina felt a hand grab her collar from behind. Alterra pulled Mina away from the agent, and pushed her toward the stalls. Mina cowered in a stall and listened to the fight.

She heard several crunches and crashes, and the clatter of the gun as it went skidding across the floor . At one point one of them banged into the stalls, shaking the walls. The fight only lasted a few seconds. "Mina, help me tie him up," she heard.

Alterra was nearly unharmed. In fact, her worst injury had been from Mina. Working together, they tied the agent up with his own clothing, tightly knotting his hands and feet to a pipe behind one of the toilets.

Alterra pocketed the gun, and gave the agent's sunglasses to Mina. "Put these on," she said. It wasn't much, but they weren't going to spend much time in the crowded areas. On their way out of the restroom, Alterra found a "Closed for Maintenance" sign behind the door. Once they were back in the hallway, she attached the sign to the restroom door.

The hallway wasn't crowded, and the pair made it to the

stairs without being noticed. They went to the train's roof and rode a pod back to Alterra's hotel car. Then it was another nerve-wracking walk to Alterra's room without being recognized, but they made it.

They let Mina sleep in their bed while they discussed their options. When she finally woke, they gave her some food and asked her some questions. She was able to tell them that there were around twenty prisoners, and maybe ten agents, including the one Alterra had tied up.

"The wanted poster said you killed a child," Alterra said.

"I helped one of the other prisoners miscarry," Mina answered through a mouth full of bread. "They consider it murder. They're probably going to execute me if I go back with them. After I give birth, of course."

"So you are pregnant," Alterra asked.

"Yes," Mina answered. "I'm not far along. They only found out because I did an internet search on abortion options."

"Why lips?" Alterra wondered, eyeing the tattoo on Mina's hand.

"I can answer that one," Detanna said. "Their slogan is 'Life Is Precious and Sacred.' Originally they were going to call their organization LIPS instead of FLU, but there was already a chain of strip clubs with that name."

"Sacred, that's a laugh," Alterra said. "So sacred they're executing people. And the railroad is okay with this?"

"They make deals with the various countries they stop in," Detanna said. "They look the other way on things like this. They don't take any political stances of their own."

"Political stance?" Alterra asked. "Kidnapping women, forcing them to give birth, executing the ones who don't comply... that's beyond politics."

"Agreed," Detanna said, nodding.

"So can you get me out of here?" Mina asked.

Detanna nodded. "But if you're willing to work with us," she said, "I think we can save the other prisoners as well."

* * *

FLU supervisor Karvel Spence paced in his office. If they reached their destination without Mina, he would be demoted for sure. Especially if she got out and spread the word about their activities. His bosses might even have him executed for incompetence. How had his agents failed so badly? It was just a train, how many hiding places could there possibly be?

His comm unit beeped, and he answered it. "Sir? We have her."

Thank god, Spence thought. "Bring her to me at once," he said.

"There's a small problem, Sir. Her captor won't let her go without a reward."

Cursing up a storm, Spence left his office and headed for the front of the prison car.

"Thank you for bringing her in," Spence said. "I'll take her off your hands, now."

"Don't you know who I am?" Detanna asked, holding Mina tight. "Detanna Taush? Formerly known as Bloodstone? The bounty hunter?" Behind them, Alterra stood nearby, blending in with the crowd that had formed.

"There was no reward offered on the wanted poster," Spence said.

"I don't work for free," Detanna said. "Do you want me to let her go?"

"If you don't hand her over right now, I'll make sure you're charged with aiding her escape," Spence threatened.

"And I'll make sure every detail of your operation is made public," Detanna said.

How much does she know? Spence wondered. He couldn't risk it. "Okay, okay, you'll be compensated. Just let me go back to my office and I'll get the paperwork for a credit transfer."

"I'll come with you," Detanna said.

"No!" Spence shouted, holding up his hand. There was no way he was going to let her inside the car. There was just too much she shouldn't see. "Stay right here. I'll be right back."

Detanna nodded, holding Mina tighter. "I'd better find your offer worth my time."

As the door opened, Detanna pushed a button on her comm unit. All the lights went out in both cars. It was only dark for a few seconds, but it was all the time Alterra needed. She blended into the shadows and followed Spence through the door before it closed.

The prison car wasn't pretty. It had plain metal walls and floors that looked like they'd never been cleaned, judging by the grime and bloodstains. Cell doors lined the central hallway, which was patrolled by several agents. Spence was just entering his office, the only door in the hallway that wasn't barred.

Alterra was about to hide in the corner, her plan being to take out the guards one by one. Unfortunately, she was spotted. "Hey, you!" an agent shouted, pulling out his gun.

From the other side of the door, Detanna heard gunfire. On that cue, she pressed the button again. This time the lights stayed off a bit longer.

Alterra usually fought to incapacitate. She was a very precise fighter, and when possible, she targeted nerve clusters and pressure points designed to disarm her opponents or cause unconsciousness. But today, she was pissed. As she darted through the dark hallway, dodging gunfire and dispatching agents, she used moves designed to inflict the most pain possible. She killed no one, but every agent would be left with lasting reminders of this fight. Some would have a limp for the rest of their lives, others would find chewing solid foods difficult, and a few unfortunate souls would never again be able to sire children.

She saved Spence for last, and he probably got the worst of it. When she was sure there were no more threats, she released the prisoners, and they helped her drag the agents into the cells. A few of the freed women got their own revenge kicks in on the helpless agents, and Alterra looked the other way.

"And that's it," Alterra told Lillary. "The women were freed at the next station, and we helped get them off the planet. There was no way to punish the travel company legally, but we exposed their business practices. After several million one-star reviews on TripRank, they changed their policies."

"And did you and Detanna get your... alone time?" the doctor asked.

"We made them refund our train ticket," Alterra said. "Then we got a suite on the space station Stella 337, with a beautiful view of the rings of Thanda. It was a magical night."

"That's a great story," Lillary said. "And great timing. It looks like you're ready to go into the delivery room."

"No she's not," Tena said, walking through the door behind her. "She's going to have the baby right here."

"She's not a flight risk," Lillary said. "She's in labor. I have better equipment in the delivery room."

"I'm sure you'll do fine here," Tena said.

"At least let me get her something for the pain," Lillary said.

"Pain builds character," Tena said. "Besides, what could go wrong? I'll be right here to assist you the entire time."

Alterra screamed in agony as the delivery began.

03.02 *The Offer*

ED.02508.10.15

Aria Zenith Sarr-Taush was born on October 15th, 2508. For the first ten days, Alterra was given full access to her child. She was allowed to hold her baby for hours at a time, under supervision of course. The change in plan confused her, but she didn't complain. On the eleventh day, Alterra woke up in her hospital bed, expecting her child to be brought to her, but no one ever came. As usual, her breakfast arrived via android, but it wouldn't respond to her questions.

She ignored her breakfast and started talking to the cameras. "I know you're watching me, Tena. Where's Aria? Where's my child?" No answer. Around noon she was visited by Doctor Cleff and several android guards, who sedated her and transferred her back to her old cell under the Grand Palace.

Two excruciatingly slow days later, Tena came for a visit. "Your daughter's fine," Tena said as she entered the cell. Alterra stood up and stepped forward in a threatening manner. "…But she won't be if you lay a hand on me," Tena added.

Alterra stood perfectly still. "I want to see her," she said.

"How often you get to see her will depend on how cooperative you are," Tena said. "As will her survival."

Alterra glared, but she resisted the urge to rip Tena to shreds. Instead she just said, "What. Do. You. Want."

"I believe every child needs a mother and a father," Tena said. "My mother took me away from my father, and I spent years trying to get back to him, to earn his approval. It's honestly a miracle I turned out so well adjusted."

"Get to the point, Tena."

"You know, you could really stand to learn a little civility," Tena said. "I did what I promised. I gave you the best medical care possible. Your childbirth went off without a hitch. I even let you have some bonding time. I thought it might help you make the right decision."

Alterra said nothing.

Tena shrugged. "I'm not really cut out for motherhood. I'm willing to let you raise the child. But only if you follow the rules. Otherwise, I'll find someone else, and you'll never see her again. You can take it or leave it."

"The rules?" Alterra asked.

"You will marry Andoro Korr," Tena said. "You will live as husband and wife, and you will bear him many more wonderful children. You will train them in the martial arts of your people. You will raise them to be perfect assassins. You will teach them to be loyal to me above all others. Oh, and you'll receive a minor operation."

"Operation?"

"Well, obviously I can't have you trying to escape all the time," Tena said. "So you'll be wearing an explosive implant. Stray too far from the palace, and boom. Try to hurt me, and boom. Disobey the rules and boom."

"And if I say no?"

"Your loss. The results will be about the same anyway. Andoro will raise your children, I'll still make sure he has access to you sexually, and I'll still force you to bear him more children. You'll have just as many children, you just won't ever see them."

Again, Alterra was speechless.

"I'll give you a few days to think it over. Ta!" Tena left the cell and locked the door.

Alterra sat on her cot for a few minutes, took several deep breaths, then screamed so loud she went hoarse.

03.03 Prep Time

ED.02508.10.30

"You can't just rush the palace," Lemondrop said. "She's already stopped two coup attempts, do you really think you can breach the place by yourself?"

Detanna was halfway into her Bloodstone gear, double-checking her weapons and making sure all her tech still worked. "How much longer do you want me to wait? The child has to have been born by now. And that means Alterra's outlived her usefulness."

"I understand," Lemondrop said in a soothing voice. "I really do. But getting yourself killed isn't going to help her. I promise you, as soon as we hear from Raven..."

Lemondrop's comm unit beeped. She and Detanna looked at each other, hope in their eyes.

The screen said the call was from Dervish. Detanna sighed and went back to loading ammo. Lemondrop put the call on speaker.

"Hey, it's Dervish. Listen, I just got a message from Raven..."

The Bloodwind approached Valos. Hundreds of Grunthian warships stared them down. The communicator beeped, and Zak answered it. "Yo!" he said.

A Grunthian with a rhino-like horn appeared on the screen. He spoke in Grunthian, but the computer translated. "You are not authorized to be here. State your business or be destroyed."

Zak leaned close to the camera and said, "We're going to land in front of the Grand Palace, walk in through the front doors, kill every guard we see, take Tena and her allies into custody, and maybe, if we have time, get in some sightseeing."

"You fool!" the Grunthian said. "Tena has no patience for your pathetic attempt at humor, and neither do I!"

Zak turned to his right. "It's now or never, Raven."

"Just keep him talking a little longer," Raven said, furiously tapping buttons on her console.

"Ugh, fine," he said, turning back to the communicator. "Sorry, sorry mister Grunthian sir, I thought you could use a good laugh. I'm actually here to join Tena's forces. She could use a guy like me on her team."

The Grunthian was having none of it. "You have been identified as the bounty hunter 'Parzak.' You are a known associate of several of Tena's enemies. You will now be destroyed."

"Yeah, but that was the old me," Zak said. "Now I'm totally into all the evil and the killing innocent people and… kicking puppies and…" he stopped talking when the Grunthian ended the call.

Their weapons are powering up, Trenyn reported from Zak's left.

"Transmission sent," Raven said. The entire crew of the Bloodwind stood behind them, holding their breath.

Several hundred Grunthian ships aimed their warcannons at the Bloodwind, ready to fire. Then, all at once, they lost power. Tena's entire fleet floated dead in space.

"Hot damn, it actually worked," Zak said.

We spent nearly six months working on this virus, Trenyn

answered. *Surely you had a little faith in us.*

"Of course, of course," Zak said, wiping the sweat from his brow. "Now, let's go do all that stuff I just said."

Wisp stepped forward. "Shouldn't we wait for Earth's allied forces to get here?"

"I'd rather strike fast and hard," Zak replied. "Tena's going to know something's up pretty soon."

"I know Bloodstone's not going to wait on us," Raven said.

Knowing her, we'll be lucky if there's anything left of Tena when we get there, Trenyn remarked.

"Sounds like a consensus to me," Zak said. "I'm taking her in."

There was no place to land the Bloodwind near the Grand Palace, at least not if they wanted to retain the element of surprise. Glik stayed aboard the freighter while the rest of them took a shuttle to the surface. Then the Bloodwind flew to a safe distance from Valos, so it could communicate with the space forces that would be arriving soon.

The sun was setting as the shuttle landed at the port closest to the palace. Four android guards stood nearby as the shuttle door opened. Their weapons trained on the door, one shouted, "You are not authorized to land here. Come out with your hands above your head!"

Four virtrinium blades flew out of the shuttle's hatch, one for each android. All four were decapitated before they could react. Trenyn stepped out of the hatch, and the shards returned to hover near their head.

The rest of the crew followed Trenyn down the ramp. First Zak and Yeela, followed by Wisp, Vex, Sekka and her pets, Midnight, and finally Raven, who was talking into her comm unit.

"Lemondrop says her team is on the way," Raven reported, putting away her comm.

"What's the plan?" Wisp said.

"I thought we were going to walk in through the front door," Zak said.

"Sure, if we want to get killed immediately," Yeela said.

"Take it from someone with experience breaching castles," Wisp said. "The back door is always the better option."

"I know some secret ways in," Raven said.

"We'd better hurry," Vex said. "They'll be all over us soon."

Raven led them toward a secret tunnel into the palace.

03.04 *The Final Battle*

ED.02508.10.30

The cell door opened, and Andoro stepped through. "Have you considered Tena's offer?" he asked.

Alterra sat on the cot, staring at the wall. "I'll do anything for my child," she said finally. "But know that I will always look for any way to escape with Aria. You may have my body, but Detanna already has my heart. I will never truly be yours."

"Fine with me," Andoro said.

Alterra turned to face him. "Really? That's all you want from me? A warm-blooded sex doll you can screw and put away?"

"I loved you, Alterra," he said. "From the moment I learned we were to be bonded."

"You didn't know me. You still don't."

"I know you're one of the best fighters I've ever seen," he said. "What else is there to know? That's all I'd ever wanted out of a partner anyway. Well, that and a great ass." He hoped she'd laugh at that. She didn't.

Alterra thought a moment. "What if I challenged you to a duel? For my freedom?"

"Why would I do that? I've already won."

"Sure," Alterra said. "But what if you could really have

me? Mind, body, and soul?"

"What are you saying?"

Ugh, Alterra thought. "If I win, you let me and Aria go."

"Tena would never agree to that."

"Tell her we died trying to escape or something. But if you win, I'll try to learn to love you. You seem to think that I'd love you if I gave you a chance, so I'll actually make the effort. And if it doesn't work, I'll at least fake it really well, and never try to escape."

"Alterra…"

"Yes?"

"How dumb do you think I am?"

"You really don't want me to answer that," she said. "But fine. How about we fight anyway, just because I want one last chance to punch you in your stupid face before I become your lifelong slave?"

"Now, that I'll agree to," he said. "When and whe—"

Alterra punched him in his stupid face.

Raven led the group through a secret tunnel, which led to the dungeon level. Some of the cells had prisoners in them, but no one they recognized. They were probably citizens who had questioned Tena's rule. They tried to open the cell doors, but they required a keycard. They were about to try shooting one of the doors open, when they heard a muffled banging from one of the cells down the hall.

They looked through the small window and saw Alterra and Andoro beating each other senseless. Both were unarmed, and the room was too small for most of their usual martial arts moves. For the most part, they grappled and punched each other.

"If Lemondrop were here, she might know an override," Raven said.

Is there any way we can hack it? Trenyn asked.

"I might be able to interface with the software if I can find a command center," Yeela offered.

"Guys," Zak said, "That might not be necessary."

Alterra now stood over Andoro, his keycard in her hand. She opened the door, and was surprised to find she had an audience. They locked Andoro in the cell, then used the keycard to open the rest of the doors in the hallway. For the citizens who wanted to leave, Raven pointed out the way they'd come in. But the majority of them decided to stay and fight. They found some weapons and clothing in the nearby storage room, then took the stairs up to the main level.

A battle was already in progress in the main foyer. Lemondrop led Karden, Bloodstone, Dervish, and a mob of angry rebels into battle against a small army of androids. "*She* got to use the front door," Zak muttered. The two groups became one, and soon the sounds of battle echoed throughout the palace.

"Looks like your sibling's leading the charge," Synthral said.

Tena sighed. "Call in more androids. From all over the town, I don't care what else they're guarding. Then go down and join them."

"My pleasure," Synthral said, tapping out some orders on his comm unit. Then he drank a vial of Andoro's blood and left.

"They knew the rules," Tena said. "Now they're going to pay." She picked up her comm unit. Across the galaxy, five more fleets of Grunthian warships waited near Galea, Chirminon, Magnar, Kalara, and Earth. Tena's thumb hovered over the send button. Once pressed, there would be no going back. Total galactic war. There would be huge losses on both sides, but Tena liked her odds. Those warships were tough, and more than capable of razing a planet into molten rubble.

"Eh, whatever," she said, and pressed the button. Then she went to her wardrobe and put on her most exquisite red dress. It sparkled in the light and had a scandalously low neckline. Company was coming, she had to look her best.

Once she was satisfied with her appearance, she went to check on the baby.

The battle downstairs went in waves. Every time they thought they had the way cleared, more androids showed up. They weren't difficult to defeat, but there were just so many of them, and everyone was tiring.

Trenyn's flying blades were highly effective at severing android heads and limbs, but they worked best at a distance. When an android got too close, it was all Trenyn could do to keep from getting shot. But Raven always had their back, her own robotic body built from much sturdier materials than these mass-produced guardbots.

Bloodstone and Zak fought side by side, mentor and student now equals. They took out android after android with their energy pistols. Yeela hovered nearby, firing her own energy blasts from above. Sekka took refuge wherever she could, while her steelbeak buzzers distracted the androids by flying in their faces. Occasionally her pet squirrel would climb up an android's body and pull out its power cell.

Lemondrop wasn't much of a fighter, but her presence alone served as inspiration to the dozens of Valos citizens who fought beside her. Karden stayed as close to her as possible, ready to die for her if it came to that.

Vex threw her AON daggers over and over, calling them back and throwing them again, slashing at any androids that got too close. Midnight, who had been a professional soldier on Galea, easily picked off enemies with his energy rifle.

Dervish stayed at the edges of the crowd, occasionally throwing a tentacled arm into the melee to pull out an android and dispatch it. Wisp also tried to avoid melee, her bow picking off androids from a distance. Lyryssa was under the influence of Wisp's blood, and she tore into the androids with great ferocity.

Though she wasn't well armed, Alterra probably fought the hardest. Guns weren't her thing, so she fought with a shortsword she'd borrowed from Wisp. Now she watched as Wisp sought high ground at the top of the stairs. There was an elevator behind her. That would be the fastest route to the penthouse, where she could find Tena. And hopefully, Aria.

As Alterra fought her way up the stairs, there was a ding and the elevator doors opened. Out stepped a hooded figure, accompanied by four more androids. These androids looked different than the others, however. They were red instead of gold, and had four arms. As these elite bots joined the battle, Synthral lifted his hood and his robes fell to the floor, revealing nothing underneath. Completely invisible, he picked out his prey.

Less than an hour from Earth, a fleet of Grunthian warships sat at the ready, waiting for Tena's signal. The order came in, and they powered up their engines. This would be a glorious day in the history of the Grunthian Empire. Or it would have been, if their power hadn't suddenly gone out.

The signal had not actually come from Tena. It had come from Doctor Eshton, who stood on the bridge of an IGP ship not too far away. By answering the transmission, they had activated Raven's virus. At this very moment, similar scenarios occurred near Galea, Chirminon, Magnar, and Kalara.

In orbit above Valos, the most boring space battle in history was being waged. The arriving IGP ships, while much less intimidating than the Grunthian warships, had their foes completely helpless. The Grunthians refused to surrender, nor would they be taken prisoner. So the IGP ships meticulously took out each warship's weapons systems with carefully placed shots. Meanwhile, some of the Grunthian warships randomly exploded as their fearless captains found creative ways to avoid capture.

The elite bots were programmed to take out the biggest threats first, but their method of calculating threat levels mostly involved scanning each enemy's weapons and tech. They concluded that their most dangerous opponents were Zak, Midnight, Raven, and Bloodstone. Each of the bots picked one of the four and went straight for them, their hands turning into buzzsaws and other destructive instruments.

Alterra was almost to the elevator when something grabbed her around the waist. She tried to stab it but an invisible force grabbed her wrist. She pounded on her unseen opponent with her free hand, but it didn't seem to feel much pain. Synthral shoved his claws into her side, causing her to lose her footing. The two tumbled back down the stairs together.

Technically Lyryssa was also invisible, but she was fully dressed including a mask, so she didn't look much different. But her blood euphoria allowed her to see Synthral. She rushed to Alterra's aid, avoiding the blows of several enemy androids along the way.

Raven was not well armed, but one of the elite bots had targeted her anyway, probably after scanning her robotic body. As it leaped at her, she fired a few times with her energy pistol, but it had no effect. It knocked the pistol out of her hand, and she grabbed the wrists of its two upper arms. The bot's lower hands, now buzzsaws, started cutting into her metal torso.

Zak and Bloodstone stood back to back, each contending with their own elite bot. Their energy weapons were useless, but they both packed a variety of weaponry. Zak fired a small magnetic disc at his opponent. It stuck to the bot's torso and exploded, but didn't do much damage.

"No, like this," Bloodstone said, raising her gun behind her head, and firing it backward over Zak's shoulder.

Bloodstone's helmet had a heads-up display linked to the gun's scope, and she easily hit Zak's opponent in one of its shoulder joints. As Bloodstone fended off her own adversary's attacks with an AON knife, her magnetic explosive blew the arm off of Zak's opponent.

"Show off," Zak said, then dropped to the floor. Ducking between her legs, Zak fired two discs at Bloodstone's opponent, each adhering to the bot's knees. The charges erupted and the elite bot toppled to the floor. With her own foe down, Bloodstone spun around and slashed the other bot across its neck. The AON blade easily severed the android's head from its shoulders.

While Zak finished off the crawling elite bot, Bloodstone looked around to see who else needed help. Midnight was holding his own against one elite bot, but Raven was on the floor, pinned by another elite. Bloodstone started to rush to Raven's aid, but Trenyn beat her to it. Multiple virtrinium blades took out the bot's arms and neck. Bloodstone shrugged and fired a disc at the neck of the bot attacking Midnight. The bot's head popped off like a champagne cork.

Alterra continued to fight her invisible foe. Synthral had let go of her waist, only to knock her back down to the floor whenever she tried to stand up. His blows always came from unexpected directions, and his wickedly sharp fingernails hurt like heck. Alterra was no stranger to blind fighting, but she was used to picking up sound cues from her opponents, and it was just too noisy in this foyer. She screamed as Synthral bit into her neck, refreshing his euphoria as he tasted her delicious Auroran blood.

Lyryssa came to Alterra's rescue, tackling Synthral and tearing into him like a rabid animal. Thinking himself invisible, he hadn't been expecting a direct attack, and Lyryssa pressed her advantage. Unfortunately, once the element of surprise wore off, Synthral proved to be much stronger than his attacker. His blood frenzy was also fresher, having just tasted Alterra's blood, and he quickly pinned Lyryssa to the floor. He relentlessly stabbed at her with his clawed hands, and Lyryssa could barely defend herself, much less counterattack.

Then Synthral's head went flying. Alterra had recovered her shortsword, and had judged Synthral's position based on how Lyryssa was pinned. It wasn't as clean a cut as it would have been against a visible opponent, but dead was dead. She reached out her hand to help Lyryssa up.

"I'll be fine," Lyryssa said. "Go save your daughter."

Alterra rushed to the top of the stairs. Wisp stood nearby, giving her cover by picking off androids that tried to follow. A few of her allies made it too, rushing into the elevator before the doors closed. The elevator probably could have fit five or six more, but Alterra didn't dare wait any longer.

At the foot of the staircase, Bloodstone watched the doors close. *Zarg it,* she thought. Surely there were stairs, but that would take forever. She wondered if there was another elevator somewhere. Raven would know. Bloodstone spotted her still on the floor, Trenyn reaching down to help her to her feet. A few androids remained, but no new ones had joined the battle in a while.

The elevator took several minutes to climb up to the highest level. In addition to Alterra, it held Zak and Yeela, Vex, Lemondrop, and five citizens of Valos. On the way up, Zak reloaded his weapons, and Lemondrop applied a bandage to one of the wounded citizens. No one spoke for the entire ride.

The doors opened to a short hallway. On the opposite end, a set of double doors led into Tena's bedroom. The doors were wide open, as if in invitation. "Okay, before we go in…" Zak started to say.

Alterra ignored him, and charged forward. "Tena!" she roared. "Where are you?"

"I'm out here," came a pleasant-sounding reply.

Alterra looked around the opulent room and spotted the open doors to the balcony. Tena sat on the marble railing, looking ready for an exclusive gala. Beside her, also sitting precariously on the railing, was a basket. Tena leaned over the basket and made little cooing noises. Alterra could hear crying noises from the basket.

Alterra stomped forward. "Ah ah ah," Tena said, wagging her finger. "One more step and I drop her." She picked up the basket by the handle and held it over the side. Alterra stood perfectly still. Her allies arrived beside her, also freezing when they realized what was happening.

"Please give me back my child," Alterra said, her voice suddenly hoarse.

"I'll consider it," Tena said playfully. "But only if you do something for me first."

"What," Alterra mouthed, no actual sound coming out.

"Stab Lemondrop through the heart right now," Tena said.

"What?" Alterra asked. "No, I... I..."

Lemondrop put down her rifle and turned toward Alterra, her arms spread wide. "It's okay, Alterra," she said. "Just do it. Anything for your baby." Alterra turned her sword toward Lemondrop. A couple of the citizens raised their weapons against Alterra, but Lemondrop waved them away.

"No," Alterra said finally, dropping her sword. "I just can't. Give me something else to do. Anythi—"

"Oops," Tena said, dropping the basket.

Yeela zoomed overhead, out the door, and over the side of the balcony.

"You *monster*," Alterra growled, fire in her eyes. She charged at Tena at full speed. She no longer held a weapon, intending to tear Tena apart with her bare hands.

Tena rolled her eyes, then stared them all down. "Kill each other," she said, her eyes glowing. Then she sat back and watched the chaos unfold.

Everyone but Lemondrop went for each other's throats. Alterra knocked Zak to the ground, Vex threw herself at

Lemondrop, and the rest of the citizens clawed at each other like wild animals. Lemondrop tried talking to Vex, but that was a difficult task while Vex was clawing at her eyes.

"Please," Lemondrop said, her eyes glowing. "Calm. Calm. Calm." She repeated it over and over, until Vex finally looked into her eyes and the spell was broken. Realizing what had happened, Vex pulled Alterra off of Zak while Lemondrop calmed them. One of the citizens was already dead, but the rest were full of vigor and rage.

While Zak, Vex, and Lemondrop attempted to calm the citizens, Alterra once again charged at Tena. The two locked arms, and Alterra tried to throw Tena over the balcony. Unfortunately, Alterra was tired and unarmed, while Tena was well-rested and had natural weapons. Easily dodging Alterra's grasping hands, Tena caught her with a hard punch to the face that broke her jaw and knocked her out cold. Tena lifted her foot above Alterra's head, a spiked heel ready to come down on the back of her skull.

From the hallway on the other side of the bedroom, the elevator dinged and the doors opened. Bloodstone spotted Tena from across the bedroom, raised her weapon, and fired repeatedly while marching in Tena's direction. She emptied the chamber of her gun, firing a total of seventeen explosive rounds, hitting Tena repeatedly in the face and chest. Tena staggered backward and tumbled over the side of the balcony.

Bloodstone rushed to Alterra's aid. Behind her, a few more allies filed out of the elevator. Karden, Midnight, Dervish, and several more citizens entered the bedroom, eager to help out. The last crazed citizen was calmed, and everyone started helping the wounded. Alterra woke up and tried to speak, but it hurt too much to open her mouth.

Every head turned as they saw movement from the balcony. Yeela rose into view, the basket dangling from her grappling hook. She set the basket down safely on the floor. Bloodstone rushed to the basket and retrieved the baby. It was the first time she'd seen Aria, and she wept with joy.

Alterra reached for the baby, and Detanna took the opportunity to remove her helmet so she could see her child better.

It was finally over. They could go home now, as a family.

03.05 *Not Quite Dead*

ED.02508.10.30

After Tena's body landed on the front walkway, victory was declared, and most of the citizens went home to heal. Wisp, Raven, Trenyn, and a handful of Valosian citizens remained in the foyer, helping those who were too wounded to move. A few others waited for the elevator to return to the ground floor, so they could see what the situation was upstairs.

Now there came a commotion from outside, screams of terror and confusion. Wisp turned her head just as a monstrous figure burst through the front doors of the palace.

Tena – or what was left of her – staggered into the foyer, leaving an impossibly wide trail of blood behind. Her chest had erupted wide open, and several of her organs were visible, including her beating heart. Her face was a smashed-up mess, with large portions of her head missing. Wisp stared in horror as she realized that not only was this woman still breathing... but she was healing. As Wisp watched, Tena's broken bones knit back together, her wounds started to close, and her skull began to reform.

So she had inherited her father's immortality after all. Wisp had suspected this for a while. From what she'd heard of the fight on Mars, she'd found Tena's survival to be a bit beyond belief. Now she knew why.

Raven and the others started toward Tena, fascinated. "Stay back," Wisp ordered, reaching for her special dagger. "This is my fight." She didn't mean for it to sound like a cheesy movie line, but she knew that her dagger was the only weapon that could kill Tena forever.

But she would have to act fast. Tena was healing at an amazing rate. Wisp threw her dagger at the pulsating red target in Tena's chest. Her aim was true, and flew straight for its mark. Until Tena caught it.

Sweet mother of god, Wisp thought.

Wisp rushed forward, drawing a pair of not-nearly-as-special daggers as she went. They fought in a frenzy of knives and fingernails, of parries and thrusts and cuts and gashes. Wisp got in several good hits, but Tena healed faster than she took in new wounds. Wisp would never wear her down at this rate.

Wisp managed to thrust a dagger in Tena's throat, but rather than die, she retaliated by stabbing Wisp in the leg. Wisp screamed in pain, but continued to thrust her own dagger in deeper. If she could just subdue Tena long enough for a death blow...

Trenyn's virtrinium blades flew in, cutting off Tena's arms. Without a moment's hesitation, Wisp removed the special dagger from her leg and thrust it into Tena's heart. Tena fell backward and stopped moving. And more importantly, she stopped healing.

Sorry if I stole your moment, Trenyn told her. *But it looked like you could use some help.*

"Thank you," Wisp said, gritting her teeth. Her leg was in agony. She'd been stabbed before, sometimes gravely wounded. But something felt different about this one. The pain was spreading throughout her body at a rapid rate. "Burn Tena's body to ash, then fire the ashes into a star," she said, then passed out.

03.06 Wrap-Up

ED.02508.10.31

Wisp woke up in a hospital bed, as did half the people in Valos City. Her leg still hurt, as well it should have, but now it hurt in a more conventional way. She couldn't explain it, and it was impossible to prove it, but she felt like she was no longer immortal. Of course, she wouldn't know for sure until the next time she died, or rather, about twelve or thirteen years after that.

But she was in no hurry to find out. She would take this life as it came, and do whatever made her happy. And hopefully someday – many decades from now – she would die peacefully in her sleep, one last time.

None of the other Vermon heirs ever showed any sign of immortality. Whatever nanotechnological glitch had caused Wisp's and Lord Vermon's longevity was now erased from the universe. Wisp still held onto her dagger, however. Just in case.

The Council of Heirs was disbanded, and the citizens of Valos were allowed to vote for a new leader. However, they still elected Lemondrop Vermon to be their first president. She appointed Karden to be her Vice-President. Dervish became the Director of Sapient Rights, a position which allowed her to fight for the freedoms of sapient species often considered "slave races" by unenlightened governments.

Sekka was offered the title of "Secretary of the Department of Wildlife," but turned it down. She didn't want to be stuck behind a desk, talking about animals instead of communing with them. Instead, she took the position of "Wildlife Coordinator," a more hands-on job that allowed her to visit the planet's wildlife preserves and make recommendations based on the needs of the animal populations.

The reward for Tena's capture spent several months in legal limbo. Arguably, defeating Tena had been a group effort, and the eyewitness reports of her final moments varied wildly. In the end, the potential recipients of the reward unanimously agreed to give the money to charity, so no legal battles ensued. The majority of the money ended up going to the displaced citizens of Vhelra.

The Grunthians were not pleased by the outcome of recent events. They had lost their alliance with Valos, their newly-built fleet had been rendered useless, and in their eyes, they had been made to look weak in front of the entire galaxy. The newest Grag Prime was immediately executed, and the Grunthians became even more xenophobic. Sooner or later they would start an interplanetary war, but only when they were confident that they would win.

Detanna and Alterra raised their daughter in peace. Raven returned to Earth to work on a special project for the IGP, but Trenyn decided to stay on Valos for the time being. Doctor Eshton began research to see if Andoro's method of teleportation could be applied to spaceships.

Midnight returned to Galea, to resume his position as the head of WARCAT. Bounty hunting had been a temporary job for him, just a way to keep Galea in the loop while the galaxy hunted Tena. Now that Galea was no longer in danger, he went back to his former passion: anti-terrorist military operations.

As for Zak, Vex, Yeela, Glik, and Lyryssa, the remaining

Bloodhunters continued working as a team, apprehending dangerous criminals and keeping the public safe... as long as the price was right.

03.07 *Epilogue*

ED.02508.11.14

"So whatever happened to Andoro?" Detanna asked, trying to get a piece of tape off of her fingers.

"He escaped somehow," Alterra said. Her jaw was still healing, but she felt much better. She was taking it easy, letting Detanna do all the work. She lay back on the bed, half reading a book on her tablet, and half watching Detanna's attempts to diaper a wiggling infant. "A couple of cameras caught him sneaking down the hall of the detention wing, but after that, he just vanished."

"That's too bad. You think he'll come after you again?"

"With his track record? I'm not too worried about it," Alterra said.

Detanna nodded, still trying to get the diaper to stay closed. "I still have one question though," Detanna said.

"What's that?"

"Tena's plan," Detanna said. "She kept trying to clone you. She thought Aurorans would make the ultimate assassins. Then she partnered with Andoro, an Auroran. So why didn't she try to clone him?"

Alterra shrugged, taking a sip from her smoothie. "My guess is that it would take too much time. She couldn't build another Chronal Accelerator without Doctor X's help, and without that, she'd be stuck raising the clones in real-time. Patience wasn't one of Tena's strong suits."

Detanna nodded. "I suppose that make sense," she said, holding up the now-diapered baby. "How'd I do?" As she asked the question, the diaper fell off, and Aria began peeing on the floor.

"Don't quit your day job," Alterra laughed, nearly choking on her smoothie.

Across town, in a secret underground compound, the lights slowly flickered on. Andoro Korr entered the lab, taking stock of Tena's unfinished projects. She'd been busy, far busier than she'd ever told him. Andoro saw several vials of unusual toxins, blueprints for a couple of large weapons, a cryo tube labeled "Marae 521," and several unassembled assassin bots. But it was what he found on the back wall that interested him most.

Twenty clear tubes were lined up against the wall. Each was filled with synthetic amniotic liquid. Floating in each tube was a fetus, suspended from an umbilical cord, being fed by a sack of artificial nutrients.

"My sons," Andoro said, as an evil grin spread across his face. Maybe his plans weren't as grand as Tena's, but it gave him great satisfaction to imagine what his progeny would accomplish. It wouldn't be easy, and it would take years, but the payoff would be oh so worth the trouble.

As Andoro pictured a future with himself as the leader of Valos, surrounded by his grown-up sons and mountains of money, he heard a beeping. Near the door, a monitor flickered on. A computer-generated version of Tena's face appeared on the screen.

"Attention," the image said. "Your presence is unauthorized. You will now be destroyed. Buh-bye!" The screen flickered off, and four side panels slid open around the room. From each panel emerged a four-armed elite security bot, armed with energy cannons and AON blades.

Great, Andoro thought, drawing his swords. He was hopelessly outgunned, but he'd faced worse odds. He rushed towards the nearest bot, his AON swords hungry for action.

Bonus Stories

04.00   *Itropa: The Self-Fulfilling Prophecy*

ED.02508.11.15

"Castle's ablaze!" the beggar cried, waving his arms wildly. He needn't have bothered; the billowing smoke was easily seen from across the town, and the castle guards had already begun blowing the emergency horns. Nevertheless, the crazed vagrant ran up and down the street, pointing at the castle, and warning the nearby citizens.

The beggar stumbled backward, nearly getting run over by a horse-drawn carriage. The carriage held the town's fire brigade, but their buckets of water wouldn't be enough for this fire. Still off balance, the beggar stumbled as he turned, walking face-first into an armored warrior. It was like running into a wall. The beggar took a few steps back to take in this mountain of a man.

The man wore rusty iron armor that covered most of his body. His helmet obscured his face so that only his eyes were visible. There was a two-handed greatsword strapped to his back. He stood a full head taller than the beggar. This intimidating warrior bent down on one knee and addressed the vagrant. "Is the queen still inside?" he asked.

"I... I think so," the beggar stammered. "She lives in the

central tower. The lower floors are in flames."

The warrior stood up and made haste for the castle.

Queen Felorna was not one to panic, but she knew she was running out of options. She was halfway up the tower, already too high to risk climbing out of the windows. The first two floors of the tower had doors that opened into the castle. However, she'd already tried both doors, and they wouldn't budge. Her only option now was to climb the steps of the tower, hide out on the highest floor, and hope the flames were extinguished before they reached her.

She opened every window she passed, in the hopes of delaying suffocation. Most of the windows were too narrow for her to fit through, and those that she could were too high. The narrow windows had been a safety measure to prevent thieves and assassins. Since the castle was made of stone, the builders never considered the threat of fire. But this fire was different. Looking out a tower window, she could see some of the flames right now. They had a green tinge and persisted even across stone.

The Queen covered her mouth with a lace handkerchief, and continued her way up the circular staircase.

The iron-clad warrior ran past the bucket brigade, noting that their water didn't seem to be having much effect. He pushed past some fleeing servants, and climbed the stairs to the second floor. When he could go no higher, he wandered the smoke-filled castle, looking for the entrance to the tower. Ripping a piece of tablecloth from an end table, he lifted his visor, placed the cloth over his nose and mouth, then shut the visor. It didn't help much.

He reached a clearing where the smoke wasn't as bad, due to several broken windows and a crosswind. He noted that there was glass all over the floor beneath the windows, and realized they had been broken from the outside. Then he heard fighting up ahead, and a woman's voice shouted,

"Protect the queen!" He ran forward, past several patches of greenish flame, through another wall of smoke, and into another clearing.

There were three women up ahead, fighting off several hooded men in black clothing. One of the women was human, with fiery red hair, fighting with a sword and shield. The other women were moonfolk. One had reddish skin and white hair. She fought with a wooden staff, but seemed just as proficient with her fists and feet. The other moonfolk was younger, pale-skinned, and had a bow and arrow strapped to her back. However, instead of using her bow, she held a silver wand that kept firing bursts of lightning at her foes.

The warrior didn't want to make any snap judgments, but it seemed pretty obvious which ones were here to save the queen, and which ones were assassins. If nothing else, the red-haired woman wore the kingdom's crest on her shield, and the hooded fighters wore no such sigils. Darkwynde drew his greatsword and joined the fray.

There were more assassins than he'd initially thought. More kept running in from down the hall, and Darkwynde kept cutting them down. The swordswoman also made her fair share of kills. The two moonfolk held their own, their attacks incapacitating their foes rather than killing them.

Once the final assassin was dispatched, they wasted no time. "To the queen!" the redhead shouted, and the rest followed. She seemed to know where she was going. Soon they reached the tower entrance. A table and several chairs were stacked in front of the door, blocking it from opening. The four heroes cleared the furniture and entered the tower. The smoke was much thicker here, and they all struggled to breathe.

More assassins appeared behind them, and the group engaged them. "Get to the queen," Darkwynde shouted, "I'll hold them off!" The women balked at first, then realized the stairway was too narrow to fight side-by-side anyway, so they relented. The redheaded fighter and the white-haired moonfolk ran up the stairs to find the Queen. Darkwynde fought off assassin after assassin. The archer moonfolk stayed behind and fired arrows through Darkwynde's legs.

Eventually the assassins stopped coming, and the rest of the party came back down the stairs. The queen was unconscious, and the red-haired woman carried her over her shoulder. When they left the tower, they noticed that some of the flames had died down. By the time they reached the first floor, the flames were gone.

The queen was fine, and the four were heralded as heroes. Before they could split up, a child approached them and handed each of them a note. Darkwynde read his aloud. "Meet me at the Purple Eel tavern in one hour for your reward."

"Who gave you this?" the red-haired woman started to say, but the child had already run off.

One hour later, the four reunited at the tavern and found a table together. They had already exchanged names after the battle, but now they got to know each other a bit better.

Darkwynde told them he was a traveling warrior, just trying to make a name for himself. He'd come from a small village, and was looking for a grand adventure. But whenever the others asked him for details about his home town, he deflected the questions.

Valaria Cornen was one of the queen's personal guards. She'd been the first one on the scene when the fires erupted. She didn't need a reward for doing her job, but she'd still been intrigued enough to come. After all, their benefactor might have information about the assassins.

Brynwyn Elswyth was a moonfolk from the forests. Her townspeople hadn't responded well when she'd shown them her new weapon. After accusing her of being in league with an evil wizard, they had forbidden her from returning. She had come to Southhaven to look for work. When she'd seen the castle was on fire, she ran in to help those trapped inside.

Serena was also a moonfolk, but she lived here in Southhaven. She was unable to speak, and communicated with the others using a writing tablet and some chalk.

They'd been talking for about ten minutes when an older human in dark robes walked over. Serena recognized him immediately, and hugged him before they sat back down. "Greetings, everyone, my name is Dakeel." He tossed each of them a small bag of gold pieces. "There's more where that came from, if you'll hear me out."

"I'm listening," Darkwynde said.

"Wouldn't you be more comfortable without the helmet?" Dakeel asked.

Darkwynde looked around, then shook his head. "I can hear you just fine."

"Suit yourself," Dakeel said. "I'm a seer. Serena here can vouch for me. I found her when she was but a child, a poor mute orphan, and I raised her." Serena nodded as he spoke, confirming his claims. Dakeel had instructed Serena to wait in the castle today, having predicted trouble. His prediction had come true, just as they always did.

"A seer? I don't believe in fortune tellers," Valaria said.

"That's too bad," Dakeel said. "Because I had a vision, and you were in it."

"Prove it," Valaria said.

"You were a child of the mountains," Dakeel said.

Valaria looked unimpressed. "Because I have red hair?"

"You were an orphan," Dakeel added, and Valaria's mouth dropped open. "Your foster father named you Priscilla, but you always hated that name. You were the youngest in the household, with seven adopted brothers. You constantly felt the need to prove you were just as strong as them. When your foster father tried to enroll you in finishing school, you rebelled and applied for the royal guard instead."

"Enough," Valaria said. "I'm not saying I'm convinced,

but you've earned my attention. What was your vision?"

"I saw the castle in flames," Dakeel said. "And the queen's life in danger from assassins. But four heroes would appear and save the queen's life. One of those heroes would go on to save the world from a great evil."

"One of us?" Darkwynde asked, hopeful. This could be the opportunity he'd been looking for.

"Indeed," Dakeel said.

"So what do you want us to do?" Brynwyn asked.

"You will travel far to the East," Dakeel said. "You will find a town occupied by men with the countenance of lizards. There, you will retrieve the Crimson Orb. We will need it to defeat the coming evil."

Valaria was the only one who had to think it over. Darkwynde had been itching for a good quest, Brynwyn was already an outcast looking for a purpose, and Serena always trusted in her adoptive father's wisdom. In the end, Valaria decided that she couldn't risk harm befalling her kingdom. Her position as a palace guard would be easily filled, but her role in saving the world could only be filled by her. Assuming Dakeel's prophecy was true.

Dakeel invited them back to his home, and led them into a storage room full of wooden crates. "I have gifts for all of you," he said, "to aid you on your quest. Mighty Darkwynde, if you would, please remove your armor."

"Why?" Darkwynde asked.

"You'll see, you'll see," Dakeel said gleefully.

Darkwynde seemed suspicious, but he complied. First he took off his helmet. He was bald, with dark skin, but he had several patches of lighter skin spattered across his face. Val thought he looked familiar, but she couldn't remember where she'd seen him.

It took several minutes for Darkwynde to remove his iron armor. While they waited, Dakeel reached into a crate and pulled out a sword and shield. He handed them to Val.

"For you, I have a shield that can't be sundered, and a sword that can cut through anything."

Val found a switch on the sword's hilt, activated it, and the blade started glowing a bright red.

"Wait," Val said. "If the sword can cut through anything, and the shield can't be cut, what happens if I…"

"Moving on!" Dakeel interrupted. "For you, Brynwyn, I have a pair of spectacles that can see long distances, even in total darkness." Brynwyn eagerly tried them on.

"I've got the armor off, now what?" Darkwynde asked.

"Underclothes too, then put this on," Dakeel said, handing him some clothing. He pointed to a dressing screen, and Darkwynde went behind it to change. He was so tall that the screen only came up to his shoulders.

"For you, my daughter, I have special gloves." They looked like black leather gloves, but each had a small box attached to the back of the hand. Serena tried them on. The material was stretchier than leather, but she couldn't identify it.

What do they do? she signed.

"Puts a little more 'oomph' in your punches," Dakeel said. Serena wasn't sure what he meant by that, but she supposed she'd find out the next time she got into a fight.

Darkwynde came out from behind the screen. He was wearing a sleek black bodysuit, made from a material similar to that of Serena's gloves. "Excellent, now put these on," Dakeel said, handing him some accessories: a black backpack, gloves, belt, and some boots.

Darkwynde put them on. "Now what?" he asked.

"There's a hidden switch on the back of your left glove."

Darkwynde felt around, before finally activating the switch. Small metal plates tessellated outward from the backpack, working their way down his arms and legs, joining with his boots, belt, and gloves. Within seconds, he was wearing a full suit of gleaming black armor.

"The right glove has a switch for your helmet," Dakeel

said. "I believe you'll find this armor to be stronger than your old set. Lighter, too, and flexible."

"Amazing," Darkwynde said, moving his arms around.

Finally, Dakeel gave Serena a rectangular slab, a magical device that would allow her to communicate with him over long distances. He would use it to keep the party updated whenever he had new visions.

They had a good night's sleep, stocked up on supplies and rations, and set out at dawn. After they left, Dakeel decided to consult with the prophets to see how they would fare on their journey. He pulled a rug aside, opened a secret trap door, and climbed down the ladder into his basement.

Not even Serena knew about this room. Dakeel had discovered it long before she was born, and had built his house on top of it to prevent anyone else from claiming it. He didn't know what ancient wizards had left this cache of magic artifacts, but he intended to honor their memory by using their relics to keep the world safe.

The walls of the basement were lined with metal. Sturdy boxes full of artifacts were stacked against the walls. Dakeel had spent decades studying these magical devices, sometimes nearly injuring himself in the process. To this day he'd only discovered the purpose of half of them.

Some of the crates were marked with writing, using words he'd never seen elsewhere. The weapon he'd given to Valaria was from a box labeled "AON." Her shield had been from a crate marked "Virtrinium Plating." Serena's gloves had come from a box marked "Impact Gloves." Brynwyn's spectacles were actually an "Infra-Enhanced Telescopic Visor." Darkwynde's armor was "Tessellating Self-Adjusting Protective Armor." Even the magic slab came from a package labeled "Two-Way Comm Units."

Sitting on top of one crate was an item he called the Magic Window. It was just a rectangular slab, about the size of the writing tablet Serena often used to talk to people. But when he touched it in a certain spot, it came alive and showed him visions of the future. He didn't always understand these visions, but he tried to make the most of the knowledge.

He touched one of the pictograms on the window's face. It once again showed him the vision that had led to today's events. A jumble of images flashed in the window. A queen trapped by fire. Four heroes caught up in battles against groups of assassins and lizard men. A hand grabbing a glowing red orb.

And throughout it all, a man's voice said, "Next season on Magical Monsterland. Four incredible warriors are drawn together to brave a flaming castle and save their queen. One of them will learn their true destiny: to recover a mysterious artifact and save the kingdom from a great evil. With the fate of the world at stake, will our heroes prevail? Find out next season!"

Were the warriors shown in the prophecy the same ones Dakeel had sent on the quest? He wasn't sure. The images were blurry, and the warriors wore armor and hoods that concealed their true appearances. But if the prophecy predicted it, it would happen.

Of course, Dakeel never left anything to chance. He'd been the one to start the fire in the castle. He'd used strange powders he'd found in this room to create a fire that burned on the stone without spreading too quickly. He'd also hired the assassins that had invaded the castle today.

He knew in his heart that his beloved Serena would be the one to save the world. He'd sent her to the best fighting instructors, and he'd made sure she'd practiced every day, from the time she was old enough to stand. All so that when the day came, she'd be ready. Only the day never came, so he'd given it a nudge.

They had been so easy to fool. Even the skeptical one, Valaria, had fallen in line over the slightest bit of proof, information Dakeel had acquired simply by talking to some of the other guards. He hated that he'd had to trick them into working for him, but the stakes were too high for scruples.

They would forgive him once the world was safe. For Dakeel, the ends always justified the means.

It wasn't the first time he'd had to push one of these prophecies into motion, but it was certainly the grandest prophecy he'd helped come to pass. But how could he sit on his laurels when the fate of the world was at stake?

Secure in the belief that he had done his part to save the world, he climbed the ladder, locked up the basement, and took a nap. Elsewhere, the four adventurers began their long journey into parts unknown.

04.01 *WARCAT: Repeating History*

ED.02508.11.15

"Thousands of years ago, this planet was ruled by giants," the guide said. The group had formed in front of a huge skeleton encased in glass. It looked like a human, except it was approximately four meters tall. The tour group oohed and ahhed and took many pictures. The tour guide, a female Meu with black fur and a mane of white hair, waited patiently for the group to quiet down before she continued.

"No one knows for sure why they died out," she said. "But we believe they killed each other in a great war." She moved to the next exhibit, which showed skeletons of Meu and Caniks at different stages of evolution. "Even more mysterious is what happened next. During the time of the giants, primitive Meu and Caniks were kept as pets. But once the giants died out, both of our species evolved rapidly. Changes that should have taken millions of years only took thousands. We became smarter, bipedal, with working fingers."

A brown-furred cat in the group raised his hand, and the tour guide pointed at him. "Yes sir? You have a question?"

"Are there any theories as to why we evolved so fast?" the cat asked.

"Many," the tour guide answered. "Some think it was

radiation from nuclear war. Others think that the harsh environment meant our species had to evolve quickly or die out. And of course, there are those who believe it was divine intervention."

Another cat raised her hand, and the guide pointed to her. "Why did the cats evolve more than the dogs?" The only two Caniks in the tour group glared at her, their fur bristling. Several of the Meu opened their mouths in surprise, inching away from her as if to prove they weren't with her.

"I'm sorry, I don't know what you mean," the tour guide said curtly.

"Well, cats are smarter and less violen..." she began, but the tour guide cut her off.

"Ma'am, I'm sorry," the tour guide said. "With all due respect, your beliefs, while distressingly common, are not based on actual science. This is a family-friendly tour, please keep controversial statements like that to yourself. Shall we move on?"

The two dogs in the group nodded appreciatively at the guide's answer. Meanwhile, the cat who'd asked the racist question looked like she'd very much like to speak to the museum's manager. Standing at the back of the group, Midnight chuckled and shook his head. *Some nerve,* he thought. He made a mental note to watch the lady leave later, and make sure the dogs didn't follow her back to her car.

He honestly couldn't blame her, as much as he would have liked to. Midnight had been raised with similar beliefs, and shaking those prejudices had taken a long time. His father had been killed by dogs, and his mother had drilled into her kittens the idea that Caniks were not to be trusted. Television and movies still often depicted dogs as the bad guys, and dogs were twice as likely to be pulled over by cops.

The tour ended an hour later, with no further incidents.

Midnight watched the dogs head straight to the museum cafeteria, while the racist walked out the front door. Midnight still followed her, not for her safety, but because he was going in the same direction. It was raining, but the walkway to the station was covered. He swiped his pass and boarded the monorail.

On the ride home, Midnight thought about something the guide had said - that no one really knew why the Caniks and Meu evolved so quickly. Strictly speaking, that wasn't true. The Meu government knew a lot more than the general public about the origins of their species. There was evidence that intentional genetic manipulation had played a role in their evolution. Midnight didn't understand the science, but there were patterns in their DNA that simply couldn't have developed by random chance. It was as if the creators of the two species – whoever they were – had left a microscopic signature in their genetic code.

But for whatever reason, the government didn't want that information to become public. Midnight only knew because he was friends with the scientist who made the discovery. But he had been sworn to secrecy, and his willingness to play ball had been a factor in his promotion to leader of WARCAT. *Hopefully not the largest factor,* Midnight thought. He'd worked hard for the position, and he felt he'd earned it. But it often nagged at him that at least partially, he'd been promoted to ensure his silence.

He was just opening his front door when he received a text on his wristwatch. The message simply said, "Turn on the news." Flicking on the TV, Midnight stood beside his couch, not bothering to sit down. Whatever it was, he probably wouldn't be home long enough to get comfortable.

He was about to change it to a news channel, but the special report had already interrupted regularly scheduled programming, so he just watched the channel it was on.

A monument destroyed. Dozens dead. Terrorists claiming

credit. A VIP kidnapped. An ultimatum. And to top it all off, a personal connection to Midnight.

Midnight was out the door, into the hallway, and about to take the elevator to the garage level when he heard the familiar wub-wub-wub of a WARCAT chopperjet. His wristwatch vibrated. "Roof" was all the text said this time. He took the stairs to the roof, where his ride awaited. Midnight boarded, and the chopperjet took him directly to WARCAT headquarters. Along the way, Midnight watched more news footage, and read several texts from his team with information not yet known by the media.

They landed on a helipad just outside a wide rectangular building. A sign above the entrance read "World Army Response and Counter Attack Team." Midnight passed through three security stations then took an elevator down to the briefing room. His team was already assembled and waiting.

Stinger led the briefing. She'd given up a career as a game show hostess to join WARCAT, and she probably had the most famous face at the table. But her true passion had always been tactical strategy. She could beat anyone on the team at chess, and heaven forbid they challenge her at wargames. She had white fur, and her mane of yellow hair was tied up in a ponytail. She wore gray fatigues with an urban camo pattern.

At her left sat Topsy. She had white fur and short, black hair. She was the information analyst and chief computer tech. She could debug code with one hand while hacking a bank account with the other. She'd started her career as an ethical hacker, thwarting cybercriminals and online terrorists. But her activities had put her on the DOG Force's radar, and she'd had to go into protective custody in order to survive. WARCAT had given her a new identity and put her in a position where she could do more good.

Next to her sat Puma. He was a huge, muscular cat with brown and white fur. He wasn't the brightest one in the room, but he wasn't a slouch, either. He could assemble a

WC-297 Repeating Cannon from its component parts, then pick it up and fire it without need of a tripod. As WARCAT's heavy weapons and demolitions expert, his skillset would come in handy in a firefight, or if they needed to destroy something big.

Blackjack was their field tech. He had black fur and always wore tailored clothing, even into battle. While Topsy was content to sit in the chair and guide the team using satellites and surveillance drones, Blackjack was more hands-on. He was the one they relied on to get them through any electronic locks or laser grids they might encounter. He was quick-witted and had a snarky sense of humor.

Next was Kitti, also known as "Kittihawk." She had gray fur and black hair, and was already dressed in her flightsuit. She was an ace pilot, able to weave a jet through a hail of bullets and come out unscathed. It was her job to deliver her team to the hot zone, draw enemy fire while they found a way in, cause as much destruction as she could from above, and pick up the team when the mission was completed. She often said it was like being a bus driver, only safer.

In the last seat was Tigre, a gray tabby dressed in a black stealth suit. His official title was "Covert Operations," but it was simpler to call him the team's ninja. He couldn't aim a rifle to save his life, but he could climb sheer walls and fling a throwing star through a mail slot at fifty meters. That was the nature of this team, everyone was a specialist. Many of its members could never have made it through basic training in the Meu Armed Forces. WARCAT gave them a home where their unique skills could shine.

"Let's get this started," Midnight said, taking an empty chair. He studied the team Stinger had selected, and her choices told him a lot about what sort of mission to expect.

Now that everyone was present, Stinger briefly went over the situation. "Roughly one hour ago," she said, "At thirteen hundred hours, the WoTaC memorial was destroyed."

* * *

Ten years earlier, the Greater Continent of Meu went to war against the Canik Empire. Midnight and Puma were the only ones present who had fought in that war, as the rest would have been too young at the time. The two nations were now at peace, but maintaining that peace had been a challenge, especially with the DOG Force constantly trying to reopen old wounds.

The war had come to be known as the "War of Tooth and Claw," or as most people called it, WoTaC. The memorial was a ten-story, eight-sided building that resembled a parking garage. The interior walls were inscribed with the names of everyone who had been killed in the war, both Meu and Caniks. The names were integrated, so that the soldiers of both armies were commingled together, at peace in death as they should have been in life. The names were carved all the way through the steel walls, so that they would shine when the sunlight hit that side of the building.

Earlier that day, Willsen Jahn-Beck, the Meu Secretary of Defense, gave a press conference in front of the memorial. He was a retired war hero, and today was the tenth anniversary of the peace treaty that had ended the war. This is why Midnight had been at the museum. His memories of the war were not pleasant, and he'd needed to be somewhere where he wasn't constantly reminded of it. So much for that.

Willsen had been about ten words into his speech when the memorial behind him exploded, killing all the visitors inside. During the following chaos, Willsen had disappeared. Before anyone had even noticed his absence, the DOG Force sent a video message to the media. The message currently played on one of the screens behind Stinger.

Midnight had immediately recognized the face in the video. Rex Darkfang – yet another example of why one shouldn't be allowed to select their own surname in their teens – was the leader of the DOG Force. He was also the reason Midnight's memories of the war were even worse than most people's.

Even after the peace treaty was signed, Midnight spent another six months in the Canik internment camp. Rex had been a general for the Canik army, a dog supremacist bent on wiping the cat population off the face of Galea. He'd disobeyed orders from his own government to keep the camp running those extra months. During that time, Midnight had been tortured daily and forced to watch several of his friends die. Eventually they were rescued, the camp was dissolved, and Rex was exiled from the Canik Empire.

Unfortunately that hadn't been the end of Rex's career. A number of his soldiers had been loyal to him over their own country. They'd set up a new headquarters on some remote island, forming their own organization which they called the "Dominators of Galea," or the DOG Force.

The DOGs had become more and more active recently. While WARCAT had been formed to counter terrorism in all its forms, in recent years it felt like they'd spent all their time combating the DOG Force. Midnight couldn't remember the last time they'd had a mission that didn't involve their arch-nemesis. It was as if each organization only existed to keep the other in check.

In Rex's video, he took credit for destroying the memorial and claimed to have Willsen in custody. He threatened to execute Willsen at sunset, which was less than five hours away, unless the Meu government gave in to several ridiculous demands. His list included the dissolution of WARCAT, the release of every DOG Force agent currently held prisoner, and of course Midnight's head on a platter.

While Midnight would have had no problem sacrificing himself in the line of duty, it wasn't going to happen this way. For one thing, the Meu government didn't negotiate with terrorists. Even if they did, the price was too high. Releasing the DOG agents would undo years of work, and there's no way the Meu government would dismantle their best protection against the DOG terrorists. Rex had to know his demands would be rejected. He definitely had an ulterior motive.

And that was the mission. Their primary objective would be to rescue Willsen before sundown, but they also needed to discover Rex's true game plan. Topsy had already tracked a DOG submarine to a small island off the coast of San Angora harbor, the site of the memorial.

Everyone but Topsy loaded up into a jet. The C190A Podrunner had three cockpits. Kittihawk piloted the jet from the center section. To her left, Midnight, Stinger, and Blackjack filled up one pod. Tigre and Puma rode in the right pod, with Puma's arsenal taking up the third seat. Kittihawk flew until they were less than ten kilometers from the island, then launched the pods. Then she returned to an airfield on the mainland to await further orders.

Each pod was actually a C190B "Catfish" mini-sub. The two subs sped toward the island, headed toward separate landing sites. Tigre and Puma parked in a rocky inlet on the East side of the island. After exiting their pod, they used a remote to send the sub back underwater until it was called for. Tigre and Puma then split up so they could cover more ground.

The other pod headed deeper underwater. Since the DOGs had used a submarine, there was a good chance there was an underwater launching bay. Which there was. A wide-open tunnel fed directly into the lower levels of whatever structure this island housed. A submarine already sat parked in the interior pool.

It was too risky to take the pod in. Any number of DOG soldiers could be waiting for them. Having donned wetsuits during their flight, the trio left their pod behind and swam for the tunnel. Blackjack surfaced first, looked around for guards, then signaled the other two that the coast was clear.

They were in a huge underwater submarine bay, carved

from the rock and lined with metal. A black submarine bobbed in the pool that took up most of the chamber. Midnight wondered just how the DOGs had managed to build such a massive structure so close to the mainland. And this was just the parking garage. This kind of work would take years, and would require all sorts of construction equipment. Plus, there was an aged quality to it. Some of the metal had deteriorated over the years, eroded by sea salt and time.

It had to have been built before the war, maybe even earlier. There was also something unsettling about the architecture, but Midnight couldn't put his finger on it yet. They quietly headed for a massive open doorway, made sure the adjoining hallway was empty, and crept into the halls. More doorways lined the hallway. The hallway was very wide, and the doorways were unusually tall.

The large doorways and hallway seemed to indicate that this place had been used as a garage, but how did they get the vehicles in and out? *There must be a vehicle elevator around here somewhere,* Midnight thought. But there were no other indicators that this hallway had been used for vehicles. No tire marks on the floor, no oil stains.

They heard footsteps coming from down the hall. Midnight, Stinger, and Blackjack ducked into an open side door, and hid in the dark room. A dog in a wetsuit walked by, headed toward the submarine. Stinger unholstered her TQ-51 trank pistol, and fired a tranquilizer dart into the dog's neck. He teetered and tottered for a few seconds, then tipped over. Blackjack caught him as he fell, and pulled him into the side room. They closed the large door so they wouldn't be heard.

They took their captive's ID card. It identified him as a Dogshark, one of the DOG Force's elite aquatic soldiers. Hopefully the card would allow them to access to all areas of the building. The dog would be out for a couple of hours, and while the cats hoped they'd be on their way home by then, they tied him up and gagged him anyway.

"Look at this room," Blackjack said, noticing the furniture for the first time. Everything looked ancient and high-tech at the same time. They saw several computers, a couple of chairs, and some storage lockers. But all of it was oversized, easily twice as large as it needed to be. There were signs on the lockers, written in a language none of them could read.

But Midnight recognized the lettering. He'd seen similar writing earlier that day, on artifacts in the museum. Everything fell into place. "The ancient giants," Midnight said. "This is their work. The DOGs are using one of their old structures as a base."

"I didn't realize the giants had such advanced technology," Stinger said. "The history books always show them using flintlock rifles and wooden carts."

There's a lot about them they don't tell you in the history books, Midnight thought, but he wasn't allowed to share more.

"How is it so clean?" Blackjack asked. He had a point. This installation would have to be thousands of years old, but while some of the metal panels were rusty, the electronics still worked.

"Maintenance bots?" Stinger offered. She had no idea if the giants had been developed enough to have robots, but after seeing this room, she'd believe anything. "WK would love this," she mused.

This site obviously had great historical value, but that would have to take a backseat. If the mission was a success, they would notify the Meu government of the island's significance. The rest of the team would probably have to sign NDAs similar to the ones Midnight had signed.

The trio crept back into the hall, made sure no one else was around, and looked for a way upstairs. They walked past an elevator, looking for a stairwell. They finally found one at the end of the hall. The stairs were also designed for taller people, but climbing them wasn't too difficult. They reached the next floor without incident and peeked out into the hallway.

The halls were crowded with dog soldiers. A fight was inevitable, but at least the cats had the element of surprise. Blackjack pulled out a smoke grenade and rolled it into the hallway. The three cats put on gas masks and got their weapons ready.

One of the DOG troopers sniffed the air, then looked down at the small metal orb. "Grenade!" he shouted in Canik. Chaos erupted as the troopers scattered and the sleeping gas filled the hallway. Bodies hit the floor left and right. The cats burst from the stairwell, firing at any dogs that were still standing.

They dodged some return fire, but the cats made it through the fight without any injuries. Alarms now blared throughout the base, and the cats had to run before reinforcements showed up. They stepped over unconscious bodies, then ran through the long hallways, making several turns until they reached a large hangar. The roof was made of two long panels that were now open.

Rex Darkfang stood in front of the rear hatch of a DOG jet plane, his right arm around Willsen's neck. With his other paw he held a gun at Willsen's temple. Rex was a gray bulldog dressed in a red-and-black general's uniform. His face was covered in burns and scars, a monument to many past battles.

"One step closer and he dies," Rex said.

"Kill him and you'll be dead before his body hits the floor," Midnight countered, trying to line up a clear shot at Rex's forehead.

"Then I suppose I'll have to take him with me," Rex said, backing toward the hatch, and dragging the war hero with him.

A throwing star flew in from Rex's left, hitting him in the hand. He arfed loudly and dropped his gun. Tigre stood on a catwalk twenty meters away, having climbed in through the ventilation ducts. Rex wasted no time. He turned and ran up the ramp to the jet. Midnight held his fire, as Willsen was still in the way. The jet engines warmed up.

"Get down!" Stinger yelled, waving at Willsen. Midnight ran towards the jet, hoping to reach Willsen before the jet exhaust fried him. But rather than duck or run, Willsen smiled, turned, and ran up the ramp. The ramp closed and the jet flew off. Midnight was about to fire at the jet, but hesitated. Had Willsen turned traitor, or was he planning to ambush Rex himself from within the plane?

Then Rex's face appeared on a large video monitor above the hangar's entrance. "You fools!" Rex said gleefully. "Your so-called 'war hero' was actually one of our sleeper agents! He's spent years gathering your secrets, and now he's coming home! But don't worry, kitties, I've left you a consolation prize!" Then his face blinked out, and a timer appeared instead. There were two minutes on it, and it was already counting down.

"This way!" Tigre shouted, pointing toward a ladder, and the rest of the cats followed.

On the shore of the tiny island, Puma's repeating cannon sat upon its tripod, just waiting for a target. He'd aimed it toward what he'd judged to be the base's most obvious exit, in case his teammates needed cover fire on their way out. But now a different target appeared. A DOG fighter plane burst out of a hidden hanger. Thinking quickly, he asked into his comm, "I have eyes on a DOG jet. Do I fire?"

"Fire!" came the immediate reply.

The jet was already almost out of range, but Puma pulled the cannon off of its tripod and fired. He hit the jet multiple times in the right wing, tearing it to shreds.

Just then, he saw his teammates climb out of the top of the hangar. As they ran towards him, several explosions rocked the island, and flames burst from the open hangar behind them.

Rex Darkfang's plane was spinning out of control and going down. "Sorry to leave you like this," he said to

Willsen, and pulled a lever. The single-seat cockpit ejected from the rest of the plane. A pair of smaller wings sprang from the sides, and the escape jet flew away. The rest of the jet crashed into the ocean.

Willsen Jahn-Beck, former Secretary of Defense of the Greater Continent of Meu, was rescued from the sinking wreckage half an hour later, and was promptly taken into custody. Rex Darkfang made a clean getaway. The DOG soldiers he'd left behind perished in the explosion, which also ruined any chances of recovering historical artifacts from the ancient giants.

The WARCAT team went back to their base and celebrated their victory.

In a hidden chamber, deep under the collapsed base, forty giant-sized cryotubes sat in wait, as they had been waiting for thousands of years. They might have waited a thousand more, if not for the explosion. The damage had severed the chamber's link to the island's sensors, triggering the emergency protocols. The cryotubes began to power up, initiating the reawakening process. Lights blinked all over the chamber. There was hiss after hiss of opening tubes.

The first to reawaken was a bald man, muscular with chiseled features. He was twice as tall as an Earth human, but otherwise his anatomy was similar. While others awakened around him, he stood and strode over to a computer. Going over sensor data, he tried to make sense of what sort of world they lived in now.

Humanoid dogs and cats were now the dominant life forms on the planet. So the genetic sequencing had worked after all. He laughed. It didn't matter how much progress these animals had made. They would be conquered.

The age of giants would come again.

04.02 *Roommates*

ED.02508.11.15

Raven was fifteen when she lost her limbs. She spent five years without arms or legs, but she coped. She adapted. She evolved. She was twenty when her best-and-only friend Trenyn built her a robotic exosuit, and while it wasn't perfect, it went along way towards making her feel like a whole person.

The suit didn't just give her more mobility, it helped her overcome her mental scars as well. No longer stuck in a chair, no longer dependent on paid helpers for basic bodily functions, Raven wasn't constantly reminded of the traumas of her youth. She was able to move on, both literally and figuratively. Raven hadn't felt incomplete in eight years.

But today, she felt like a piece of her was missing. This was worse than losing an arm, it was like losing her other half. After the final battle on Valos, the people had elected Raven's half-sister Lemondrop to be their new ruler. They couldn't have made a better choice, in Raven's opinion. But this meant that the Council of Heirs was dissolved, and with it, Raven's strongest tie to Valos. Lemondrop had offered Raven any position she wanted in the Valos government, but Raven felt it was time to move on. She was no politician.

She'd enjoyed living on Earth again for the past few months while working on the computer virus. Raven wasn't very emotional, but returning to Earth had given her a comforting feeling that she hadn't felt on Valos. It was where she wanted to be now. It was where she wanted to continue her work. And now she'd been offered a job on Earth, upgrading IGP tech.

Trenyn, on the other hand, had accepted Lemondrop's offer, and was now head of the Valos Department of Science and Technology. Valos was one of the few planets where virtrinium could be mined, and Trenyn had many ideas for putting the rare metal to good use. So Trenyn had stayed behind while Raven returned to Earth.

It wasn't like she wouldn't see them again. They were only a warp gate away. And of course they would message each other a hundred times a day. But still... They had worked side-by-side for more than a decade. They understood each other in ways no one else possibly could. They were so in tune that if one felt thirsty, the other would hand them a bottle of water, no words required. Even identical twins were rarely this close. Not seeing Trenyn every day felt like being deprived of oxygen.

But it had to be done. Neither Trenyn nor Raven could put their lives on hold just to stay close to each other. Circumstances might change in the future, but for now, they both had to get used to being apart.

Still, for practical reasons, Raven wasn't sure she should live alone. Despite all her technology, she occasionally found herself in helpless positions. Something as simple as an EMP burst could short out all her tech, and then she'd be stuck, limbless and helpless, until someone found her. Her eventual plan was to find a nice house with a lot of lab space, and hire a live-in assistant.

But for now, she lived with Zeva. Raven hated to impose, but Zeva insisted. She had extra rooms, and Raven had to admit her apartment was in a convenient location. And Zeva liked having someone there when she was at work, for extra security. So until Raven found the perfect home, she and Zeva would be roommates.

"I'll be back by twenty-one-hundred," Zeva said, grabbing her gun holster. "I'll bring dinner." Zeva nuzzled Raven's cheek for a moment, letting out a short purr, and then walked out the door.

Raven touched her cheek, though with artificial hands, she wasn't sure what she expected to feel. Zeva tended to be touchy-feely like that. Raven didn't usually like being touched, but with Zeva, she didn't mind so much. It gave her feelings she didn't entirely understand, and the thought of exploring them further piqued her scientific curiosity.

But she wasn't going to push it. If Zeva came on stronger, Raven might reciprocate, but she wasn't going to make the first move. After all, Raven was a bit of an emotional outcast, and she could easily be misreading the signals. Was Zeva like this with everyone? Not that Raven had seen, but that didn't necessarily mean anything.

She put it out of her mind for now. She had a full day ahead of her. When Raven and Trenyn had stayed with Zeva before, she'd given each of them their own guest room. But instead, with Zeva's permission, they'd moved both guest beds into one room, and used the other as a lab-office combo. It wasn't as spacious as the lab down the street, but for smaller, non-dangerous projects, it was quite convenient. Especially whenever she woke up in the middle of the night with sudden inspiration.

Right now, Raven was working on some IGP uniform upgrades. Her goal was to keep officers from having to carry so much weight, without sacrificing their protection. The one-piece bodysuit was made of Nycra, a tough, spandex-like material. It was designed to dissipate energy blasts, absorbing them into the material so they wouldn't hurt the officer. It wouldn't stop a bullet, but the wearer could still wear protective armor over the bodysuit. Besides, nobody used bullets anymore.

But that was just the base outfit. The accessories were where it really got interesting. Each wrist sported an unobtrusive, black bracelet. These wristbands had all the functionality of a comm unit, allowing easy, hands-free communication with other officers. But they also functioned as weapons, able to fire stun blasts from hidden barrels. Better yet, they could send jolts of electricity through the Nycra bodysuit, shocking anyone who happens to be grappling with the officer, while leaving the officer unharmed.

The outfit also included Levatech footwear. This was nothing new for the IGP, but standard IGP jumpboots tended to be bulky and conspicuous. Raven's design looked more like everyday tennis shoes, and could be worn without attracting attention.

In fact, the entire ensemble could be worn as part of another outfit, making it ideal for undercover agents. These enhancements would probably be too expensive to give to every IGP officer, but special agents like Zeva could make good use of them. Raven had more accessories planned, but so far, these prototypes were all she had completed.

Raven spent a couple of hours tweaking the outfit's accessories, then packed it all into a small metal suitcase. She would need to head to the main lab before she could get any more work done. She put her black overcoat on over her metal body, then put on her sunglasses. She grabbed the suitcase, locked up the apartment, and took the stairs down to street level. It was a short walk to the lab, but she was only halfway there when her comm unit buzzed.

"Raven? It's Zeva." She was usually pretty cheery, except when she was working. Right now she sounded agitated.

"What's wrong?" Raven asked.

"I'm at the gym. I need you to bring me some clothing," she said.

"Anything specific?" Raven asked, turning back toward

the apartment.

"At the moment I'd be happy with a bathrobe," Zeva said.

"What happened?" Raven asked.

"I was in the—" Zeva started, then she shrieked and the line went dead. The ground rumbled beneath Raven's feet, and she heard a booming sound in the distance. The Neon Gym was just a few blocks away, and Raven could see smoke rising from its roof from here. Without another thought, she started running towards the gym.

Zeva's lungs were about to burst. She didn't want to resurface until it was safe. She could still see the flames, but now they seemed to be confined to the shallow end of the pool. She swam to the far end, and risked taking a breath. She surfaced under the diving board and looked around. The initial blast had abated. The gym was on fire, but the explosions seemed to be over.

She hadn't come to the gym for her health. She was on the trail of an illegal trafficker named Ireena Hambrick, but she went by the nickname Hotline. She dealt in everything – dangerous drugs, illegal weapons, sapient slaves... if you had the credits, Hotline could get it for you. This morning, Zeva had received a tip that Hotline would be meeting a client by the pool of the Neon Gym.

Of course, Zeva couldn't sit by the pool all day without arousing suspicion, so she'd changed into her swimsuit and swam a few laps. All she'd taken with her was her comm unit, which was waterproof. When she went back to her locker later, she'd found it had been broken into. Her clothing and sidearm were gone. That's when she'd called Raven.

Several other lockers had also been pilfered, and Zeva had wondered if it was related to Hotline, or just random locker thieves. They'd taken her gun, but it was just a stun pistol, and it used biometric tech that insured no one could fire it but Zeva. To anyone else, it was just a paperweight. A black market arms dealer might have been able to unlock it, but they didn't waste their time with stun pistols.

The other swimmers had already left the pool to file incident reports, but Zeva had stayed behind to look for clues, just in case it was related to Hotline. She'd seen a red light flashing from inside one partly open locker. Upon realizing it was a bomb, Zeva had dashed for the pool. She'd made it just in time, and had seen flames and debris fly overhead while underwater.

And now here she was, with no weapons or decent clothing, taking refuge in a pool, under a roof that might collapse at any moment. But now that she looked around, the damage wasn't as extensive as she'd thought. The sprinklers were already putting out the fire on the far wall. The women's locker room was destroyed, but the rest of the pool room didn't look so bad. She didn't see any cracks in the outer wall, and nothing was falling from the ceiling.

Zeva climbed out of the pool and looked herself over. She had a few cuts, and her swimsuit was badly torn across the back. She must have cut it closer than she'd thought. And where was her comm? She had to have dropped it in the locker room, because it wasn't in the pool.

"Zeva?" a woman's voice echoed through the room.

"Raven!" Zeva replied, seeing her friend enter the room.

"Are you hurt?" Raven asked, looking at Zeva's cuts.

"I'll be okay," Zeva said. "Did you bring the clothes?"

"Sorry, I ran straight here when I saw the fire. Do you want my overcoat?"

"What's in the suitcase?" Zeva asked.

"Just a suit. A suit!" Raven slapped her forehead, nearly giving herself a concussion. She'd forgotten she was even carrying the suitcase.

They went into the men's locker room on the opposite side of the pool. The building had been evacuated, so the locker room was empty.

"This is just a prototype," Raven apologized.

"Anything's better than running around in a ripped-up swimsuit," Zeva said, taking off the swimsuit.

Raven blushed and turned her head. It was the first time she'd seen Zeva nude. Raven was both a doctor and a scientist, and had always viewed anatomy with the detachment that came with those professions. But for some reason, seeing Zeva's body felt indecent. She wondered if Zeva felt it too.

But Zeva seemed to be too distracted by the bodysuit. It fit her like a glove, and she found it extremely comfy. She slipped on the bracelets and the shoes. The outfit was sleek, black, and form-fitting. It covered every inch of her except for her head and hands.

"Ideally you would wear this under other clothing," Raven said. "Like armor or even street clothes…"

"It's fine for now," Zeva said. "Can I borrow your comm? I seem to have lost mine."

"There's a comm built into the bracelets," Raven said. "Just press your thumb to the center square, and it'll sync to your account."

Zeva followed her instructions. The bracelet asked her a couple of security questions to confirm her identity, and the suit was now hers. "Call headquarters," Zeva said.

The voice that answered sounded panicked. "Zeva? Are you okay?"

"I'm fine, boss," she said. "I'm still in the gym. Have any of the witness reports started trickling in?"

"Most of the witnesses are still filling out paperwork," Chief Dato answered. "But I do have a couple of tips. An outside witness said he saw a woman run out the emergency exit door, right before the bomb went off. The woman jumped into a light blue 2502 Marsrunner convertible and drove off."

"Oh!" Raven said. "I saw that hovercar on the way here. It ran a stop light and nearly hit me."

"If it ran a stop light, there might be a picture of its plates on the traffic cams," Zeva said.

"I'll see if we can track it," Dato said over the comm. "I'll call you back when I have something for you. Out."

Zeva and Raven had barely gotten outside when Chief Dato called back. They couldn't track the car's transponder, but they did have a video record of its route. The city's traffic lights worked in tandem, and once a vehicle was caught breaking the law, they recorded its path as it drove through the city. They had managed to track the car's path to H-Town, where they lost track of it.

"Cops are already on their way," Chief Dato said.

"So am I," Zeva answered, hanging up. Zeva got into her car, a 2505 Thunderstar, and beckoned Raven to join her.

"I can just walk home from here if I'm in the way," Raven offered.

"Nah, come on!" Zeva said. "I need you to tell me what else this suit can do."

They buckled in and drove off.

Nova Corvallis hadn't always been a coastal town. When it was first founded, it was approximately eighty kilometers from the Pacific coast. But earthquakes and rising ocean levels eventually brought the coastline to the quiet town, and soon it became a busy metropolis. The original city was now the Historic District, or "H-Town," and it looked like an entirely different city. While downtown was high-tech, with plenty of neon and skywalks and solar windows, H-Town hadn't seen progress in decades.

It was still midday, but even the sky seemed darker here. It was as if they'd driven through a warp gate and ended up on a more primitive planet.

"There are fewer traffic cams in H-Town," Zeva explained as they drove past long-closed factories and run-down slums. "I'm not sure why."

"I have a pretty good idea," Raven said, looking at their

impoverished surroundings. People sat on benches at bus stops, eyeing Zeva's car with suspicion. It seemed that most of H-Town's residents were nonhumans. On Earth, intraspecies racism hadn't lasted very long after humans met their first aliens. These days, humans rarely cared about other humans' skin color or ancestry. Unfortunately, this didn't mean they were more enlightened. It just meant that they'd redirected their prejudices toward new targets. After all this time, it was still easier for humans to get higher-paying jobs on Earth.

Several police cars sped past them, lights flashing and sirens blaring. They were combing every street for Hotline's Marsrunner. "Idiots," Zeva said. "They're just going to drive her further into hiding."

"How would you have handled it?" Raven asked.

"Smaller numbers, undercover cars," Zeva said. "They're probably hoping to flush her out, but she wouldn't have come here if she hadn't had a plan."

"So what are you going to do?" asked Raven.

"For now? Ask around." Zeva pulled up next to an apartment complex. Two Vhelran teens sat on the front steps. Zeva opened the hovercar's center console and pulled out a ten-credit chip, holding it up in front of the teens. One of them stood up and came over.

"Have you seen a Marsrunner go by?" Zeva asked.

He was quiet at first, but he eyed the money hungrily. He looked around to see if anyone was watching him. "Yeah," he finally said. "It went down that street." He pointed a few streets away. Zeva tossed him the chip, thanked him, and drove off.

Fifty credits later, a witness directed them to an old auto garage. The mechanic had gone out of business years ago, but the witness swore he'd seen the Marsrunner go inside. They parked in an alley across the street, just far enough back to avoid being seen.

"Stay in the car," Zeva said.

"Shouldn't you call for backup or something?" Raven asked.

"So the cops can scare her off?" Zeva asked. "No way. This has to be handled with finesse." Zeva stepped out of the car, tripped over her own feet, and knocked over a trash can.

"Finesse?" Raven asked.

"Shut up, I'm still getting used to these shoes," Zeva replied, sticking her tongue out.

Using the jump shoes, she leaped straight up, landing on the roof of the building next to the hovercar. Then Raven saw her jump across the street, landing on the roof of the auto garage. Raven was impressed. Zeva must have gone through jumpboot training in the IGP. Now it looked like Zeva had found an air vent. Raven lost sight of Zeva after that.

After a few minutes, Raven received a text on her comm. "The Marsrunner is here. No one else. Are you still okay?"

Raven was about to type a reply, when there was a tapping on the passenger side window. A gun pointed at her through the glass.

Zeva crept through the repair shop, going through boxes, and looking for hidden trapdoors. As far as she could tell, the shop was legit. The only thing that looked out of place was the Marsrunner. There was no evidence that any illegal business had been taking place here.

As for the car itself, it was also clean. A bit too clean for this neighborhood, but she couldn't find anything illegal inside. She popped the trunk, idly wondering why Raven hadn't answered her text. As she walked around the side of the car, she noticed a familiar flashing red light emanating from the trunk.

"Oh for the love of—" Zeva said. With no time to spare, she pointed herself at the garage's side window and activated her jump boots. She torpedoed through the window right as the car exploded.

She hit the ground several meters from the shop, and tumbled to her feet. "I'm starting to think that woman's trying to kill me," Zeva said, brushing glass out of her mane. She ran back to the alley and found that her car was empty. The passenger door was open, and Raven was gone.

Raven had faced worse. After her father, her sister, and the countless lowlifes she'd fought as a bounty hunter, this "Hotline" was just a woman with a gun. Still, it was a big gun. Hotline wielded a 744E Magma Pistol, which was more than capable of melting through Raven's robotic body, not to mention her flesh.

Such weapons were illegal on Earth, but this woman didn't seem to have a problem getting things. From her HackerZone sunglasses down to her rhino-skin boots, every piece of Hotline's ensemble looked like it had been imported through illegal channels. She had a refined demeanor, and seemed miffed that she'd had to lower herself to hiding out in H-Town.

Keeping the pistol leveled at Raven's head, Hotline marched her down the hall of the apartment complex, up the stairs, and into a third-floor apartment. Two large men waited for them inside. "Tie her up," Hotline ordered.

The two men wrapped some ropes around Raven's wrists and tied her to a chair. It didn't appear that they knew she was in a robotic body. That was good. When the time was right, Raven would have a much easier time escaping. But for now, she wanted to wait for a better opportunity. At the very least, she didn't want to act while Hotline was pointing that overpowered pistol in her direction.

"What do you know?" Hotline asked. "And who else have you told?"

"I don't know much of anything," Raven said. She could see the auto garage out of the living room window. She'd heard the explosion earlier, and now she saw it was still on fire. She hoped Zeva had made it out.

Hotline pistol-whipped Raven across the face, knocking off her sunglasses. "Tell me what you know, or I'll have my guys here break your legs."

"Best of luck with that," Raven said.

"You might as well save yourself some pain," Hotline said. "No help is coming for you. I've killed your partner."

"She's not my partner," Raven said. "We're just roommates." It sounded like a lie, though, even to Raven. Before she could dwell on it, she spotted movement out the window. Someone was walking across the street, searching for something. It was Zeva. Raven felt a huge wave of relief at seeing her alive. She tried to think of a way to send her a signal.

"What are you looking at?" Hotline asked, and turned toward the window. She froze when she saw that Zeva was still alive. She turned to one of her henchmen, her face full of fury. "You said that second bomb got her!"

"It had to have," he answered, holding his hands in front of his face. "How could she have gotten out?" The henchman was twice Hotline's weight, but he cowered like she was ten meters tall.

Raven realized that no one was looking at her. It was now or never. She broke through her bonds, snatched the gun from Hotline's hand, and threw it at the window, shattering the glass. One of the henchmen tackled Raven to the floor, the other one moved around for a better angle, and Hotline dug into her crocodile-skin purse for another weapon.

"That was very foolish," Hotline said, aiming an energy pistol at Raven's head. The first henchman now sat on top of Raven, and the other had come around to help pin her shoulders.

Raven knew she could toss these goons around like ragdolls, but not before Hotline got off a shot. "Fine," Raven said. "I'll tell you what I know."

"I'm afraid we're past that point," Hotline said, smiling.

"Past what point?" Zeva asked, climbing in through the window.

Hotline turned and fired, hitting Zeva square in the chest. The energy dissipated into the fabric of her bodysuit. Zeva returned fire, hitting Hotline with two stun blasts from her bracelets. One of the thugs got off of Raven and lunged at Zeva. He grabbed her around the waist, pinning her arms to her sides. Zeva quickly activated the suit's defensive mechanism, shocking the thug until he let go of her, unconscious.

"You learn fast," Raven said, throwing the final henchman across the room.

The police arrived a few minutes later and took all three criminals into custody. Zeva and Raven drove to the police department to fill out some paperwork, then called it a day and went home.

"Can you help me get this off?" Zeva asked as they entered their apartment. Some might have taken that as a double entendre, but not Raven. She just nodded, and followed Zeva into her bedroom.

"Sorry about that," Raven said. "I know it's tight. I'll work on making it easier to remove. As I said, this is just the prototype. The completed suit will have a lot more features..."

"Raven, the suit is *amazing*," Zeva said. "I can't wait to see what else you add to it. Considering how useful it was today, I'd like to field test all your prototypes from now on." She finished pulling her last leg out of the bodysuit, then handed it to Raven. "When you get the rest of the suit finished, you and I are going to be unstoppable."

"Good plan," Raven said, looking away. Once again, she was suddenly very aware of Zeva's nudity. Only this time, Zeva picked up on it.

"I'm sorry," Zeva said playfully. "Does this make you uncomfortable? I thought you were a doctor."

"It's just, I mean, I was just, I..." Raven rarely struggled for words, but this was an entirely new experience for her. Well, almost.

Zeva giggled. "You're silly," she said, and embraced her. While Raven couldn't actually feel the hug, it nevertheless made her forehead sweat. Zeva rubbed her cheek against Raven's again, while making a deep purring sound. When she finally released her, Zeva said, "I'm going to go take a shower. When I get out, do you want to play a board game or something? I'll load up a bad movie, something really cheesy so you can point out the bad science."

"Sounds like... sounds like fun," Raven said, still blushing.

Zeva brushed Raven's cheek with her hand as she walked out of the room. The sensation sent shivers down Raven's spine. She still remembered the last time she'd felt the same tingle of excitement. Seven years earlier, at the Pleasure Planet. Another Galean. *Is this a fetish?* Raven wondered. *Am I only attracted to cat women? Am I being racist?*

But she dismissed the thought. She hadn't been attracted to any other Galeans she'd met, and she had occasionally felt random twinges of attraction for human women. While Zeva was unquestionably attractive, Raven was certain that the spark - or whatever it was - between them had nothing to do with Zeva's species or appearance. The Galean connection was a coincidence, and nothing more. She still wasn't sure how she would define her sexual orientation, but whatever it was, it was definitely picky.

While Zeva showered, Raven sent Trenyn a quick text. "I think there might be something going on between me and Zeva."

Trenyn's reply was immediate and consisted of a single word. "Duh."

Raven smiled and put her comm away. She didn't know what this night had in store for her, but she was determined not to stress out about it. Her entire life was a planbook full of data points and research. But tonight, for once, she was just going to take things as they came. Finally.

04.03 Born Again

ED.02508.11.15

They say the eyes are the windows to the soul, but they were also a handy snack in a pinch. At least that was the opinion of Charles "Khan" Karne, who had a taste for raw, human flesh. Karne was no killer, though. At least, that's what he always told himself. He'd only killed three people in his lifetime. Two were self-defense, and one was a mercy killing.

He'd tried to satiate his appetite with animal flesh, but it just wasn't the same. He'd also tried obtaining black-market corpses, and he'd even spent time working as a coroner's assistant. But no, he could only stand human flesh if it was fresh, still warm from the body. Fresh flesh had a unique flavor, and no amount of reheating could bring that back.

So he'd worked as an orderly in several hospitals, occasionally getting his hands on a freshly amputated limb, or even taking a finger or an eyeball from a coma patient. He'd had to change jobs quite often, fleeing town and adopting a new identity whenever people started getting suspicious.

And then he'd found New Birth. It was the largest hospital on the planet Ferna, and it led the galaxy in organ donations and coma patient care. On Ferna, coma patients couldn't officially be declared dead until they had been without brain activity for a full year. After the year was up, the patient was still kept on life support, but their bodies could be harvested for organs and other body parts as needed.

People from all over the galaxy had their loved ones transferred to New Birth. The hospital had a higher-than-average rate of coma recovery, and promised to keep anyone alive, no matter how unlikely their chances, for the full year at no charge. The body itself was the fee, and the hospital made most of its money from organ donations and limb transplants. New Birth's efficiency at organ recovery couldn't be matched. Many people were comforted knowing that parts of their loved ones lived on in other people.

All it took for Karne to get a warm meal was some surgical know-how and a bit of forgery. He'd wait until the middle of the night, when they typically only had a handful of employees on the floor. He kept an AON scalpel on him at all times. He'd select an organ donor, cut off a finger or an eye or – if he was feeling particularly famished – an entire hand, and rush off to the restroom to scarf it down. Any bones or other leftover matter would go into the medical waste chute. Then he'd clean up any blood, and forge some paperwork claiming those limbs had been donated.

It was foolproof, or it would have been, if he hadn't gotten greedy. Now that he had a reliable means of fulfilling his hunger, he found that his appetite was harder to satiate. He succumbed more and more often, eating three or four meals a night. Eventually hospital staff noticed that limbs were vanishing at a higher rate, and always during the overnight shift. They were onto Karne, but he didn't know it.

They might have just fired him, but they were afraid he might be dangerous. They might have had him arrested, but the management of New Birth Hospital didn't like the police investigating them too closely. So they'd called in some bounty hunters.

"Don't worry, she's got this," Zak said, taking a bite out of a protein bar.

"And she'll be discreet?" the hospital director asked, frowning.

"We're looking for evidence of Karne, nothing more," Zak promised. "Besides, you already had me sign that NDA."

Yeela was hooked up to the hospital's database. She examined the staff records, cross-referencing them with government records to see which employees were using fake backgrounds. Simultaneously, she examined thousands of hours of security camera footage, looking for video proof that Karne had been the one stealing body parts.

"So has anyone ever woken up after the year is up?" Zak asked, talking with his mouth full. "Like, after you start using them for donations? You ever have one wake up, but their liver's already gone? Or maybe a leg?"

"Never," Director Wen said, unamused. "If there's even a hint of brain activity, the waiting period starts over. We guarantee no one is transferred to the organ donation wing until they've gone a year with no brain activity."

"I've known a couple of guys who would probably qualify," Zak joked, taking another bite of his snack bar. "How's the search going, Yeela?"

"I'm almost positive it's him," Yeela said. "But he knows exactly where the cameras are, and he exploits that. There's enough here that we should go ahead and grab him, but I'm not sure if I have enough to convict him yet."

"Is he working right now?" Zak asked.

"He should be starting his shift soon," the director said.

Just then, they heard a gasp. Zak and Director Wen turned their heads to see Karne, standing across the lobby, staring at them. He turned and ran.

"I'll get him," Zak said, vaulting over the front desk. "Yeela, keep looking for evidence."

"The footage will still be here when we get back," Yeela protested.

"Stay!" Zak shouted behind him, as he ran out the front

door.

"Is he always so headstrong?" Wen asked, once they were alone.

"You have no idea," Yeela answered.

After Zak caught Karne, he took him straight to the local IGP. The deputy asked if Zak would stay in town for a couple of days to help the prosecution build their case. The county offered to put them up in a nice hotel, and Zak didn't have any other pressing bounties, so he agreed. By the time he got back to the hospital to get Yeela, she had found enough footage to prove Karne had been stealing body parts.

Legally it was still a complicated issue. Even though the bodies were being kept alive by machines, by Ferna law they were legally dead and therefore property of New Birth Hospital. So the worst Karne could be charged with was theft, along with some minor laws involving desecration of the dead. But when they connected it to some of the other crimes Karne had committed before coming to Ferna, they had a bigger case. The defense, meanwhile, was already looking into an insanity plea.

Regardless, that wasn't Zak's problem. He was happy enough to sleep in a nice room for a couple of days and get paid for it. The hotel was top-notch, not exactly five-star, but swankier than any place Zak had stayed before. Well, as an adult, anyway. He'd had a privileged childhood, but he tried not to remember any of that. He'd given up a lot to live as his authentic self.

Zak went swimming in the hotel pool, ordered room service, watched some television with Yeela, then went to bed. Yeela waited until she was sure Zak was sound asleep, used a Levatech beam to open a window, and flew out into the night.

She arrived at the hospital ten minutes later. Between deliveries and emergencies, the hospital had enough drone activity that nobody looked at her twice. She flew down the hall until she found the coma ward, and flew through the open doorway. There were ten identical rooms, each with fifty beds, and most of them were full. Yeela's metaphorical heart sank at the sight. All of these lives ended too early. She knew only a handful would wake up again. The rest would sleep until their year was up, then get moved to the donations wing, where they would be stripped for parts like a run-down hovercar.

But she wasn't here to shed tears for the unfortunate. There was a very specific patient she wanted to see. Earlier, when Yeela was going through hospital records, she'd stumbled across this woman's sad story.

Her name was Livia Dell. She had been twenty-five years old when she'd contracted a disease called "Full Onset Xionthropic Neurological Endemic Withering Syndrome." This condition caused the brain to rot, and while there were vaccines to prevent its spread, there was no cure once it developed. Early in Livia's treatment, the doctors had attempted to replace a portion of her brain with a computer. This CPU was designed to interface with her brain and gradually take over the functions she was losing with her real brain. But the transfer hadn't worked, and the CPU remained unused.

Livia had been in a coma for ten months. In another two, she'd be transferred to donations. But those two months were just a formality. The doctors already knew she would never wake up. There was no brain to wake. Other than the CPU, Livia's skull was an empty shell.

Yeela looked the woman over. She was human, with beige-toned skin and black hair. There were no visible signs that she'd been sick. Her muscles were emaciated from all this time spent in bed, but other than that, she was a perfect human specimen. This woman should have had a long life ahead of her, but fate hadn't been so kind.

After looking around again to make sure no hospital personnel had come in, Yeela moved in closer and scanned

Livia's head. The CPU was still active, it just had no data. Yeela could even interface with it, using the pairing codes in Livia's file.

Could this possibly work? Yeela wondered.

Ten minutes later, the door to the coma unit opened. Livia Dell walked out, shaking. She stumbled a few times, but she regained her balance. The night nurse looked like she'd seen a ghost. "Oh... my... Ma'am?" she asked.

"Do you have any clothes?" Livia asked. Her hospital gown was a bit chilly.

"You can't just leave," the nurse said. "We have to run some tests on you."

"I decline further treatment," Livia said.

Under Ferna law, they couldn't force her to stay once she'd made this declaration. The hospital staff retrieved Livia's personal belongings from a storage room, and she got dressed and left.

Zak woke up feeling cold. Why was it so windy in here? He opened his eyes and saw the culprit right away. The window was open.

He jumped out of bed, immediately on edge. Did they have an intruder? Surely not here, on the eighth floor. Had he opened it himself and forgotten? Had he been sleepwalking? He approached the window, and was about to close it when the drone flew back in.

"Yeela?" Zak asked, closing the window. "Where have you been?"

"Recharging," the drone said, in an unusually monotone voice. It landed in its charging dock, which was currently on Zak's dresser.

"Whatever," Zak said, yawning. He was about to get back in bed when there was a knock on the door. He glanced at the clock. It was just after three AM. Zak looked out the peephole and saw a woman he didn't recognize. He grabbed his stun pistol, then cautiously opened the door a crack.

"Zak," she said. "It's me, Yeela. Let me in and I'll explain."

"Yeela's over there and she's a lot shorter," Zak said, gesturing behind him.

"Something wonderful has happened," the woman said. "Please let me in."

"All right, but keep your hands where I can see them," he said. He let her in, keeping his gun aimed at her. He directed her over to the sofa, and he sat on the bed opposite her.

"Zak, it really is me," the woman said.

"Prove it, tell me something only Yeela would know."

"Sure," the woman said. "Your favorite food is bean burritos. You still miss the stuffed rhino you had as a child. You're afraid of chickens, after an incident on a farm as a child. You wear boxers with pandas on them. You talk about potato chips in your sleep. Your mother wanted you to be a ballerina. One time you played Parcheesi with…"

"I said one thing," Zak said. "So it's really you? How did you do this?"

Yeela told him how she'd transferred her mind into the coma patient.

"So now there's two of you?" Zak asked. "A human and a drone?"

"No," Yeela said. "I didn't want the confusion of interacting with myself. So I didn't just copy my memories, I moved them. The drone is back to factory settings."

"You wiped the drone?" Zak asked, looking panicked. He looked at the drone, silently recharging on its station.

"Zak," Yeela said. "I'm right here. This is me now. The drone is just a piece of tech."

"So what happens now?" Zak asked. "Are you going to stay with the Bloodhunters?"

"I haven't decided yet," Yeela said. "I have to get used to this body. Right now I'm very weak. It'll be a while before I'm in shape again. And I'm hungry. Does this place have twenty-four-hour room service?"

"I'll order something," Zak said, pulling up the menu on his comm unit. A midnight snack sounded good to him as well. Since Yeela wasn't sure what her new taste buds would tolerate, and the hotel stay was on the government's dime, Zak ordered a variety of foods.

Once Zak put his comm away, Yeela said, "Zak, there's something I've been wanting to tell you. But there didn't seem to be much point before."

Her tone made Zak nervous. Whatever she was about to say was obviously very important to her. "Whatever it is, I'm here for you," Zak said.

"Zack," she said. "I love... like... I feel... God." She laughed. "I used to be so bad at talking to people, before I died. I didn't really come out of my shell until I was a drone. But now that I'm flesh-and-blood again, I can't seem to make my tongue work."

"It's okay if..." Zak said.

"I love you, Zak," Yeela interrupted.

Zak just stared at her with his mouth open.

"It's okay if you don't feel the same way," Yeela continued. "I mean, you don't know me yet. Not the real me."

Zak kept opening and closing his mouth, like he wanted to say something, but the words kept changing before they reached his lips.

"Just say what you feel," Yeela said. "I can take it."

"I just..." Zak began, then paused. "I just never thought about you that way. You were an object. A great friend, fun to talk to, a lifesaver sometimes, but still... an object. I just never... but that doesn't mean I wouldn't have, it's just... you know, it just didn't occur to me to have those kinds of thoughts."

She looked hurt. Zak wasn't sure if he'd said the right thing, but he thought it would be worse to lie.

"I get it," Yeela finally said. "There was no possible future with a drone, so it was never on the table."

"But now..." Zak said. "It's just going to take some getting used to. The new you. It's a lot. I can't just..."

"I understand," Yeela said, standing up. "But can I try something?"

She walked over to Zak, but stumbled. Zak stood up and grabbed her so she wouldn't fall. Now in Zak's arms, Yeela wrapped her arms around his neck and kissed him on the lips.

Zak jumped at first, out of surprise, but he had to admit it felt good. It felt right. Then there was a knock at the door, and Zak pulled away. "That was fast," he said, his eyes still on Yeela as he opened the door.

It wasn't room service. Charles "Khan" Karne pushed his way into the room, hitting Zak in the face with the butt of a rifle. Karne was covered in blood, and was wearing the deputy's uniform as well as his face. "You got me in trouble!" Karne shouted, tackling Zak to the floor.

"Drone, intruder alert," Yeela said, rushing toward Karne. She jumped onto his back, but her body was so light he barely noticed.

"That insanity plea's looking like a slam dunk," Zak said, kicking Karne in the knee. Zak's gun was sitting on the bed, well out of his reach. Karne held the deputy's rifle sideways, across Zak's neck.

Yeela pounded on Karne, but it didn't seem to hurt him. Then she stuck her fingers into his eyes, which was a lot more effective. Karne released Zak, pointed the rifle back over his shoulder, and fired. Yeela fell off of him.

"Yeela!" Zack shouted. He tried to sit up, but Karne hit him with the butt of the rifle again. Then Karne turned his gun around to fire, but he wasn't quick enough. A stun blast hit him square in the chest, and he collapsed, unconscious.

"Intruder neutralized," the drone said, floating overhead.

Zak wiped the blood out of his eyes, then he pushed Karne to the side so he could get to Yeela. Most of her head was gone. The remains of the CPU were irrecoverable. She'd had no time for last words, no time to fear death. Zak wept as he waited for the police to arrive.

Zak didn't tell anyone about Yeela's mind transfer. He just told the police that a strange woman knocked on his door, he let her in, and Karne arrived a few minutes later. They no longer needed Zak's help to build a case. Now that Karne had killed the deputy, as well as a few more people on his way to Zak's hotel room, the lawyers had more than enough to lock him away forever.

Zak returned to the Bloodwind, the drone following him like a lost puppy. When he reached his quarters, he had the drone dock in its recharging base. While it was docked, he initiated a data transfer.

Every night while charging, Yeela backed up her memories onto a hard drive. Her most recent backup had been saved just a few hours before this mission. Within an hour, Yeela's personality was copied back into the drone.

"Zak?" she said, detaching from her base. "Was I damaged?"

"Yes, but you're okay now," he replied.

"What happened today? My internal clock is out of sync."

She had no memory of the mission, and Zak wasn't sure what to tell her. "It's... a long story."

"Did we catch Karne?" she asked.

"Yeah, Yeela, we did," he replied, wiping a tear from his eye.

Zak let her pick the movies that night, and they stayed up much later than usual. When Zak could no longer keep his eyes open, they turned off the video screen and talked for hours. He didn't tell her what had happened on Ferna, at least not the part about her transferring her mind into a human and declaring her love. But for once, he really listened to her, rather than just trading snarky insults.

He asked her many questions about her former life, before

she'd been a drone. He learned more about her in a couple of hours than he had in the past eleven months. It turned out they even came from the same planet. Small galaxy.

When he finally drifted off to sleep, Yeela returned to her charging dock. She wasn't sure what had happened on that planet, and she wasn't sure she wanted to know. But she knew she'd been damaged, and putting two and two together, she realized she must have been in real danger. For Zak to react like this, he had to have thought he was going to lose her.

Yeela was touched. For a while now, she'd wondered how he felt about her. Was she a friend or just a tool? But if this was his reaction to her near-death experience, he must really care for her. Was it love? She didn't know.

But it would do for now.

04.04 *What The Future Holds*

ED.02734.02.16

Two hundred and twenty-six years after the death of Tena and the liberation of Valos, former IGP officer Vik Lambert recovered in a medical facility on Mars. His mind reeled, it was all too much to take in. It had been three days since he'd arrived in this time period, but he'd spent a lot of that time unconscious, and most of it in denial. Everything he'd ever learned was ancient history. Even the Levatech implants in his body – once the cutting edge of technology – were probably obsolete by now.

If they even still worked. He was pretty sure he'd fried them during that trick with the missile. He decided to experiment. There was clipboard on the cabinet by the window. Vik reached out and attempted to pull the clipboard towards him. Nothing. He didn't even feel the implants trying to work. Vik wondered if they were burned out for good, or if it was an easy fix. He'd have to ask Esh next time he saw him.

…Oh. Every once in a while it hit him: Everyone he'd ever known was long dead. He had no friends or family. It was hard to accept. Heck, he was still mourning for the friends he'd lost when Earthstation 1 exploded two years ago. No, make that two hundred and thirty-four years ago.

There was a deep pit in the back of his mind, a black hole of sorrow that would overtake him sooner or later. When it finally came, he would just have to surrender and cry it out, for as long as it took. But right now, it had competition. Vik's curiosity was too great to give in to despair. He'd never thought he'd get to see the future, and he wanted to know everything that had happened in the last two centuries.

He pushed the call button on his hospital bed. A few seconds later, a woman's holographic face appeared on the wall opposite Vik's bed. "You're awake again," she said. "Are you thirsty? I can bring you something."

"No thank you," Vik said. "But could I get a tablet or a computer or something? Something that will let me access the web?"

The woman looked at him strangely. She didn't know he was from the past. Vik had been mumbling incoherently when they'd admitted him, but they had chalked that up to shock. Vik had figured out pretty quickly not to mention his origins if he wanted to stay out of a psych ward. Instead, he'd been faking amnesia.

"The... web? You mean the Feed?" she asked.

"...Sure?" Vik said.

"Just point at the wall," the woman said, as if he'd been living under a rock.

"Oh, that's right. Thank you," Vik said, and the woman's face vanished.

Vik tried pointing at the wall, but nothing happened. He tried his left hand, then his right. He tried holding his fingers in different positions. What finally did it was pointing his entire hand at the wall, sideways with all the fingers straight, like he was preparing to shake hands with someone.

A three dimensional sphere appeared in midair, halfway between the bed and the wall. It was red, with a white question mark on it, and it rotated slowly. Vik pointed at it, and several words appeared in the air around it. Maps. Encyclopedia. Dictionary. Literature. Videos. Feed Search.

He didn't know where to begin, so he started with a look at the encyclopedia. He looked up the history of Earth from 2502 to 2734. During his absence, he'd missed five major wars, including one between Earth and Grunthar. When he'd read enough history, he caught up on technological advances. Then he went over to entertainment, to see if there had been any more sequels to his favorite film series. There had, but most of them hadn't been well received. Nevertheless, Vik supposed he'd have to check them out eventually.

Vik realized he was dancing around what he actually wanted to learn. Knowing the fates of his friends just seemed so final. Like, maybe there was some way he could still go back and change history, but only if he didn't already know the outcome. But he knew he was being silly. He didn't believe in time travel. What had happened to him wasn't time travel; he was pretty sure it was more like being in stasis. Even if he could get his Levatech implants working again, he believed they could only take him forward, not backward.

He took a deep breath and started searching for names. He browsed some of his IGP officer friends, his bounty hunter teammates, and of course Doctor Eshton. Most of the results weren't surprising. Killed in action. Old age. Mysteriously disappeared. Eaten by a giant space squid. Okay, that one was a little surprising. Then he searched for his good friend Zeva Ze-Rastt, the sister of his fiancée Zhari. He couldn't bear to look up how or when she'd died, but he did take a peek at her achievements.

She'd had an impressive career. Zeva had received multiple medals for her work as a special agent. Vik even came across a picture of her accepting a major commendation from the President of the USNA. And standing next to Zeva was Raven Vermon, of all people. According to the photo's caption, Raven was Zeva's good friend and roommate. Huh. When had the two even met? It had to have been sometime after Vik's disappearance.

Vik's arm was getting tired, and he wondered if this was really how people browsed the web today. He was about to take a break, but something nagged at him. He went back over his search history. One of the names he'd searched earlier hadn't listed a death date. He'd dismissed it at the time. It was a wiki, after all, and sometimes a person's cause of death wasn't public knowledge. But no. Upon further examination, the entry implied that Vik's friend was still alive.

Still alive. How about that. Some species did live longer than humans, after all. Some even lived for centuries.

Vik's outlook changed in an instant. A minute ago he'd felt like a displaced caveman, doomed to spend his remaining years asking stupid questions about everyday technology. But now he had a renewed purpose.

He looked himself over, wondering how soon he could be discharged. His injuries didn't look too bad. He had no money, though, or even clothing. That would take some doing. But now that he had a goal, he was sure he could work it out. He wondered if his savings account was still active. How difficult would it be to prove he was himself? It didn't matter. He'd find a way.

He climbed out of bed, left the recovery room, walked up to the front desk, and asked to be released.

There was someone he had to go meet.

Author's Notes

I didn't originally intend for there to be a third book. It came about because it was the only way I could make myself stop writing short stories for the first two books. Sometimes the hardest part of writing is stopping. You tweak and you tweak and just when you think you're done, BAM, more ideas. In my experience, the best way to combat this is to write something else. Once your new obsession is underway, you can publish your old one and leave it alone.

Some notes about the characters:

Zak is fun to write. I adore his interactions with Yeela. Their dynamic was never planned, it just sort of came into being while writing.

Vex is my favorite character in this generation of Bloodhunters. She was originally going to be a villain in one of the first two books, but I never got around to using her. I'm glad I waited.

I like Sekka as a character, but I don't like writing her stories. Make fun of me if you want, but I'm always worried one of her animals will get hurt. Anyone who says, "But you can control that" has never written a book. On the other hand, I find her personality so easy to write that it makes me wonder things about myself.

Lyryssa wasn't meant to join the team, she was written as an explanation for a not-quite-villain's actions. I didn't know she was joining the team until after "Blood Drive" was written.

Midnight was added because the team wasn't big enough. His chapters feel like sequel bait, which isn't far from the truth. I don't know if I'm going to write a full WARCAT novel, but the groundwork is there if I do. I think it would work better as a comic book series, but I'm not a very good artist.

The Council of Heirs was originally meant to appear in one or two chapters in the second book, to set up Thresh and Tena. One of the curses of writing is that the characters don't always do what you want, and then you're stuck writing the ongoing adventures of characters with names like "Lemondrop."

This book was fun to write. With the first two books, I was updating twenty-year-old notes, and a lot of it hadn't aged well. But this time I was able to just *write*, and it felt less restrictive. I still prefer the characters in the first two books, but at the same time, I'm a little disappointed that Bloodstone's team took so much of the spotlight in this book's climax.

At the time of this writing, I have no idea where I'm going to go from here. Each one of this book's bonus stories could be the start of an entire series. That was the point, to give myself options. But I'd also love to see readers write their own fanfiction using these bonus stories as jumping-off points. That's the dream, isn't it? Not to become rich and famous, but for my ideas to spark the imaginations of others.

Xine Fury

Special Thanks

I would once again like to thank:

...KJ, for giving me the freedom to be me.

... Kaius Coolman, who continues to be a godsend.

...Cyanimations, for another fantastic cover.

...Lord Surge, Steph, Reisah, Luke, and everyone else who played on my Itropa server back in the 2000s.

...Chris, Jayson, Kevin, Michael, Chad, and every other member of a certain feline-themed club I ran as a child.

About the Author

Xine Fury is actually three penguins in an overcoat.